# ~~BRONTË'S GAP YEAR~~
## Magnolia's packing list

Travel light! You're going to be
carrying all your own clothes and you'll
probably buy stuff as you go.

- ☐ First Aid kit
- ☐ ~~Paints, pens and notebook~~
- ☐ Toothbrush, toothpaste,
  hairbrush, sunscreen, moisturiser
- ☐ Hiking boots, trainers and flip flops
- ☐ Sheet sleeping bag, a towel, a sarong
- ☐ One nice dress
- ☐ T-shirts, shorts, bikinis,
  knickers and ~~a~~ bra**s**
  **4**

### *What the hell am I doing?*

# Cathy Bramley

# somewhere only we know

ORION

First published in Great Britain in 2025 by Orion Fiction,
an imprint of The Orion Publishing Group Ltd.,
Carmelite House, 50 Victoria Embankment
London EC4Y 0DZ

The authorised representative in the EEA is
Hachette Ireland, 8 Castlecourt Centre, Castleknock
Road, Castleknock, Dublin 15, D15 XTP3,
Republic of Ireland (email: info@hbgi.ie)

An Hachette UK Company

1 3 5 7 9 10 8 6 4 2

Copyright © Cathy Bramley 2025

A CIP catalogue record for this book is
available from the British Library.

ISBN (HB) 9781398713925
ISBN (Export Trade Paperback) 9781398713932
ISBN (eBook) 9781398713956
ISBN (Audio) 9781398713963

Typeset by Born Group
Printed and bound in Great Britain by Clays Ltd, Elcograf S.p.A.

www.orionbooks.co.uk

For Phoebe and Isabel
Make your life spectacular, love Mum xxx

# Prologue

'Mum!' Brontë waved a hand in front of my face. 'Stop grinning at me.'

'Never.' I helped myself to another California roll from the box. 'It's such a nice surprise to see you. I'll fall asleep with this smile on my face.'

Tonight I was supposed to be at book club. This month's choice had gripped me to the last page. The story was a warning to slow down your life and pay attention to the people you love. But then Brontë had invited herself over and I chose to heed the book's lesson and put her first.

My daughter snorted softly. 'Nutter. I'm happy to see you too, and be home.'

I knew that one day another house would be her home and her visits would be less often. I didn't want to think about that yet.

We were sitting at my kitchen table with the doors open to the garden. It was a summer's evening in the Cotswolds and we'd started off outside, but a breeze had blown us back inside.

I sneaked another look at her while we took turns to spear sliced ginger onto chopsticks and plunge them into wasabi. Our taste buds were similar; we both adored strong flavours, the hotter the better.

Her face held the gifts of youth which we take for granted until they begin to elude us: smooth skin, bursting with collagen, a scattering of freckles highlighting her cheekbones, teeth sparkling white. When she smiled, I saw my younger self reflected in her features, but her liquid brown eyes and dark curls she owed to her father. I delighted in her vivaciousness, and I knew that even when she was older, a mother herself maybe, I'd never tire of looking at this girl of mine.

'So.' Brontë looked at me from under her lashes, cheeks flushed. 'I have news.'

I put down my chopsticks, heart already fizzing with pride. 'I knew it.'

She laughed. 'You always know it.'

'The spontaneous dinner date, the sushi, you *paying* for the sushi.' I listed the clues. 'I learned the language of Brontë Jones a long time ago. I'd say I'm fluent.'

Sushi had been her go-to celebratory food since her tenth birthday when instead of a party, she'd opted for a trip to Tate Modern for the two of us, followed by sushi for lunch. Never one to follow the crowd, my daughter.

Normally I paid for our takeaways. Brontë had recently graduated and was saving every penny for her move to London. This time when she'd offered, I let her pay. There was a feeling of self-worth that came from being able to treat someone. I understood that.

'I think I can still surprise you,' she replied, tilting her chin with a touch of defiance I recognised as my own.

She swallowed hard, her fingers reaching for the Tiffany pendant that I'd bought her for her twenty-third birthday in April.

Her obvious nervousness at whatever she'd come to tell me made me want to squeeze her tight. I loved that she shared so much with me, that I was the first person she called with news. She'd achieved so much, knocked it out of the park on every challenge she'd set herself. School, art college, uni and, last week, she'd landed her dream job.

'Let me guess,' I said, topping up our soda glasses. 'Saatchi & Saatchi want you to start earlier?'

Bronte let out a shaky laugh. 'Not exactly, but you're in the right area.'

She'd set her heart on working in Saatchi's art department since attending a guest lecture one of their directors had given at university. The selection process for their graduate scheme had been brutal, but her talent shone through and they'd offered her a junior position starting in September. I couldn't have been prouder.

'Okay.' I raised an eyebrow, my mind racing through the possibilities. 'Um . . . I give up.'

'Wait there.'

She scrambled up from the kitchen table, darted out into the hall and returned carrying the hobo patchwork bag she'd picked up from a yard sale. It suited her style, but reminded me of something my mother had had in the eighties. I tried not to go back to those times if I could help it; my relationship with my own mother was the opposite of the bond Brontë and I shared.

'So here's the thing.' She sat, plonking the bag on her lap. 'I'm going to be working until I'm an old woman. Like, I don't know, seventy or something.'

I nodded. 'You and me both, kiddo. And that's all right.'

I liked working, being busy and useful and knowing that I would be able to support Brontë financially until she could support herself. When she left home for uni I immersed myself even deeper into my career, filling the aching gap she'd left behind. I was in my mid-forties now and couldn't imagine feeling different any time soon.

'Yeah, I know.' Brontë frowned. 'But there's so much world to see. And if I don't go and explore now, I might never get the chance.'

'Of course you will!' I argued. 'You're so young! You'll have time off, holidays . . . and you'll get used to making the most of weekends.'

'Listen, Mum, I've decided to go travelling in January,' she blurted out. 'Take a gap year. Before I start work – my graduate job, I mean. Obviously, I'll need to work in a bar or something to save up. I'm going by myself initially and then I'll meet Harry midway through – he's got an internship first. I should have enough cash by January. The flights are the main problem. I need to book them now and I was wondering if you could lend me the money. I'll pay you back.'

'Whoah, slow down,' I cried. 'A gap year?'

She nodded, willing me with her eyes to support this crazy idea. I had not expected this; I was staggered.

'What?' I couldn't believe my ears.

'Where's this come from? Harry? Has he put this into your head?'

I'd always liked her boyfriend until now. He was a lovely lad, and they were well suited, and had been together for three years all through university.

'Mum!' Brontë looked appalled by the suggestion.

'Sorry, sorry.' I pressed my hands on the table and took a deep breath. I never spoke to her like that. Ever. 'It's a surprise, that's all.'

'To answer your question, Harry has nothing to do with it. This is something I've wanted to do.' She glanced at me then looked away. 'Ever since I read your diary from 2000.'

'My . . . ?' A rush of heat flamed my face.

Her eyes widened in panic. 'You said I could have it.'

'I remember.' I'd only ever kept a diary once, and it was too full of memories to throw away. She'd found it amongst my things when she was looking for photos for an art project a couple of years ago. I'd let her keep it. The things I'd written about were as important for her as they were for me. The last thing I'd expected was that it would trigger a desire for a gap year.

She pulled two books from her bag and pushed them across the table. One was my old diary, the other was a notebook covered in her illustrations. A map of the world with dotted lines leading away from the UK. Aeroplanes, backpacks, turtles, flowers, beach towels and palm trees . . . She referred to them as doodles, but her drawings were much more than that. *Brontë's Gap Year* was written across the front, each letter of each word in a different colour. The cover alone was a work of art; I could only imagine how detailed the inside would be. The pages had that tell-tale waviness to them which told me that she'd painted on them. This book – this plan – must have been weeks, possibly months in the making.

'I'm confused,' I said, attempting to stay calm. 'This is the first I've heard about you wanting a gap year.'

'Because you've always told me to put details into my plans, otherwise they're just dreams. So I wanted to get everything lined up, my itinerary finalised first. Can I show you . . . ?'

'*Finalised?*' I launched into her before she ended her sentence. 'Darling, you've accepted a job, you can't walk out before you've even started.'

'Actually, I haven't accepted,' she said, shrugging her shoulders. 'They gave me a week to respond.'

'I'm speechless.' I dropped my head into my hands.

'So I have responded.' Brontë's voice cracked, and she paused to sip her water. 'And I've asked them to let me defer for a few months. Possibly a year.'

I couldn't believe what I was hearing. 'They're one of the biggest creative agencies in the world, with their pick of young hopefuls. I doubt very much they'll be willing to make a concession for someone who has apparently changed her mind about joining them.'

'Perhaps they'll think that I'll come back a more rounded person with a new perspective on the world.' Brontë fingered the cover of the notebook. 'I've got some cool places on my list; would you like to see?'

'Or they might think that once you've had a taste of travelling, you'll struggle to settle into work,' I said, deliberately ignoring her question.

She gave a sigh so full of sadness that I almost backed down. But this was a mistake. She'd had her sights set on this company for so long. I wondered whether it was a case of cold feet.

'*You* did it,' she countered. 'You had your trip to Bali. And don't you dare tell me that you regret it because your diary tells me otherwise. Look.'

She flicked through the pages of my old diary until she came to a photograph of me. My heart stuttered in my chest; it had been years since I'd seen this. I was in a bikini on white sand at the edge of turquoise water. I looked tanned and beautiful, and although you couldn't tell from the picture, I was posing for Jackson, my arms reaching up to the sky, one foot kicking up behind me. But the most striking thing was the smile lighting up my face. This was a girl having the time of her life. Even without knowing anything about her, you could see she was in love.

Brontë was staring at me, waiting for an answer.

'Of course I don't regret it! But this isn't about me.'

The photograph had unnerved me. My words came out sharper than I'd intended and Brontë flinched.

'All I want is the opportunity to look as happy and free as you do there. A break between education and my working life, that's all. I want my Bali moment.'

'And you can have it, I'm sure,' I said, tempering my tone. 'But you don't need to take a gap year to do it.'

'Fine.' She closed the lid over the remaining sushi and shoved it in her bag. I ached with regret that the evening had taken such a turn. 'I hoped you'd support me. I guess deep down, I knew you'd be like this. So closed. All you think about is work. *Your* career, *my* career. But you know what? There's more to life than work.'

'Wow.' My hackles rose. 'That's easy for you to say, but growing up with no financial security wasn't easy. Neither was having a mother whose responsibilities didn't even stretch to making sure there was food in the cupboards. I've thought about work to make sure you never have to feel that way, to make sure you know the value of being independent, to give you the opportunities I never had.'

Brontë began to stack the used crockery. 'And yet as soon as I make an independent decision you throw it back in my face.'

'That's not fair!' I snapped. I was offering my opinion. That was all.

'Nothing's fair, Mum,' she snapped back, jerking to her feet. 'It's not fair that you didn't get to graduate from university, and it's not fair that you had to look after Auntie Kat while you were a kid, or that you had to work two jobs to put a roof over our heads. But I can't be the one to right those wrongs for you. You've got to stop expecting me to follow in your footsteps. Or at least the footsteps you never got to take. Independence means me going my way. Doing what I want without being pressured to live the life you should have had.'

'I see.' I stood up too fast, panic making my legs feel heavy and my head light. My vision blurred with tears, and there were already tears streaking Brontë's face. 'I had no idea you felt like that. I'm sorry I wanted so many good things for you.'

'I'm sorry too,' she said stiffly. 'I'm sorry that I've done all this work, put so much into this travel itinerary because I wanted to impress you, so you could see what this trip meant for me. But you won't even look. Thanks a lot.'

I shook my head. 'You've already contacted Saatchi before speaking to me, so I hardly think my opinion matters.'

'Of course it matters.' She glowered at me, putting on her jacket. 'I want to do this, Mum. And I'd hoped . . . well, I'd hoped maybe you could join me at the end. You never take your annual leave from work. How about it? Fancy a holiday on the other side of the world?'

My stomach twisted at the idea of her being on the flip side of the globe. I'd only been on a long-haul holiday once. I hadn't done much travelling since.

I exhaled slowly, forcing myself to calm down. She and I never quarrelled. We were best friends, and this felt horrible and alien. I wanted to make things right between us. I glanced at the book and took in the words *Brontë's Gap Year* again. I had to salvage the situation; I didn't want us to part on bad terms.

'Will you do something for me?' I asked, catching hold of her hand. 'Will you think about it for one more week? Make sure that this is definitely what you want.'

Brontë groaned. 'I've already thought about it.'

'Please,' I said. 'And it'll give me a chance to get used to the idea too.'

She chewed the inside of her cheek, weighing up my proposal. 'And if I do that, and still want to go, do you promise you'll give me your blessing?'

'I promise,' I said, although the words stuck in my throat. 'Let's have dinner again next week, and if you're determined to go, we'll look through *Bronë's Gap Year* together. What do you say?'

'Fine, then. It's a deal.' She sighed again, but this time a small smile lit her face, and with it, my heart.

But for Brontë next week never came.

# Chapter 1

I ran the tap, holding my hands under the stream of hot water, my thoughts a million miles away. January had rolled around and Brontë would have been heading off on her trip. I could visualise her, dashing around at the last second, stuffing phone chargers and toothpaste and one more book into her rucksack. I'd have been following behind, her shadow, blurting out random things such as reminding her not to eat the ice, or to always tell someone in the hostel where she was going, and asking if she had taken a photo of her passport in case of emergency. And she'd have been laughing and rolling her eyes and pointing out that we'd had this conversation many times, that she knew what she was doing, and I should stop worrying and trust her.

I'd have driven her to the airport and hugged her for the longest time and tried to focus not on my fears, but on my pride, on the fact that my daughter was heading off to the other side of the world, alone, full of confidence and excitement and that this was exactly what I wanted for her.

A hot tear tracked down my face and I brushed it away as Anna, my boss, emerged from the toilet cubicle.

'I bloody hate that man,' she said with a scowl.

The man in question was Kevin Armstrong with whom we were having a business lunch. He was so awful that this was our second trip to the ladies, both of us needing a breather from his self-obsessed twaddle. He was the procurement manager for Vap-A-Rise, a chain of e-cigarette stores which had sprung up on the high street like weeds over the past few years. We were the lucky people tasked with persuading him to sign on the dotted line for a three-year e-commerce management and training package with our company ShopSwift.

'Hate is a strong word,' I replied, pulling towels from the dispenser to dry my hands. A whisper of a remembered conversation made my breath catch.

*'I hate PE,' Brontë grumbled as I handed over her sports bag one school morning.*

*'Hate's a strong word, darling.' I kissed her forehead, realising that I barely had to stoop to do so anymore. 'Think of it as not your favourite.'*

*'Physics is not my favourite; PE is actual torture.' She pulled a face. 'But I'll try.'*

*And she would, I thought; my girl gives everything her best shot.*

I blinked away the memory and made room for Anna at the sink.

'Yeah, well, I have very strong feelings towards our future client, Maggie,' said Anna, darkly.

'I hear you.' I dropped the used towels into the rubbish bin and picked up my bag.

'I mean where does he get off, telling us that he doesn't like to do business with women because they're crap at golf?' Anna continued. 'Perhaps I should have let Lee join us after all.'

My hackles rose but I didn't let it show. Lee Masters was a sales manager like me, and foaming at the mouth that he hadn't had the chance to seal this deal with Vap-A-Rise. No doubt Kevin would have preferred all-lads-together Lee, but I'd been the one to make the initial contact with Vap-A-Rise and I didn't give away my sales leads easily. My team handled the higher-value clients with multiple locations. Lee's team looked after the smaller customers. He was constantly trying to poach my accounts, but to no avail. My strength was client management and Anna knew that. I looked after people, I knew what they needed and delivered it. Lee promised customers the earth to gain a rapport with them. Unfortunately, he didn't always deliver, and Anna knew that too, and yet somehow he always managed to come up smelling of roses.

'The idea of Kevin possessing even one iota of sporting prowess is ludicrous.' I ran a hand over my hair, smoothing any flyaways. I wore it poker-straight, but the slightest hint of damp in the air and the unruly kinks returned. 'I'd like to show him what I can do with a nine iron.'

Anna paused from applying her lipstick. 'Do you even know what a nine iron is?'

I gave myself a cursory glance in the mirror. I avoided it as much as possible now. There were only so many times you needed to see your eyebags when they looked like hollowed-out avocado skins. 'No. But I'm pretty sure he'd know about it if I whacked him in the balls with one.'

She sniggered. 'Let's take a rain check on that until we get the deal in the bag, shall we?'

The deal in question wasn't only worth a significant amount of money to ShopSwift, it was important to me too. It could be my ticket to promotion to sales director and a seat at the boardroom table when Anna's father Ron retired in a few months' time. It would be between Lee and me; I really wanted it to be me.

My phone vibrated with a text from the depths of my bag. It was from George, my junior sales executive.

When will you be back? I've written an email and I'd like you to read it before I send it.

Twenty-one-year-old George had been with me for three months and still came to me for things which by rights he shouldn't need help with. But it felt good to be needed, so I didn't pull him up on it. Besides, what he lacked in experience he made up for in his eagerness to do the right thing. I typed back an update before answering my boss.

'Don't worry, I'll keep my opinion about Kevin to myself – my eye is firmly on the prize. You know how ambitious I am.' I looked at Anna, hoping that my meaning was clear.

'You're the best salesperson we have. But . . .' She paused, resting a hand on my shoulder. 'I worry about you. You are okay, in yourself, I mean?'

I detested that question; what did it even mean?

'Absolutely,' I said, heading for the door. 'Let's go and wrap this meeting up, shall we?'

An hour later and we were almost finished. Anna had been checking her watch for the last twenty minutes, as keen to get out of here as I was. If it wasn't for the company we were keeping, lunch would have been enjoyable. Give him his due, Kevin's choice of venue, the Lock and Barrel, was a lovely pub with an impressive menu and a fabulous view of the canal. A row of narrowboats was moored outside and on the opposite bank, a flock of sheep grazed in the field.

Our waiter appeared to clear the table and asked if everything was okay.

'It was delicious, thank you.' I smiled as I handed him my empty coffee cup.

'You know, you're a lot more attractive when you smile,' said Kevin, with a leer.

Beside me Anna sucked in a breath.

And you're a lot more attractive when you keep your mouth shut, I thought. I could almost hear Brontë's voice in my ear. *Go Mum! Don't let him get away with that.*

'ShopSwift don't employ me to be attractive,' I said instead. 'They employ me because I deliver results. For our company and for our clients too. Which is why I'm confident that we will not only provide you with the best e-commerce package on the market, but we'll exceed your expectations. So,' I leaned forward, fixing him with an intense look. 'Do we have a deal?'

Kevin gave me a cocky smile, wide enough for me to see that it had been some time since his backside had graced a dentist's chair. He picked up his brandy glass and swirled the liquid around a couple of times. A double measure of a label which had cost even more than the dozen oysters he'd insisted on ordering at our expense. My dislike of the man was growing exponentially.

'I'll sleep on it,' he said, throwing the rest of his brandy down his throat. 'Thanks for lunch, ladies. Now I'll visit the little boys' room and be on my way. I'll be in touch in a week or so.'

He pushed his chair back from the table, causing the feet of it to screech across the flagstone floor. He stumbled against the table next to ours and it suddenly struck me that he might be tipsy. We'd had a bottle of wine with lunch; Anna and I had barely touched ours as we were both driving. He'd been sipping a gin and tonic when we arrived, and now the brandy. Anna and I rolled eyes at each other.

'A week or two?' I shook my head in despair. 'This is turning into the longest negotiation in history.'

'Arsehole,' she muttered, handing her credit card to our waiter.

'How do men like that get so far up the career ladder?' I fumed. 'How do they get away with saying shit like that?'

'Because we let them?' she replied wryly. 'Although I thought your reply was brilliant, Maggie. You put it much better than I could have done.'

Rubbish. I liked Anna but I knew full well that she wouldn't have said anything to jeopardise winning this contract.

'Let's get out of here,' I said with a shiver. 'Two hours in that man's company and I need a shower.'

Once the bill was settled, we walked out to the car park and bumped into Kevin leaning against the no-smoking sign, a cloud of smoke billowing from his e-cigarette.

'Are you waiting for a taxi, Kevin?' Anna asked. 'Because I'm sure Maggie wouldn't mind giving you a lift. I'd offer myself but I've got another appointment to get to.'

My heart sank. I'd do it, of course, but I'd rather stuff my shoes with stinging nettles than spend one more minute with Kevin Armstrong.

'No problem, although Uber is probably the quickest,' I suggested.

My phone buzzed, and I glanced at it, thinking it would be George again. It was my mother.

Hello Magnolia, I hope you're well, darling? Long time, no see. Are you free at the weekend? Perhaps you could pop over?

I felt my jaw tighten, not fooled by her one bit. She wasn't interested in whether I was well or not. She only got in touch when she wanted something. Usually money.

'Taxi?' Kevin scoffed, shaking a bunch of car keys. 'Why would I need a ride when I've got my own car?'

My reaction was so severe, so instant that I felt every hair on my arms stand on end.

'You're not driving?' I stammered. 'You've been drinking.'

'Maggie's got a point, Kevin,' Anna agreed. 'You might be over the limit.'

He gave a dismissive laugh and patted his stomach. 'This body was built to take alcohol. If anything, it sharpens my reflexes.'

The smugness of him. Bile rose in my throat.

Kevin was struggling to stand without swaying. It was people like him who . . . I shook the image from my head, the one of Brontë in the mortuary, the one which tortured me night after night as I lay awake in the silent hours before dawn. She and Harry had been walking home after seeing a film, two kids minding their own business, when a drunk driver lost control and the car mounted the pavement.

'Is that right?' I stepped forward and swiped the keys from him. Any pretence of liking the man had evaporated. 'Oh dear, look what I've got. Reflexes not so sharp, after all.'

'Give those back,' Kevin demanded, one hand outstretched, the other clasping his e-cigarette.

I gripped the keys to my chest. 'Only if you promise not to drive.'

'What the hell is this?' His eyes slid from mine to Anna's. 'Give me my keys, now.'

'Maggie,' Anna warned. 'Don't do anything you might regret.'

I pinned her with my stare. 'Oh believe me, I won't.'

Kevin lunged at me, but I jumped sideways out of his path and without me to break his fall, he staggered forward and crash-landed on his knees.

'Shit. Ouch!' He sat back on his heels and looked at his hands. Beads of blood appeared from under the grit. 'Help me up, for God's sake.'

'I'm so sorry.' Anna leapt forward to assist, taking his elbow. 'Maggie didn't mean that to happen, it was an accident.'

He continued to protest and swear as she found a tissue in her handbag and brushed his hand.

Blood thrummed in my ears as I watched them through a haze. His attitude to drink-driving had triggered the rage

I worked so hard day after day to suppress. I'd been unable to save my child from people like him, but I'd do anything to prevent someone else from going through this living hell.

I looked down at the car keys in my hand, then across the car park to the canal on the other side of the fence.

Fatigue, anger, adrenaline swirled like a cyclone inside me and before I had a chance to weigh up the consequences, I threw the keys as high and hard as I could. They sailed over the fence and landed with a faint splash in the water.

'Oh Christ.' Anna pressed a hand to her mouth, eyes wide with horror.

Kevin loomed over me, his fist clenched. 'You mad bitch.'

'Mad? Mad?' I spat at him. 'Damn right I am, I'm bloody furious. It's people like you—'

Anna gripped my shoulder. 'Go home, Maggie, I'll deal with this.'

'She's going nowhere,' Kevin blustered. 'I'm calling the police.'

Anna nudged me in the direction of my car. 'Please, it's for your own good. I'll sort this out.'

I ignored my boss, not taking my eyes off Kevin for one second.

'Be my guest.' My body was taut with tension. 'I dare you. One whiff of your breath and they'll be very keen to know about your intention to drive.'

'And this.' Kevin jabbed a finger at me, spittle gathering in the corners of his mouth. 'Is why I hate doing business with women.'

'Why, because we can outsmart you?' I needled.

It was unprofessional of me, but I didn't care. I felt untethered, wild and ready for a fight.

'Go now, Maggie,' Anna ordered, her voice dangerously low. 'I'll see you in my office tomorrow. Nine a.m.'

The look on Anna's face: pity, disappointment, revulsion sent a wave of nausea from my stomach to my throat.

'I'm going.' I turned, my legs shaky with nerves as I walked to my car. I climbed in, lowered my head to the steering wheel and waited for the beat of my heart to slow before setting off.

Oh Magnolia Jones, what have you done?

# Chapter 2

The next morning, I got to the staff car park at seven-thirty and waited in my car for Anna to arrive. I planned to intercept her before she reached the office. Whatever she had to say, I'd rather no one overheard, especially Lee – not that he ever turned up before nine. By the time her car pulled in, half an hour later, I was cold and my muscles stiff, but I rushed to greet her.

'Anna! Hi!'

'Jesus, Maggie.' Anna clutched her chest as she climbed out. 'You scared the life out of me.'

'Sorry, sorry, it's . . . well, you know what it is.' I rubbed my arms to get some life back into them. 'I've been on tenterhooks since yesterday. And when you didn't answer my call—'

Anna shut the driver's door and walked to the passenger side to retrieve her laptop bag. 'Or your emails, or your WhatsApps or texts, or the voice note you sent me four hours ago which woke me up.' I winced; not getting enough sleep was her main topic of conversation after the diet of her six-year-old and her husband's inability to stack the dishwasher. 'Because I said I'd see you at nine.'

'You did, I'm sorry.' I registered that Anna wasn't making eye contact. Not a good sign. 'I needed to know what happened after I left. And what's going to happen to the contract.' I swallowed hard. 'And to me.'

Anna looked at me properly. 'You look like shit.'

No surprise there. I hadn't even bothered going to bed. The idea of lying in the dark staring at the ceiling and dwelling on my increasingly pointless future had been too depressing. Instead, I'd brought my duvet to the sofa, made a plate of toast and watched every single video I possessed of Brontë and cried and laughed and cried some more until my tears ran dry.

'I know. A lump of very repentant shit.'

She cracked a smile. 'Come on, get in my car. We'll go to the drive-through and get coffees.'

I was desperately in need of a caffeine hit, but I glanced over my shoulder at the office. 'Shouldn't we . . . ?'

It was past eight o' clock. I hadn't arrived at work this late since Brontë had left home and gone to university. That first hour of the morning when the corridors were quiet and nobody bothered me was my most productive. Now I'd be behind for the entire day. Assuming, that was, I still had a job.

'No we should not.' Anna jerked her head at the car. 'In. We can talk on the way.'

I did as I was told, scenario after disastrous scenario playing out in my head as she got in.

I must be getting fired, why else wouldn't she even want me in the building? Did she think I was dangerous? Or was this her way of sparing me the humiliation of being dismissed in her office with other employees within earshot? Or perhaps she thought it would be easier to have this conversation while she was driving so that she didn't have to look me in the eye while she cut me adrift from my job – my only remaining lifeline, the frame around which I shaped my existence.

'Okay,' she said, once she'd driven out of the car park. 'What's going on?'

'Nothing, honestly,' I protested.

'Seriously?' Anna stared at me grimly. 'After yesterday's antics, you're going with *nothing*?'

I'd told her as soon as I came back after a short stint of compassionate leave that I didn't want to talk about Brontë at work, that it was the only way for me to maintain a professional attitude without breaking down every five minutes. But it looked as if I wasn't going to be able to get away without giving her something.

'The bog-standard losing your twenty-three-year-old daughter stuff.' I stared out of the window, avoiding her eye.

'Want to talk about it?' she asked gently.

I felt a lump in my throat. 'Brontë would have been going travelling about now. I can't stop thinking about what should have been the most exciting time of her life and instead . . .'

'Oh bloody hell. I'm sorry.'

'Instead, people like Kevin Armstrong behave like arseholes, treating drinking and driving like it's a joke, oblivious to the destruction they cause.'

'I totally get it.' Anna nodded. 'It's natural to be angry. Anger is part of the grieving process. When my granddad died, I—'

And this was why I didn't want to talk about Brontë. Because other people felt obliged to share their own stories – which nine times out of ten did not compare to mine at all. Her *granddad*, for heaven's sake.

'I'm aware of the grieving process,' I interrupted. 'I'm fine. Of course, I'm sad, but I'm dealing with it.'

'I don't think you're dealing with it at all.'

'You sound like my counsellor.'

'So you are getting therapy?' She looked pleased. 'That's great.'

'No, of course I'm not.' I folded my arms. 'I already know what they'd say, and I don't need to hear it.'

An uneasy silence descended.

'Look,' Anna began again, 'I'm under pressure from the board.'

'Don't fire me,' I blurted out. 'I know what I did was bad.'

She gave me a sideways look.

'Okay, worse than bad, it was unforgivable.' My stomach lurched as I realised the hole I was digging. 'No, *unacceptable*. That was what I meant.'

'Maggie, I appreciate you have experienced a major trauma, but we cannot have our staff, especially senior managers, verbally and physically abusing clients.'

'Of course not, and I regret what I did.' I didn't regret it at all, even now, faced with losing my job. 'I promise it will never happen again.'

'Damn right it won't.'

My shoulders slumped. Of course it would never happen again — because I wouldn't get the chance. I was out of a job.

We arrived at the drive-through and Anna pulled the car up to the hatch and shouted her order. 'Flat white with oat milk, please. Maggie, what do you want?'

'A second chance?' I said meekly.

She raised her eyebrows and waited.

'A large cappuccino with an extra shot, please,' I supplied.

'Coffee fiend,' Anna said, chuckling. She paid and we pulled up to the next window to collect our drinks.

'So? What happened with Kevin after I left?' I took the lid off mine to blow on it.

Anna put hers in the cup holder in the central console and we headed out of the car park.

'We went back inside the pub. I got him another drink — coffee, before you ask — and he demanded a plaster for his cut hand. Honestly, you'd have thought it was severed at the wrist, the way he was cradling it and sucking it any time anyone went near him. I offered to drive him anywhere he wanted. Assured him that ShopSwift would cover all his expenses getting the keys replaced, et cetera.'

'I'm sorry you had to deal with my mess.' I did feel guilty about that; Anna would have had to arrange for someone else to collect her son from after-school club because of me.

'He called his wife to bring him his spare car keys. She was fuming.' Anna let out a giggle. 'She was only little, but my God she had a good set of lungs on her.'

'Poor woman, being married to him,' I mumbled.

'She took one look at Kevin, sniffed his breath and let rip. I got the impression it wasn't the first time she'd been called to rescue him. Before he had a chance to protest, she'd frog-marched him outside and bundled him into her car. I wouldn't have wanted to be in his shoes on the drive home.'

I conceded a smile. Whatever came next for me, at least I'd prevented another accident caused by too much booze and not enough common sense.

'I guess I've cost us the business.' I sipped my coffee; it was too hot and burned my throat. It felt like a penance, and I gulped again, blinking away tears of pain.

'We won't be working with Kevin Armstrong.' Anna took a bend rather quickly and I grasped the cup with both hands. 'The managing director of Vap-A-Rise called me last night.'

'Oh God.' I held my breath, shame pulsing through me. The managing director, Peter Rufford, was a sweet man. When he'd found out about Brontë, he sent me a voucher for a spa day. I hadn't used it yet – I hadn't wanted to book a day off – but it was a thoughtful gesture. 'So Kevin told him what happened?'

Anna nodded. 'His wife made him own up. Peter fired him for gross misconduct. Apparently, he'd been given several warnings about his drinking, and this was the last straw.'

'Good.' I didn't normally wish anyone harm, but Kevin ticked all the boxes for reasons never to set eyes on someone ever again. 'And the contract?'

'It's ours.' She grinned. 'Just the paperwork to sort out, but we did it, Maggie.'

'Oh, thank heavens.' I felt light-headed with relief.

We'd put hours into our pitch; the mood at work was going to be celebratory for the next few days. I hoped I got the chance to join in.

'I got the impression that we may have even done Peter a favour by giving him a reason to remove Kevin from the company,' Anna continued.

'So I didn't screw it up after all.'

'Lucky for you, no.' Anna slowed as we approached a queue of cars. 'But *your* MD isn't impressed with you either.'

'Don't fire me,' I repeated my plea. Without Brontë, without my work, who was I? What was my purpose? What was the point of me? 'I've lost Brontë; I can't lose my job as well, I'll . . . I'll have nothing left.'

'Maggie, that's not healthy.'

She frowned, but there was kindness in her eyes, and I sensed that she was exasperated rather than angry. She took a sip of her coffee while we were stationary.

'It gets me up in the morning,' I ploughed on. 'It keeps me looking ahead, without it I'd . . .'

I'd be forced to look backwards, to rerun every parenting mistake I'd made, relive every occasion when I'd lost my temper, and wish, wish, wish I could have those moments again to do better. I should have listened to my bright, funny girl more, and given her my words of uninvited wisdom less. And I especially should have given her the opportunity to tell me more about her gap year when it was so obvious that she was excited about it. But I didn't want to say these things to

Anna because I could see she was worried about the state of my mental health.

'I let you down yesterday,' I said. 'But it was a one-off. I want to prove to you and to the rest of the board that when your dad retires, I'm the obvious choice to fill that empty chair.'

Anna's father, our CEO, started the business in the eighties. It was one of the first companies to supply electronic cash registers to small retailers. Over the last fifty years Ron Swift and his team had moved with the times, always at the forefront of retail technology. Anna had worked in every department, learning the nuts and bolts of the business, making her way to managing director. Yes, she'd always known the top job would be hers, but she'd earned it and when she became CEO, there'd be a vacancy at director level. A vacancy I wanted to fill. As did Lee Masters.

'You're the best salesperson we've ever had,' Anna said, as we reached the front of the queue at a set of traffic lights.

It was manned by a crossing patrol person wearing a fluorescent-yellow coat, holding a STOP sign. A stream of kids flooded into the road.

'Thank you, I appreciate that.' I felt the load on my shoulders lighten.

'But as it stands *right now*,' she paused to pull the lid off her coffee and blow it as I had done, 'Lee is the one who has the stability and . . .'

'Are you saying I'm unstable?' A tremor of fear rocked through me.

'. . . the people skills,' she continued.

'I'm bad with people?' I said, affronted by the insinuation.

'And whose values are more closely aligned with those of ShopSwift – i.e. tolerant and inclusive.'

'I'm very tolerant!'

'Try telling that to Kevin Armstrong.'

I couldn't argue with that. 'If we're talking company values, I had to have a word with Lee last week about posting fart videos on the internal messaging system.'

Anna smirked. 'I quite like them.'

I threw a hand up in despair. 'If sharing puerile jokes is what gets you promotion, then I'm done for.'

'So right now,' she said, circling back, 'I can't say you'd be my first choice. Because I'm not even sure that ShopSwift is the place for you.'

I gulped. 'You can't be serious?'

So, this was how my career ended. One rash moment in twenty years of exemplary service – and game over. And if work wasn't the place for me, then where was? Nowhere, that was where.

Silence descended and I willed the lights to change to break the moment. Anna looked as if she was hating this conversation as much as I was. Eventually the lights turned to amber, but a last-minute flurry of kids appeared, and the crossing person stood their ground resolutely, still holding up traffic.

'You need a break from work,' Anna said gently. 'I wouldn't be doing my best by you, not only as your employer, but as a friend, if I didn't intervene. You need to switch off completely, no emails, no phone calls and certainly no middle-of-the-night messages.'

'I can't think of anything worse.' I waited for her to point her finger and do a Lord Sugar on me. I could almost see the words *you're fired* forming on her lips.

'Come on, Maggie,' she chided. 'There's more to life than work.'

That was exactly what Brontë had said the very last time I saw her. She'd accused me of putting work before everything. At the time it hadn't been true. I loved my daughter above all else. But now she was gone.

'Not for me, there isn't,' I murmured. 'Not anymore.'

'What you did yesterday was not only a sackable offence, but a huge error of judgement on your part.' Anna tempered her words with a sympathetic tone. 'You're on the verge of being what Human Resources would term a loose cannon. And we can't have that.'

'I understand.' I pictured myself at home, scrolling through vacancies, updating my CV, cold-calling possible employers, and had to suppress a shudder. 'Look, I admit that I've struggled this week, thinking that Brontë should be on the other side of the world by now. It's unsettled me, that's all.'

'I'm not sacking you,' Anna announced.

My insides unclenched. 'Thank God, thank you.'

'I'm trying to support you during this . . . difficult time you're going through by insisting that you take a break.'

'I can do that,' I replied. I'd agree to anything if it meant putting this behind us. 'My sister is always telling me to use her cabin in the Lake District. I'll go there for a few—'

'Months,' Anna jumped in before I could say *days*. 'A few months. Call it a sabbatical. A non-negotiable sabbatical.'

'Months?' My jaw fell. 'We're too busy for that! There's the Vap-A-Rise contract, plus a hundred and one projects in the pipeline, and George is still on probation. I want to make sure he gets the support—'

'We'll manage all that.' Anna was firm. 'No one is indispensable, Maggie, not even you.'

My heart knocked against my ribs as I processed what she was saying. If the company didn't need me, then who did? I literally couldn't think of anyone. I'd built my life around those who'd needed me. First my sister Kat when she was young, until she met her lovely husband, and then Brontë and lastly, ShopSwift. Now nobody needed me.

'Take some time off, find your spark again,' Anna continued.

Panic flared in my chest. 'How am I supposed to do that?'

'I don't know. But I do know that you won't find it sending emails at three a.m.'

I shook my head. 'I appreciate the offer and the thought behind it, but a sabbatical is the last thing I want. I'm sorry, Anna, but the answer is no.'

'Is that so?' She raised her eyebrows.

For a few seconds, we stared at each other, but I held my ground. She couldn't make me, could she?

The lights changed to green. Anna stuffed her cup down into the holder before putting her hand on the gear stick and preparing to drive off.

What came next was one of those moments when time stretches interminably. In the split second we started to move, my eye was caught by a pram hovering on the edge of the pavement. The woman holding it released one hand from the handlebars to bring her phone to her ear, and the pram jolted forward, its front wheels tipping down into the road.

'*Stop!*' I screeched at the top of my lungs, bracing myself against the glove box.

Anna hit the brakes. The car slammed to a halt, causing the coffee in both of our cups to spill.

'What the *hell*, Maggie?' she yelled as boiling hot liquid splashed over her hand.

The woman, oblivious to the panic she'd caused, laughed into the phone, and pulled the pram back onto the pavement.

'It's fine,' I said, breath whooshing from my lungs. 'False alarm. Carry on.'

'What, with a third-degree burn to my hand?' Anna shot back. 'You're too kind.'

I barely acknowledged her; my heart was hammering hard against my ribs. What if the pram had gone into the road, what if Anna had accelerated, what if . . . ?

'I'm sorry, I saw the mum and baby and panicked,' I stuttered.

'Maggie!' Anna snapped, startling me. She pulled the car over and let out a sigh of exasperation. 'Now do you see why you need a sabbatical? You can't carry on like this. You're permanently on edge, and I'm constantly expecting you to fall off the cliff at any moment.'

I watched, numb, while she shook the coffee off her hand and found a tissue to wipe the spillage from the central console. Was that how she saw me? And others? I thought I was doing all right, coping.

'A holiday, yes, that's a good idea,' I conceded. 'But that's all I need.'

'You've lost your darling girl, your heart is broken, your soul deserves to be soothed.' Anna gave my arm a little pat. 'Take three months off and use them to gain some perspective. Life is short, Maggie.'

'Don't.' I flinched and looked away.

'Sorry,' said Anna meekly, 'this is raw for you, but you know I'm right. Go out and explore the world, find something that you like more than work.'

There wouldn't be anything, I already knew that, but I could see I didn't have much choice.

'And then?' I asked. 'What happens when I get back?'

She held my gaze. 'You come back to work and if you still want to be considered for a place on the board, I'll support your application.'

My eyes welled with tears; I recognised a lifeline when I saw one.

'Thank you,' I mumbled.

'So?' She stared at me with anticipation. 'What do you say?'

'Okay.' The sound of a death knell rang in my ears, but what choice did I have? 'I'll take the sabbatical.'

# *Chapter 3*

'I'm opening a bottle, want to join me?' I said to my sister Kat on the phone later that evening.

It had been quite a day. Once we'd got back to the office, I'd worked like a demon, first composing an email to the rest of the company explaining that I was taking a break with immediate effect, and then meeting each of my team individually to delegate my workload and put a positive spin on my departure. After updating Anna and finessing the terms of my sabbatical with Human Resources, I'd left the building for the last time until April. Now I was home again, the house felt emptier and quieter than ever and without my distraction technique of pulling out my laptop and checking emails, I needed some company.

'But it's a work night!' My sister did a fake gasp.

'It is,' I replied. 'And it isn't.'

'Please don't talk in riddles, I'm not as clever as you.'

I tutted at her. 'Don't put yourself down, you're amazing, remember that time when—'

'Mags!' she cut in. 'Now is not the time to be my cheerleader. What's up?'

She was the only person who I allowed to call me Mags. Actually, there was one other person, but I didn't count him because that was a lifetime ago.

'Everything.' I heard rustling noises. 'What are you doing?'

'Putting my coat on.'

'You're the best.' I already felt better.

I'd known she'd come. Saying no to people or animals wasn't an option for Kat Winkleberry. Hence her ever-expanding menagerie of cats, rabbits, and chinchillas – not forgetting the blind dog she'd adopted from Macedonia or the gang of birds that hung out on her patio for the seed she bought in bulk.

'Andy? I'm going over to Mags's for wine,' she shouted to her husband, not bothering to put her hand over the phone.

I winced at the assault on my ears.

'Maggie's drinking? On a work night?' I heard Andy yell back. 'Bloody hell. Give her a hug from me.'

'Tell him thanks, hug appreciated,' I said.

'On my way, sis,' Kat said with a slam of the door. 'Hang on in there.'

We lived close to each other in the Cotswolds village of Honeybourne, and within ten minutes her bicycle was parked in the narrow hallway of my cottage, where it would remain for the rest of the night. She always walked home if she had more than two glasses of wine. I loved having her nearby and she felt the same. We'd had each other's backs since we were kids, there at the drop of a hat, or as now, the tweak of the corkscrew. I was five years older than her and, growing up, I'd been the one she'd turned to. These days it worked both ways.

'I lost my job today.' I poured us both a glass of Pinot Grigio while she divested herself of coat, cycle helmet and boots.

Kat froze, one boot dangling from her foot. 'Sacked? No way.'

'Technically, I avoided being sacked, but I'm not allowed back into the building from now until Easter.'

My sister kicked off the boot, sank onto the sofa and accepted the glass of wine. 'I'd normally say cheers at this point, but it doesn't feel appropriate. Can you sue?'

I wrinkled my nose. 'It's my own behaviour which landed me in this mess.'

'Oh dear.' She looked at me solemnly.

I cocked my head. 'You don't seem surprised.'

Kat produced a bag of crisps from her bag. 'Do you remember when Mum made a load of elderflower wine, thinking she'd sell it for a fortune; it did nothing for ages, and one day every single bottle exploded?'

I nodded – the carpet had been so sticky we'd had to get rid of it and make do with second-hand rugs to cover the draughty floorboards for the next two years.

'Not something I could ever forget. Why?'

'Because, Maggie,' she said softly, 'you've been bottling up your grief since Brontë died. It was only a matter of time until you blew your top. Like that elderflower wine.'

'Rubbish.' I felt my jaw tighten. 'I'm not bottling anything up. I'm getting on with my life, keeping busy. Let me tell you what happened today. I bet you'd have done exactly the same.'

Over wine and Kat's sweet chilli crisps, I brought her up to speed with the last twenty-four miserable hours of my life.

'I had to agree to this sabbatical, as we're calling it, because otherwise I won't have a shot at being promoted to the board and Lee–bloody–Masters will get the job instead.' I added a log to the fire, prodded the embers viciously with the poker, and plopped back down beside her.

Kat looked at me for a few moments. 'Oh Maggie, I'm so sorry.'

I'd expected her to at least giggle at the bit where Kevin Armstrong's car keys landed in the canal. But her hand reached for mine.

'Me too.' I smiled, grateful for her sympathy. 'I hope this encourages him to get help with his drinking. He didn't endear himself to Anna or me, but I don't wish him ill.'

Kat huffed. 'If I'd been there, he would have been swimming home. How dare he think it's okay to drive after boozing?'

We locked eyes. Losing Brontë had hit her hard too. The two of them had adored each other and Brontë had babysat for Kat's little boy Sam ever since he was born. He was nine now, and I felt a pang of guilt for not seeing my nephew enough recently. I loved Kat and her family dearly and enjoyed being in their company, but returning to a silent house, after spending time in their boisterous family home, brought me down to earth with a bump. Sometimes it was easier to be alone all day than to be reminded of what I was missing.

'Exactly,' I said indignantly. 'So now, I've got three months to kill before I can get back to work and reassert myself as a professional who'd be an asset to the board.'

I shuddered, remembering Anna's use of the words 'loose cannon'.

'So, what are you going to do?' Kat set her glass down and tucked her feet underneath her.

I appreciated her not saying something motivational like *see this as an opportunity for growth*. Tonight, I didn't want to be motivated, I wanted someone to take my side and rant at the unfairness of everything.

'This place could do with a makeover, I guess. It's been years since we . . .'

My voice petered out. I looked around my living room with its open fireplace, honeyed oak beams and the squishy velvet sofa Brontë and I had picked up for free from Facebook Marketplace. We had decorated this room together. She'd been obsessed with the colour teal and insisted on a feature wall around the fireplace. 'Maybe not. I don't know, Kat,' I said wearily. 'What do other people do with time off?'

'Don't ask me,' she scoffed. 'I haven't worked since having Sam and I still never seem to have a minute to myself.'

Kat's phone made a trumpet sound. 'Sorry, that's a notification from the lost pets Facebook page.' She looked at the screen. 'Good news! Mintie the Westie has been reunited with her owner.'

Kat's life was full to bursting. Hobbies, commitments, volunteering, running their cabin as a holiday let in the Lake District, on top of looking after Andy and Sam. Perhaps this was my wake-up call to start a hobby. Perhaps I should rejoin the gym, or grovel to my old book club and see if they'd take me back.

'You could rescue a dog. Company for you, and think how happy you could make an old dog,' she suggested.

I held up a hand like a stop sign. 'No way. I'd be heartbroken when it died. I couldn't handle losing anyone else.'

'A puppy then?'

I shook my head. 'Too much responsibility. I don't want to be tied down. What if I want to go away?'

She gave me a quizzical look. 'You don't like travelling.'

'I haven't done much recently,' I admitted. 'But I was going to ask to stay at your cabin in the Lakes.'

'Oh no! We've let it for six months to someone.' She pulled an apologetic face. 'You don't want to go there on your own at this time of year anyway: too cold, too remote. You need people around you. No, come on, top me up and let's brainstorm.'

'Do we have to?' I sloshed wine into her glass.

I didn't agree with her about needing people. People asked questions like: *What do you do? Are you married? Do you have kids?* People were hard work.

'It'll be fun,' she replied. 'And I won't hold you to anything. So, if you could do absolutely anything, money no object, what would it be?'

'Easy.' I helped myself to a handful of crisps. 'Time-travel. I'd go back to the day Brontë came to tell me about her gap year. I'd say that it was a brilliant idea and that I wanted to hear all about it. And she'd leave the house knowing that she had my full support and approval.'

My sister gave me a chastising look. 'You need to stop beating yourself up about that.'

I shook my head. 'I should have done better. I let her down.'

'Not true. You held her up all her life. She knew you always had her best interests at heart. You made her feel loved and heard and seen. She knew how precious she was to you.'

Tears pricked at my eyes. *Hello again, grief.* I could go for days without it playing out in public, and then suddenly here it was, raking its talons down my spine.

Kat scooched up the sofa and put her arm around me. I rested my head on her shoulder.

'I miss the person she was,' I murmured, accepting a tissue. 'And I'm grieving the loss of the things I was looking forward to for her. Like getting her first home, telling me she'd met "the one" – which might even have turned out to be Harry.' I paused, sparing a thought for Brontë's poor boyfriend, wondering how he was. The injuries to his ribs and arm would have healed, but the mental scars would never leave him. Was he thinking of the gap year too, or had he moved on, met someone else? I wasn't sure I wanted to know. And, I wasn't convinced he'd want me to. His parents had updated me with his progress in hospital after the accident, I'd asked them if he wanted me to visit, but was told he didn't want to see me. I'd been relieved; seeing him alive in a hospital bed after only being able to see Brontë long enough to identify her body would have been more than I could have borne. We'd sent each other a few messages since the funeral, nothing more. Probably for the best; the only thing we had in common was loss.

'It's natural to grieve those things.' Kat soothed, kissing the top of my head.

'I miss my daughter and I miss the family I'll never have,' I went on. 'I even miss hearing about her adventures on that bloody gap year.' I sat up and scrubbed at my tears. 'I'm sorry, you must be fed up of me going on about her.'

'Magnolia Jones,' said Kat sternly. 'I will never be fed up. Ever. And I know it's nowhere near the same thing, but you are my family, and you'll always have us. Okay?'

I managed a watery smile. 'Was I a good mum?'

'Oh Mags.' Kat blinked away tears. 'Brontë idolised you. She used to come round to my house before your birthday and at Christmas and ask for help choosing a gift for you. Last year, she bought you that sundress, do you remember?'

I nodded. It was a pretty white kaftan. I hadn't worn it yet. Last year I'd only ventured as far as Edinburgh which, although beautiful, had not been the place for floaty cotton.

'She wrapped it up at my house. I can even recall what she said. Mum's such a brilliant role model, I hope I can make her as proud as I am of her. I can see her wearing this on a beach looking glamorous. Maybe she might even join me when I . . .' Kat stopped and made a choking sound.

'When I . . . ?' I prompted, sensing she was about to say something important. 'Kat, when I what?'

She bit her lip before answering. 'Go travelling next year.'

I stared at her as the words sank in.

'You knew? She told you before she told me?'

Kat swallowed. 'I didn't know the details, only that it was something she was planning.'

'I see.' I was stung that Brontë had gone to her aunt before telling her own mother. Had she been nervous to tell me?

I felt a churning of self-loathing in the pit of my stomach. Clearly she had been, and with good reason, as it turned out.

'Don't take it personally, Mags. She'd said that she was working on her itinerary and that as soon as it was finished, she was going to give you a presentation. It was you she wanted to talk to properly about it.'

I pictured her that night she came over with sushi, her eyes bright with news.

'And when she tried, I refused to listen, I wouldn't even look at her notebook.' I stared at the twisted tissue in my hands. 'I still can't bring myself to look at it. There's all sorts of stuff I haven't been through yet. Her uni work, letters, drawers full of mementos, all sorts. They're all up in her room.'

Her housemates had brought her belongings back when they moved out. The girls had been so good, insisting on packing up Brontë's room for me. I'd shut the door to her bedroom after they'd gone and had never been in there since. One day I'd have to deal with her things, I knew that. But that day was not today.

'Do you think you should?' Kat asked. 'There could be something important in amongst her things.'

I shook my head. 'I've sorted the main stuff, closed her bank accounts. She was a saver; I'd drummed that into her. She had quite a nest egg.'

'Which I suppose is yours now. What are you going to do with it?'

I shrugged. 'Save it, I suppose.'

'What for? Beige cardigans and sensible shoes for when you're in your dotage?' she chided. 'Come on, let's think. Why don't you do something spontaneous with it, something Brontë would love?'

'Like what?'

'I don't know, a holiday somewhere sunny. You've got time, and it would do you good to get away.'

The thought of leaving England right now, while the weather was cold and the days were long and dark, did appeal.

'Maybe. But where?' I didn't have a special place like other people that I returned to summer after summer.

'Think about where you've always wanted to go.' Kat tipped the bottle over my glass, but there was no wine left. She got up and headed to the kitchen. 'Hold that thought.'

I'd negotiated a paid leave of absence with Anna, so financially I'd be fine. Plus, I'd been putting money aside for years to help Brontë get onto the property ladder. I could afford to go anywhere I wanted, but did I really want to go on my own? I'd had Brontë with me on every holiday for the last twenty-three years. I couldn't imagine going away without her.

There was a loud pop from the kitchen and Kat returned with the bottle of sparkling wine I'd had chilling in the fridge for months.

'Kat! That's expensive, I was saving that!'

'Of course you were,' she said with a smirk. 'But in the spirit of being spontaneous, what the hell.'

I laughed. 'True. Besides, it's not often I get given three months off.'

It would be the longest time I'd ever spent away from the workplace. In twelve weeks I could circumnavigate the globe if I wanted to. I could almost hear Brontë's voice cheering me on, telling me to have an adventure.

'That's the spirit.' She poured me another drink with a flourish.

'Kat.' I straightened up as an impulse overtook me. Perhaps it was time to do something I'd been putting off. Maybe now was the right time to hear from my daughter again. 'Will you do something for me?'

'Anything.'

'Would you fetch Brontë's gap-year book? It's in her room, on the desk.'

Kat took a sip of her fizz. 'Are you sure?'

My heart rate stepped up a notch. The book was a physical reminder of my failings that night. I'd never even been tempted to look between the covers. But six months had passed since I lost my girl. If she were alive, she'd be on that trip and I'd know all about it.

I nodded. 'It's time. I can't change the past, but I can show an interest now, see what she'd planned to do.'

Without another word, Kat set down her glass and left the room. I listened to her footsteps on the stairs, the creak of the floorboards overhead as she entered Brontë's bedroom. Sounds I'd heard a thousand times in so many forms over the years: the hesitant tread of a toddler, the skip of a little girl, the stomp of a frustrated teenager, through to the tiptoe of a young woman returning in the early hours from a night out, doing her best not to wake me. Footsteps that I'd never hear again.

Two minutes later, my sister was back, and I pulled myself from the depths of my memories. As she put the book on the coffee table in front of me, a piece of paper fluttered down to the floor.

'Whoops.' She retrieved it and handed it to me. 'Must have been stuck to the back.'

'It's a letter from Saatchi,' I said, scanning the letterhead. It was dated the day after our sushi night. I hadn't seen it before. 'She'd asked to delay the start of her job so she could have a gap year. This must be the reply. I wonder what they said.'

Kat leaned across and we read it together.

*Dear Brontë,*

*I'm writing in response to your request to defer the start of your employment. Your trip sounds amazing. You've certainly picked out some great locations. With my employer's head on, this is disappointing, as there's a project I'd scheduled for you to work on. But with my old hippie-at-heart head on, I applaud you. Travelling gives us a chance to discover the*

*world, experience different cultures, and learn who we are
with no one to impress but ourselves. So I will approve your
deferral. And I will look forward to hearing how travel has
changed you and try not to be too envious.*

*Bon voyage,*
*Neville Mortimer*

I read it twice, my eyes lingering on the line about learning who
you were. Neville might have been writing it for me. Without
Brontë to mother, without my team to manage, who was
Magnolia Jones, who did she want to be?

I shook my head, ashamed. 'Even her new boss was more
supportive than I was.'

Kat flapped a hand. 'It was easy for him to say that – it
wasn't his kid. Nice guy though.'

'She thought they'd approve of her plans,' I said, remembering how she'd countered my worries with her positive
outlook. 'I'm glad she got to read that letter before she died.
Good for her. No doubt she'd have told me all about it the
next time we met. So she could have had it all: the time to
travel and the job she'd wanted. She was a smart cookie.'

'A gap year.' Kat sighed with longing. 'Can you imagine?
Complete freedom, a few clothes stuffed in a backpack, no
responsibilities, no one needing you. Why do kids have all
the fun? I think mums should get a chance to go. Why isn't
mum's gap year a thing?'

'Because I imagine most families would come apart at the
seams without Mum there to organise everything. Women are
the engine room of the family machine. Usually,' I added as
Kat gave a soft snort.

Our mum hadn't been like that. It had been up to me to
steer us to safety when she landed us in deep water. An event
which happened all too often.

'True,' she said. 'Talking of Mum—'

I cut her off immediately. 'We aren't.'

'She's worried about you,' Kat persisted. 'We know how short life is. Don't you think maybe it's time for you two to reconcile?'

I shook my head. 'I'm angry. At life, at the man who took Brontë from me, with myself, and I'm still angry at Mum. It's not fair. She lost me when I was twenty-three through being an irresponsible mother. And even though I did everything I could to support my own daughter, I lost *her* at twenty-three anyway. How is that fair?'

'It isn't, Mags. None of it is. But keeping Mum out of your life won't change that.'

'She sent me a text yesterday asking to meet,' I told her. 'I didn't reply.'

My relationship with my mother through my teenage years had only survived by a thread. After the reaction I got from her when I told her I was pregnant with Brontë, I cut ties altogether. I'd been better off without her. Now we only saw each other sporadically, usually at Kat's instigation.

I had a vision of Mum crying during her granddaughter's funeral and all I could think of was that she'd advised me to have the pregnancy terminated. If I'd listened to her, Brontë would never have existed.

'She bought a car a few months ago, you know,' Kat added. 'A Mini. Brand new. So I think she might have got on top of her finances.'

'Better late than never,' I said, refusing to be drawn.

'Think about it, okay?' she begged. 'She has two daughters. It would be nice for her to see both of them now and again.'

I fell silent, shutting down the topic. Neither of us had a relationship with our dad. His choice. He'd pulled further and further away from us after leaving the family home. By the time Brontë was born he'd moved to Galway. I'd let him know the details of Brontë's funeral, but he hadn't attended. At least Mum had been there, I supposed.

I pulled Brontë's book onto my lap. Instantly I felt a connection with her. I traced a fingertip across the cover illustrations, imagining her concentrating, her brow furrowed as she drew them. What had she written on these pages? Where had she wanted to go, what had she wanted to see, to experience?

'Are you going to open it?' said Kat, reading my mind.

'I will,' I said with a sad smile. 'But these pages contain her plans for the future. When I've read this notebook, she'll never be able to share anything new with me again.'

Suddenly my heart thundered as an idea began to form. A crazy, spontaneous idea that was about as far away from anything I'd normally contemplate as possible. Maybe I didn't have to go away without Brontë. Maybe there was a way to take her with me, for me to stay connected. Here was an itinerary all mapped out, one full of the places that Brontë had wanted to visit.

'Hey.' Kat put her hand on mine. 'If you've changed your mind about reading it, I understand.'

My eyes skimmed over Brontë's illustrations of palm trees and sunglasses, dolphins and turtles, kangaroos and cocktails . . .

'I think you're right about me needing a holiday,' I said.

I could see a hundred doctors and would put money on all of them telling me I needed to take some time out. But could I leave home with all its memories of Brontë behind me? In this house, I could conjure her up so easily.

Except, if I followed this itinerary, I wouldn't be leaving her behind. Brontë could be my guide, and that way we'd be in it together. I wouldn't lose her; I could make new memories that she would become a part of.

'Brontë will never have this adventure, but I could,' I said.

'What are you talking about?' She frowned.

'Her gap-year trip.' Goosebumps ran down my spine. 'I could do it for her, follow the footsteps she's already set out for me. I haven't been travelling for twenty-four years. It'll do me good to get out of my comfort zone.'

'Maggie, the comfort zone is exactly where you should be right now,' Kat said, horrified. 'I won't be able to hop on my bike and be with you in ten minutes if you're on the other side of the world.'

'You told me to be spontaneous!' I protested.

'Two weeks in Greece would tick that box. There's no need to take on a young person's gap-year adventure. We're talking rucksacks and hostels and shared bathrooms. You'll hate it.'

Part of me knew she was right. But a bigger part of me had something to prove. To Anna: that I could take a break and return as the ideal candidate to sit on the ShopSwift board. To Kat: that there was more to me than work. And most importantly, to my darling Brontë: that her gap-year adventure mattered to me.

'For the first time in my adult life I don't have a goal,' I said quietly. 'This book in my hands would give me that. And I can't think of a better way to honour Brontë's life.'

We stared at each other.

Every holiday I'd been on since Brontë had been born had been carefully researched, planned around what I knew she'd like. This one was no different, except that the planning had been done by her instead of me. And there was no one I trusted more than my daughter.

'Me neither.' Kat brushed a tear from her cheek. 'If you're sure you want to do this, I'll support you. I'm proud of you, Mags.'

I smiled through my tears. 'I haven't gone yet.'

'On that note, I guess we'd better find out all the places you'll be going to.' Kat nodded to the book, but still my fingers hesitated to open it.

'I don't know.' I'd thought about this book so many times over the last six months. It had become a symbol of everything I regretted about my relationship with Brontë; most of all, for not sharing her excitement about her proposed trip. 'I want to savour each page, read it as I go along.'

She looked doubtful. 'You're going to turn up at the airport with your suitcase, turn to page one and buy a ticket?'

I squirmed. 'I don't think I can be quite that spontaneous. How about we find out the first destination?'

'If that's what you want,' Kat said, bemused, 'go for it.'

Very slowly I opened the cover of *Brontë's Gap Year* and read the first page.

*The Adventures of Brontë April Jones, 2023.* Beside me, Kat breathed a little sigh.

*Can I show you, Mum?* Brontë's voice rang in my ears, and I tried hard to blot out my negative response. I should have looked then, but at least I was doing it now.

The next couple of pages consisted of her contact details, a packing list and a rundown of vaccinations she'd need.

'I'll read those later,' I said, impatient to find out where she'd planned to go first.

The heading of the next page caused Kat and I to gasp aloud, and the words began to swim in front of me.

'Will you read it?' I asked shakily, pushing the book onto my sister's lap.

Kat cleared her throat. 'Sandwiched like the easy-going child between its two bossy siblings, China and India, is Nepal. It might only be small, but it's home to the world's tallest mountain, Mount Everest, and the backpacker's favourite, Kathmandu. This is the perfect place—'

'Stop!' I said. 'Save the rest, that's all I need to know.'

'Wow.' Kat closed the book and handed it back to me. 'So now what?'

'Looks like I'm going to Nepal.'

'Are you sure this is wise?' She chewed her lip.

'No, but I'm doing it anyway. Mum's Gap Year is on.'

## Brontë's Gap Year

Nepal looks like the perfect place to kick off my adventure. Harry is jealous he can't come with me for this bit. I wish he was, but you know what they say, absence makes the heart grow fonder (hopefully). Anyway, it'll do me good to start off by myself, be independent. The landscape will be like nothing I've ever encountered. I want to get as close to Everest as possible. I went up Mount Snowdon on a school trip years ago and Mum was freaked out enough with that. God knows what she's going to think about the Himalayas. There are also jungles, rivers, elephants, temples . . . loads of cool stuff. I'm probably going to be here for six weeks, more if I love it. I've never challenged myself physically, so this is my chance to find out how I cope when my body is pushed to its limits.

PACKING LIST

Still to be finalised but . . .

- Travel light! You're going to be carrying all your own clothes for a whole year and you can buy stuff as you go.
- First Aid kit
- Paints, pens and notebook
- Toothbrush, toothpaste, hairbrush, sunscreen, moisturiser
- Hiking boots, trainers and flip-flops
- Sheet sleeping bag, a towel, a sarong
- One nice dress
- T-shirts, shorts, bikinis, knickers and a bra

DAY ONE

Check into the Ganesh Guest House. Explore Kathmandu! Ride in a rickshaw! Learn to say thank you and hello in Nepali. Buy a SIM card. Go shopping, but do not go wild, Brontë Jones – remember your budget. Get a good night's sleep, you're gonna need it.

# Chapter 4

## Nepal

The arrivals hall in Kathmandu was chaotic, noisy and four-and-a-half thousand miles from home. My eyes were gritty, and I couldn't remember the last time I'd gone this long without a shower. I had begun to fantasise about a decent cup of coffee and fresh underwear.

Edgy and overwhelmed, I nudged my way through the swarm of travellers. Stay positive, I thought. I'd done the hard thing; I'd arrived in Nepal and my mini gap year was underway. What had started off as a crazy notion had quickly turned into a challenge I was determined to complete.

After finding out that Brontë's intended first stop was Nepal, Kat had said goodnight and headed home. I'd taken Brontë's gap year book to bed with me and read through the first couple of pages. Brontë had been right: I *was* freaked out by the mention of the Himalayas. I'd have been worried to death if I'd known she was planning to go mountain climbing. Funny how your perspective changes; given the choice between an adventurous child and one I'd never get to hug again, well, that wasn't a choice at all.

The following morning, I'd booked a one-way ticket to Kathmandu before I'd had chance to talk myself out of it.

Then I'd reserved a room for two nights at the guest house Brontë had mentioned. Preparing for the trip had given me a goal and a deadline, something to focus on other than the fact I had been banned from work for the next three months.

Since then, I hadn't even opened Brontë's book. She was going to be my guide, I was going to go where she wanted to go, I'd allow the adventure to unfurl as I went, letting her surprise me with her words and delight me with her drawings every time I turned a new page. I already knew I'd be heartbroken when I reached the end, but right now, the connection I had to my girl was giving me something positive to cling to.

Once through customs, and reunited with my suitcase, I found myself in a large area opening on to the street. A crowd of taxi drivers, tour guides and hawkers waved at the new arrivals, shouting to attract business. My driver would be waiting somewhere, but a sign for the ladies' toilets drew me like a magnet. I had no idea how long the drive would be to my hotel and no woman my age would pass up the chance for a wee, so I joined the queue.

'First time?' The woman in front looked me up and down. She was wearing serious trekking gear, her mouth partially obscured by a fringed scarf around her neck.

I was in the white kaftan Brontë had bought me, perhaps not the most practical choice, but it had felt symbolic to wear something chosen by her as I embarked on her journey.

'In Nepal, yes. A spontaneous trip on my own.'

'Wow, that's brave.' The woman looked sceptical. 'I've been many times. But never alone.'

'It must be good then,' I said, ignoring the comment about not travelling solo.

She gave a dry laugh. 'Either that or I'm a sucker for punishment.'

I hoped it was the former. 'Any tips for a newbie?'

She listed them on her fingers. 'Don't drink the water. Don't get money out of ATMs without checking the fees – it's practically extortion. Avoid the local brew; only drink branded spirits. I'm serious about that – I heard of someone who lost their eyesight drinking unlicensed booze.'

'Right, thanks,' I said, beginning to wish I hadn't asked.

The woman hadn't finished. 'Never accept the first price you're given on anything – you must always barter. Always keep an eye on your bags. Let your hotel organise your transport. Never, ever get into a car which stops on the street for you, or heaven knows where you might end up. And don't, under any circumstances, stroke stray dogs, no matter how cute they look. Rabies is not pretty. Oh, and don't touch the cows either,' she pulled up her sleeve and showed me a red mark on her arm. 'Ringworm.'

'That's quite a list of don'ts,' I said nervously. 'Are there any dos?'

'I didn't mean to put you off.' She laughed airily. 'Go slowly, take time to acclimatise yourself to the altitude, and listen to the advice from the experts.'

'I'm not trekking to Base Camp,' I told her. A pair of Nike trainers and a bobble hat was the extent of my outdoor kit. Right now the temperature was in the low twenties and inside the building it felt muggy. Hopefully, I wouldn't even need the hat.

'What *are* you doing here then?' she asked. A cubicle became free, and she darted towards it. 'Oops, sorry, I'm desperate.'

Which saved me from replying that I had absolutely no idea.


'Your room is not ready, mam.' The man behind the reception desk of the Ganesh Guest House returned my passport to me after photocopying it.

'Oh dear.' My heart sank. So much for that shower I'd been dreaming of.

'Do not worry. You may leave your suitcase here and come back in a few hours.' He waved an arm to the space behind his desk where a heap of rucksacks were piled on top of one another.

It didn't seem very secure. Everything I needed was in that case, and probably a number of things I didn't, since I'd had to pack for every climate. I'd even brought a small tin containing some of Brontë's ashes, so that I'd always have her with me. I'd be devastated if I lost that tin.

'Thank you.' I glanced outside. Most buildings were either boarded up or abandoned; there was a pile of rubble on the opposite side of the street and the view of the sky was obscured by an overhead lattice of thick cables and wires, some of which hung dangerously low. Was I ridiculous to be attempting this trip, I asked myself? I could have been on a beach in Florida now, watching the sunset with a cold drink in my hand.

'You'll be quite safe, honey,' a woman piped up in an American accent. She was sitting on the floor with her laptop plugged into a power point, a steaming cup of tea beside her. 'Five minutes in that direction,' she jerked her head, 'you'll be right in the centre of things. There's even a Starbucks if you're not up to experimenting yet.'

'Thanks.' I replied, mildly affronted that I looked like someone who would only stick to international chains when abroad. Starbucks, though . . . what an unexpected treat.

'Perhaps you would like our chauffeur, Lila, to take you somewhere?' asked the receptionist.

The chauffeur, who'd been watching TV in the lobby, gave me a toothless smile and waved his hand towards the minibus which had collected me from the airport.

'That's very kind, but I think I'll take a walk and get some air.' My knuckles were still white from the journey, and I was feeling queasy.

The hotel was costing me about twenty pounds per night, so I hadn't expected to be picked up in a limo. But neither had I expected the taxi to be crammed with five large men on what seemed to be the equivalent of an Indian stag weekend, or missing a driver's door, seat belts, and a chunk of the floor near my feet where the metal had rusted through.

I picked up my backpack and, remembering the warning from the woman in the loo about leaving luggage unattended, I collected my suitcase and set off through the narrow pot-holed streets in search of coffee.

'We're not in Honeybourne anymore, Toto,' I misquoted to a small fat puppy fast asleep behind a lamppost. I bent to stroke it before the dangers of rabies came back to me, and straightened again. 'Sorry, pup. Better safe than foaming at the mouth.'

I knew from the guidebook I'd bought at Heathrow that the tourist centre was called Thamel. And within minutes I found myself in an area where ribbons of fluttering prayer flags criss-crossed the streets. It was crowded, colourful and confusing; a cacophony of sound making my head spin. People advertised their wares at the tops of their voices; they tooted car horns, revved scooters, and blasted music from doorways. My ears rang with the melodic sounds of singing bowls being thrust in front of me and demonstrated by insistent sellers. Cashmere pashminas, silk scarves and yak blankets in every size and hue were waved at me, along with buddha statues, incense sticks, and elephant-printed baggy trousers.

Brontë would have loved it, but I was tired from my travels, overwhelmed by the hustle and bustle. Plus, I was having major regrets about bringing my suitcase with me. What had I been thinking? It was impossible to steer the wheels over the cobbles and I kept bumping into people. I felt stupid, naive and very alone.

Finally, my senses overloaded and my stomach rumbling, I found a café with a menu in English, which lured me in with the smell of freshly roasted beans and the promise of high-speed internet.

As soon as I was settled with a large coffee and a cake, I logged onto the wi-fi.

Instantly a barrage of emails came in from ShopSwift. George wanted me to read over a report he'd written, the finance department had a raft of queries on recent invoices, Anna messaged to wish me luck and remind me that under no circumstances should I respond to any work emails and, disturbingly, Lee wanted details of the terms I'd agreed with Vap-A-Rise. I answered all the emails except the one from Lee, to which I replied by reiterating Anna's instruction not to do any work and referring him to her. I felt a prickle of unease at the thought of him muscling in on my clients as soon as my back was turned, but there was absolutely nothing I could do about it.

Correspondence complete, I FaceTimed Kat.

'Mags!' my sister squealed. 'Thank goodness you're still alive. I haven't slept since dropping you off at the airport.'

'Ditto.' I said, yawning.

'Hey, I bumped into your friend Sadie yesterday.' Kat stifled a yawn of her own. 'She had no idea you were going away and said you haven't been at book club for months. Why's that? You loved it.'

A memory flashed up of the last time I'd seen the group; the anxious expressions, the too-tight hugs, all of them walking on eggshells, trying to say the right thing.

'I left,' I confessed. 'I made them feel awkward. No one likes to moan about their kids when your friend's only child is dead. I felt like a constant reminder to them to count their blessings.'

'Oh Maggie.' Her expression melted. 'That's so sad.'

I shrugged. 'That's life. Anyway, I've lost my reading mojo, so it's probably for the best. So do you want to hear about my trip so far?'

I told her about my two long flights and the journey to the guest house in the rickety minibus and how I'd seen a cow wandering down the street on its own. I missed out the bit about the doom-monger with ringworm at the airport.

A waiter approached me to take my empty plate. 'Can I get you anything else, mam?'

I was still hungry. I'd only eaten airline meals and snacks for the last twenty-four hours. I tried to see what other customers around me were eating, but all I could surmise was that they were enjoying it, whatever it was. 'Yes please, what do you recommend?'

'First time in Nepal?' He nodded at the guidebook on the table.

I nodded.

He opened his arms wide. 'Then it has to be *dal bhat*.'

'Sounds great,' I said, not quite sure what I'd agreed to.

'What's Brontë's itinerary for the next few days?' Kat asked.

'Not sure. I'll read the next page while you're on.'

I tugged *Brontë's Gap Year* from my backpack.

She was there in every drawing, every stroke of the pen and I took a moment to drink it in.

'Her intention was to end Day One with a good night's sleep,' I told her, 'and you'll get no arguments from me there. I'm thinking a comforting audiobook and a long lie-in tomorrow.'

'And tomorrow brings . . . ?' My sister did a drumroll with fingertips on her table.

I turned the page and read the headline. A cold shiver ran down my back. 'Oh no.'

'What is it?' Kat leaned closer.

'Rise and shine!' I read out loud. 'This is the big day. Register with the Everest Base Camp Guys at eight a.m.'

Below was a collage of images of snow-covered mountains, wooden huts, people whose smiles beamed out from inside furry hoods. At the centre was a paragraph which looked as it if had been printed off a website:

> Join us for a two-week adventure of a lifetime! Immerse your-self in the natural beauty of the world's highest mountain, let us take you higher than the clouds and discover endurance levels and strength within you that you never even dreamed of. Experience the thrill of suspension bridges across chasms, the charm of Sherpa villages and a warm Nepalese welcome in tea houses as we climb to the Everest Base Camp.

'Bloody hell, Mags! You can't go there.' She clapped a hand to her mouth.

'I can,' I said automatically. My heart was pounding but I didn't want Kat to sense my fear. 'I can do anything I put my mind to.'

'Please don't do anything foolish. People die going up Everest.'

'I think that's climbing to the summit,' I corrected her. 'Base Camp is not as treacherous.'

But it would be tough going, and I was far from fit. I had been so weighed down with sadness since losing Brontë that I'd probably only done 10,000 steps in the whole of December.

'But still really dangerous,' Kat squeaked.

'I've committed to this trip; I can't fall at the first hurdle,' I told her.

'But do you *want* to do it?'

'This isn't about me,' I tried to explain. 'It's about Brontë. Okay, I haven't trained for it, and I don't have the right clothes, but I can buy what I need.'

'Brontë wouldn't expect you to start flinging yourself around mountains. This was her dream trip,' Kat said firmly. 'Hers. There might be lots of things that you don't want to do on those pages. Are you going to do them all regardless of how miserable or scared they make you feel?'

'Yes!' I shot back, adding more quietly, 'Probably.'

'Of course you're not!' she retorted. 'You're going to make this trip work for you. If Brontë had designed it with you in mind, it would have been kaftans instead of crampons. Am I right or am I right?'

I conceded a smile. 'You're a bit right.'

Kat shook her head fondly. 'You idiot. Look, promise me you won't rush into anything. Take a breath and think it through.'

'I promise.' Although I might go back and buy that puffa jacket I'd seen.

'Mam?' The waiter slid a plate between me and the phone and bowed as he walked away.

'I'd better go. My food has arrived.'

'What is it?'

I looked at my dinner: a pile of wafer-thin poppadoms, two bowls, one of rice and one containing something brown, and a tiny pot of something fragrant. 'Not sure. Curried lentils by the look of it.'

'Sounds absolutely delicious and good for your digestion.' She gave a snort. 'Glad I'm not your roommate tonight.'

'I haven't got a roommate,' I said. 'I have a private suite, darling. The best that the Ganesh Guest House has to offer.' Which wasn't saying a lot.

I promised to keep in touch, and after we ended the call, I opened my internet browser and searched 'Nepal trekking for beginners'.

Kat was right about the lentil curry, it was delicious. Was she right about the trekking too? Was it one step too far? How far would I go to carry out my daughter's wishes?

# Chapter 5

## Nepal

'Your room, mam.' A young member of staff opened the door and set my suitcase over the threshold.

I took a quick look at the piece of paper I'd put in my pocket. 'Dhan-ya-bad,' I read out.

My waiter had patiently taught me how to say 'thank you' and I'd written it down on the back of the receipt from the café. I'd looked it up since and this was not how it was spelled, but written phonetically I'd have a chance of remembering it.

The boy grinned, no doubt impressed at my mastery of his language, and handed me the key to room 106 with a small bow.

I repeated my only word of Nepali and bowed back to him. I locked the door as soon as he'd left and looked around, trying not to grimace.

It resembled a prison cell, except perhaps not as clean. Twin beds, separated by a small nightstand, a thin folded towel at the end of each one. A window overlooked a row of air-conditioning units which thrummed loudly. The person in the room next door had the TV on full volume. Above me someone flushed the toilet and it sounded as if water was cascading through my ceiling. I consoled myself with the fact that not only had I brought ear plugs with me, but I was so tired that I'd probably be able to sleep on the street with that puppy I'd seen earlier. Moving into the bathroom, I found a stained bath and a chipped toilet bowl; but on the upside, the light was so dim I could barely see anything at all. My bed was calling, but first I needed to wash away the grime from the journey.

The shower over the bath only produced a dribble of luke-warm water when I turned on the tap, but it was better than nothing. I checked the door was locked, stripped off and showered and washed my hair as quickly as I could.

Ten minutes later, I was searching for my new satin pyjamas in my suitcase when I heard the unmistakable scrabbling noise of a key being inserted in the lock of the door. I froze, holding my breath, my heart thumping. I was only wearing a towel. Looking around for something to throw on, I picked up a hoodie.

The handle jiggled as whoever was on the other side wrestled with the lock.

'Who is it?' I inched towards the door, struggling to tug my hoodie over the bath towel turban I'd got wrapped around my hair. I got my head into the hood, but the rest of it stayed wedged on my shoulders.

The rattling stopped.

'Your roomie,' said a woman's voice. 'Have you got the key in the lock by any chance?'

American by the sound of her.

'Yes. But I don't have a roomie.' I opened the door a fraction and peered out into the narrow corridor to find the woman I'd met in the lobby earlier shrugging a large rucksack off her shoulders. 'You must have the wrong room.'

'Ah, shoot.' She looked at the key in her hand. The fob was carved with the number 106.

A family group chose that moment to pass by, forcing the woman to lean in through my open door, knocking her rucksack over onto my legs as she did so.

I staggered backwards and the rucksack hit the floor.

'I'll run back down to the lobby and sort it out.' She gave me an apologetic smile. 'Can I leave my bag here, save me lugging it all the way?'

'Sure.' I tugged it inside with one hand, the other making sure my towel didn't drop off.

The woman strode away, and I shut the door, wedging the backpack against it. By the time she returned, I was wearing my pyjamas. This time she wasn't alone. The man from reception was with her.

'Mam,' said the man, addressing me nervously. 'On behalf of the Ganesh Guest House I am very sorry. But there has been a mix-up.'

'What sort of mix-up?' I looked from him to her.

She shrugged apologetically. 'A double-booking sort of mix-up. You and I have both been allocated this room.'

I glanced over my shoulder and indicated my stuff everywhere. 'But I've already unpacked.'

'No problem,' said the woman. 'I never unpack, so you can keep all the drawers.'

'But why do we have to share?' I said to the man. 'Can you not put this lady, er . . .'

'Tiff,' she supplied.

'Could Tiff not go in another room?'

'This is impossible,' explained the man. 'Our hotel is full except for one spare bed in the men's dormitory.'

'Listen, it's not ideal, but you won't even know I'm here,' said Tiff. 'It's one night and I'm leaving early in the morning.'

'Thank you, mam,' said the receptionist, bowing as if the matter was settled. 'The management are very grateful.'

'Hold on!' I gripped the front of my pyjama shirt. 'I specifically requested a private en suite room.'

'I am very sorry, mam. We have only one private room. Somehow this lady booked it also.'

'Look, I'm not crazy about it either,' said Tiff, casually. 'But I'm as entitled to this room as you, so why don't we agree to get along?'

I let out a breath. 'I've never shared a room with a stranger.'

'Never?' Tiff wrinkled her nose in disbelief. 'Not a traveller, huh?'

'Not since I was twenty-two.'

I had a sudden image of how Brontë would have dealt with this mix-up if she'd been here instead of me. She'd have opened the door wide and welcomed the other woman in. Maybe I was going to have to be more like Brontë on this trip. I was supposed to be letting her guide me, after all.

'And actually, I had the time of my life on that trip, so I guess it's about time I did it again. Pleased to meet you, Tiff, I'm Maggie. Come in.'

'How early are you leaving tomorrow?' I held out a bag of peanuts for Tiff to help herself.

'Thanks.' She took a handful. 'Five a.m. maybe?'

I'd cleared my things off one of the beds for her, but she'd insisted that she didn't need any other space. I'd left her to work on her laptop while I dried my hair and now we were both sitting on our beds, sharing my snacks and drinking bottles of the local beer Tiff had fetched from the hotel bar.

'Right.' My heart sank. I'd been looking forward to a slow start to the day. On the plus side, I'd have the bathroom to myself again. My stomach was protesting about all the lentils I'd eaten earlier.

'I'm taking a flight tour around the Himalayas,' Tiff told me. 'It's my second trip. It was so foggy the first time I couldn't see

58

a thing. This time I'm hoping I get some good pictures. But if I don't,' she shrugged, 'well, I guess I'll be back a third time.'

'You love Nepal that much?' I said with a hint of scepticism.

'Absolutely I do,' she confirmed. 'But officially I'm here for work.'

'So this is a business trip?'

'Yep.'

She had a brand-new phone and an expensive-looking laptop and her rucksack looked very professional.

'So why are you staying in such a cheap hotel?'

She grinned. 'I was thinking the same about you in your silky PJs and your fancy suitcase.'

I smiled back. 'Touché.'

'You strike me as a woman who likes a hotel room with a safe and a proper coffee machine and nice toiletries.' Tiff's eyes sparkled with mischief. 'Definitely not one where you end up sharing a tiny twin room with a beer-swilling American.' As if to press home her point she belched softly. 'Excuse me.'

I would have liked a safe; I'd been contemplating sleeping with my passport, credit cards and Brontë's notebook under my pillow until Tiff turned up. 'You're not wrong. But I asked you first.'

'Well.' She tilted her head back, threw a peanut up in the air and caught it in her mouth. 'Life has a habit of going off at a tangent until you're so far away from yourself that you forget who you are. Are you with me?'

I nodded politely.

'Staying somewhere unpretentious and authentic, travelling with a backpack instead of a flashy case on wheels,' her eyes wandered to my nice spinny case and back to me, 'brings me back to the girl I was at eighteen, who was so certain of who she was and what she was going to achieve in life. Staying in a guest house like this helps keep the money in the local area instead of lining the pockets of the global chains, and it's like pressing my reset button, I guess.'

I studied her. Mid-thirties, maybe. Far enough away from eighteen to have changed completely, at any rate. 'Do you honestly think you're the same girl?'

'I know I am.' She slurped her beer. 'There's a little more junk in the trunk, but that internal flame still burns the same. How about you?'

'Why am I here at this guest house?' I asked. Tiff nodded. 'My daughter chose it.'

'Is that her?' Tiff pointed to the framed photo of the two of us I'd brought with me from home.

'Yes, that's Brontë on her twenty-first birthday almost three years ago. My only child.'

'She has a beautiful smile, and you look so alike. I bet she thinks her mom is cool, coming to Nepal on her own?'

I shook my head. 'She was the cool one. She died last year.'

Tiff groaned. 'Oh shoot, Maggie, I'm so sorry.'

We fell silent and both drank our beer. I was used to this pattern. I always felt so sorry for the other person as they racked their brains to follow my revelation with something which didn't sound clichéd that I usually ended up talking for England. I needed to get better at that.

'She was going to take a gap year and go travelling,' I said. 'Had it all mapped out. So I'm taking her place, to her honour her memory. Nepal was the first stop.'

'Wow. That's brave.' Tiff raised her beer bottle across the gap between our beds and I chinked mine against it. 'Kudos to you, lady.'

'Not brave; naive,' I argued. 'I found out today that she was going to trek to Everest Base Camp. Which means I'll be doing it instead. My sister isn't happy about it. Quite honestly, I'm not thrilled, but that was the deal I made.'

'With that suitcase?' Tiff gave a bark of laughter.

'No, obviously not,' I said haughtily. 'I'll buy what equipment I need.'

She looked at my Nike trainers. 'I'm assuming you've got walking boots already. Because you can't do it in new boots, they have to be worn in.'

That was a good point; imagine if I ended up with blistered heels and I had to keep going despite the pain. I'd hate that.

'How's your fitness level?' Tiff went on. 'Even the base camp is like a 5,000-metre climb. It's a physically challenging trek at high altitude. You can't rock up and say a single ticket to EBC, please. And you can forget having a private room – they'll laugh you off the mountain.'

'I think I've proved I can share if push comes to shove,' I said primly.

'What about the rest of your group, huh? They'll have been preparing for months, saving their money for this trip of a lifetime, bucket-list-level expedition. Don't you think it might be a teeny bit selfish to tag along and slow everyone down?'

'Okay, fine, I get it,' I snapped.

She was so annoying. Correct, but annoying.

'Well, that's a relief,' she muttered under her breath.

I could sense that she was dying to laugh. I didn't blame her: the stupid middle-aged English woman who thought she could trek the world's most treacherous landscape on a whim. *I can do anything*, I'd claimed hours earlier to Kat. What an idiot.

I wished I could laugh at myself. I used to be able to, years ago, when life had felt like one big adventure, when I'd got by on finding solutions to life's challenges and brushing off mistakes as part of the learning process.

But now the stakes were too high to laugh it off. I had three months to tick off all the things Brontë wanted to see and do. I'd made her a promise. I didn't want to let her down.

I let out a long sigh.

'Hey, I didn't mean to come on so strong.' Tiff swung her feet to the floor and turned to face me. 'I'm sorry.'

'It's okay,' I replied, feeling teary. 'I wasn't thinking it through, that's all. Seeing the mountains up close was Brontë's number-one reason for being in Nepal. I have to find another way to do it, preferably one which won't require an oxygen mask.'

Tiff grinned. 'That's easy. Come on the flight tour tomorrow with me. You won't get closer than that.'

She opened her laptop and tapped at the keyboard. 'Want me to book you a seat?'

'I . . .' I tried to concoct a reason to refuse, but other than the fact that I'd have to be up before dawn, I couldn't think of one. Tiff's idea was a great compromise and flying would be a damn sight easier than walking. 'Why not. Yes please.'

Within minutes, I had a seat on board the 6:30 a.m. flight with Yeti Airlines and a plan for the day. Between us on the nightstand lay *Brontë's Gap Year*. I gave it a kiss and settled down to sleep, feeling closer to my daughter than I had in months.

'Thank you,' I said into the darkness once we'd turned the lights out an hour later. 'I'm glad the guest house was double-booked, and I got to meet you.'

'Save your thanks until tomorrow,' said Tiff. 'Apparently my snoring could wake the dead.'

I snapped on the light and rummaged around for my ear plugs. 'I don't suppose you'd mind waiting for me to fall asleep first, would you?'

From the other bed came a low rumble which grew into the sort of noise I hadn't heard outside of a sea life centre. So that would be a no.

Nepal absolute definites:

Trek to Everest Base Camp

Visit the Boudhanath Stupa and see the prayer flags

Take art materials into a school (maybe even do some art with the kids???)

Bathe an elephant. Harry did this in Sri Lanka and the photos he got are awesome.

Visit a women's empowerment project. Mum told me that if you put other people at the centre of your world, you'll always feel fulfilled. I love that. This trip feels self-indulgent, so my aim is to give back as much as I receive.

# Chapter 6

## Nepal

Six-thirty a.m. on the tarmac at Kathmandu's domestic airport was a chilly and drizzly place to be. Beside me, I could sense Tiff's disappointment as we headed towards the tiny aeroplane that awaited us.

'I'm not a morning person,' she'd informed me when first her alarm and then mine had jolted me from sleep. 'Please ignore me until I've had at least two cups of coffee.'

I was with her on the coffee front. I'd kept quiet and retreated into the bathroom to talk to Brontë while I got dressed (only in my head – I didn't want Tiff to hear me) until Tiff had knocked on the door to chivvy me along. So far, we'd only had one coffee and I was keeping conversation to a minimum.

'Oh my Lord, will it even get off the ground?' hissed the woman in front, clinging to her partner's arm. 'Looks like it's held together with elastic bands.'

'Look at that, Diane.' Her partner slowed to peer at the propeller as he walked past. 'Get a pigeon caught in one of those and we're dead in the air.'

'Don't say things like that, Steve,' she tutted.

I wasn't usually a nervous flyer, but that was the last thing I needed to hear. I'd been on bigger buses.

'Asshole,' Tiff muttered, tugging up her hood against the rain. 'It's precisely because it's so small that we can get so close to the summit. Still up for this?'

I was doing this for Brontë. Whether I was up for it or not was irrelevant. 'A bit scared,' I admitted. 'Thanks to Steve.'

'Fear and excitement are two sides of the same coin,' she replied. 'Let's choose excitement today.'

'That's a brilliant way of looking at it. Thanks.' I smiled gamely and tried to ignore the way the steps were shaking under Steve's weight as the couple ascended ahead.

'Namaste!' A member of cabin crew greeted us on board and waved us to seats.

The flight wasn't full, which meant that Tiff and I had window seats with no one beside us, me on the row in front of her. The group boarded speedily and we were soon taxiing along the short runway.

Steve and Diane were sitting opposite, Steve at the window, taking shot after shot on a big camera. His wide shoulders encroached into Diane's space, forcing her to lean into the narrow aisle. I doubted she could even see the window, let alone the view.

I stared down through the rain over Kathmandu as we ascended, leaving the city behind, the tight grid of streets swiftly giving way to the lush greenery of hills and valleys. My ears popped as we climbed higher and higher, at last breaking through the layer of cloud until the aircraft was flooded with a blinding light.

Almost immediately, the Himalayas came into view in the distance and the change of mood inside the cabin was palpable. Noise levels began to rise, people leaned across to take pictures and the cabin crew wandered up and down pointing out sights to each passenger.

I was mesmerised by the view: snow-capped peaks of varying shapes and sizes as far as the eye could see, the tallest of which were encircled by gossamer clouds. Brilliant white contrasting with a sky so blue that the only shade I could think of to describe it was 'heavenly'.

In that moment, I was proud of myself: I'd been in the country less than twenty-four hours and already I was about to see the first item on Brontë's list.

Tiff prodded my shoulder. 'You must be my good luck charm. We're gonna get an incredible view. This sky is insane.'

I turned and beamed at her. 'You see, you didn't need a second cup of coffee after all.'

'Oh I do,' she replied, 'but there's no toilet on this aircraft and I didn't want to take any chances. So, you're glad you came?'

I nodded. 'It makes up for only getting three hours' sleep last night. You weren't kidding when you said you snore. You sounded like an injured sea lion.'

'Now wait a minute, lady. You can wear ear plugs to protect you from snoring. Whereas your gas? There was no escaping that, even with my pillow pressed over my face. What did you eat for dinner yesterday, rotten eggs?'

'Dal bhat,' I muttered, mortified. 'I don't think I've ever eaten so many lentils in one sitting.'

Tiff snorted. 'Better get used to it, princess. It's the Nepalese equivalent of a sandwich.'

'Excuse me, dear,' said Diane, waving to attract the attention of the stewardess. 'There isn't a life jacket under my seat. Neither is there one under my husband's.'

'No, mam, we do not keep them on board.' She tapped the instruction diagram on the back of the seat in front of Diane. 'See this picture? The cushion you are sitting on is your flotation device.'

'I see.' Diane's face turned a peculiar colour.

'A cushion?' Steve spluttered loudly. 'So, all that's saving me from death on a mountainside is a sodding cushion?'

'Don't make a fuss, Steve,' his wife whimpered. 'I don't feel safe as it is.'

'Me?' He snorted. 'Says the woman who ran screaming into the corridor last night when she saw a cockroach.'

'Cockroaches?' I turned to look at Tiff.

She raised an eyebrow. 'Better get used to those too.'

I instinctively scratched my scalp.

'Would you like to visit the cockpit?' the stewardess said to Diane. 'You get an excellent view of the mountains, and our experienced pilot will show you how safe we are.'

'I can't move,' said Diane, her bottom lip trembling. 'I'm frozen to the spot.'

A smiling man in a pilot's uniform appeared from the cockpit. 'Ladies and gentlemen, I would like to invite you one at a time to—'

'Whoah,' cried Steve, rising out of his seat, his safety belt straining across his lap. 'Get back to your chair and keep your eyes on the road, pal.'

'It is okay.' The pilot held his hands up. 'My colleague is flying the plane, there is no need to—'

The last word of his sentence was lost to the screams of the passengers as we hit a pocket of turbulence and the aircraft pitched and rolled like a canoe in rough waters. Both the pilot and the stewardess lurched forward, almost losing their footing. The pilot retreated swiftly to the cockpit while the stewardess rearranged her features into a smile.

'We're crashing,' screamed Diane, gulping in air. 'We're all going to die. I can't die now; I've got Harry Styles tickets.'

'Everyone please remain in your seats,' the stewardess said calmly. 'There is nothing to worry about. The captain knows what he is doing.'

I gripped the armrest, trying not to think about what would happen if we crashed on a snow-covered mountain. So much for me taking the less dangerous route to see Mount Everest.

'I think we're almost there.' Tiff prodded me again once the turbulence had disappeared.

My eyes roamed the skyline. There were so many mountain peaks ahead of us that even knowing it was the tallest one didn't help to identify it. 'Where?' I said, reaching for my camera. 'I can't pick it out.'

'We are approaching Everest,' said the stewardess.

The plane banked sharply to the left.

Diane let out an ear-piercing shriek. 'I want to get out.'

The stewardess handed Diane a paper bag. 'Breathe into this.'

'Off you go then,' Steve grunted. 'Don't forget your cushion.'

'We're crashing. I can't breathe. I can't . . . Oxygen, oxygen.' She leapt to her feet and choked as if someone was strangling her.

'Jesus Christ,' Steve said through clenched teeth.

'I'm going to have to ask you to sit down, mam, or we will have to turn the aeroplane around and go back.'

'No way,' Tiff muttered, 'over my goddamn body, not this time. Sit down, honey!'

'I'm going to throw up,' Diane moaned, burying her face in the bag.

'Is there a doctor on board?' said the stewardess, looking alarmed.

'A vet would do,' Steve added with a snigger. 'Preferably one who could put her out of her misery.'

I couldn't bear it; the wild look in her eyes was terrifying, and that husband of hers was the one who needed putting down.

'Me!' I put my hand up. 'I'm medically trained.'

'Thank you, thank you,' Diane garbled, discarding the paper bag. 'Can I get your strongest drugs, please?'

I ignored Tiff's look of surprise, moved to Diane's side and took her hands. 'Look at me, focus on my face. Let's breathe together. In and out, in and out.' I kept my voice low and calm, and my eyes on her.

'That's the final straw, Diane. I'm leaving you at home from now on,' her husband grumbled. 'I paid good money for this trip for your birthday, and you had to ruin it with your drama.'

'Sorry, Steve.' Her words escaped in wheezy gulps. 'But I don't like heights. Or flying, or confined spaces.'

I heard Tiff mutter, 'Asshole,' and I tried not to smirk.

My mum had had a panic attack once. Kat and I hadn't known what to do so we'd run next door to fetch our neighbour, a retired army officer. He didn't know what to do either so had thrown cold water over her and shouted in her face. She'd given him a black eye for his trouble. I taught myself how to deal with the situation after that. I learned to spot the warning signs too: a build-up of bills on the hall table, another one of her get-rich-quick schemes backfiring, a visit from the landlord. Her first response was to ignore trouble for as long as possible until inevitably there was no escape. Her second was to let it overwhelm her. The older I got, the more difficult it was to stay sympathetic when she'd invited trouble in so readily and regularly.

Steve unclipped the buckle on his safety belt and pushed past us.

'Where are you going?' Diane wept.

'The other side,' he said, throwing himself into my seat. 'I'm not missing Everest because you're being hysterical.'

'My name's Maggie,' I said to Diane to distract her. 'Short for Magnolia, which my mother chose because she thought it would make me appear interesting.'

'I feel faint,' she replied.

'Can you wiggle your toes?'

69

'Yes.'

'Well done. Circle your shoulders?'

Diane did what she was told and after a few more breaths, I could see her getting on top of the fear. 'Are we nearly there yet?'

*'Are we nearly there, Mummy?' Brontë's face was pressed up against the window of the train. Her first trip to London. Her exuberance as she told the lady opposite exactly what the day held in store had given the other passengers around us so much joy that I'd been filled with pride.*

Diane squeezed my hand hard, and I snapped back into the present.

'We are, Diane, yes.'

'Maggie?' Tiff poked her face around the seat. 'Sit down. You're going to miss it.'

I stood up slowly, bringing Diane with me, and guided her into the seat beside her husband. Then I swung myself into the seat beside Tiff, keeping one hand on her arm.

'I've got you, Diane,' I said, 'I'm right behind you.'

'And here we are,' said the stewardess, proudly, gesturing towards the window. 'That is Mount Everest.'

'Yes, sir.' Tiff nodded gently, a smile of bliss on her face. 'That's what I'm talking about.'

'Absolutely breathtaking.' I gazed out of the window in awe.

I was looking at the roof of the world, the highest point on our planet. It felt like such an important moment, such an achievement, a privilege, one I'd only got to experience because of Brontë. Everest stood regally above its neighbours, crowned with snow that sparkled in the sunlight as if it were coated with diamonds. Brontë's birthstone: an April baby. My heart twisted; I would have given anything for her to be on this plane instead of me. Anything. But this was the best I could manage.

'This is where you belong, darling,' I murmured. 'On top of the world.'

'Champagne?' Our stewardess appeared with a tiny trolley.

'Yes please,' replied Tiff and I together.

It was the quickest hour of my life and before I knew it, we were almost back at Kathmandu. Diane and Steve returned to their own seats for the second half of the flight and so did I.

As we prepared to descend through the clouds, Tiff plonked herself in the seat beside me.

'That was impressive, what you did back there with Diane. You almost missed seeing Everest yourself. That would have been quite a sacrifice for a stranger.'

'It was nothing. I was worried she'd have a full-blown episode and we might all miss it. And her husband wasn't helping.'

'He should never have brought her on this flight. Selfish people like that who are unaware that they're spoiling it for others make my blood boil.'

'I know. You made that perfectly clear last night, when I was planning to trek to Base Camp,' I reminded her.

'Yeah, well, I take that all back now.' She smiled sheepishly. 'You're a cool dude, Magnolia.'

I grimaced. 'Only my mother calls me that. I'm Maggie. Please.'

'Sure,' Tiff said, holding up her hands. 'Sorry. Are you really medically trained?'

I looked across at Diane, who'd calmed down and appeared not to be speaking to Steve. 'No, I work in sales for e-commerce systems. But I have got my first-aider certificate.'

She laughed. 'It worked anyways; you talked her round. What a trip. Glad you came?'

'Absolutely. It's a big tick on Brontë's list, and now I can move on to the next.'

'More importantly, you loved it. I saw it in your eyes,' she said with a grin.

That wasn't the most important thing: fulfilling Brontë's dreams was my one and only goal. But I let it go. She wouldn't understand and it wasn't worth arguing about.

The plane landed soon afterwards. Once we were decanted onto the tarmac and into the terminal, the group began to disperse. Out of the corner of my eye, I saw Diane blowing her nose and Steve shaking his head impatiently. The two men were nothing alike physically, but I suddenly thought of Kevin Armstrong and his odious attitude.

I ran after him and tapped him on the shoulder.

'You're the woman who helped Diane.' He puffed his chest out. 'Sorry about her.'

'My friend thinks you're an asshole, Steve,' I said, smiling an apology at Diane.

Behind me I heard Tiff choke.

'I disagree,' I continued before he had chance to interrupt, 'because at least assholes are useful. You knew your wife wouldn't like that flight, but you booked it anyway. And then when she had a panic attack, you abandoned her.'

'How dare you.' Steve turned puce with anger, and his mouth flapped open and shut like a guppy.

'If I hadn't intervened, she could have been a danger to herself and others. We might even have had to cut the flight short.'

'And I would not have been happy,' Tiff piped up.

Steve dismissed us with a wave of his hand. 'Women, overreacting as usual. You should learn how to keep calm under pressure.'

'Steve, dear, I think I've lost your passport.' Diane tugged at his arm.

His hands flew to his head and he gawped at her. 'What? What? Are you kidding me? Jesus Christ, Diane!'

She winked at us. 'Only kidding.'

He rolled his eyes. 'Very funny. Not.'

'So do you know what you're going to do now, Steve?' I said briskly.

'Back to the hotel for a nap,' he said. 'Not that it's your business.'

'No. You're going to ask Diane what she'd like to do next. And then you're going to do it. Right, Diane?'

She nodded. 'Right.'

'Oh my God,' said Tiff as we walked away. 'You called me your friend.'

I giggled and she giggled and by the time we found the driver from our guest house and climbed aboard the rusty minibus, we had tears rolling down our cheeks.

'Back to Boston for me tonight,' said Tiff, rolling her head from side to side to stretch her neck. 'What about you?'

'Lots more to see. I'll show you my list.' I took *Brontë's Gap Year* out of my rucksack and turned the pages until I came to the bookmark I'd stuck between the pages to ensure I didn't flick too far ahead.

I let Tiff read it for herself.

She cocked an eyebrow. 'You're happy to do the elephant stuff?'

'I've been on an elephant before, I'll have you know.'

Early morning before the sun rose too high. My arms round Jackson's waist, kissing his back, the elephant's thick dry skin against my legs . . . a day of pure exhilaration, memories as vivid as the day we made them.

Tiff gave me an appraising look before picking up my bookmark. 'Cute.'

'Brontë made it for me.' It had a photograph of her sitting on my knee while I read to her. The other side contained a quote from Betty Smith.

'*The world was hers for the reading,*' Tiff recited.

'Teaching her to read was one of my greatest pleasures.' I smiled at the old photo. 'I'll never forget the first time she read a whole book to me, the wonder on her face as her brain made sense of the story. We read together every night after that, taking turns until she was twelve. When she hit her teens, she'd only let me read to her if she was ill. I think she still loved it secretly but was too proud to admit it. When she grew up, we'd read by the pool on holiday and swap books.' I was going to miss those trips. 'Those were my favourite sort of holidays.'

Tiff started scrolling through her phone, checking emails, and it made me think about ShopSwift. I wondered whether Anna was letting Lee take over the Vap-A-Rise contract. But I brushed the thoughts away. No one is indispensable, Maggie, not even you, Anna had said.

Tiff looked up from her phone. 'I can't help thinking that somewhere more upmarket than the Ganesh would suit you, where you can join an organised tour for the rest of your time in Nepal.'

'Possibly. But that's not what Brontë planned to do.'

She narrowed her eyes. 'What are you doing here, Maggie? I mean really?'

'Keeping my promise to Brontë,' I said simply.

'You've come all this way and you're only going to focus on what your daughter wanted?' She sounded incredulous. 'What's in it for you, what are you getting out of the trip?'

'That *is* what's in it for me. I'm going to do as many things on Brontë's list as I can in the time I have available and then I'm going to go back to the UK and get on with my life.'

She studied me. 'Maybe it could be more than that.'

I glared at her. 'Don't try to tell me that something positive can come out of losing my only child. Because I don't want to hear it. If you dare give me any of that *trust the universe* crap, you and I are going to fall out.'

'I wasn't going to say that.'

74

'Good.'

She called out to the front of the minibus. 'Lila, is there a place around here we can buy art materials?'

'There is, mam, we go now?'

'Yes please.'

'That's really kind of you,' I said, surprised.

'After that we can tick off some of the other things, if . . .' She drew a breath, her eyes sparkling, 'you consider doing something for me.'

'Okay.' I was intrigued. 'Fire away.'

'I co-run a volunteer project in the Chitwan valley; it's called One World. We could use someone like you. Someone – no offence – mature, to help with kindergarten. Those kids would love some new art stuff, by the way. You'd get your own room and you'd be able to complete the rest of your Nepal list while you're there. I think you'd get a lot out of it.'

'So are you asking me to become a volunteer?' My brain wound back twenty-four years to the beach in Bali. I'd loved living and working alongside the locals; I'd had to prove myself worthy of their respect. What was that guy's name? The one who'd resented all the volunteers . . . ?

'That's right. What do you say?'

'Am I not too old? Won't the others be eighteen-year-olds on a gap year?'

'So what?' She shrugged. 'They'll love you. And I bet you'd enjoy their company too.'

'You might be right.' I nodded slowly, remembering how much fun it had been when Brontë had brought her friends round for drinks before heading out for the evening.

'Cool. Say the word and I could organise transport today.' Tiff raised her eyebrows in anticipation.

'So soon?' I had no idea where the Chitwan valley was. My plan had been to go back to the guest house and work out what I was going to do with the next two weeks, when Brontë would have been trekking.

'Did they tell you that the Ganesh is fully booked again, so you'll be sharing with someone new tonight?' said Tiff. 'In case that helps you make a decision.'

I laughed at her tactics. 'Will I be in the Chitwan valley by dinnertime?'

She grinned. 'You sure will. But maybe lay off the dal bhat tonight. For everyone's sake.'

# Chapter 7

## Nepal

Tiff had two hours before she had to head to the airport and catch her flight home. We quickly worked out an itinerary for me to see as much of Brontë's list as possible and checked that Lila was happy to drive.

I liked Tiff. She was brash and forthright and served her opinions with a side of sarcasm, but she had a big heart and a *Why not?* attitude that was starting to rub off on me.

Our first stop was at one of the most sparsely stocked supermarkets I'd ever been to. I bought paper and pencils, paints, stickers, anything I thought young children would like. When I came to pay, it was such a small amount that I went back and loaded up with more until Tiff reminded me that I'd have to carry all this stuff with me.

We piled it into Lila's minibus, and while he drove us out of town to the Boudhanath Stupa she began to tell me about her love affair with Nepal. And I listened without interruption, my own thoughts intertwining with hers.

'My first trip was in 2014. I'm from New Jersey originally. The mountains and valleys and rivers and ancient temples, *phew!*' – she mimed her brain exploding – 'blew me away. We talk about something being old in the US if it reaches a hundred years. People drive cars older than that here.'

'I'd noticed.' I nodded at the hole in the floor of the minibus and we both smiled.

'But the best thing was the instinctive trust people had in each other. We were invited into homes to drink tea with the family, treated like special guests. We never do that at home, we're suspicious if someone even phones us unexpectedly.'

I had a sudden flashback to the time a few months ago when my friend Sadie knocked on my door and I hid in my bedroom until she'd gone. She must have known I was in. The lights were on, and my car was parked outside. The relief I felt, when she'd given up and left, had me sweating and shaking! I knew she was there because she cared, but I wasn't ready to be cared for. I realised now that I'd been wearing a suit of armour since Brontë died, scared that if I lifted the faceguard all my emotions would pour out and I'd never be able to scoop them back in again.

'So anyhow, there I was, on holiday with my husband, soaking up the culture, buying up all the prayer flags and pashminas and elephant trinkets I can fit in my bag. I wasn't naive; I could see that there was poverty and lack of healthcare and stuff, so I knew it wasn't a cakewalk for the Nepalese. But there was a spirituality which ran through the lifestyle which I'd never experienced before and that appealed to me. When we got back to the US, my husband chalked it up as *been there, done that, what's next?* But I wasn't ready to let it go, I felt connected. And then the earthquake struck here in 2015.'

I remembered the news coverage at the time, the displaced families, children left orphaned, parents missing presumed dead, the devastation to the country's basic infrastructure. 'I saw it on TV. Brontë was old enough to understand the news and I remember trying to shield her from the images of crying children.'

Seeing the loss and the suffering had made me hold Brontë even closer than usual. I was always like that when stories of child abuse or murder hit the headlines, desperate to know my own child was safe from harm.

Tiff shuddered. 'It was the plight of the kids that did it for me too. The timing of the earthquake coincided with us finding out we couldn't have babies. Or more accurately that I couldn't have babies. He was very reassuring, it didn't matter, we had each other, we could have a family another way yada, yada, yada. But as my dreams of a family were crushed, I felt my sole purpose in life had gone.'

She looked out of the window and cleared her throat.

We were the same, I thought. Different circumstances but the same. The various facets of our lives: family, work, love, home overlapping smoothly like tectonic plates to create a life we took for granted. And all it took was for a fault line to appear and the whole thing – and life as we knew it – exploded. It had happened to both of us.

'You had your own personal earthquake back then,' I murmured. 'I'm still in the aftershock of mine.'

'On the TV, I saw news reports of people who needed help, kids facing a hopeless future. And I knew I had to be there.'

'That is such a selfless attitude. When Brontë died, I shut myself off,' I told her. 'Some parents who lose their kids launch awareness campaigns to prevent stuff like that happening again. Not me. I split my time between binge watching *Game of Thrones* and working even longer hours than I'd done before.'

She smiled. 'It wasn't selfless. I think at the start I probably thought that being with people who were having an even shittier time than me would make me feel better about my life. In the end it was a lesson in endurance and acceptance. With my husband's blessing, I quit my job and flew out to volunteer here for three months. The experience nearly killed me, but it healed me too. It made me appreciate what I did have instead of focusing on what I didn't.'

I let her words sit with me for a moment. Was it too much to hope that this trip of Brontë's would heal me too? I felt my eyes sting and blinked quickly to stop the tears.

'So it helped?' I asked.

'For a while. But by the time I got home he'd met someone else. And I crumbled all over again.'

'Oh Tiff.' I almost reached for her hand, but changed my mind.

Physical acts of sympathy were always the ones to tip me over the edge. A hug, a squeeze, a pat on the arm and I was a goner. Something told me Tiff liked to keep a public veneer of toughness over her feelings. Like me.

'They say you don't miss what you never had. Not true at all. I missed the children I'd assumed I'd have running around my yard. I missed the family I never got to clear up after, the weekends at Little League and the homework projects I'd never tear my hair out over.'

'I get it,' I said, nodding. 'I feel the same about losing my daughter. I can't stop grieving for the things she hadn't achieved yet, plus all the milestones I'd thought would happen someday, being a grandmother, a mother-in-law, those sorts of things.'

Tiff exhaled. 'Oh Maggie, that's tough. It's a double loss, isn't it? Like my husband swapping me for a woman who could give him what I'd wanted to give him. My first thought was to adopt an orphan from Nepal, then I thought that instead of helping one kid, I could help lots.'

'And you did it?' I marvelled, completely in awe of her resilience. 'You're very inspiring, Tiff.'

She chuckled. 'I have my moments.'

The minibus came to a stop.

'Mam?' Lila turned and gave us his toothless grin. 'Entrance to Boudhanath, through there.'

He pointed towards a grand archway between the buildings.

'We'll pick you up in an hour,' said Tiff, sliding open the door for me.

I climbed out and waved them off and, taking Brontë's gap-year book from my bag, I'd let her be my guide.

## Brontë's Gap Year

The Boudhanath Stupa!!

I'm not one for bothering with tourist traps but I've seen this come up so much on TikTok that I know I've got to see it. It's meant to be very spiritual. It's basically a massive monument said to house the remains of Buddha and people walk clockwise around the perimeter all day long, either praying or taking it all in. The huge white building in the centre looks like a mandala from up above and there are gold bits too. It probably cost millions to build and it's centuries old. There's a place high up where you can get drinks and if it's not packed, I'll go up and take photos, do a bit of people watching. See if I can spot any good-looking Buddhist monks.

Top three things to get pictures of: the prayer flags which are strung right up to the spire at the top, the gold tower with the painting of the all-seeing eyes and the spinning prayer wheels.

There's a mantra that people chant while they're walking round: *Om mani padne hom*. I looked this up. It literally means praise to the jewel in the lotus. But really it's about trying to find the Buddha in ourselves.

I can't believe I'm writing this down, but I've been wanting to explore my spiritual side recently. We're not a religious family, so I haven't been brought up with the rituals of the church.

I asked Mum once what she believed in and she said love, taking care of others and saving ten per cent of what you earn for a rainy day. I agree with those (although she has the saddest love life known to humanity), but I'd like to think there was something bigger than us out there, someone with a master plan making sure we don't do anything stupid like blow up the entire planet to win an argument.

Maybe I'll become a Buddhist. At least I'd get to be reincarnated and live forever. I'd like that, as long as Harry joins me. Or maybe I'll light a candle while I'm there and send loving thoughts to my mum who'll be missing me. I might light one for my dad too. I wonder what he believes in.

# Chapter 8

## Nepal

'Dhan-ya-bad, Lila,' I carefully enunciated an hour later, climbing back in the minibus.

'All good?' Tiff's eyes narrowed.

She must have been able to tell I'd been crying, but she didn't say anything.

'All good,' I replied, getting my guidebook out of my bag to avoid looking at her.

I'd read Brontë's words while sitting quietly with a coffee in the rooftop café overlooking the magnificent white dome. I thought about Harry, how he was coping with his grief, and what he was doing with his life. It melted my heart the way she managed to weave his name into most of her itinerary entries. They'd been together for three years and I'd got to know him well during that time, but they were young; I'd never really considered that they'd be each other's 'happy ever after'. Now reading her thoughts about him, I wondered if I'd been too dismissive of their relationship. What if they had gone the distance and he'd eventually become part of my family? I forced myself to recall those first few days and weeks after the accident. I'd been too numb to think about anyone or anything. In my head Harry was badly injured, but he'd mend; his parents would still have their son in their lives. My Brontë, on the other hand, was gone forever. I made my mind up, sitting alone above the stupa, that I'd get back in touch with him, check how he was doing, let him know that if he wanted to talk about my daughter, I'd be there to listen.

I'd watched the monks deep in contemplation while I finished my drink, smiling to myself when I saw a good-looking one. I'd listened to the hypnotic chanting of a group of women connected by the repetition of their mantras and I'd taken pictures of the fluttering prayer flags. Before leaving I'd lit a candle for Brontë, and thanked her for bringing me a moment of peace amidst the chaos of this beautiful place; and then I'd lit one for her dad because she would have liked that. Should I have done more to find him? I closed my mind to the guilt and reminded myself that I'd done the best I could at the time. There was nothing to be gained by questioning my decisions now.

I left the candles burning and joined the pilgrimage for one lap around the stupa. I leaned into my grief for once, allowing my tears to fall freely instead of keeping my emotions locked inside. And it had felt cathartic.

'Where now, mam?' Lila asked.

'Here, please,' I said, showing him the page in my guidebook for Shree Pashupatinath, the oldest Hindu temple in Kathmandu. 'It's not on Brontë's list, but I've read about it and if there's time, I'd like to go.'

'Maggie, it's a wonderful temple, but it's also a site for funerals.' Tiff pursed her lips. 'I don't think you're ready.'

'You've known me less than twenty-four hours and you're making decisions for me?' I said, bemused.

'I'm looking out for you, that's all,' she replied. 'I know that place well, and I think experiencing the raw grief of others won't be healthy for you.'

I felt a rush of warmth for this new friend of mine. 'Thank you, I appreciate that. But this trip is forcing me out of my comfort zone. I can cope, I assure you. Sorry Lila, Shree Pashup . . . er . . .'

'Okay, mam,' said Lila, solemnly.

'He agrees with me,' Tiff murmured.

'Tell me more about the project in Chitwan,' I said, changing the subject. 'And your job in the US. Who do you work for now?'

'I work for the only woman who can put up with me.'

'Your mum?'

'Nope. Best boss in the world.' She gave me a mischievous look. 'Me. Gives me all the time off I want to come to Nepal.'

Lila stopped the minibus outside the entrance and I gathered my things ready to get out.

'I'm not happy about this,' said Tiff, sliding open the door. 'So I'm coming with you.'

'I'll be fine, but happy for you to be my tour guide,' I conceded, secretly grateful for the company.

The temple was a huge place consisting of many separate buildings along the banks of the Bagmati river. The main building had an ornate copper roof topped with a gold spire. Through an open gateway we could see glimpses of a giant golden statue of a bull. Tiff pointed out places of interest as we followed the path down to the river. 'This is one of the most important cremation sites in Kathmandu,' she explained. 'Hindus believe that it is a very special place, not only to be cremated but to die.'

'Oh gosh,' I said, sucking in a breath as we passed a group of mourners carrying their departed loved one on a stretcher. Ahead, I could see a row of stone platforms lining the river-bank, most of which were topped with smoking funeral pyres.

Tiff gave me a concerned look. 'Happy to carry on?'

I nodded. There was a reverence to the atmosphere here, a sense of peace and acceptance, a far cry from the oppressive pain which had hung over Brontë's cremation.

We continued walking in silence, watching young men washing the feet of the dead in the waters of the river, and sobbing women arranging garlands of marigolds over orange satin sheets, the outlines of the bodies visible beneath them. None of it was being done behind closed doors.

'Still okay?' asked Tiff, as I stumbled over a tree root.

'Not really.' I fixed my eyes on a place further along the riverbank where clouds of black smoke filled the air. A group of men lowered a wooden stretcher onto a plinth by the water.

We stood at a respectful distance as the family piled chaff onto the body and set fire to it. Flames engulfed the body and people began to wail. A few metres away, the fire on the next plinth was almost burned through; all the mourners had gone. A man worked his way along the riverbank with a broom, sweeping debris into the waters of the river.

I gasped. 'Is that . . . is he . . . ?'

Tiff nodded. 'Sweeping the remains into the river? Yes.'

I was shocked. Apart from the small pot that I'd brought with me, Brontë's ashes were safe at home. Wherever they were finally scattered, it would be somewhere precious to her, and I would make sure it was a moment to remember.

'It's so barbaric,' I said croakily. 'Our funerals are so tidy and organised, we dress our dead in their own clothes, even put make-up on them to make the sight of them more palatable.'

'Death is part of life here,' Tiff explained. 'The human body has no meaning after death. The quicker it can be disposed of, the quicker the soul can reach the next stage of enlightenment, which is reincarnation.'

'It seems very matter-of-fact,' I argued.

She shook her head. 'We might do it differently, but for Hindus this ritual is every bit as sacred as ours.'

I'd agonised over every detail of the service we'd held for Brontë. An image flashed into my mind of her pale weeping friends singing along to 'A Thousand Years' by Christina Perri, traumatised to have lost one of their own. Harry, on crutches, head bowed, flanked by his parents, hadn't sung. He'd remained silent throughout, even disappearing at the end without joining the line of mourners who'd come to hug and kiss me, offering condolences. It was supposed to have been a celebration of her life. But really, what had there been to celebrate?

'Shall we go?' Tiff asked, noticing me shudder.

'Yes please.'


An hour later we were back in the lobby of the guest house, having packed up our room. My transport to the Chitwan valley was on its way, and Tiff was waiting for Lila to take her to the airport.

The manager had offered us free drinks as an apology for the room mix-up, but all we wanted was water.

I rested my head against the back of my chair and heaved a sigh.

'You okay?' Tiff asked.

'What am I doing here, Tiff?' I said wearily. 'I'm a knackered, middle-aged woman doing the gap-year trip of a twenty-three -year-old. I'm ridiculous. Why am I not doing something incredible like you?'

She gave me a half-smile. 'You're not ridiculous. You've suffered a traumatic event, through no fault of your own. What comes next can be a choice. For me, I can't make the whole world a better place, but I'm trying to make it a better place for some. I work hard but I have the freedom to balance it with my passion project. You have freedom now too.'

My body tensed; I couldn't bear it when people tried to persuade me that there was a positive side to losing my only child. 'Don't go there.'

'Freedom is a wonderful thing, Maggie. You don't value it yet, but you will.'

I wondered when her loneliness had tipped over into freedom. Because I doubted mine ever would. 'How did you get to be so wise when you're still so young?'

'Wisdom doesn't come with age; it comes from experiencing things you don't always want to.'

'Even that was wise,' I countered. 'I envy you, not for what you've been through, but for how you got back up, how you found new purpose. How do I move forward when all that I love is in the past?'

'I dunno.' She shrugged. 'By loving yourself, I guess, by believing that there is a purpose for you, and you don't know what it is yet.'

I shook my head. I wanted to believe her, but I couldn't.

'This trip you're doing for your daughter, it's your earthquake. Don't let yourself drift through this trip, don't let it be a series of tick boxes. Dig deep inside you, use this time to find what makes *you* tick. This is your life. Yours. I know you're grieving. I can see it in your smile: it's only eighty per cent true. But it's okay to feel joy, and have fun, and take pleasure from being someplace new. Your purpose is already inside you, waiting for you to notice it.'

I touched my face, and tried to remember the last time my cheeks ached from smiling so much.

*'Mum! Stop grinning at me.'*

*'Can't help it. It's such a nice surprise to see you. I'll probably fall asleep with this smile on my face.'*

A minibus pulled up outside the guest house. Its roof rack held a mountain of luggage and curious faces were pressed to the windows; my ride was here.

88

'To Chitwan.' Tiff raised her water bottle and tapped it against mine.

'To Chitwan,' I chorused, 'and to finding the missing twenty per cent of my smile.'

# Chapter 9

## Nepal

'Namaste.' A petite woman with shiny black hair greeted us as we climbed out of the minibus, her hands together in prayer. She had a flower tucked behind her ear and wore a green tunic with matching trousers trimmed with pink braid. 'Welcome to the One World Project in Chitwan. I am Meena.'

Two young men in One World staff T-shirts scrambled onto the roof rack and helped the minibus driver to unstrap our luggage.

The drive had taken four hours from Kathmandu, with a couple of stops en route for surprisingly good coffee and snacks from roadside sellers. My fellow travellers were three eighteen-year-old boys, all friends from school, and fresh off a long-haul flight from London. While they slept, I listened to my audiobook and composed a WhatsApp message to Sadie and the rest of my book group, updating them on my whereabouts and asking if it would be okay to join them again when I returned home at Easter. Replies came back instantly from all of them with a resounding yes, interspersed with countless questions about my trip, expressions of envy and requests for updates. The conversation left me glowing. It was only a small step back to normality, but it felt good to ease myself back into my book-loving community.

We'd traversed hills and valleys, followed the path of sparkling rivers, honked our way through busy towns – at one point I'd seen two men on a scooter, the one at the rear holding a goat across his lap – and finally entered the Chitwan valley.

It was early evening and several degrees warmer than Kathmandu. I pressed my hands into the small of my back and stretched, drinking in the blue sky and inhaling air fragrant with the smell of tropical flowers.

We each introduced ourselves and the boys were led away to their room by the men.

I looked around me, taking in my new surroundings. There were two single-storey buildings: a long L-shaped one where the boys had gone and a second rectangular one which looked like it contained classrooms. Outside was a fenced-in area with brightly coloured outdoor toys, a swing and a couple of little tricycles. The kindergarten, I presumed.

'Tiff has told me about your journey,' said Meena, gesturing for me to follow her.

'From the UK to Nepal?' I said, falling into step beside her.

'About your daughter, your journey from loss back to life.' She smiled kindly. 'I hope Chitwan is good for you, and you find what you are looking for to take onward with you.'

'Thank you, Meena.' I didn't know what I was looking for, nor where to look. But if time was supposed to be a healer then at least I knew I had that, and that was a start.

'The volunteers are out on a walk down to the river now, so it is very quiet. Please, follow me. I will show you to your bedroom. Tiff says you need a room to yourself?' She looked at me, as if trying to gauge what reason I had for the request. I'd never felt more like a diva in my life. I hoped Tiff hadn't said anything about the lentils.

'I wouldn't say *need*,' I said, making light of it. 'More of a preference. Sometimes it's nice to have company.'

'I understand. I will let you decide.' She ushered me across a bare concrete yard and into the accommodation block.

'There is space in one of the girls' rooms. This one.' Meena opened a door and gestured for me to take a look. The smell of ripe bodies wafted out. There were two sets of bunk beds separated by a slim gap. You could have probably held hands with the person in the opposite bed. The floor was decorated with trainers and discarded clothes and tiny bikinis hung from the bedframe. The spare bunk was on the top – of course it was. I didn't know what was worse: the thought of climbing the ladder, or having three young pairs of eyes averting their gaze from the horror of my big bikini bottoms hanging next to theirs.

'And there is a single room . . . ?' I said, backing out of the dorm.

'Of course.' Meena nodded and showed me through the next door. This room was so narrow that I'd have to walk sideways to pass the bed, but it had a door and a window and I wouldn't need to use a ladder to get into bed.

'This is perfect,' I told her.

'You can find places to eat in Sanaura village tonight – from tomorrow all your meals will be provided. Breakfast is at seven in the dining hall. The children arrive at eight. Namaste.'

She left me to settle in and I sat down on the bed and unzipped my suitcase. But the floor space was so tiny that once it was open, I realised I'd blocked myself in. I clambered over and slid it under the bed. Then I reached inside, took out my toiletries and arranged them on the small chest of drawers at the end of my bed. I thought wistfully of my triple wardrobe at home, my dressing table and the mirror with the lights around it and my own private bathroom.

But then I also remembered that my cottage despite all its home comforts had felt like an empty shell with the heart ripped out of it, and that for now being in cramped quarters and sharing a bathroom with strangers was easily a better option.

I opened my bedroom door to go in search of the bathroom, and in stalked a scrawny tabby cat.

'Hello.' I bent to stroke it, but it dodged my hand and jumped up on the bed. 'Oh no you don't, fleabag.'

I lifted it off the bed and it lashed out, scratching my hand.

'Ouch. It's like that, is it?' I set it down in the corridor outside my room and shut the door firmly behind us both.

I opened the bathroom door and screamed as two cockroaches came scuttling out. I glanced downwards, expecting them to be followed by the rest of their army. The coast seemed clear, so I stepped inside. There was no other word for it other than disgusting. It smelled of drains, the tiled floor was slippery, and every square centimetre of space was covered with other people's toiletries. I resolved to keep my ablutions to a minimum for the next two weeks; the less time I spent in there, the better. I grabbed my bag and headed out of the camp to explore.

The shops were shutting up for the day, but I bought water and fruit and followed a sign to the Rapti river. I passed men cooking spiced meat over charcoal, stalls selling savoury snacks, and people selling bottles of cola and beer straight from coolboxes.

The quay down by the river was lively too. Little boats strained at their moorings and clusters of children fished with pieces of line. A man wearing a nautical hat was trying to sell boat tour tickets to a large family, and a group of young Chinese men were taking it in turns to snap selfies with the setting sun as a backdrop.

I took a seat on an empty bench at the river's edge and let my senses tune into the new neighbourhood. The gentle slosh of the water, the sulphur scent of the washed-up debris on the riverbank, the soft heat of the dying sun on my skin, an insistent whine from a mosquito . . . My eyelids fluttered, a wave of weariness reminding me that I'd barely stopped to catch my breath since I'd arrived.

The bench shifted and I opened my eyes to see I'd been joined by an elderly couple. They nodded to me and then, hands interlinked, her head on his shoulder, they gazed out across the water and pointed things out to each other.

A pang of loneliness washed over me.

It had been a while since I gave up dating. How had Brontë put it? Oh yes, I had the saddest love life known to humanity. Charming, although there was more than a grain of truth in it. Seeing her so happy with Harry had made me think about dipping my toe in the dating pool again, but nothing had come of it. Kat said I was too fussy; I preferred to think I had high standards. Maybe now it was time to look for love again. Maybe.

I shook away the thought and stood up, deciding to get back to my accommodation before it got too dark.

There were bars and restaurants on my way, but I wasn't tempted to stop. I didn't usually mind dining or drinking alone, but tonight I couldn't face it. Even the one playing Coldplay and decorated with thousands of pretty fairy lights couldn't lure me in.

'Hey, Maggie!' yelled a voice from somewhere behind me.

I turned to see a group of young people crowded round a table loaded with beer bottles, their faces lit by the lights strung above them.

'Hey,' I waved back.

'Join us!' shouted one of the boys from the minibus.

I walked towards them, feeling every one of my years. There were about twelve of them, boys and girls. All around Brontë's age.

'Thank you, you're very kind. But I've had a long day and I don't want to cramp your style,' I said.

'Babe, you are rocking those jeans,' said one of the girls, taking her feet off a chair and patting it for me to sit. 'You're the stylish one. And look, snap!' She held up her foot. We were wearing the same Birkenstocks. 'I'm Izzy, by the way.'

'Yeah, come on!' said another girl, waving her beer bottle in the air. 'We're swapping stories with the new boys.'

The boys who'd only smiled shyly on the drive here were now full of energy, possibly alcohol-fuelled. One of them looked particularly glassy-eyed.

'I could have one, I suppose,' I relented, despite the fact that my pyjamas were calling. 'What's everyone having?'

The gang erupted into cheers as I climbed over the wall to join them and caught the eye of a barman.

Two hours later, I'd forgotten about my pyjamas. I was on first-name terms with Krishna the barman, and Izzy had persuaded me to sing 'Maggie May' with her on the bar's rudimentary karaoke machine. Everyone cheered at the end of our terrible duet, and I resumed my seat gratefully.

'So what's your story?' asked a girl called Naomi, setting a beer in front of me.

I puffed out my cheeks. 'Honestly? My daughter died at twenty-three. This was meant to be *her* gap-year trip. Now it's her mum's gap year instead.'

The group fell quiet.

I could have kicked myself for ruining the mood. 'Sorry, I probably shouldn't have said anything.'

'Oh Maggie, that's so sad,' said Izzy, jutting out her bottom lip.

'Mums are great, aren't they?' mumbled a curly-haired boy called Colin.

'Yeah,' said a couple of the others morosely, as if suddenly hit by a wave of homesickness.

'To mums!' Naomi cried, raising her beer bottle.

'To mothers everywhere.' Another boy drummed on the table with his fingers and whooped.

'To mums!' yelled everyone else.

I raised my beer bottle but kept quiet; I couldn't bring myself to toast my mum. Even after all these years.

# Chapter 10

## Maggie, England, 1992

I was so trembly with hunger when I got home from work that it took me ages to fit the front-door key into the lock. It had been a long day. I had a Saturday job at a local hair salon, and I worked from the moment it opened until the last client had gone, the basins had been washed and the floors swept. I worked too long for a fifteen-year-old, but I wasn't complaining because I needed the money. The hourly rate was low, but I earned big tips by making tea and coffee, always with a biscuit, and remembering the names of their pets and children. I never took lunch with me, because usually someone bought cakes in to celebrate something. But today there'd been nothing. And there were only so many complimentary biscuits you could eat without feeling sick.

As soon as I opened the front door, I smelled food. Really nice food.

'Come in, sit down,' Mum shouted from the kitchen, 'you're just in time for Chinese takeaway.'

I hooked my coat over the others at the end of the stairs. This was weird. Firstly, Mum sounded really happy. Secondly, we never had takeout food.

'Wow, Mum.' I stood in the doorway staring at the steaming cartons on the table and gave Kat a questioning look to see if she knew what was going on. 'That's a lot of food.'

Last night we'd had so little in the house that my sister and I had had to get creative with a vegetable stock cube, handfuls of dried pasta, the last squeeze of the tomato puree tube and the stalk of broccoli which I'd insisted on keeping after Mum had cut tiny florets off it. We'd made soup and pretended it was delicious. Tonight, it seemed we had enough money to buy a banquet for six, despite there only being three of us.

'I thought we deserved a treat. Me and my girls.' Mum beamed, wafting a hand grandly towards the table. She was very glamorous, my mother. All my friends were in awe of her. Today she was wearing a satin kimono and had a big dragonfly clip in her long hair. She had an eye for spotting good clothes from charity shops; her wardrobe was bulging with beautiful, if impractical, clothing.

'Mum sold something. So we're rich.' Kat's cheeks flushed with excitement. She crunched into a prawn cracker and closed her eyes. 'Mmmm.'

At ten years old, Kat was easily impressed by Mum's grand gestures. Lucky her. I, on the other hand, was immediately suspicious.

Mum tutted at her. 'Trust you to blab.'

My stomach lurched. Not again. My eyes roamed the kitchen, looking for clues. What had she sold? She had nothing of value left, at least not that I knew about. Her jewellery was long gone, and what we did still own was second-hand. I poked my head into the living room. Everything was still there. Although I couldn't imagine her being able to sell our ratty sofa which the previous owner's cat had scratched to shreds, or the TV which only had two working channels.

Mum's ethos in life was that everything would work out in the end and there was no need to stress. She paid bills only when she'd had at least two reminders and legal action was mentioned. She spent money as if it would spontaneously combust if she left it in her purse. Kat and I had a small savings account, but Mum couldn't get to it. Dad had made sure of that before he packed his bags and moved out declaring that she was impossible to live with – but handily forgetting that we would still have to. Dad, I'd come to realise, liked a drama-free life. Why he'd ever thought Mum would be the woman for him was beyond me.

The only thing left that I could think of which might be worth something was not hers to sell. Not even Mum would dare touch that.

'Mum?' I demanded. 'What have you sold?'

She sighed theatrically, avoiding my eye. 'Let's enjoy our food, shall we? I've gone to a lot of trouble to fetch this. Can we, for once, not ruin the occasion by talking about money?'

No. I stared at her, feeling sick. Please say she hadn't.

I bolted from the kitchen, took the stairs two at a time and flung open my bedroom door. I knew straight away that she'd been in there; the cuff of my winter coat was sticking out of the wardrobe – I'd never have left it like that. I dragged my chair to the wardrobe, plunged my hands right to the back of the top shelf. It wasn't there. The box containing Granddad's World War Two medals had gone, his standard-issue Bible, even the little silver frame with the photo of him in uniform. I polished that frame once a month with a special cloth to keep it shiny. His collection of commemorative coins had gone too.

I sat down on my bed to get my breathing back in check and pressed my hands to my eyes so that I wouldn't cry. Granddad's precious things were irreplaceable, not of particularly great value, but priceless to me. Once my heart had stopped racing, I went back down to confront her.

'How could you do that, Mum?' My throat burned with emotion, and it took all of my strength not to yell at her.

'Oh, darling.' Mum put a plate in front of me. 'They were up there gathering dust. No good to anyone.'

'They were mine. Granddad left them to me. You had no right.'

It was the fact that she was so blasé about what she'd done – not a shred of remorse – that made me so angry.

'I haven't sold them, anyway; I've pawned them, which is not the same thing.' She gave me a fond smile, as if to imply I was overreacting.

'It is, if we don't have the money to get them back!' I blurted at her.

She flapped a hand. 'Something will turn up.'

'And my bike? Does that mean I can get that back too?' Kat piped up.

'Well?' I glared at my mother. 'Answer her.'

Kat's bike had disappeared to help with last month's bills. My sister was the sweetest girl, genetically wired to see the best in everyone, and hadn't questioned it when Mum had told her the news. I vowed to get it back for her. As soon as I could. I'd take on another job if I had to, to pay for it.

'Look, Magnolia, I had the opportunity to get in on something which could make us a fortune, all I needed was—'

'Stop!' I jumped up from the table, jamming my hands over my ears. 'I can't listen to any more of your fairytales, Mum. Kat and I depend on you, we're kids, we need you to be responsible with money. This, this . . . easy-come, easy-go lifestyle of yours isn't working. Why can't you look for a proper job instead of gambling your way from one bill to the next?'

'A proper job? I'd die if I was stuck in an office. I'm a free spirit. I wasn't born to labour.' Mum pouted and pushed her chair back from the table. 'Thanks to you, I'm not hungry now. You've ruined dinner. And you complain that I waste money.'

In that moment, I'd never hated anyone more. I knew it was wrong to hate, but she was a parent, she was supposed to put the welfare of her kids before anything and certainly before the latest dubious deal that came her way. Mum never wanted to earn money the hard way. It was always a quick fix, instant gratification. I was never going to be frivolous with money like her. I'd save so I always had enough for emergencies and to look after Kat, and when I had my own family, I'd instil those values in them too.

I put my hand out. 'Give me the rest of the money. You can't have spent all of it. It's mine and I want it back.'

Mum's face contorted with rage. 'Don't you speak to me like that. Have some respect.'

'I've got respect for Granddad, and he didn't earn those medals for you to fritter it away on sweet-and-sour pork.' I kept my hand held out.

'Ridiculous,' Mum muttered angrily, reaching for her purse.

'That Kat and I can't trust you to look after us?' I jutted out my chin defiantly. 'I agree, Mum. It is.'

# *Chapter 11*

## Nepal

*Thump thump thump.*

'Wake up, Maggie, I think I've got something to say to you,' sang a strangely youthful Rod Stewart.

'What, what?' I mumbled, waking with a start.

I sat bolt upright, only to regret it. My head spun and my stomach pitched wildly as if I was on a sinking ship. I lay down, gripping the edge of my narrow bed, nausea rising up my throat as I closed my eyes. That was weird, dreaming about Rod Stewart.

'Maggie!' There was another thump on the door. I clutched my head to stop the banging. 'Let me hear you say whoah, whoah, yeah, yeah! Come on, Maggaroo, you were singing it last night.'

Was I? I groaned as fragments of my antics came back to me. Who called me *Maggaroo*? What the hell was happening? 'What do you want?'

'I'm opening the door now, okay?'

I checked my boobs were still inside my nightie. They had a habit of trying to escape during the night. All good. I found a gap in the mosquito net and poked my face out. 'You may enter.'

'Jeez. You look rough.' Colin grinned and did a pointy finger dance while swinging his hips. The move rang a very alarming bell. 'Worth it though, eh?'

'I'm not sure yet. Did I dance on the table last night?'

'Dancing queen . . .' Colin sang in falsetto and I clamped my hands over my ears.

'Oh God.'

I had a vague recollection of playing a drinking game too. What had possessed me? I'd let my hair down for the first time in ages. The kids had been so friendly and welcoming and fun. It had brought back fond memories of Brontë and Harry having their friends around in the summer and dancing and singing under the fairy lights in the garden. I'd missed their laughter, the fast-paced banter, the in-jokes and the internet memes they would chant before collapsing in fits of laughter. 'I don't normally drink. Well, not much anyway.'

'If you say so.' He winked.

I squinted at him through barely open eyes. 'Why are you in my room?'

'It's time to rise and shine. There's a wake-up rota. It's my turn today. Did you like my wake-up Maggie May song?'

'Loved it.' I slid my hand under my pillow to check the time on my phone, but it wasn't there, which was worrying. I sat up again and patted around a bit more. No sign. Damn it. I was always meticulous about having my phone with me, keeping it charged, in case Brontë ever needed me. Less important now, obviously. 'You're very young to know Rod Stewart songs.'

'I looked it up on Spotify after you sang it last night. Here's the cat. Morning, Bob.'

The cat who'd scratched me yesterday streaked around Colin's legs and ran underneath my bed.

'Ah, he's climbed into your suitcase. Your phone is down there too, by the way.'

'Thank goodness.' I sighed with relief as Colin passed the phone through the mosquito net to me. 'Not about the cat; it's a vicious thing.'

It would have to stay there for now. I didn't have the energy for a battle.

Colin turned to go. 'Breakfast in fifteen mins. Don't go back to sleep, okay?'

'Okay.' I closed my eyes.

'*Breakfast!*' Someone thumped on my door. Not Colin this time; a girl.

'Shit.' I rolled myself out of bed, staggered to the door and opened it.

'Morning, Magster, ready for your first day at kindergarten?'

She wore a long skirt, flip-flops and a T-shirt with the One World logo on it.

I rubbed my eyes. 'Remind me who you are again?'

'Naomi!' she giggled.

'Why do you look as if you haven't got a hangover?' I said, running my fingers through my hair and getting stuck in a matted bit at the back. Why was everyone so young and full of energy? I needed someone as old and haggard as me to even things out.

'Because I haven't.' She looked puzzled. 'It was a quiet one last night, we were all back by eleven.'

'Right, right.' My mouth felt like I'd swallowed gravel. 'I might skip breakfast. Just have coffee.'

She sucked in a breath. 'Not a good idea. We're going on a walk this morning to where the elephants bathe. The kids are super-excited. You're gonna need energy. Also, they don't have coffee here, only tea.'

'No coffee? You're kidding.' I could have wept.

I swallowed down two headache tablets with the dregs of the water in my bottle and blinked at my phone. It was completely out of charge.

I plugged it in to give it a quick blast in case there were any important messages from Kat or the office, grabbed my toiletries bag and headed to the bathroom to work a miracle.

I'd managed to go to the loo, brush my teeth and scrape my hair into a bun, when there was a soft knock on the bathroom door.

'Maggie! Are you in there?'

'I am,' I shouted back. 'Hold on.'

I was not used to having company in the morning. Yesterday, Tiff barking at me to hurry up for our flight. Today a succession of youths chivvying me along. I wanted to be left alone to sleep.

I opened the door to see another one of the girls from last night. Somehow, she'd found time to put immaculate French braids in her hair.

'Hello,' I said dully. 'You are . . . ?'

'Izzy.' She grinned. 'You are funny. Your phone has been ringing. Like a lot. Like non-stop. I thought you'd want to know in case it was urgent.'

I thanked her, went back to my room and glanced at the notifications on my phone. One good morning message from Kat which made me smile, but I'd also got a couple of missed calls from George and three from Anna which wiped the smile off again. Something must have happened. In trepidation, I shut my door and called Anna immediately.

'Thank heavens,' Anna blew out a breath. 'Sorry to bother you, but can you help me sort out the invoicing for Renways?'

'Is that all?' I let out a sigh of relief. 'I thought something drastic had happened. I left all the details in a spreadsheet in a folder marked *Invoicing for Renways*.'

'I know you did,' she said, groaning, 'but I've deleted the formula by accident and now it's a mess. I need you, Maggie.'

I glanced at the time. 'I can try, but I'm late for my first day at kindergarten already, due to being hungover, and we're going on a walk to see elephants, so I need to get going.'

There was a pause on the line.

'So many questions about that sentence.'

I rubbed a hand over my face. 'I can imagine. Can I ring you back later?'

'Okay,' Anna said. 'An hour? Two, preferably not more than three.'

'Have you asked George?' I suggested. 'He's pretty good with spreadsheets.'

'Um, no,' she replied, shiftily.

'Why?'

'He's helping Lee and I didn't want to disturb him.'

'George is working for Lee? Why?' I demanded.

Lee, the office joker who wanted to be liked more than he wanted to manage people effectively. The man who was currently first in line for the directorship.

'Because . . . because . . . oh hell,' she muttered. 'Because I've had to give the Vap-A-Rise business to Lee because I had too much on my plate.'

'Anna!' I gasped. 'My team worked hard for that business. *I* worked hard for that business.'

I gritted my teeth, thoroughly annoyed about the whole situation and aware there was very little I could do about it other than complain. I wondered what George thought about that. Not much, probably. Which might explain the missed call I'd had from him.

'I've made a mistake,' said Anna. 'I said we could manage without you, and we can't.'

'I thought nobody was indispensable,' I reminded her, pleased nonetheless.

'I meant nobody except you,' she said with a sigh. 'How long are you—'

The end of her sentence was interrupted by a strange yowling sound from under my bed. I dropped down and peered underneath. Nestled in my open suitcase on top of the blanket I'd bought in Kathmandu was that mangy cat. And beside it was what looked like two kittens . . . Oh my Lord, there was another one coming.

'Anna, I'm going to have to go, there's a cat giving birth on my new yak blanket.'

'What the hell? Yak?'

'Yes, although *yuk* might be a better description.' Why was all this happening to me today? All I wanted was a decent cup of coffee and another two hours in bed. 'I'm not sure I'll be snuggling up in that any time soon.'

'It sounds like you've got your hands full,' Anna said.

'I'll call you later. I promise.'

Izzy appeared at the door as I ended the call.

'The cat's giving birth?' she gasped.

I gestured for her to join me. Both of us lay flat so we could see what was happening. The cat was busy cleaning her babies.

'Ah. She must have felt safe in your room.' Izzy sighed wistfully. 'And that's why she chose your suitcase. You should feel honoured. If I was going to give birth, I think I'd have come to your room too.'

'Thanks. I think. Although please don't.' We got to our feet. I was now far too late for breakfast, but I did need some water at least. 'Come on, let's give her and her babies a bit of peace.'

'Was that your work phoning you while you're on holiday?' she asked as we headed across the yard towards the dining room. Outside the gate, parents and their little ones were already waiting for it to open.

I nodded. 'Some problem they can't solve without me.'

'That must be annoying.' She looked indignant. 'People should be allowed to take a break without their employer hounding them.'

'Actually, I quite like it. It makes me feel useful,' I told her.

Outside in the courtyard, an old-fashioned bell rang and Izzy made for the door. 'In that case,' she said over her shoulder, 'you're going to love it here. Come on. Kindergarten has started. Prepare to be extremely useful for the next four hours.'

I stuffed my partly-charged phone in my pocket, wedged the door so that Bob and her kittens could get out and tried not to think about caffeine as I joined my new young friends outside to greet the children. I hadn't had a clue where Brontë's itinerary was going to lead me, but I'd certainly never have guessed I'd be a childcare volunteer in Nepal. Which proved that even at my age, life could be full of surprises.

## Brontë's Gap Year

By the time I'm reading this page, I'll be trekking in the Himalayas. The actual Himalayas. So I'm going to give Future Me a pep-talk to remind myself why I'm doing this . . .

Brontë, you don't like heights, you're not even that keen on walking and you've never trekked along mountain trails before. So you were being a bit ambitious when you chose one of the most treacherous routes in the world for your first expedition. But I'm so proud of you for doing it anyway. It's OK if you don't love every minute of it, it's OK if you have a little cry when your boots rub your heels. You're doing this to challenge yourself and push yourself beyond your limits. And of course to see Mount Everest. It'll look great on your CV, so Mum will approve once you've peeled her off the ceiling when she finds out about it. And Harry is going to be so impressed. He didn't actually come out and say it, but I think he doubted you'd go through with it. Also, think ahead to when you've got teenage kids who think they're cool and you're an embarrassment. You'll be able to whip out the photos and say *Now who's the cool one?*

There will be moments in these two weeks where you'll freeze with fear. (That trek on Day 9 from Gorak Shep looks horrific.) But I want you to remember that thing you read* about leaning into being scared. That doing the thing that scares us the most is how we grow and learn. And there's that other phrase: failure is not an option. No idea where I read that. But I don't agree with that one. Failing at things sometimes is healthy. Not that you're going to totally fail, but I know you'll beat yourself up if you have a bad day. So remember this. Making mistakes, failing at stuff makes us more resilient. It makes us pick ourselves up and have another go. (Like when you learned to ride your bike.)

You're going to ace this, Brontë, and you're going to grow a lot on this trip. I'm leaving some pages free now for you to journal in. I'm not usually a journal type of person, but then I'm not a mountain explorer either and look at me go. Write down your thoughts, so you can remember how you felt when you were on top of the world.

xoxoxo

*I didn't read it anywhere. It was something Mum said when I came back after a bad driving lesson all shaky because I'd nearly crashed the car at a roundabout, and vowed never to get in the driver's seat ever again. She was right, of course. Good old Mum, so wise, always there with the right words at the right time. She'll be missing me by now. And I'll be missing her.

## Mum's Gap Year

---

Darling girl,

I've reached those pages you left free in your itinerary for journaling, and I hope this is okay, but I'm going to write in them instead.

It is so bittersweet to read your travel itinerary. I can even hear your voice when I read it. I didn't want to be the one doing this trip – it was yours. I'd rather be at home, missing you, refreshing my emails every few minutes in case you've managed to find somewhere with internet. Instead I'm here in Nepal wishing you could have seen the things which you have so beautifully illustrated and written about. I put off looking inside the pages for months because I felt guilty, but I'm so glad I've done it now. I feel like I'm learning little snippets of new things about you, how you feel and what's important to you. Although when you talk about the children you assumed you'd have, it breaks my heart all over again. You'd have made a wonderful mum, and I would have spoiled my grandchildren rotten. I feel a thrill of love every time you mention me, and so far, it has all been good. I especially love the way you leave yourself positive messages. I might start doing that myself. And now we know that I wasn't as wise as you thought, that I don't always say the right things at the right time. I asked you to give it another week before committing to doing the gap year, to fully think it through. But *of course* you'd already given it a lot of thought because that was the sort of person you were. It was me who needed to get used to the idea, not you.

I'm still only in the first of the places you wanted to visit, but already I can see how much you'd have thrived and flourished doing this trip. We use throwaway comments about how short life is and how we should grasp every opportunity to fill our time with joy. But how many of us do that, purposely seek out a life filled with moments of happiness?

It touches my heart to see the other young people I've met express their personalities and lose their self-consciousness without the constriction of their lives back home, and I wonder how changed you would have been by the experience.

Okay, confession time. I'm supposed to be following your itinerary to the letter, and you know me, I do like to stick to the plan, but I've gone off-piste by coming to Chitwan rather than doing the Everest Base Camp trek. I hope you understand why and you're not disappointed in me. It was my new friend Tiff's idea, and – touch wood – it's working out well.

You'd love Chitwan. I'm the oldest volunteer here, no surprise there, the others are kids. Even Meena the boss is only thirty. They are boisterous and fun and never seem to get hangovers, unlike your lightweight mother. When I first arrived, I thought I'd feel uncomfortable without anyone my own age. Instead, I seem to have become the camp mum and I'm leaning into the role with pleasure. Sometimes I remember with a jolt that I don't have a daughter on this planet anymore. I can be having a lovely day and then, wham, there it is. Do you remember that ice bucket challenge and the shock of being drenched in cold water that leaves you gasping for air? That's the feeling I get. And I get it at least once a day. There are other times when you're so close by, I can sense your smile and feel the warmth of your love. At those times I feel like the luckiest woman alive.

I'm getting emotional, so let's talk about the One World project. I'm more than halfway through my time here already. It is flying by; I can't remember a time when I've felt so busy. The children start arriving while we're still having breakfast. We see them jostling to be first through the gate, while their parents and carers stand and chat. Some little ones are brought by older siblings, who abandon them as soon as they arrive. But everyone looks out for each other, so it's not a problem. There's no free nursery care here, which was why Tiff and her partner set up this charity project: to help parents get back to work. There are four groups of children and a qualified nursery worker in each one. The volunteers act like extra pairs of hands. We each have a buddy. Mine is Colin, who is great fun and a real sweetie. He has fallen for the eldest sister of one of the children and always makes sure he's at the gate when she arrives. He and I like working with the older kids best. They adore him and hang off him like monkeys, climbing up his legs. They have a quieter relationship with me, bringing me flowers, taking me to see things they've found, or scrabbling onto my lap if they've hurt themselves or they're feeling sad. When that happens, I read them a story to

III

cheer them up. Before long I have a little gang leaning in to listen. You used to do that, do you remember? Bath, bed and as many books as you could persuade me to read. You knew all the words to *How Much Do I Love You?* and you insisted on looking at every detail of the illustrations before I was allowed to turn the page.

I shouldn't have favourites, but there's one boy who melts my heart, called Hom. He's a shy little thing, with the most beautiful brown eyes and lashes. He brings me a gift every day. Sometimes a marigold, sometimes a leaf, or a shell. He took my hand and brought me to meet his mum yesterday. She can't be much older than you and she is clearly a devoted mother. Meena told me that she lives with her father, who is very strict and does not want her to go to work and thinks she should stay at home to look after him. It makes me realise how lucky I am to have grown up in a country where I had the choice of what to do with my life. I chose to have you and I'd choose you every time.

Today is Sunday and the other volunteers have gone on a trip to the national park. There's a trip most weekends, so the kids see as much of their host country as possible. I also think it's because Meena and the rest of the staff need a break from their exuberance and noise for a day or two. They were picked up in an open-sided jeep after breakfast and headed off for a safari and won't be back until this evening. I've stayed behind, not only because I heard they have tigers here, but because there's a market in the village this afternoon. It's run by a women's empowerment project (something you had on your list to visit!) and everything on sale has been made by local women. I've promised Meena I'll go and have a look. Her sister makes tablecloths and I know I'll want to buy one.

Meena is an inspirational woman. She has so many plans for the One World project. She wants to start running English classes for teens and reading classes for women. She has such a passion for improving the lives of the people in her community; I've no doubt she'll succeed. Seeing her run this project has made me really think about my relationship with work. I've only been gone from ShopSwift for a few days, but Anna is feeling my absence. It has been a real boost to my confidence to know that I'm needed by someone now that you're no longer here. Do you remember us joking that you'd always need me even when you were seventy, that you'd still be phoning to ask how to get grass stains out of your socks. Without you, I've been relying on work to fill that sense of feeling needed. My job has always been a route to financial security for you and me, but it has never been a passion like it is for Meena. And being dependent on work isn't a healthy way to live, is it? I'm beginning to think that I'm going to have to find something more to pour my love into. Because a job is never going to love me back.

I must go, but I need to tell you about the kittens. The camp cat, Bob, has become the most dedicated mother to her five kittens. Naomi and Izzy made them a proper home in one of the sheds, so we were able to move them out from under my bed. They are tiny, and haven't opened their eyes yet and Bob has barely moved from their side. One of the kittens wasn't doing well and couldn't latch on, so I risked getting in close and helping it out. I thought Bob would rip my hands to shreds but she closed her eyes and laid her head back down. Poor thing is exhausted. I remember those early days of motherhood and I only had one baby! Being with the cat family takes me right back to the day I met your dad. Except on that occasion, it was puppies rather than kittens. Anyway, you know the story, and you've read my diary. But I wanted you to know that the memories I have of him are still with me. They always will be.

I'm sitting in the yard beside the children's play area in the sun right now. Kat says it's been snowing at home – and here I am in a T-shirt with factor fifty on my face. It's been a while since I've considered myself the lucky one, but today is coming close. Meena is waving to me from a window, which I think means it's time to head into the village. I must remember what you said about not going wild when I go shopping.

I love you, darling, you'll always be my baby, even if we can't be together. I was worried that my memories of our life together would fade, but they get brighter every day. Thank you, sweet girl, for sending me this trip. I'd never have had the courage if it hadn't been for you.

Love

Mum xxx

# Chapter 12

**Nepal**

'A lot of people came to our village after the earthquake,' said Meena. 'They had nothing. Many women and children settled here, but the men had to leave to find work. Some of them send money back to their wives, but not all. For the women it is hard to work and care for their families. At first there were no jobs.'

Meena and I were walking along the main street towards the community hall where the market was being held. It was the first time since she'd shown me to my room that we'd spent any time alone. She was quiet on the outside, but I'd seen her deal with two drunk men who tried to break into the camp last week. This woman had a core of steel that I wouldn't want to mess with.

'The village feels quite buzzy now, so I guess things have improved?'

She nodded. 'The tourists have found Chitwan. And mostly this is good for us. They have money to spend in our shops, they buy food and drink at our restaurants.'

'Only mostly?'

'It makes our young people feel restless and want to leave the village. They see people on holiday with money to spend. Even the volunteers who come to help us are only here because they can afford to work without wages. We have lost many of the younger generation to the cities in search of adventure and better pay. And we need them here to bring money into the community.'

'Young people will always be restless,' I said, pulling Meena out of the path of an ox and cart plodding stealthily past us. 'Always wanting to see whether the grass really is greener on the other side.'

'This is true.' She laughed. 'In Sanaura, if we want rice, we grow it, we harvest it, we lay it out to dry in the sun. Only then can we cook it. Kathmandu offers rice today without the work or the wait. Young people prefer the rice from Kathmandu.'

The image made me smile. I remembered planting sunflower seeds with Brontë one year. Every day she would run outside expecting to see a fully grown sunflower in the garden. We had to start growing mustard and cress in the end for faster results. But the day the sunflower finally flowered, she had been beside herself with excitement. She fetched her soft toys out into the garden and set up a picnic by the edge of the flower bed to celebrate. Such a sweet memory.

Suddenly a small boy leapt out in front of us and flung himself around my legs.

'Maggie!' exclaimed my favourite little boy.

'Hello, Hom!' I squatted down to his height and looked around for his mum. She was hurrying towards us, a heavy bag of vegetables over one arm.

'Namaste,' I nodded to her.

'You have met Shila?' Meena said, introducing us.

Hom's mum nodded shyly. 'Namaste, mam.'

Hom tugged his mother's arm and whispered something in her ear. She set her bag on the floor and reached into her pocket.

'For you,' she said, in hesitant English and held out a necklace identical to the one she was wearing.

Hom bounced around us and chattered away excitedly.

Meena laughed, ruffling the little boy's hair. 'He says now you can be as pretty as his mama.'

'Thank you, Shila, and thank you, Hom. I agree, you have a very beautiful mama.'

Shila pressed a hand to her cheek and smiled. 'I make it for you to say thank you. You make Hom happy and that makes me happy and then life is good.'

That was so true. When the ones we love are smiling, then so are we.

'You made this yourself?' I said, turning it over in my hands. It was a delicate elephant pendant within a row of tiny colourful beads.

She nodded. 'I do them for friends.'

'Then your mama is clever *and* beautiful, Hom. Do you sell them?' I stooped so that Meena could fasten the necklace for me. 'I'd like to buy one for my sister, and I'm sure all the volunteers would buy them too.'

'No, no, I could not sell them, it is not possible.' Shila's face clouded.

'I understand,' I said, hurriedly, sensing her discomfort. 'I'm very honoured that you have given me one of your necklaces. I shall treasure it for ever.'

I thanked them both again and we continued on our way.

'I wonder why she said it wasn't possible?' I mused.

'Her husband disappeared after Hom was born, so she lives in her father's house,' Meena explained. 'Since Shila's mother died, she has been looking after him and Hom. She is a smart girl and wants to work, but her father is old-fashioned and will not let her. She will probably not even have money of her own.'

'What a shame.' I glanced back over my shoulder to see Shila walking away, that heavy bag of groceries hanging from her shoulder.

'Equality has not reached every corner of Nepal,' said Meena, following my gaze. 'There is a gradual cultural change, but it will take several generations for us to accomplish what a woman like you has already achieved.'

'Me?' I batted away her compliment. 'I haven't achieved anything special. The thing I'm most proud of is raising my daughter – and Shila is doing as good a job as I ever did.'

Meena shook her head. 'Travelling across the world without a husband would be a great achievement for a woman in Chitwan.'

'If I'd waited for that to happen, I'd never have gone anywhere,' I replied.

'For him to give you permission?' Meena looked scandalised.

'No, for me to get a husband in the first place,' I said, amused by her expression. 'I've never been married. By the time my daughter was born, her father wasn't in my life anymore.'

'Maggie, I am very sorry to hear that.' She shook her head sadly.

'Don't be,' I reassured her. 'He was a wonderful man, and we were very much in love, but we were young and wanted different things from life. Besides, without a husband I was able to bring Brontë up the way I wanted to. We had a very special relationship.'

I felt the familiar tightness in my throat. It had taken me a long time to be able to talk about my girl in the past tense. I hated that it was now becoming automatic.

'A child to love is a precious thing, but a man to love,' she fanned her face, 'that is very important too. Especially in the UK where the nights are cold.'

'Meena!' I gasped, pretending to be shocked. 'I've been warm enough over the years, thank you.'

In truth my love life wouldn't fill a single page of a notebook, but she didn't need to know that.

'And now?' Meena probed.

'Oh, look, we're here,' I said, changing the subject.

At the entrance to the market, a dance troupe of elaborately dressed young women were about to begin their routine. Music blasted from a speaker and so any further conversation was impossible.

The hall was packed with shoppers, many of them tourists, and trade appeared to be brisk. Meena was soon swallowed up by members of her family and for the next twenty minutes or so I meandered along busy stalls of savoury snacks, spices and chutneys in glass jars, felt toys, embroidered table runners, carved wooden boxes, knitted hats and scarves and handcrafted rugs. But the products weren't the stars here, the women were. The smiles, the passion, the pride in what they had made resulted in a joyful atmosphere. It made me want to buy everything. I did buy a lot, including a tablecloth from Meena's sister. At one end of the room, there was a table festooned with coloured flags and a banner pinned to the front advertising 'Chitwan Women In Business'. There were no products for sale on the table, but a woman sat behind it with a notepad and a pile of leaflets. Her berry-red nails matched her lipstick exactly, and her outfit marked her out as someone who liked to be noticed.

'Thank you, lady.' She indicated my bags and beamed. 'You have supported our businesses and we are very grateful.'

'I am the grateful one. I've managed to buy lots of things to take back to England with me.'

'We hold our market every month. Please come back, tell your friends.' She handed a leaflet to me.

It wasn't written in English, but the photographs told me all I needed to know. There were pictures of smiling women handing out awards, making clothing, tending rows of seedlings, groups with their arms around each other. It was about women supporting women.

'I'll have left Nepal by then, but I'll pin this up on the noticeboard,' I promised. 'It looks like a fun organisation to be a part of. If I was staying longer, I might want to join myself.'

Her eyes lit up and she pressed a business card into my hand. 'Here is my email address and this is my name: Rina. I would like international partners. You could help us.'

'I'm not sure what I can do from the UK, but I'm flattered. Thank you.'

'Many of our ladies have not been to school and cannot read or write. But they are smart and want better lives for their families. We help them plan their business and give them small loans to buy what they need to get started. There is no help from the banks for small businesses like the ones our ladies have, so we do it ourselves. We need sponsors, we need space in the big hotels to hold our markets . . . many things.'

I thought of Shila and her jewellery. Belonging to a group like this might give her the support she needed to gain some independence.

'So you help people's dreams come true.'

The woman wagged a finger. 'Not dreams, business plans.'

I tucked the leaflet into my bag.

A conversation with Brontë wafted through my head: *You've always told me to put details into your plans, otherwise it's just a random dream.*

'Of course,' I said, my vision going a little misty. 'I stand corrected.'

Meena appeared beside me ready to leave, and I said my goodbyes.

'Shila should join the group,' I said, once we were outside again. 'I'm going to give her this leaflet.'

Meena shook her head sadly. 'Shila will already know about it. The market has been running for a while.'

'Oh. You think her father won't let her?' I let out a breath of frustration. 'Why do men get the last word?'

'I don't know,' she shrugged. 'Ask him yourself. Look, they are there on that cart.'

About to disappear from view was a wooden cart being pulled by a large white ox. Hom sat in the back waving to everyone, Shila beside him. I could just make out a man holding the reins in the driver's seat.

'I will ask him,' I said, making a spontaneous decision. 'Right now.'

I sprinted after the cart as fast as my Birkenstocks and heavy bags would allow.

'Maggie, wait!' Meena gasped. 'I didn't mean it.'

'Well, *I* did,' I said, determinedly. 'Wish me luck.'

# Chapter 13

**Nepal**

'This is very kind of you and your father,' I said to Shila, trying to maintain polite eye contact with her father while he helped me from the cart, which was tilting precariously. The ox had had enough and was trying to lie down. Hom was dancing on the spot, clearly enjoying watching me wobble about.

We were outside their family home, about a mile out of the village. At least I think it was about a mile; I'd never travelled by ox before and it was difficult to judge the speed. The houses were sparse and each one was surrounded by a large plot of land. Shila's had rows of vegetables on one side and a tangle of trees and flowers on the other. A plastic table and chairs sat outside the door and underneath was a collection of toy cars.

Her father, Govinda, didn't speak English, but Shila was doing an admirable job of translating for us both. He waved some green leaves at the ox to get it moving and took it around the back of the house.

My plan had been to catch up with the cart and talk to Shila in front of her father about the women's business group. But as soon as I'd flagged them down, her father had insisted on me coming back to his house to drink tea with them. I'd accepted on the basis that I'd have more chance of convincing him to let his daughter make a go of her jewellery business in a place where he felt at ease. Also, I was nosy and was curious to see a Nepalese home. So here I was.

Shila showed me to a seat at a table in front of the house and dashed inside to make tea. Hom followed her and returned carrying a half-bald chicken. He handed the chicken to me unceremoniously and burst into a fit of giggles when I tucked it under my arm and stroked its patchy feathers.

Govinda reappeared, shouted at Hom and gave me a dazzling smile – at least it would have been if he'd had more than one front tooth. He removed the chicken from my grasp and set it down on the ground.

'Tea!' announced Shila, setting a loaded tray on the table.

She handed me a mug and I inhaled the steam; lemon and ginger. Govinda looked on in disbelief when I turned down the offer of sugar, and tipped three big spoonfuls into his own.

'Please,' said Shila, pushing a plate of plain biscuits towards me.

Govinda stopped stirring his tea, waiting to see if I took one. I wished I knew more about guest protocol in Nepal; perhaps it was rude to say no to anything. I took a biscuit to be on the safe side.

'What do you do for a living, Govinda?' I asked. I took a sip of my tea while Shila translated.

Hom climbed up onto his grandfather's lap and laid his head on the old man's chest.

'He build houses again after the earthquake,' Shila told me. She turned to her father and said something else. Govinda waved a hand at her irritably and said something in reply. Shila frowned at him and banged her mug down on the table.

'What are you saying?' I wanted to know.

'I said that he works too hard and I am afraid that one day he will die and I will be alone with no money. My father says that I should find a husband and he will look after me. I am not going to do that.' Shila shook her head defiantly. 'Ever.'

'Would that be such a bad thing?' I suggested.

'A new husband will not love Hom like his own son. I would rather be alone than have a marriage like that. I can look after myself and Hom.'

My heart went out to her. I had had almost this exact conversation with Kat a decade ago. 'I totally understand,' I said softly.

She and I were from totally different backgrounds, but we shared a fiercely independent streak, and a desire to put our own potential happiness to one side for the sake of our children.

Govinda gave Hom a biscuit and spoke again.

'He wants to know if you are married,' said Shila.

I shook my head. 'Like you, I didn't want to be married either, but it seems to be easier for a woman in the UK to make her own choices about her life than here. I was able to be a mother and have a job to earn money to look after us both.'

Shila repeated this to him and the conversation became heated. I felt awful for causing this conflict, but I only hoped that my presence would help Shila in some way.

Shila turned to me to explain. 'My father thinks that the men in our village must do the work and I argue and say this is not true in every family.'

I took some of the things I'd bought out of their bags. I showed them the beautiful gifts I planned to take back to England with me. 'These are all made by local women from Chitwan. The ladies make money so that their husbands can relax at home.' I mimed putting my feet up and closing my eyes. Govinda laughed this time.

'He thinks you are funny lady. He says that his father taught him that he must look after his family. He is a proud man.' Shila shook her head. 'When my grandfather was alive, my father argued with him all the time, saying that times change and the old man was wrong. Now my father is the same as him.'

'Govinda,' I said, leaning forward to address him directly, 'we want more for each new generation that comes along. When Hom is a man he could go to university, travel to America, become a doctor, anything he wants. Your daughter wants to earn her own money, to buy things for her son. She wants to provide for Hom the way you provided for Shila. She wants a chance to show you what she can do.'

While she relayed what I'd said, I pulled out the leaflet I'd picked up from the market. 'Shila, you do not have to do this alone. There are people – *women* – who can help you, who want to nurture talent like yours, to bring more employment to the village.'

'I know about this, but he does not listen to me,' she said sadly.

'I had a daughter once,' I said. 'She was the most precious thing in the world to me. The biggest mistake I made was to not listen to her. Loving someone means allowing them to do what their heart is telling them, even if it hurts to do so.'

Govinda shook his head and spoke again.

Shila sighed. 'He says he doesn't understand why you care.'

'I care because having a goal gives you purpose and having a purpose makes you feel happy. We only have one chance at life, and we all deserve happiness.'

'My father says you are a very wise woman.'

'Please thank him and tell him that I learned the hard way.' I took off the necklace that Shila had given me and placed it on the table in front of Govinda. 'Why don't you tell your father what making and selling jewellery would mean to you? Don't take no for an answer, keep trying, and make him listen to you. You can do it, Shila, I have faith in you.'

The young woman pulled her lip between her teeth, lines of uncertainty furrowing her brow. Govinda slurped his tea and spoke again harshly. Finally, Shila spoke, handing him the leaflet and forcing him to study it. He pored over the pictures, asking questions which Shila responded to with confidence and respect.

After a pause in the dialogue, Govinda smacked his hand down on the table and said something to Shila, a grin forming on his lips.

Hom giggled but Shila scowled and answered him back in a sharp voice.

'What is it?' I asked, unsure whether the conversation had taken a turn for the better or worse.

'I am sorry. He is playing a game with us. He says that he will let me join this group if you will try his food.'

'Really? That's a fantastic result, congratulations, Shila.' I pressed my hands together in prayer. 'Thank you, Govinda.'

Govinda set Hom down and went inside.

'You don't understand. My father makes pickle. It is . . .' She poked her tongue out and mimed fanning her face.

'Spicy?' I suggested, helping her out.

She nodded. 'Like fire. We eat it with a potato snack.'

I gave her a supremely confident smile; spicy food would be no issue for me. 'No problem, I'm happy to play his game.'

He returned with a plate of sausage-shaped croquettes and a small dish of chutney.

'Aloo chop,' he said, pointing at the croquettes. He picked one up, dipped it in the chutney and bit into it. Then he gestured for me to do the same.

I picked one up, dipped it hesitantly into the chutney and took a bite. The first sensation was one of sour limes, the second was a fiery burst of chilli.

'Wow!' I nodded, blinking as my eyes started to water. 'This is good. Spicy, but good.'

All three of them stared at me with suspicion. Govinda gave a gleeful laugh and said something to Shila.

'He says it is good for cleansing,' said Shila gesturing to her stomach.

Good, I thought, I'd eaten lentils at least twice a day since I'd been here and I was feeling bloated.

'Aloo chop,' Hom sang out. 'Aloo chop.'

'I love it,' I puffed my cheeks out and exhaled before dipping it into the chutney again.

Govinda beamed and gave me a round of applause. Shila waved the leaflet in his face and kissed his cheek. And just like that, she was in.

That was the easiest sales negotiation I'd ever done, I thought half an hour later as I prepared to leave.

'I cannot thank you enough.' Shila placed her hands together in prayer and bowed.

'You did the hard work yourself,' I said, returning the bow. 'Stay strong, and make sure he sticks to his side of the bargain. I hope you'll have a stall selling your beautiful jewellery at the next market. Good luck.'

Govinda gestured to the cart and pointed to me.

'Thank you, but I'm going to walk. I need the exercise after all that delicious food.' I patted my stomach, and he walked away laughing to himself.

'Take these.' Shila handed me some of the leftover aloo chop, wrapped in square of cotton. 'For the others at the kindergarten.'

I thanked her, gave a sleepy Hom one last hug, and set off. It was one long straight road back to the village, and so even though the light was beginning to fade, I wasn't worried about finding my way back.

I thought about Tiff as I walked. I'd googled her since I'd been here. In her day job, she was a mix engineer in the music industry. She'd worked with everyone from Beyoncé to Harry Styles. A woman at the top of her game. And yet still she found time and energy to run the One World Project. Food for thought, Magnolia Jones, I mused, comparing her rich life to my own sparser one. Food for thought.

A scuffling noise from behind brought me back from my daydreams. There was someone following me, I could sense it. I heard heavy breathing and every hair on my body prickled. Oh God. I glanced left, right and ahead but there was no one in sight to call to for assistance. I picked up my pace, feeling my heart gallop with fear. The faster I walked, the faster the person behind me must have been moving, because the sound of panting felt as close, if not closer. I was too scared to turn around. My throat felt as if it was closing up, and I wasn't sure if I could scream for help even if I'd wanted to. And then something touched my bag. I looked over my shoulder, let out a high-pitched squeal and started to run. I was being chased by four dogs. A rag-tag of shapes and sizes but the leader of the pack had long legs, sharp pointed ears and drool dripping from its jaws.

I pushed myself as fast as I could, and the dogs started to bark. I started to cry, convinced that they were going to attack me. I hadn't had a rabies shot; there hadn't been time and I'd foolishly thought I wouldn't need it. How wrong I was. My bags were weighing me down and I considered dropping them, but then I'd have no weapon at all; at least I could swing these at the dogs. Why hadn't I accepted that lift from Govinda? Why did I always have to be so bloody independent?

One of the dogs jumped up at my bag. I batted it away, but it jumped again.

'Go away. Get down.' I lashed out, swinging the bag at the leader.

But a smaller black dog, its eyes hidden in matted fur, lunged at my ankle. I tried to kick it away, but missed, almost losing my footing. All four dogs were barking now and I was shaking in terror.

'What do you want?' I shouted.

The cloth wrapping the aloo chop caught my eye at the top of my bag. Could they smell the food – was that it? I slid my hand into the bag, pulled out the still-warm potato croquettes and flung them into the road as far as I could. They scattered on the ground and the pack of dogs scrambled after them. I let out a sob of relief and ran as fast as I could in the opposite direction. I rounded the corner and pressed myself up against the wall, my lungs screaming with pain from sprinting. I stood there, trembling, letting the adrenaline subside and the tears dry up. Finally, my legs stopped shaking. The dogs hadn't returned and I felt brave enough to carry on. I'd only taken a few steps when I felt the first gurgle in my stomach. A minute later there was a full-on cyclone going on in there. Good for cleansing, I remembered Shila translating for me. I had a feeling that the bloat was going to come to an end very soon – hastened, no doubt, by my brush with a pack of wild dogs. I really hoped I could get back to the camp in time.

As I speeded up again my phone beeped with a text message and I grabbed it, grateful for the distraction. It was from George. I smiled at seeing his name; I missed my trainee, his hesitant comments in meetings, his earnest expression. I hoped Lee was looking after him. His probation was a formality as far as I was concerned; he had the potential to go far in the organisation, like I had.

I swiped the screen to read what he had to say.

*

Sorry I've not been in touch, the boss said I shouldn't disturb you. But I've decided to resign from ShopSwift. Thought it only fair to let you know. Hope you're having a good time. G

I felt a wave of disappointment and wondered what could have happened to prompt this. I would have given it more thought, possibly even replied, had my stomach not made a series of gurgles.

Oh God. I needed a bathroom urgently. I marched on, starting to sweat. By the time the One World camp came into view, I was dripping with perspiration and my stomach felt ready to explode.

As I got closer, I noticed a crowd outside the gates. That was odd. There were only ever people at the gates at the start and end of kindergarten and today we were closed. Where was Meena? I spotted the volunteers amongst the crowd. Was the gate locked? A series of cramps made me catch my breath. *Please don't let the gate be locked.* I was going to have to rush past them all yelling that I couldn't stop. How embarrassing; everyone would know I was desperate for the loo. They were all very open about their bowel movements, but I liked to maintain a bit of decorum in the bathroom department. That might all be about to change.

There was a lot of screaming going on. And shouting and . . . holy moly, was that a cricket bat waving about in the air? Whatever was going on, everyone needed to clear a path because I was going in.

Naomi and Izzy spotted me and raced over. Their eyes were bright and I suspected that they were enjoying the drama.

'Keep back, Maggie. You need to stay safe,' said Naomi, breathlessly.

'What's happening?' I pressed a hand to my stomach.

The girls garbled the story between them, neither of them quite able to drag their eyes away from the scene.

'You know that girl that Colin has been seeing?'

'Her dad has found out about it, and he's not happy.'

'He's threatening to hit him if he goes near his daughter again.'

'With a cricket bat.'

'Colin's bricking it.'

'I know that feeling.' My stomach released an almighty gurgle as if someone had pulled the plug out of a full sink and I let out a groan.

'You look really pale, Maggie.' Naomi took a step back.

'And sweaty.' Izzy wrinkled her nose. 'Are you going to be sick?'

'I can't wait,' I muttered. 'I can't.'

I pushed my way through the crowd. Meena was standing in front of the angry father, holding her hands out, trying to placate him. It didn't seem to be working. He had the cricket bat raised above his head and was jabbing his finger at Colin. His daughter was sobbing and a group of boys were surrounding Colin for protection.

I marched up to the irate Nepalese man, conscious that fear was not making things any easier for my poor pickled bowels.

'I'll take that.' I pulled his arm towards me and plucked the cricket bat out of his hands.

The man was so surprised that he didn't even put up a fight.

'You're being ridiculous,' I said, putting the bat behind my back. 'Give your daughter some credit; Colin is a lovely boy. I'd have been delighted if my daughter had brought him home. Why don't you get to know him instead of trying to knock his head off? Please translate for me, Meena. Now excuse me, I'm in a hurry.'

I sidestepped him, shuffled through the gate and ran across the yard, leaving the man stunned into silence. Gosh, I could be brave when the situation called for it.

'Maggie is a literal goat!' I heard someone shout, which was a bit rude.

I made it to the bathroom just in time, dropped the cricket bat and launched myself at the loo. Through the locked door I heard the others whistling and cheering and I let out a laugh which turned to a sob as the adrenaline of the last hour seeped from me.

What a day. Maybe I'd sleep tonight, despite the lumpy mattress that was almost impossible to get comfortable on. What I'd give for a bath and a chance to relax and a little bit of peace and quiet, but I had another week of this.

It dawned on me in that moment that I had the freedom of choice. Nepal had been a blast, the people were lovely, I'd made memories to last forever, and being away from home had been the tonic I hadn't known I'd needed. But I was done here.

I'd had enough of fighting my way in and out of the mosquito net, plugging my ears so as not to hear the scuttle of cockroaches across the bedroom floor. I'd had enough of waiting for the bathroom to be free and wading across a heap of sodden towels to get to the shower. This place would have been perfect for Brontë; she would have flourished and grown in confidence. But this sort of travelling belonged in my past, when everything was new and exciting and I'd been open to having adventures. Tiff had said that I shouldn't simply tick boxes on this trip, it should be about what I wanted. The truth was that I was not the wide-eyed and carefree adventurous girl I'd been at twenty-two. And right now, I had a sudden yearning for home.

# Chapter 14

Maggie, Bali, 2000

I kicked off my flip-flops, unzipped my denim cut-offs and waded straight into the ocean. The water was smooth, hardly a ripple. The sun, still not quite risen, had painted stripes of pink, orange and blue in the sky.

The pictures in the brochure I'd been shown at uni had not done this place justice at all. Our accommodation was right on the beach. I had never been anywhere so beautiful, seen skies as blue, or waters so clear. I was twenty-two years old, high on sunshine, giddy with the freedom that lay ahead. All the part-time jobs I'd had over the last few years to pay for this had been worth it. For a whole month, I'd be based here, in a coastal village in southern Bali, fulfilling a long list of dreams, volunteering on a turtle conservation project.

I dived, taking long strokes along the ocean bed. Then with my lungs screaming for air, I powered my way back up to the surface, sweeping my hair back from my face.

I turned onto my back and floated like a starfish, relishing the sensation of warm water on my skin. The last time I'd been in the sea had been swimming off the rocks in Wales with Kat, my dad sitting morosely on a towel fully dressed, an umbrella over his head while we swam in the rain. It had been our last family holiday. Mum had refused to leave the caravan, sulking because she'd wanted a week in Greece. I'd lasted approximately ten minutes before hypothermia had begun to set in. Mum still hadn't been to Greece. Dad had kept the caravan when they split but never invited Kat and me to stay in it with him again. Anyway, I had a whole month away from home and I wasn't going to waste a single second dwelling on my parents.

Instead I closed my eyes and let the sun warm my face.

'Paradise,' I said aloud.

It was my first day and I'd woken early. The other three girls in my dormitory were still sleeping, but I had been too excited to wait for them. By the time I'd arrived last night, tired and sticky from my long journey, the daylight had all but faded. And once we'd been shown our rooms, and I'd been allocated a bunk, the view had been all navy sea and sky and a million pinpricks of starlight. Very lovely, but hard to get my bearings.

'Cool, huh?'

Startled, I spun around, planting my feet on the ocean bed to see who'd spoken.

There was a boy wading towards me, brown eyes twinkling and a friendly smile revealing white teeth. His body was lean and toned, the waistband of his boxer shorts visible above the top of his shorts. He was beautiful.

'Very cool,' I squeaked. I mean, literally squeaked.

He dipped below the water and bounced back up again, shaking droplets of water from his hair. 'D'you arrive last night?'

I nodded. 'And I'm in love already.'

'Is that right?' He flexed an eyebrow and grinned.

'With Bali? Yes, of course.' If he was trying to embarrass me, he'd got the wrong girl – I'd happily match him for boldness. I ducked down into the water, kicking my legs to move away from him. 'I've never been this far from home.'

He swam after me. 'Australian?'

'With this complexion?' I indicated my pale skin. 'British.'

He pressed his hand to his forehead. 'I get that wrong all the damn time. I'm Jackson from the US.'

His accent was gorgeous.

'Maggie. Pleased to meet you. And seeing as you asked nicely,' I teased, 'you *may* join me for a swim.'

His eyes danced. 'Why, thank you, but I've been sent to tell you that you're not allowed in the water by yourself. It might seem like paradise, but the current is very strong; even the locals can get into trouble. You never swim alone, and you always make sure someone knows where you are.'

'Oh. Right,' I replied, slightly crushed and failing to hide it, as the current dragged me away from him. 'Thanks.'

'Hey, no problem.' He held out a hand, which I grasped, and he tugged me towards him. 'Anyway, it's breakfast time. Are you hungry?'

'Absolutely starving,' I said with relief. 'I could eat a horse.'

He looked down at me and grinned. 'Anyone ever tell you you're cute?'

'All the damn time, Jackson,' I said, cheekily, mimicking his voice. 'All the damn time.'


That evening it was our induction to the turtle conservation project, and I waited with six other new volunteers beside the turtle hatchery on the beach. Underfoot, the sand was still warm, and I watched in awe as a giant sun slid below the horizon, sending flames of crimson and gold out into the sky. Light shimmered on the water and children splashed and played in the shallows nearby.

I'd spent the day swimming, exploring the village and getting to know the other volunteers. My hair was wavy and wild from the salt water, my skin tender from the unaccustomed sun. I already felt sunkissed and blissfully happy.

The man in charge of our turtle induction was called Utt. He was short and squat with bulging biceps and scars on his forearms. He gestured to us to gather closer.

'Listen up! The rules of turtle hatchery. No talking. No smoking. No torches,' he barked.

'No problem, we'll be *utterly* silent,' someone at the back sniggered.

Utt scowled as we all laughed. 'Hahaha. New joke. Very funny. Everyone inside.'

'He hates us,' said a voice behind me, breath soft in my ear.

Jackson. Where had he appeared from? I felt something tighten inside me, and realised I'd been hoping to bump into him again.

'*Utter* hatred,' I replied with a grin.

I followed the others up the steps and into a low-ceilinged, ramshackle hut built from mismatched planks of wood.

The space was almost entirely taken up with a raised wooden bed. It looked like a children's homemade sandpit on stilts.

There were rows of little flags poking out of the sand with a date and a number on each one.

'We collect turtle eggs from beach at night and bring in here to bury them again,' Utt said, delivering his lines flatly. 'We mark where we bury with a label. You can see when they were collected and how many eggs in each clutch. When they hatch we release them back into water at night. Until then we do not dig up, we do not disturb. Any questions?'

Hands shot up.

'Yes?' Utt pointed at a girl I'd met earlier, Hannah from Canada.

'Why do you collect up the eggs instead of leaving them where they're laid?' she asked.

'To protect them, of course,' he replied, looking at her as if she was an idiot. 'From predators, from humans, from tourists who won't leave them alone.'

'Sorry, sorry, sorry, I'm late. Had to call home, my grandma is ill.' One of the tallest boys I'd ever seen came thumping up the stairs, out of breath.

'Careful, Hugo!' someone yelled.

'Arghh!' The latecomer hit his head on the ceiling at the top of the steps, lost his balance and lurched forward. He crashed into the turtle bed, snapping the wooden edge and causing sand and a clutch of eggs to pour onto the floor.

There was a beat of horrified silence.

'Oh my God,' I whispered under my breath. 'This is turtle extermination not conservation.'

'Utter nightmare,' Jackson muttered.

'Out!' Utt screamed. 'Get out, all of you.'

He pushed his way around to the broken side of the bed, saying something in his own language which I guessed was not polite.

'Sorry, everyone,' said the tall boy, rubbing his head. 'Did I miss anything?'

'No,' said Jackson, offering his hand to help him up. 'Unfortunately not.'

Everyone trooped out quietly, some biting their lips to keep in their laughter, but I hung back.

'Utt, can I stay and help you mend the turtle bed?' I asked.

'No, no.' He waved me away but then a corner of his mouth lifted. 'But thank you, miss.'

'Call me Maggie.'

Unwilling to leave until I'd convinced him that we weren't all bad, I watched him for a moment rescuing the eggs that had dropped to the floor.

'Rich kids. Come to Bali for a holiday. Not interested in preserving our wildlife, only want to party,' he muttered.

'I'm sorry. I'm not a rich kid.' I'd saved up for this trip, waitressed and worked the night shift at a supermarket twice a week all through this year at uni while my friends went out clubbing.

He laughed, shaking his head. 'You fly on aeroplane, you a rich kid.'

'I'm sorry,' I said again, although this time I wasn't sure what I was sorry for. I didn't feel rich, but it was all relative, I guessed. All Utt saw was a young adult who had the time and means to play at looking after turtles. He wasn't to know how much effort it had taken for me to get here. I said goodbye and left him to it.

Outside on the beach the other volunteers were making plans to go to a bar. In the last few minutes, the sun had vanished, and the evening had turned to night.

'Are you coming?' Hannah asked me.

I nodded. A beer sounded great. I hadn't showered or done my hair and I was still in the bikini and shorts I'd worn all day. But it didn't matter here. Nobody cared.

'See you around,' said Jackson, touching my arm.

'Are you not joining us?' I said, disappointed.

He shook his head. 'Got stuff to do.'

In the next second, huge raindrops started to fall from the sky. Slow at first and then torrential. Everyone started to yell and scream.

'My hair!' yelled Hannah, racing for cover.

'Run!'

'See you at the bar.'

'First one there grab a table.'

But Jackson and I didn't move. The rain was warm and soothing to my salty skin. I could feel raindrops on my eyelashes, and I blinked them away.

'How is that even possible?' I held my hands out. 'The sky was perfect a few minutes ago.'

'It's still perfect,' said Jackson, tilting his face upwards.

'For the fish maybe,' I scoffed.

'For me.' He looked me in the eye. 'Because now I've got you to myself.'

The compliment took me unawares and I felt a pulse of excitement. 'Looks that way. What about your stuff?'

'So, do you like puppies?'

I laughed. 'What sort of question is that?'

He gave me a lazy smile. 'I don't know. A genuine one?'

'I mean, ask someone if they like dogs and it's fine to say *No, I don't*. But puppies? What sort of person can say no to them?' I replied.

He grinned. 'Got it. So do you like puppies or do you *think* you should like them?'

'Take me to the puppies already,' I said, shoving his arm.

We took a detour via the volunteer kitchen, where one of the cooks had left a bag of food ready for him to collect, and headed around the back of the camp and into trees. The rain had stopped as abruptly as it had started, and the air smelled fresh and earthy. It was dark and Jackson produced a torch and lit a path for us.

'Poor Utt,' I said, feeling guilty. 'He really doesn't like us, does he?'

'You can't blame him for being permanently mad. He must get fed up with a bunch of party animals turning up every two weeks supposedly to help him.'

'I'm not a party animal,' I said.

'Nope, sorry. Don't believe you,' Jackson teased.

'Okay,' I conceded. 'I do like to party, but I want to be useful too.'

'Good, because I'm going to put you to work any minute.'

'I was looking forward to Utt's induction,' I said, following the beam of torchlight.

'I can continue your education. Ask away.'

'You know about turtles already?'

He nodded. 'Sure. I've been here four weeks. Some of the eggs that Hugo crushed were collected by me. Really glad I stayed up half the night for that.'

'So why were you there tonight at the induction?'

'Shush.' He deflected the question and took my hand. 'We need to keep our voices down, we're here.'

In a clearing ahead of us, a makeshift kennel had been made from a broken wooden crate, and sheltering inside was a scrawny mongrel lying on her side on an old towel. Six puppies were cuddled up against her, two at her teats.

'Hello, girl.' Jackson crouched down towards the mother dog and held his hand out for her to sniff. She lifted her head from the ground and gave a low growl.

'Is this safe?' I said, keeping myself tucked behind him.

He smiled. 'Why, do you only do safe things?'

I liked his eyes. And his smile. And his arms. His arms especially.

'I followed you into dark woods, didn't I?'

'True.' He laughed softly, scratching the dog's ears. The dog leaned into him and stretched out her legs. 'You're safe. She trusts me. She's just being a mom.'

'Not all *moms* do that.' I tried out his American word, making light of the fact that my mother had stopped looking after me years ago. My dad too, I thought: he was as much to blame, checking out of mine and Kat's life seemingly with ease. He didn't even phone anymore, left it up to us to make contact.

He met my eye with curiosity but didn't pry. 'Can you give her some food from the bag?'

We'd never had a dog at home, and I wasn't comfortable with this one. Quite apart from the almost certain fleas, the flashing eyes following my every move unnerved me.

'I'll pass.' I knelt beside him and reached out warily to the nearest puppy. The mother didn't seem to mind, so I gingerly picked it up.

'Chicken.'

'A chicken who's attached to her fingers, thanks very much.'

While the mother was gobbling down the food Jackson had brought, we checked over the puppies in turn. I didn't fully understand what we were checking for, but he seemed to know what he was doing, and I enjoyed giving them all a cuddle.

'So what happens next?' I asked.

I heard his breath catch. 'Um, we can walk back along the beach, maybe go for a drink, if you like?'

'I meant when you leave Bali. What happens to the dog and the puppies?'

'Oh, right.' He rubbed the back of his neck. 'I don't know the answer to that. I'm taking it day by day, doing what I can for her and her little family while I'm here. Hopefully things will work out, which is pretty much my philosophy on life.'

'That's your master plan for your future?' I teased.

'What's wrong with that? I'm gonna surf, dive, live by the beach forever.' He tipped over the old can that served as the dog's bowl and topped it up with fresh water from the bag. 'Okay, girl, take care of those babies.'

'You must have rich parents to support you, in that case,' I said, replacing the puppy I was holding and getting to my feet.

Jackson pointed the torch back the way we'd come, and we picked our way through the undergrowth.

'Not at all. I'll get a job, pay my way. Work to live and it won't even feel like work because I'll be living the dream. One day I might even open my own surf school, who knows.'

Our arms were touching, his skin sending tiny electric shocks along mine.

'Ha! So you do have a plan,' I pointed out.

'The only plan I have is to please myself. No responsibilities.'

He smelled of heat and sunscreen and boy, and I felt a gathering of desire in the pit of my stomach. 'Except a grumpy dog and six puppies.'

'Except them.' His eyes glinted with mischief, making my heart speed up.

'So . . . no girlfriend?' I asked coyly.

'Nope. You?' He shook his head, not looking at me.

'I don't do boyfriends.' I stopped walking.

'You don't?' He raised his eyebrows.

I met his gaze brazenly and smiled. 'I do boys, though, in case you wanted to kiss me.'

He drew me in close and gave me the best kiss of my life.

'I knew it,' I said, laughing, reaching my arms around his neck to do it again.

It was only my first day. I had a hunch that I was in for an awesome four weeks.

# Chapter 15

## Nepal

I was back in the Ganesh Guest House in Kathmandu, sitting on one of three beds in my hotel room, on the phone to Kat with Brontë's journal in my lap.

Every time I looked at it, I had a creeping sense of unease that I wasn't fulfilling my promise to complete the rest of her trip. But I felt differently about her itinerary now. I knew I'd enjoy turning each page, reading her words, tracing my finger over her drawings. I'd feel connected to her wherever I was, as long as I had the notebook.

'It is the right move,' I said to Kat. 'The time away from home has been cathartic, it's made me realise that I'm a homebird, I like my creature comforts.'

'Wise choice,' said my sister with discernible relief. 'And there's plenty of time until you go back to work. Maybe if Andy doesn't mind, you and I could take a little trip somewhere. A week in Spain maybe, get a bit of winter sun?'

'Sure,' I agreed – although my enthusiasm was half-hearted. Now I'd experienced the landscape of Nepal and the pride to be had from independent travel, I wasn't sure I wanted to settle for something as straightforward as a package holiday again.

'But first I need to find out what's been going on at work. I've had a message from one of my staff threatening to quit and now I can't get hold of him.'

'You're a good boss, Mags, and a good person. I can't wait to see you.'

'Thank you. Me too. I love you.'

There was a pause down the line.

'Oh Mags.' I heard a wobble in her voice. 'You haven't told me that for years.'

'Yes, I have.' I frowned. Hadn't I? Maybe I hadn't. Thinking about it, I'd become adept at downplaying my emotions. It had seemed safer somehow.

'It doesn't matter,' said Kat, ever the peacekeeper. 'You've said it now. I love you too.'

At that moment there was a knock at the door and I got up off the bed. 'There's someone at the door – probably my room mates. I'll message you as soon as I know my flight times.'

There hadn't been a single room available at short notice, so I'd taken a bed in the triple. Last time I was here, I'd met Tiff and that had worked out well, so I was prepared to go with the flow. It was only one night, after all.

I opened the door to let in two women. We introduced ourselves and I sat back on my bed to let them unpack. They were a couple from the UK, travelling together for the first time. Marta was a yoga teacher and Skye had her own catering business.

'First time in Nepal?' I asked.

'Yes,' Marta. 'Any tips?'

I remembered the list of don'ts that I'd been given at the airport when I'd arrived and shook my head. 'Nothing you won't figure out for yourselves. You'll love it.'

'Where have you been so far?' asked Skye. From her rucksack she was pulling out a succession of brightly coloured garments in sharp contrast to Marta's neutrals.

'Yes, tell us,' Marta joined in, making herself comfy on her single bed. 'I love other people's travel stories.'

'Okay,' I said, pulling Brontë's book towards me again. 'It all started with this . . .'

The two women listened enthralled as I told them what had happened to me since accepting my enforced sabbatical. It wasn't until I voiced my story out loud that I realised how much I'd been through in the last few weeks. From my decision to follow Brontë's path to my arrival in Nepal; the shock of reading that my daughter had planned to trek to Everest Base Camp; meeting Tiff; dealing with Diane's panic attack at 30,000 feet . . . to volunteering in a kindergarten and the dramas that went with it.

'A cat actually gave birth in your suitcase?' Marta and Skye's eyes were out on stalks.

I nodded. 'Bob. She was ferocious when I first met her. Hardly surprising under the circumstances. It's the wild dogs you have to watch for. Especially if you've got any food on you. Unless it's homemade pickle. They'll soon leave you alone if you feed them that.'

Skye shook her head. 'I can't believe you took a cricket bat off an angry man and told him he was ridiculous.'

Marta snorted. 'You are a legend.'

I laughed. 'Desperate times called for desperate measures.'

'Think of all the stories you've got to tell the grandkids one day.' Skye must have seen the look on my face because she clapped a hand over her mouth. 'Maggie, I'm so, so sorry, that was insensitive of me.'

'It's okay,' I reassured her. 'I won't have Brontë's kids in my life, but that doesn't mean there won't be other children to wow with my stories. Who knows what the future holds?'

'That's a wonderful attitude,' said Marta, reaching across the gap between the beds and touching my arm. 'I believe that the universe has endless possibilities waiting for us. All we have to do is notice them.'

'You might be on to something there.' I smiled, glad I'd met these two.

'So where are you off to next?' Skye asked, nodding to the book.

'Ooh yes,' Marta added. 'After such an exciting adventure in Nepal you must be keen to see what Brontë has written on the next page.'

I gazed down at my darling girl's book, picturing the intricate drawings and the words which let me into her innermost thoughts. This book held her dream trip, a detailed plan of the things and the countries she'd felt compelled to see. Months of adventure and new experiences, places that no doubt I'd never been, and she'd never go. Then I pictured myself arriving back in the UK, putting the key into the lock and opening my front door to a cold, empty house.

Same old life, same old job, same old me.

No.

I couldn't go home. Not yet. I wasn't ready after all. She and I had more places to go.

I ran my fingers over the top to locate my bookmark. I'd left it by the last entry for Nepal. Slowly I opened the book, spurred on by the anticipation on Marta and Skye's face. 'It's been a long time since I was open to adventure, but let's see, shall we?'

*Brontë's Gap Year*

---

G'day Australia!

I had no idea until I started researching this trip how hu-u-u-u-ge this country is! I'd do it all if I could, but there's that boring thing called a budget – my mother taught me well. Koalas, kangaroos, didgeridoos, kookaburras, Sydney Harbour Bridge, the Opera House, Bondi beach … literally so many iconic things to see in this place.

So I'm starting in Sydney. Harry's Uncle Pete moved to Australia for ten pounds when he was eighteen. It's going to cost me a lot more. I'm thinking, maybe get some work? Loads of backpackers work on farms, so it shouldn't be too tricky.

Harry is planning on visiting his uncle in the Blue Mountains for a month, and if the stars align, he should be there the same time as me. If he hasn't got fed up with waiting for me and gone off with somebody else by then, we'll be meeting up. Joke! He WORSHIPS me. And we'll be missing each other like crazy, so Australia will be the place for lurve. Maybe I'll persuade him to earn some money with me, although I can see him fitting in more behind a bar with a cocktail shaker in his hand than shearing sheep, but you never know . . . After that, who knows, travel up to Byron Bay, learn to surf maybe? Apparently my dad was a surfer dude, so hopefully it'll be in my genes and I'll ace it. Anyway, first stop is a hostel on Kent Street, bang smack in heart of Sydney . . .

# Chapter 16

## Maggie, Bali, 2000

Midnight was my favourite time and the beach was my favourite place. Lying next to me, his fingers laced through mine, was Jackson, who was very quickly becoming my favourite person on the planet. Today he'd spent hours trying to teach me to surf. I hadn't mastered it, but I had enjoyed being rescued repeatedly by him.

'I wish I could stay here forever,' I murmured.

Jackson's hand squeezed mine. 'Me too.'

So, this was it. First love. I'd spent hours listening to my friends mooning about how perfect their boyfriends were, and I'd spent almost as many hours comforting them when those relationships finished. Never once had I imagined the sweet bliss I'd feel when it happened to me. I felt like a Disney princess, permanently smiling and my heart full of joy. I was half disappointed not to see a gang of tiny animals and birds following me when I looked over my shoulder.

I wanted to tell him that I loved him. But I didn't want to spoil the moment in case he laughed or looked horrified, or reacted in any way that showed me I'd got it wrong.

Jackson and I had volunteered to do night patrol. Mostly

because no one else liked to do it, and it meant we had the beach to ourselves. So far we hadn't seen any sign of turtles climbing up the beach to lay their eggs. Technically, we could both go back to our rooms now if we wanted to.

I still slept in the girls' room and he still slept with the boys, but as the days passed, we were finding more and more ways to spend the nights together.

We were at the narrow end of the beach, our feet inches from the water. Every so often a wave would rush up the sand and touch our toes. Behind us in the trees, the occasional hoot of a bird would interrupt the incessant buzzing of cicadas. The sky was clear tonight, and the longer I stared at it, the more stars appeared. Millions upon millions of glittering diamonds. This was the most exotic and romantic place I'd ever been.

'Maybe we should sleep here.'

Nights were hot and sticky in Bali; the heat in the dorm when all four of us were in was oppressive. But out here on the beach with damp sand beneath us and a faint ocean breeze cooling our bodies, it was bliss.

Jackson's hand stroked the length of my arm. 'When you say sleep . . . ?'

'Of course, I forgot,' I said innocently, deliberately misunderstanding him. 'We're supposed to be working.'

'Then how about a kiss to keep me going?'

'Another one?' I teased. 'If you must.'

I'd always liked boys. I was confident and flirty, the girl in my group sent to approach a crowd of boys with the 'my friend fancies you' messages. I had the one-liners and the cheeky smiles, all the banter. I was still that person, but with Jackson my smiles were warmer, my sharp edges smoother, my heart in a constant flutter. My feelings for him were, at times, too big for my body. I'd never been in love before so I had nothing to compare this to, but he had lit a fire inside me that I could never imagine burning out.

He turned onto his side to face me, his cheek resting in his palm. 'I must.'

He pulled me tightly into him and kissed me with an intensity I'd never known until I'd met him. His lips, his scent, his skin against mine gave me a headrush. I never wanted this to end.

This was a holiday fling, I kept telling myself. My stint as a conservation volunteer would end and we'd go back to our normal lives. Me to finish off my degree and a career in psychology, him to living by the beach and following his dream. But it didn't feel like a fling; it felt as if I'd found my person. The person I wanted to share my secrets with, the one I looked for in the crowd, the one I wanted to tell whenever I saw something amazing. He had even changed the way I saw myself. He'd helped me to discover the real me, the Maggie who could do anything, who could have adventures and shoot for the moon and not worry about paying next month's rent.

'How have I only known you for three weeks?' I murmured, snuggling into his neck after the kiss ended. I traced the muscles of his chest with my fingertips and felt his breath catch as my hand moved lower.

'The best three weeks of my life,' he said huskily.

I propped myself up to look him in the eye. 'Really? That's so sweet.'

'Yeah.' He grinned. 'I've always wanted to work with turtles.'

'Hey!' I punched him playfully.

'Mags.' His tone had changed and my eyes found his. 'I don't want this to end.'

'Me neither.' It would, I knew it would, but I didn't want to let reality in. Not yet.

He kissed my fingers. 'I can't stop thinking about you. I'm happier when I'm with you. I even laugh harder when I'm with you. Is it me, or . . .'

'It's not you.'

He stared at me with those beautiful brown eyes. 'So what do we do?'

I gazed at him uncomprehendingly. 'We enjoy what we have while we have it?'

His smile wavered. 'That's not the answer I was hoping for.'

I bit the inside of my lip, wishing we hadn't strayed into this territory, which felt too deep and dangerous for me to navigate.

'We've got totally different lives, Jackson. I can't drop out of uni. I can't fail. I can't give up because of a whim.'

'I'm a whim?' He pulled back to scan my face, uncertainty in his voice.

'No, of course not.' I rolled towards him again, hooking one leg over him, pressing my body to his. 'But holidays aren't real life. This paradise is only temporary. I've been working towards getting my qualifications for years. I'm so close.'

'Damn,' he teased. 'I'm losing my touch, I was convinced you'd be ready to throw it all away and live the dream with me.'

I grinned, relieved that the awkward moment had passed. 'I can't live your dream, Jackson, I have to live mine.'

'But mine's way better than yours.' He shuffled down so we were eye to eye. 'Come on, admit it. We could sleep under the stars every night. You could wear a bikini every day and I could rub in your sun lotion and try not to get horny doing it.'

His head dipped to my collarbone and as he kissed me, a spark of desire ignited inside. How could I even contemplate saying goodbye to this boy?

'You're selling it well,' I conceded. 'But I know what I want, and that's to be a psychologist. I want to work with people, help people be their best selves.'

'You can do that anywhere there's people.'

'Not if I want to be paid well for it.' I touched a hand to his face, willing him to understand. 'And I want to put roots down, have my own house.'

'I'll build you a beach hut,' he said, kissing my mouth.

It wasn't easy to concentrate anymore, especially as I was tempted, but I thought about how unsettled my childhood had been and how all my life I'd craved security. 'I want a place to call home, I guess. Somewhere I know will be the same every time I come back to it, no surprises.'

'Nooo!' He pretended to look horrified. 'Your twenties are the time to live big, explore, try everything.'

He was right, I knew he was right. But there was a need deep inside that wouldn't let me go.

'My whole life I've seen my mum get fired up about something, only to give up as soon as she hits a bump in the road. I've seen it happen over and over. I made a commitment to finish my education. I need to prove to myself that I'm not like her.'

'You're here.' He extended his arm to take in the beach, the sky, the ocean. 'You're already not like her.'

'Thank you.' I smiled, my heart beating with joy for him. 'But do you see why I have to go home?'

He was silent for a moment. 'What I see is a beautiful girl with a beautiful heart, and I'm not ready to let her go.'

I rested my hand on his chest, felt the slow, steady heartbeat beneath the wall of lean muscle. 'We still have a week.'

'Not enough,' he whispered, rolling onto me, and supporting his weight on his forearms.

It would never be enough, I thought, but it was all we had.

# Chapter 17

**Australia**

I opened my eyes and blinked in the afternoon sunlight. So this was Australia.

I'd only planned to lie down for a few minutes and read the next entry in Brontë's book, but two hours had passed, and I'd had the most delicious nap. Outside my giant picture window the sky was the perfect shade of blue; I stretched, revelling in the crisp cotton sheets and the most comfortable mattress I think I'd ever lain on. Or perhaps I was comparing it to the biscuit-like consistency of my bed in Chitwan. Quite possibly.

My first impression of Sydney was one of colour, joy and all-round gorgeousness. I'd arrived by taxi earlier this afternoon, and already knew I'd made the right decision to follow Brontë's itinerary and fly down under.

My last night in Nepal had been unexpectedly lovely. Skye had heard of a bar in Thamel which had live music playing, and insisted on me joining them for a drink. We spent a couple of hours singing our hearts out to covers of a random assortment of songs, from Coldplay to Beyoncé, and eating our way through piles of delicious little dumplings called momos. Then we walked down to a temple, and Skye and Marta stood beside me while I sprinkled some of Brontë's ashes beside a golden statue adorned with garlands of marigolds. It had been a moving ceremony, completely unplanned and unrehearsed. But somehow it felt right to be leaving a tiny part of her in the country she'd so wanted to visit for herself. And now it had given me a plan, I would do this in each of the places she'd written about in her book. I felt confident that Brontë would approve, and it made my decision to carry on with her gap year more meaningful.

Brontë had written down the name of a hostel for her first night in Australia. I'd googled it and while it looked perfect for a twenty-three-year-old on a budget, I was ready for a bit more comfort. So, I'd checked into the Intercontinental Hotel, a two-minute walk from Circular Quay.

There was a posh coffee maker on the table opposite my giant bed. It made me think of Tiff, and how she'd teased me for staying at the Ganesh Guest House. This room had all the luxuries she'd said I'd prefer. She wasn't wrong. She'd been really understanding about my need to leave Nepal when I'd emailed her about my change of plan. And rather than be annoyed, she'd asked if I'd consider coming back sometime. I hadn't committed either way, but it felt very nice to be valued.

I got up, made a coffee, raided the complimentary biscuits and took them to the seat underneath my window.

I sipped my coffee, watching the world go by. Ahead of me was the vast green space of the Royal Botanic Gardens, further afield, the water with its rugged coastline, inlets and coves leading out to the North Shores and the Pacific Ocean. And if I pressed my face to the glass and looked to the left, I could see the shell-like structure of the Opera House.

Wait until Kat saw this view. I grinned to myself as I fetched my phone, took a picture and sent it to her. A message pinged back immediately.

Poor you! hashtag thoughts and prayers. Currently minus three degrees here, even the dogs don't want to go outside. P.S. Sorry I shouted. I miss you, that's all. We haven't gone this long without seeing each other since you went to Bali. I was being selfish.

Don't worry about it. My fault for chopping and changing my mind. I need to do this, Kat, not just for Brontë but for me.

I'm glad and it's about time! Send me photos of Sydney and I'll try not to be too jealous. Off you go and enjoy yourself xx

I would be doing that very soon. But first, George had asked to FaceTime me, and his call was due any second.

Right on cue, his face appeared on my screen. I recognised the background: he was sitting in one of our meeting rooms at work.

'Hello, boss. Wow.' His eyes widened as he caught sight of my location. 'Cool view.'

'Very cool,' I agreed. 'And I'll be out there exploring it as soon as I've found out what's been going on. I thought you were happy at ShopSwift?'

'I was.' He rubbed his thumb along his jaw. 'But I'm working for Lee now. He has a very different management style to you and I don't think he likes me. My probation period is up in four weeks. He probably won't offer me a permanent contract. I don't want that on my CV, so I think I should cut my losses and leave before I get kicked out.'

He wouldn't be getting kicked out if I could help it. Good junior staff who turned up on time and were conscientious workers were gold dust. Bloody Lee Masters, I thought, gritting my teeth. Lee was the king of office banter and wanted everyone to like him. George was earnest and hard-working and probably didn't even look up from his laptop when Lee was holding court – which must irk him immensely.

'You'll encounter lots of different management styles in your career,' I told him, hiding my irritation. 'Not all of them will suit you.'

'He had a go at me the other day for not speaking up in a client meeting. But I couldn't get a word in – he doesn't know when to shut up. The client kept looking at his watch, but Lee didn't get the hint.'

I laughed at that. Poor George. 'I'm sure whatever you wanted to say was valid.'

'You know me,' he said glumly, 'I'm happier doing the data analysis for client pitches than the presentations.'

'Then tell Lee that,' I urged him. 'Don't be afraid to express yourself. Ask for what you want. Then you have reasons to quit if the company can't accommodate your request or won't listen to you.'

'So you think I should stay?'

'It's not up to me, it's your decision. We spend most of our waking hours at work, so if you aren't enjoying it, then you need to do something about it. Life's too short, George. Besides, you're only in your twenties. Now's your time to experiment, try different things, explore your options.'

'I guess.' He paused. 'I thought you'd be disappointed.'

'I am,' I admitted. 'You're an asset to ShopSwift. And I'll miss you when I come back.'

'You're definitely coming back?' He brightened. 'That makes me feel better about staying. Lee doesn't think you will. He's taking bets on it.'

'Is he now?' I felt my hackles rise. *He wishes*, I thought to myself. 'Look, at the risk of being indiscreet, George, that sort of comment from Lee is unprofessional. He's entitled to his opinion, but at his level of seniority, he should be keeping his thoughts to himself. It's unsettling for my team, of which you're an important part, and it's incorrect.'

George nodded earnestly. 'I didn't join in. I keep my head down. There's a lot to do on Vap-A-Rise at the moment.'

He gave me a nervous look as if not sure whether he'd spoken out of turn and I reassured him that Anna had already told me.

'I'll be back, I can't afford not to work,' I told him. Although I was missing my job a lot less than I thought I would.

'You're good at sales,' he said a touch wistfully. 'My goal was to be promoted to sales manager one day, like you. But my heart's not in it.'

'Interesting,' I said, encouragingly. 'One thing I've learned is that you're allowed to change your goal. It should serve you and no one else. If pursuing it doesn't make you happy, then it isn't the right goal. But there are loads of opportunities at ShopSwift and we'd be foolish to let you go.'

George grinned. 'Thanks, Maggie. Thanks for believing in me.'

'Okay, now off you go and wow them with your talent, and start believing in yourself.'

'Thanks, boss.'

No sooner had we ended the call than my phone buzzed with a message from Anna.

And THAT'S why I bloody miss you! That was amazing. Thank you!

I shook my head in amusement.

You heard us talking?!

Yep. I totally eavesdropped that whole conversation. Zero regrets.

He's a good kid. Let's not lose him.

Understood. I don't suppose I could tempt you to cut your sabbatical short? That I do have regrets about.

I hesitated before typing my reply. I glanced back out at Sydney Harbour looking glorious in the sunshine, and thought about the person I needed to contact. I might not be in my twenties anymore, but now was my time to explore my options.

I sent her a photo of the view in lieu of a reply.

WOWZERS. The view from your ShopSwift office can't compete with that. Go and enjoy yourself!

Now that was an order I could get on board with.

*Mum's Gap Year*

Darling Brontë,

I've followed your journey to Australia. It took me two flights and twenty-five hours from Nepal, but oh my word was it worth it!

For the last few days I've been in full-on tourist mode. I've plastered on the sunscreen, packed water and my guidebook into my backpack and set out each morning to explore the city. And for the first time since leaving the UK, I am truly relaxed. It goes without saying that you would have had a ball here. You'd have loved the outdoor lifestyle, and knowing it's so cold at home this winter makes the sunshine even sweeter.

All the wonderful things I'd heard about Sydney are true. The people are friendly, the weather is always glorious, and I don't think I'll ever run out of new places to discover. So far, I've taken an early ferry to Manly and had brunch at Fairy Bower beach, stuffed myself on the famous afternoon tea at the Queen Victoria Building, lost track of time in the biggest bookshops I've ever been in, and sipped deliciously cold white wine at the Opera Bar watching the sun set over Harbour Bridge. On Sunday I whiled away a happy few hours in the Rocks learning about the early settlers and spent far too much money browsing the market stalls that line the cobbled streets. And the next day, I walked the coast road from Bondi to Coogee. Yesterday, I woke up feeling lonely, so I joined a tour group. Our guide took us to see quirky architecture, street art, galleries and coffee shops, and we ended up at a craft brewery! I'm still a bit lonely. I realise now how much I relied on you to confide in, to share stories with and chat to on WhatsApp throughout the day. I need to expand my circle again, 'find my tribe'. I've had my head in the sand since I lost you, even deserting my book group! I've rejoined them now, you'll be glad to know. We're reading a T. M. Logan thriller, though I'm only in contact with them via WhatsApp. It's a start at least, and I'm going to make time to renew connections with people again.

Talking of connections . . . I'm writing this while on a train. I've done a brave thing and made contact with Harry. Your Harry. He's staying with his uncle in the Blue Mountains, so he's meeting me at the station in Leura and is going to be my tour guide for a couple of days. I'm so nervous about seeing him again; I feel guilty for not being in touch with him since you've been gone. But this is my chance to make it up to him. He's such a nice boy and clearly loves you very much. In a way he reminds me of your dad and how besotted with each other we were.

Sometimes I miss you so much that it's all I can do to get out of bed in the morning and face the day. But I know that waking up is a privilege that you'll never get again, so I try to remember that and make the most of my time on this earth.

Love for always

Mum xxx

# Chapter 18

## Maggie, Bali, 2000

It was two in the morning, Jackson and I were on duty in the turtle hatchery; Utt was outside patching up a hole in the side with wood. A dog had found its way inside the hut earlier and only Jackson's swift intervention had saved the eggs from getting eaten.

Sixteen baby turtles had hatched in the last half an hour; they were scuttling around the enclosure adorably, so tiny and perfect that it was hard not to keep picking them up for a closer look. Much to Utt's bemusement we'd given them all names. There was one more egg showing signs of hatching and once it did, we'd be releasing them together.

'Here he comes,' said Jackson, peering down at the egg as a fin appeared through a crack in the shell.

'I think it's a she,' I said, leaning close to him. 'What shall we call her?'

'Okay, how about Tina?'

'Tina Turtle.' I snorted. 'Perfect.'

'She's simply the best,' sang Jackson in a falsetto voice, 'the last one out of the nest.'

'No singing,' Utt shouted.

'Why?' I called, 'is it bad for the turtles?'

'No. It is bad for me,' he shot back, hooting with laughter.

'I used to sing in church when I was a kid,' Jackson replied, pretending to be insulted. 'All the church ladies loved my voice.'

'I love your voice too.' My heart gave a little squeeze, imagining how cute he must have looked dressed in his smart clothes, his curls neatly brushed, his little voice wavering on the high notes. I scarcely recognised myself these days. When had I become such a soppy romantic?

Jackson's lips brushed mine and his hands went to my waist. I could feel the heat from his skin and a pulse in my throat began to throb. I couldn't get enough of him. In the rare moments we weren't together, he was all I thought about. I was infatuated with him, and he with me. Our days were full of fun and sunshine and laughing and kissing. It couldn't be love; we hadn't known each other very long. But whatever it was, I was having the best time ever.

'We can't, not here,' I breathed, melting into him as he pulled me closer. 'Utt can hear us.'

There was a thud from outside as if Utt had dropped something, followed by a muttered curse, and we stepped back from each other reluctantly.

'Let's go release these babies,' Jackson said softly.

I picked up Tina gently and put her in the bucket along with the rest, then we made our way out to the beach. Utt left his tools and came with us. He'd never admit it, but I reckoned he liked Jackson and me.

The air was still, the waves barely making a sound, and a full moon hung in the sky above the ocean tingeing the night with an eerie silvery light.

'Perfect turtle-releasing conditions,' said Jackson. 'We won't even need a torch.'

'Not too close to the water,' Utt instructed us. 'Here is good.'

'Why?' I set the bucket down on the sand. 'If we go nearer, the babies haven't got so far to go.'

'The journey to the water is important for them,' he explained, squatting down beside the bucket. 'This is when they learn about where they are from. They will always find their way back here to nest and lay their eggs.'

'Lucky them,' I said, thinking there were a lot worse places to return to.

'Imprinting.' Jackson nodded. 'A few seconds in this place and it's enough for them to make memories for life. Amazing.'

'I think I've probably done that too,' I said, catching his eye.

He grinned at me. 'Same here.'

Utt transferred the hatchlings from the bucket onto the sand, taking care to orient them the right way so they were facing the shoreline. Jackson and I kept watch to make sure there were no dogs about to leap onto our brave little creatures.

'I feel like a proud father every time,' said Utt, brushing the sand off his hands. 'We take care of the eggs, keep them safe, and then the time comes to set them free. But we will always remember this day when we let them go.'

'Like my mom and dad, when I left the States,' Jackson said. 'My dad trying to tuck dollar bills into my pocket and my mom crying because she thought she'd wanted me to go and have my adventure until the moment I was actually doing it.'

My mum hadn't said anything like that, only wanting to know where I'd got the money to pay for my air fare and asking whether, if I was that well-off, I could lend her some to get her hair done. I'd given Kat money from my savings to tide her over while I was away. She hadn't been able to have a job because she'd been revising for her A-levels. She'd almost cried with gratitude.

The baby turtles crawled towards the water, their tiny fins flailing as they mastered the art of movement. It was an incredible sight to witness.

'Look at that,' I marvelled, 'so instinctive, the way they run to the sea, to freedom.'

We moved down the beach with them, like parents whose kids had just learned to walk, wanting to give them independence, but remaining close enough to intervene if necessary.

'Who can blame them,' Jackson said. 'Isn't that what we all want – freedom?'

I thought about that for a moment and decided that it wasn't what I wanted long term. I was enjoying my freedom this summer but eventually I wanted security, especially financially. I wanted to know what was coming, I wanted to have a plan and stick to it. Freedom represented the unknown to me and I didn't feel equipped to cope with that.

'Have you ever wanted to travel, Utt?' I asked.

'Oh no,' he said, shaking his head as if it was the last thing he'd ever wish to do. 'People travel to search for something they do not have. I have everything I want. My family, this beautiful country. My roots are here, my soul is at peace here.'

The passion in his voice brought a lump to my throat.

'That's lovely,' I said. 'My soul is at peace too.'

I thought of what lay ahead for me back in the UK and I felt my spirits sink. My final year at uni, the paper I would have to write, my tiny room in the shared house. I liked university, but I was ready for it to be over, for my life to start. But leaving here, saying goodbye to Jackson, was going to be the hardest thing I'd ever done.

'Ooooh,' Jackson teased. 'She's finally weakening, Utt, I think we're winning her round.'

I laughed. 'Bali has my heart, that's for sure.'

'You watch them until they reach water.' Utt got to his feet and picked up the bucket. 'I go back now. See you tomorrow.'

'Goodnight, Utt,' we said in unison.

'We'll make sure they stay safe,' I added.

He turned back and raised a hand in a wave.

'She is a good woman,' he said to Jackson. 'Good heart, good head.'

'I know,' said Jackson, earnestly holding my gaze, and I was glad that the moonlight hid my blushes.

'So it's only Bali that has your heart?' he murmured once Utt was out of earshot.

'Well,' I said, closing the gap between us and taking hold of his hands. 'Bali will always be associated with the happiest summer of my life, and you may have had something to do with that, so . . .'

'Come with me,' he blurted out, sliding his fingers along my shoulder to the back of my neck. 'Let's keep travelling. I want to go to Thailand next, I've heard it's even more beautiful than here.'

'I can't,' I said, trembling as he stroked a hand down my back. 'I've got to get home.'

He groaned. 'When do your classes start?'

'October.'

'There you go!' He grinned. 'That's months away.'

'I know. But my job! I have to earn money.' I rested my cheek on his chest, inhaling the scent of him, feeling his lungs rise and fall.

'Mags, you have your whole life to earn money. Put your sensible life on hold, stay free for a bit longer. Be like those little turtles and choose freedom. We'll go by train, stay in a hostel. It'll be so cheap. Come on, what do you say?'

I gave him a small smile. 'You make it sound so easy.'

He picked me up and swung me around. 'It *is* easy! Say yes.'

Another month of loving this boy, of having an adventure I'd never forget, of setting aside the responsibilities of home . . .

'Yes,' I said with a bubble of laughter. 'I say yes.'

# Chapter 19

## Australia

Harry was waiting on the platform of Leura station, standing tall and broad-shouldered. His attention was on his phone screen, giving me a chance to study him, this boy who'd captured my daughter's heart. T-shirts, shorts and trainers, all black: his taste in clothes hadn't altered, I noticed. Brontë had looked like an exotic bird next to him in her thrift store florals. Yet now he looked unrecognisable from the image I had of him at the funeral last year. Then his entire demeanour had been one of a young man defeated by life, his stance bent and his pale face doing its best to mask his emotions. His dark wavy hair was shorter than it had been last time I'd seen him. He'd got a suntan too; I remembered Brontë complaining last summer that he only had to look at the sun and he turned brown.

A look of recognition crossed his face. He smiled, raised his hand.

I felt an ache of sadness that it was me, not Brontë, stepping off the train to meet him and wondered if the same thought had occurred to him. Their faces would have been lit with love and excitement. He'd have swept her up and kissed her, ignoring the looks from other passengers. I knew this because he'd picked us up from the airport once and I had looked on fondly and with slight envy at the youthful exuberance of first love.

I walked towards him, dragging my suitcase behind me, conscious of the fluttering of butterflies in my stomach. Was this a strange thing to be doing, meeting my dead daughter's boyfriend, ex-boyfriend? Was she even his ex? That sounded wrong, as if they'd chosen to part ways rather than being ripped apart through the actions of someone else.

'Harry!' I smiled shakily as I approached him. 'I made it. Thanks for meeting me. It's good to see you.'

'Hello, Maggie.' His eyes roamed my face. Brontë and I looked alike – had looked alike. Everyone told us so. He was looking at an older version of her, a version which would never exist. 'Good trip?'

'Really good.' I reached for my water bottle and took a sip, conscious of my dry mouth. 'I loved watching the landscape change the further away from the city we got. I love Sydney and the ocean, but the hills and all the trees, and looking at the countryside . . .' I was aware that I was rambling, but couldn't shut up. 'Well, it's beautiful. Only a hundred kilometres away, but it feels like I'm in a completely different place.'

He nodded. 'It's a world away from the city. I'm looking forward to showing you around.'

'You look great.' My voice broke as I said it, and with it, my heart all over again.

I was pleased to see him looking well; of course I was. But whereas he was a picture of health, my daughter was dead. He'd survived the accident with cracked ribs and broken bones – Brontë had lost her life. Seeing him so young, so alive, delivered a punchy reminder of what I'd lost. For a few seconds, I could do nothing other than stare, the beat of my heart crashing in my ears.

His smile was tentative. 'I'm getting there.'

His voice still sounded the same, but there was a new, more adult edge.

We stood awkwardly opposite each other, arms by our sides, the enormous loss we shared standing between us like a fracture in the ground after an earthquake.

'Come here.' I opened my arms and Harry almost fell into them. 'I need a hug.'

'Me too.' I heard the wobble in his voice, and hugged him tight.

Underneath his T-shirt I could feel his shoulder blades. There was less of him than before and the thought that he'd been suffering to the point of losing weight sent a wave of shame through me. I'd been so wrapped up in my grief that I hadn't paid enough attention to the hearts of others around me who'd lost her too.

'I'm sorry I've not been in touch more,' I said, pulling back to look into his blue eyes.

He shook his head. 'I'm the one who should be apologising. But I couldn't face . . . I couldn't . . .' He rubbed his face roughly. 'Shit.' Then, 'Sorry. I didn't mean to swear.'

'It's okay, Brontë's not here to tell you off.'

He gave me a bemused look as if to say, *really, you're making jokes?*

'We're in the way, here. Is there somewhere to get coffee?' I asked as a family with a double buggy and a teenager pulling two suitcases attempted to squeeze past us without falling onto the tracks.

He rubbed his stomach. 'Yeah, actually, I'm starving.'

I had a flashback to all the times he and Brontë had showed up at my house and he'd said the same thing. Within minutes they'd be in the kitchen raiding the fridge. 'When are you ever not starving?'

Harry grabbed the handle of my suitcase, his head shaking slightly. 'You sounded exactly like her then,' he murmured.

He still loved her, I realised with a pang.

'What do you think she'd say about us meeting up in Australia?'

'She'd say . . .' He shook his head and smiled. 'She'd say, *Charming, where's my bloody invite?*'

I laughed, grateful to release some of the tension that had been building. 'That is exactly what she'd say.'

I took his arm. I'd never done that before, but it felt right. And together we headed down the hill towards the centre of town.

Leura's high street was not at all what I was expecting. The buildings on either side of the road had a familiar Edwardian feel about them, with ornate balconies and little gable windows set high up in the eaves. There was a plethora of boutiques, art galleries and restaurants, many of which were painted in pretty pastel shades. Down the centre of the road was a wide grass verge full of mature trees, which Harry informed me had earned the town the description of 'the garden village'. We stopped outside the Leura Café and Deli and he gestured for me to go in.

The interior was divided into two: a deli at the front selling an array of salads and pies, pastries and sandwiches; and a café behind with a glass wall at the back. We chose a table with an incredible view across what Harry informed me was Katoomba, another popular town in the Blue Mountains. Harry tucked my suitcase out of the way, and we ordered – coffee for both of us and banana bread for him – and for a moment my brain froze. I shifted in my seat, fumbling for the right words. This was the first time we'd been alone together since Brontë died. In fact, he and I had never spent any time alone; Brontë had always been there.

He seemed to feel the same and for the next few minutes we traded banal comments about the café, the menu and the view.

I remembered that our last face-to-face conversation had been stilted, a few exchanged words before the funeral service. I had no clear recollection of what had been said. The day had gone by in a blur of tissues and tears, and platitudes and promises from everyone to help with anything, anything at all. And now here we both were, four thousand miles from home, facing each other across a café table; the two most important people in Brontë's life.

After we'd exhausted our small talk, we finally looked at each other directly.

'There's so much I want to say,' I began, 'but now I'm here, I'm struggling to find the right words.'

'Yeah.' He ruffled his hair, self-consciously. 'Same here. It feels a million years since I sat in your cottage in Honeybourne making pancakes with . . .' He clenched his jaw and glanced away. It struck me that he hadn't said her name out loud yet.

'Look, we're here now and we've got plenty of time to chat,' I told him. 'Let's take the pressure off and not worry about the big stuff yet.'

'Cool.' He shot me a grateful smile. 'It's . . . it's good to see you, Maggie. Weird to have you sitting opposite me in a café in the Blue Mountains. It's like two worlds colliding.'

He laughed gently under his breath, but it was without humour.

'I think you'd got an internship lined up for last year,' I said, changing the subject for him. 'How did it go?'

Before he had a chance to respond, someone called his name and we both looked up to see a man approaching our table carrying a takeaway coffee and a paper bag.

'G'day, my friend.' The man patted Harry's shoulder.

'Karl.' Harry stood and shook his hand.

'I won't interrupt you,' said Karl, giving me a look of apology. 'But I wanted to say thanks for the post you tagged us in.

We sold out of the poetry book you linked on your story. The author was really pleased too.'

'No worries.' Harry looked uncomfortable with the compliment. 'Happy to help.'

'Well, I appreciate it, mate.' Karl sipped his coffee. 'There's a proof of a new book arrived at the shop that I think you'll like. I'll save it for you. Drop in again soon.'

'I did a post on Instagram about his bookshop,' Harry explained once his friend had gone. He cleared his throat. 'And, er, the internship thing didn't work out.'

'Oh?'

He scooted his chair in closer to the table and kept his eyes lowered. 'My head wasn't in the right place for it, so I left.' He shrugged. 'They were good about it; said I can come back next year if I want.'

I nodded. 'And so you decided to travel instead?'

I knew from our recent WhatsApp conversations that he'd been travelling since the New Year, staying in the Blue Mountains with his uncle for a while planning to go to New Zealand and on to the Philippines. An impromptu gap year, he'd called it. I hadn't needed to ask why.

'Yeah, I wanted to be somewhere new, no memories, you know?' He looked up at me from under his dark lashes. 'I hope that doesn't sound bad?'

My heart ached. 'No, Harry, it sounds entirely reasonable. Going away and getting a fresh perspective on life is a great idea. I'm doing something similar myself.'

He grinned. 'It was a surprise to get your message. The last place I expected you to be was Sydney.'

'Hey, guys,' said our waitress, putting her tray down on the table. 'Sorry for the wait.'

She was a petite pretty girl with long curly hair and dimples, and the sight of her brought a blush to Harry's cheeks.

'Hey, Lola,' Harry replied, sitting back to make room for her.

Lola's eyes widened as if she hadn't expected him to remember her name. 'Oh, hi, Harry.'

Their eyes met briefly, and I may have been imagining things, but I suspected that there could be some chemistry between them, given a bit of encouragement. I watched as Lola clumsily set coffees in front of us, spilling some onto the table, Harry mopping up with a napkin. I took a deep breath as a pang of sorrow pierced my side. Someone new could be a good thing for him; I wanted him to be happy, but it was only natural that it also brought Brontë's absence into sharp focus.

Lola walked away and I tried not to notice as Harry's eyes followed her.

'Actually, you might know more about my plans than I do.' I picked up my spoon and swirled it through the froth on the top of my coffee.

He whistled under his breath when I got Brontë's gap-year book out of my bag and slid it onto the table.

'No way. I don't believe it.' He whistled under his breath, reaching out to touch the cover so tenderly that my heart squeezed. I was her mother, of course this was hard for me, but Harry was not much more than a boy and he'd been through the trauma of a terrible traffic accident and witnessing his girlfriend's death. 'May I?'

I nodded and Harry picked up Brontë's book, turning it over, smiling at the illustrations on the cover. He opened it and my bookmark fell out from the page marking the Blue Mountains.

He smiled wistfully. 'I feel like I know every page of this book. We worked on it together – her itinerary, I mean, not the actual design. She spent hours drawing it. Did you like her weather wheel? I think that was my favourite part.'

'I haven't seen that yet,' I told him. 'I've only read as far as her plan to come here, to meet you in the Blue Mountains.'

His brow furrowed. 'I'm not following you.'

Over our coffees and his banana bread, which he insisted I try, I explained how I was discovering Brontë's journey page by page, savouring her entries and following her path. I told him about my experience in Nepal and how I almost went home, and how it dawned on me before booking a flight back to the UK that somewhere along the line, the trip had become as much about me having an adventure as it was about doing it for Brontë.

'And that was when I found out I'd be coming to Australia.'

He laughed in disbelief. 'That's . . .' He threw his hands up and leaned back in his chair. 'Genius! And if you don't mind me saying, really wild of you. She always told me that the secret to your success was to plan every detail. Yet here you are, winging it.'

*My success.* I let that sink in for a second, imagining her talking to Harry about me. Pride fizzed through me.

'"Winging it" is the perfect description,' I agreed, 'but I think when you've been through a tough time, like you and I both have, getting by is an achievement in itself.'

He took a breath as if he was about to say something but then seemed to think better of it.

'When I say I'm using her itinerary,' I continued, 'I realised early on that there'd be times when I wouldn't be able to follow in her footsteps exactly.'

'So, Everest Base Camp?' he said with a hint of humour in his eyes. 'Yes or no?'

'I could easily have done it,' I said primly, and then returned his smile. 'But I didn't have the shoes.'

He burst out laughing. 'Between you and me, I don't think she was totally sure about it. I think you made the right decision.'

I knew I had; my time at the One World Project had taught me a lot about myself. I wouldn't have missed that for anything.

'I've read that she was planning on travelling to the Gold Coast with you. I can easily do that too. So here I am, raring to go.'

He swallowed hard. 'Right. Okay, sure.'

I laughed. 'Your face. I'm only teasing. I'm going to stay for a couple of nights, then I'll head north by myself.'

'Are you sure?' he blustered. 'I mean, I could borrow my Uncle Pete's car . . .'

I laid a hand on his arm. 'I'm sure. She wrote – and drew – so beautifully about the Blue Mountains that I knew I had to visit. And seeing you again was too good an opportunity to pass up. I think she'd have liked this. Us meeting up again.'

He let out a deep breath. 'Yeah. I think so too. I wish . . .'

He tailed off and settled for finishing the last mouthful of cake instead. 'Let's go, shall we?'

'Sure.' I caught the eye of a waitress and asked for the bill and within minutes we were heading for the door.

I could see how difficult it was for him to express his emotions. He was suffering, that much was obvious, and he still hadn't managed to utter Brontë's name. I'd meant it when I'd said that there were lots of things I wanted to say, and it looked as if he might feel the same. Maybe I'd be able to help him with that while I was here. Maybe these next couple of days together would be good for both of us.

# *Chapter 20*

## Australia

The next morning after breakfast, Harry collected me from my guest house in Leura with a promise to show me some of his favourite spots in the Blue Mountains.

'Sorry about the state of this vehicle,' he said, brushing crumbs off the passenger seat before he'd allow me in. 'My Uncle Pete has a lot of good qualities, but hoovering his car is not one of them. Cleaning anything at all doesn't feature highly on the list, if I'm honest.'

It was an elderly estate car with bumper stickers on the rear and dents on every door panel. Someone had drawn *Clean me* in the thick layer of dust covering the bonnet. Harry was meticulous, often resorting to tidying Brontë's room when the mess got too much for him. His uncle sounded like the complete opposite and I was intrigued to meet him.

'Harry, the last time I accepted a lift off anyone it was in an ox and cart, which was dusty, bumpy and not in the least bit fragrant.' I laughed at the surprise on his face. 'Believe me, this is luxury, and please thank your uncle for letting you have his car to chauffeur me today.'

We headed away from Leura, passing the little restaurant

where I'd spent a serene couple of hours last night over a water-melon juice mocktail watching the sunset over the mountains from a white bandstand in the garden. After leaving the coffee shop yesterday, Harry and I had had a walk around Leura until it was time for me to check into the guest house, where he'd left me to my own devices.

I'd pondered asking if he wanted to join me for dinner but had decided against it. The couple of hours we'd spent together had been enough to break the ice, and this morning things felt more relaxed between us.

The drive to our first stop only took ten minutes, even with Harry slowing down so that I could see some of the wonderful street art painted on the houses in Katoomba. From the research I'd done on the train, I knew that I'd be in for a visual treat on our walk today. We were steering clear of the main tourist routes and were seeking out some secret spots recommended by Uncle Pete. There were motor homes, minibuses and plenty of cars filling the car park and lining the road, but Harry passed them by and found a parking spot under a shady tree. We set off with backpacks and sun hats following a path into dense woodland.

'This trip,' Harry asked once we were on our way. 'You're going to visit all the places included in her travel journal?'

'Yep. That's the plan. Each time I turn a page it's like having a whole new conversation with her.'

'I'd love that,' he said softly.

'It's brought me a lot of unexpected joy already.' I allowed a beat of silence to follow, acknowledging how lucky I was to have her itinerary to discover. 'I put off looking at it for months. And now I know why. I think I was meant to do this trip. I'm intrigued to see what Bronté has in store for me.'

He turned to look at me, a flicker of something crossing his face. I couldn't make out if it was impressed or alarmed.

'Exciting,' he said.

'It has been, so far. I think she'd be glad all her research hasn't gone to waste.'

Soon we were walking uphill on a twisting path towards Echo Point in Katoomba. I was staying close to Harry and warily watching for spiders. The sun was beating down in a sky barely marked with fluffy clouds, but the dappled shade of the eucalyptus trees provided enough cover to keep me from overheating. The air was fragrant  with the aroma of tea tree. Somewhere beside us, a kookaburra laughed incessantly, making Harry and me laugh too.

He stopped beside a gap in the trees and indicated for me to take in the view. 'Waterfall.'

Harry wasn't big on detail. I didn't mind. I'd been taking pictures of signposts and *You are here* maps; so I could go back and check what I'd seen later if necessary. I was happy just to spend time in this beautiful place, with him.

I knew we were looking out at Jamison Valley. And far beneath us was indeed a waterfall. Even from this distance we could hear the water crashing down into the river below.

'Wow.' I gazed with awe out across the landscape and up at the huge sky. 'Makes me feel very small.'

'Me too.' Harry waited while I took some photos and then we continued on. 'I come out here sometimes to remind myself how small my problems are in the grand scheme of things.'

I almost prompted him to explain, but decided against it at the last moment. He could tell me in his own time. We carried on for a few minutes in silence until we came to a lookout point, a flat platform enclosed with railings.

'This is my favourite view.' Harry walked up to the railings, took two bottles of water from his rucksack and handed one to me.

I recognised the rock formation on the opposite side of the valley. It was one of the most iconic landmarks of the Blue Mountains: three sandstone peaks in a row.

'The Three Sisters!' I exclaimed. 'This is beautiful, Harry. Thank you for bringing me here.'

For a few minutes, we stood together, sipping our water, lost in our thoughts, the lush bluey-green of the eucalyptus forest providing a stark contrast against the orange and brown mountains. The sky was so clear that we could see for miles and miles.

'I'm sorry,' he blurted out, turning to me. 'I'm sorry I didn't come round and see you after . . .'

He left the end of the sentence hanging. 'I couldn't face being in your house. Not without her. I feel very guilty about that.'

I was close to tears and so was he. I wanted to hug him, but knew that if I did, we'd both end up crying again. So instead I bumped against his shoulder. 'Nothing to apologise for. It was a horrendous time and an impossible situation for both of us.'

'I know but she is, I mean, she *was* the centre of your world. I knew how much you'd be suffering. I should have done more.'

'I'm not your responsibility, Harry,' I assured him. 'But thank you. She *was* the centre of my world and when she was taken from me, I felt hollow.'

'Me too,' he murmured.

'I'm sure,' I said, softly.

Above us, two aeroplanes passed by one after the other, their white vapour trails at first intersecting and then fading in a cornflower-blue sky. I'd allowed Harry's presence to fade from my life, encouraging it even. Was that the right thing, the natural way of things, or would there always be a thread of common ground to connect us? 'When your parents said that you didn't want visitors in the hospital, I was partly relieved. I couldn't face you either. And I still feel guilty about that. I should have made an effort to check up on you, to give you an opportunity to talk about her. Young people shouldn't have to experience the death of someone they're close to like you did.'

'No, they shouldn't. But then neither should parents. Can I ask you something?'

I met his eye and nodded. 'Sure.'

'How did you cope, you know, afterwards, once the funeral was over?'

'I don't think I did, Harry.' I suppressed a shudder, not wanting to revisit those dark days and weeks. 'Instead of finding something else to fill the void in my heart, I simply put on thicker armour to protect myself, not really letting grief in.'

'I was the opposite. I felt as if my skin was paper thin for the first couple of months. I got sick of people telling me to stay strong.' He tensed his jaw, his dark features clouding over. 'Why? Why should I be strong? If you can't collapse under your feelings when something like that happens to you, when can you?'

'I agree with you, although it took me a while to come around to thinking that way. I suppose it's only now, by leaving my home and my job, that I can see what I was doing. At the time I thought I was coping, but I was doing the exact opposite.'

'I loved her,' he said, gazing into the distance. 'I'd never been in love before. I know we were still young, but it felt like we had a future together.'

'She loved you too,' I told him, resting my arm around his shoulders. 'And it doesn't matter how old you are, love isn't interested in numbers.'

He gave me a crooked smile. 'I like that idea.'

We were joined at our viewing point by another couple of tourists and moved over to allow them access to the best angle for their photos. As soon as they'd gone, we resumed our position by the railings. I got out my phone and took some pictures of the view, and then a selfie of Harry and me which I'd send to Kat later. We set off again, heading further along the track. The terrain was on a slight incline but nothing I couldn't manage in my trainers.

'So how are you doing now?' I asked him. 'We're seven months on from the accident.'

'Changed.' He gave me a sad smile. 'It's made me question everything. Sometimes I feel like what's the point in trying, working hard, being the best that you can be? Because that's what she did. Every day. She was always so driven.' He looked at me. 'You did that for her, you fired her belief in herself.'

'That was my job,' I said, quietly proud. 'It's every parent's job.'

'Other times I think about that night non-stop. It plays in my head like a movie I can't turn off.' He shuddered and for a moment I worried that he was going to talk about Brontë's last seconds of life, something I had no desire to hear. I knew that once I knew the details, I could never unknow them. 'Nothing could be worse than what I witnessed that night, and I think to myself, if I can survive that, I can survive anything.' He came to a stop and pressed a hand to his forehead. 'Oh shit, I'm sorry, Maggie, I shouldn't have said that.'

'Hey, it's okay.' I reached for his hand. 'The simple truth is that you're still here. I'm still here. Our lives have to go on. We have to live with the loss of Brontë. You're right: from the moment she was born, in fact from the moment I found out I was pregnant, she became the centre of my world.'

'So what are you going to do?'

I shrugged. 'I'm still working on that, but at least I am working on it now instead of pretending everything's okay.'

We rounded a bend and came to another lookout place, smaller this time, and stood shoulder to shoulder looking out across the mountains.

'I feel so guilty, you know? I got up and walked away from that accident. I'm alive and she's not.'

I met his eye. 'You know deep down that that's not something to feel guilty about, don't you?'

179

He gazed out at the green valley below us. 'Do I? It was guilt that kept me from being in touch with you too. I thought you'd find it hard to see me still here when—' His voice cracked and he shook his head, as if impatient with himself. 'Sorry.'

'Look, I feel guilty too for what I said about her gap-year plans. The final time we were ever together, and we argued. I'll never forgive myself.'

He frowned. 'What do you mean?'

'She didn't tell you?'

'She phoned me on her way home from your house and told me what you'd said. She didn't mention a row though.'

'What did she say?' I asked, bewildered.

'Let me think. Oh yeah.' He smiled wistfully. 'I can't remember the exact words, but she said something along the lines of: *Mum's so smart. She wants me to think it all through for one more week before I commit to taking the gap year. She reminded me how much I'd wanted the Saatchi job and how much I'd be giving up if I went travelling now. And if I'm being honest, I have gone a bit crazy with some of my plans. I've already emailed Saatchi about deferring my start date, so it's too late for that. But I am going to think hard about some of the . . . er . . . other stuff.'*

Harry stopped abruptly, looking a bit shifty.

'Other stuff?' I prompted. 'What do you mean?'

He raised his eyebrows. 'To do with her travel plans. You want me to tell you?'

I sucked in a breath. I was curious, but the not knowing had its benefits too. 'Yes. No. Oh, I don't know.'

Harry smiled at my indecision. 'I helped her with the research. I could tell you about the whole trip, but you said you're enjoying turning each page and learning new things. If you come across something you don't want to do, you can always choose not to do it.'

'Good thinking. I'll do that.'

He seemed relieved. 'But to go back to feeling guilty about that day. Honestly, don't. If anything it reinforced how supportive you always were. She said it would have been so easy for you to go along with her ideas and not challenge her. But she said that's not what you do; you face up to life's challenges. And you held a mirror up to her so she could face hers too. There had been aspects of her trip she wasn't sure about; talking to you made her really consider everything. So you see, there's nothing to feel bad about.'

'Really?' My voice cracked and my chest began to burn. 'Do you really think that?'

'Maggie, oh God, I'm sorry.' He grabbed hold of me and held me tight. 'I didn't mean to make you cry.'

I hadn't even been aware I was crying, but now with my cheek pressed into his shoulder, I felt hot tears soaking his T-shirt.

I made a noise somewhere between a laugh and a sob and released myself from his crushing hug. 'I know it doesn't look like it, but you've made me the happiest I've been since she died.'

'Okay, wow, I'll have to take your word for that.' He gave me a wry smile, fetching a packet of tissues from his rucksack and handing them to me.

I blew my nose and wiped my eyes as a small tour group joined us. Embarrassed, I stepped to one side and gazed at the view, avoiding eye contact with them. Harry took photos and even offered to take one of the group for them.

'Do you want to know why I like it here so much?' he asked once they'd gone.

'Go on.'

'Because so much of this area of New South Wales was devastated by bush fires a few years ago.'

I'd seen it on the news and been reduced to tears watching animals being rescued from the flames, but I hadn't made the connection that the Blue Mountains had been one of the worst-hit parts of the country. 'That was heartbreaking to see.'

'When I first arrived in Australia, I was a mess,' Harry told me. 'I was up all hours of the night, pacing, too wired to sleep, but too depressed in the day to get out of bed. I'd lost my appetite and couldn't even think about the next day, let alone the next week or month. So my uncle brought me up here. He told me that for a while the beautiful place we're looking at now was too sick for life to continue. Trees reduced to charcoal, wildlife decimated, hope extinguished. He said it was impossible to believe it would heal. But it did eventually. Slowly, bit by bit, month by month. There are bound to be scars, but Uncle Pete reckons eventually those scars will be invisible to anyone who doesn't know what happened.' He took a breath. 'He said my scars would be the same.'

'Your uncle sounds like a very wise man.'

He laughed. 'Uncle Pete is one of a kind. I'm hoping you'll meet him. He's invited you to have dinner with us tonight. Will you come?'

I'd be staying at the guest house for another night, but I hadn't made any dinner plans. 'I'd love that. Thank you.'

We picked up our bags, ready to go back the way we'd come. Harry put a hand on my shoulder and made me turn to take in the view one last time.

'If the Blue Mountains can recover from trauma like that then so can we, Maggie,' he said, giving me a squeeze.

I'd never felt as removed from my normal life as I did in that moment: on the opposite side of the world, dwarfed by the most incredible scenery. I felt small, but at the same time brave and powerful. My physical journey here might have been easy enough on planes and trains, but the mental load had been heavy – was still heavy. But Harry was right, we had life and we had hope and the rest would come in time.

I met his blue eyes, so earnest and brave, and smiled. 'We can, Harry. We bloody can.'

# Chapter 21

## Australia

Harry's uncle lived in a small house surrounded by forest. From the inside, it was like sitting high up in a treehouse. It was charming and rustic and owned by someone who cared more about the outdoors than interiors. The backyard consisted of a patch of ground populated by random buckets, pots and even an old bathtub stuffed with herbs and vegetable plants. The area was enclosed by some of the largest ferns I'd ever seen, and it felt as if it wouldn't take much for nature to smother the house entirely, like the castle in Sleeping Beauty.

'I was a ten-pound pom.' Pete sprinkled his bottle of beer liberally over the barbecue coals and hooted with glee at the sizzle. 'Best ten quid I ever spent in my life. Left Liverpool when I was eighteen, never looked back.'

Pete was divorced, retired and living his best life. I don't think I'd ever met someone so content with his lot than this bushy-bearded, cuddly man. He reminded me of a koala bear, complete with the hairy ears.

'That must have been quite an adventure for someone so young,' I said, sipping my own beer. I'd stopped off at a shop and bought a couple of bottles of wine for my host. He'd accepted them graciously before popping the top off an Australian lager and shoving it into my hand.

'And one long adventure ever since,' Harry said, adding, 'if you believe all his stories, that is.'

'Oi, cheeky.' Pete flipped some prawns over on the barbecue. One fell onto the ground. He picked it up, brushed the grass off and replaced it on the grill.

'You won't look back either.' He waved his tongs at me. 'I can tell when a woman's happy; I'm an expert. There's a flush to your cheeks. You love it here – don't deny it.'

I surreptitiously touched my beer bottle to my face to cool them down and wondered upon what basis he'd decided he was an expert.

'Maybe if I was young, like Harry,' I said. Or like Brontë would have been if she'd come here instead of me. 'But I have a job to go back to – so as much as I love it, I'll have to go home eventually.'

'Ah, work.' Pete threw his arms in the air. 'Ruins all the bloody fun, doesn't it?'

'Only if you're in the wrong job.' Harry held a platter out while his uncle piled on griddled tuna, prawns and vegetable kebabs.

Pete laughed. 'Very true, mate, very true.'

'Not that I know exactly what work is,' Harry added.

Pete wiped his hands on his apron and mussed up his nephew's hair. 'You take as long as you need. You've been through the mill.' He met my eye. 'You both have. Come on. Let's eat.'

We ate at a solid wooden table on stools that Pete had made from logs. It wasn't quite sunset but the sun had sunk below the trees and the light had taken on a soft golden glow, making our al fresco setting feel very romantic. The food was delicious. Vegetables bursting with flavour, the fish and seafood fresh and the salad Harry had made with an Asian dressing set my tastebuds alight.

'Actually, I have sort of got a job,' Harry said, once we'd finished eating. 'I'm an accidental influencer.'

'Instagram?' I asked, remembering the encounter with the bookshop owner this morning.

He nodded sheepishly. 'I started posting about four months ago. I've got about thirty thousand followers.'

'Fiddling about on your phone is a job, is it?' his uncle teased.

'Not on your phone, maybe,' Harry shot back. 'Uncle Pete's phone will be in the Imperial War Museum one day, as part of the early communication devices exhibit.'

'It makes calls, which is all I ask of it,' replied Pete, getting to his feet. 'And talking of which, nature's calling, so excuse me. I'm off to point Percy at the porcelain.'

'Sorry about Uncle Pete.' Harry winced. 'He's great but he doesn't have a filter. I think he's lived on his own too long.'

I laughed. 'I'd better take note, or that will happen to me. He's a lot of fun, which is probably what you need.'

Harry nodded. 'I do. He's got me laughing again, that's for sure. But I also need to learn to express my feelings better too. You can't keep them locked up inside your head forever. It's toxic.'

'That was the mistake I made,' I told him. 'When I came back to work after taking compassionate leave, I asked my boss to ensure that no one mentioned Brontë. I didn't want to talk about her at work. But it must have looked weird seeing me acting as if nothing had happened, and it meant that they weren't able to show me any sympathy, which probably made them feel awkward. And as for my friends, I cut myself off entirely.'

I could see now how unhealthy it was. All it would have taken was for me to have one conversation about Brontë with each of them, and then we could have all moved forward with Brontë's death being part of my narrative instead of a taboo subject.

'Me too.' Harry took a swig of beer. 'For the first three months after the funeral, I told myself that I needed to accept she'd gone and get on with my life. You know, be a man, get over it.'

'Oh Harry.' I sighed. 'I'm so sad that I wasn't there for you. I should have helped you more. And grieving doesn't make you less of a man, it makes you more of a human. I'm sorry I wasn't around to say that to you.'

'Thanks,' he replied. 'I'm learning that now, but back then I wasn't thinking straight. I saw a girl in London once with hair like hers. I don't know what happened, but for a second, I was totally convinced it was her. I ran after her, shouting her name. I grabbed her arm and then the guy she was with shoved me. Then it all came pouring out of me. I cried for days. That's how my Instagram started. Stuff about how I felt. All the other people on Instagram talking about loss were older than me. So, I decided to say the words I needed to hear. Turns out there are loads of young people like me dealing with grief.'

My chest swelled with emotion. He'd faced his demons a lot sooner than I had, dealt with it a lot more positively too. 'I'm in awe of you. Brontë would be so proud.'

He gave me a subdued smile. 'I think so. Especially as it's starting to earn me a bit of money. It's not the career I had in mind for myself, but then neither was the last year. I'm going to do it until I figure out what comes next.'

'It's a brilliant idea. I'll have to follow you on Instagram.'

'I'm called @HarryHurts on there.' He sucked in a breath. 'I should warn you, it can get a bit raw. My posts are a safe space for people to express their grief. There's a whole lot of difficult emotions on display.'

'If you can handle it, so can I. It sounds like you're helping others as well as yourself.'

We smiled at each other, and I thought what a great judge of character my girl had been in choosing him.

'Drum roll, please!' Pete cried, returning with an enormous dessert. 'Pavlova. My speciality. Make room.'

'Wow, I'm impressed,' I said, stacking the dishes to give him space to put the plate down. 'It's a wonder you're still single, Pete, given your culinary skills.'

'It's a mystery, Maggie,' he replied, wiping his hands on the seat of his shorts. 'Fancy a slice, do you? The pavlova, that is.' He nudged me in the ribs and hooted at his own joke.

'Let me,' said Harry, intervening when he noticed my bemused look. 'You've done enough work this evening.'

Pete nodded at my phone, which was displaying Harry's Instagram page. 'Told you about all his groupies, has he? Not surprising, a good-looking lad like him. He's got all the ladies after him.'

'I'm not interested,' Harry said gruffly, thumping a dish of pavlova in front of his uncle.

Pete pulled a face at me. 'Touchy subject,' he said in a stage whisper.

'Where do you think I should go next on my travels, Pete?' I asked, redirecting the conversation.

He spread his arms. 'Why would you want to leave the Blue Mountains?'

'Good question. I guess because I promised myself that I'd do what Brontë can't anymore.'

Harry asked if I wanted dessert, but I asked if I could have a glass of wine instead. While he went inside to fetch it, I told Pete about Brontë's gap year and how she'd planned on exploring the Gold Coast with Harry. How doing this trip in her place was my way of staying connected to her, but also giving me a chance to find some peace and happiness for myself.

The outside lights suddenly clicked on automatically and I noticed how dark the night had become. Pete lit candles in a couple of hurricane lanterns and set them on the table. From the kitchen we heard the sound of a cork being pulled from a bottle.

'She must have been a special girl. There are no words that'll make it better.' Pete patted my leg amiably. He lowered his voice. 'But I do know that in time you will grow from what life has thrown at you. I also know that happiness isn't something you find, it's something you make. A happy life is a conscious decision. That kid's still working on feeling like he deserves one. Sounds like you are too.'

I was taken aback by his insight and how he had flipped from boisterous banter to tender words of encouragement. My throat felt too tight to reply and I squeezed his hand instead.

'She and I were planning on getting work in the Hunter Valley,' Harry told us, returning with a large glass of red wine. 'There are hostels you can stay at, where they pick you up, take you to the vineyards and drop you off again at the end of the day.'

'It's harvest time right now.' Pete shovelled Pavlova into his mouth. 'Plenty of work picking grapes for those who want it. And you obviously like your wine.'

'I do.' I ignored his light-hearted jibe and took a large mouthful of smooth-bodied Australian Merlot.

I could see myself wandering between the vines, picking bunches of grapes in the sunshine, enjoying the camaraderie of being part of a team. 'But I don't like hostels. The days of sharing a bedroom are over.'

'I'm sure you'd make an exception for the right person, eh?' Pete waggled his silvery eyebrows, each the size of a moustache.

'Never say never,' I replied cheerily.

I wasn't about to get into my love life with him – not that there was much to tell.

'That's the spirit.' Pete clunked his beer against my glass.

'You've got contacts in the Hunter Valley, Uncle Pete,' said Harry, coming to my rescue. 'Can you help?'

'Loads of hotels in those parts.' He scraped his plate clean and gave a satisfied sigh. 'There's even one with a spa if you're feeling flush.'

'I'm not the spa kind,' I told him. 'I'm a doer. But if there's work to be done, I'm your woman.'

His eyes glinted. 'Plenty to get your teeth into around here then.' He gestured to his backyard.

'I was thinking of that winemaker friend of yours,' Harry persisted. 'The one whose wife left him?'

Pete scowled. 'Nasty business, that. Ran off with his winery manager, leaving her kiddie behind too.'

'Poor man!' I commented. 'Poor child too! How sad.'

'Jono's rushed off his feet with the harvest.' Pete looked at me speculatively. 'I think you'd fit right in there, Maggie.'

'I'll give it a go.' I hoped he didn't mean I'd fit in because we'd both had a bad time recently and we could share our tales of woe.

'I'll show you the website.' Harry got out his phone, scrolled through quickly and held it out to me. 'Ruby Creek.'

The website showed valleys lined with vines, rows of oak barrels, bottles and bottles of wine, smiling people gathered together, wine glasses raised. There was a message on the home-page advertising temporary work starting immediately. When would I ever get another chance to bring in the Australian grape harvest?

'I wouldn't want to earn money, but if Jono could put me up in his house, I'd happily help him out for a week or two.'

'Free labour?' he chuckled. 'I imagine he'll snap your hand off.'

I was going to go for it. I would be far happier being busy and helping someone out than wandering from place to place soaking up the sun.

'Then will you ring your friend please, Pete? It sounds perfect for me. That's where I'd like to go next if Jono will have me.'

Pete whistled. 'You sure make your mind up fast. I'll call him now.' He got up from the table and went inside, muttering, 'Now where did I put my phone?'

'Good decision,' said Harry, finishing his beer. 'It'll be fun, and if nothing else, you're guaranteed good wine with dinner.'

'I'm really excited about it,' I told him. 'Oh God, am I being insensitive? Do you mind? I mean, this was something you'd planned to do with Brontë, and I've steamrollered over it.'

'Don't even think about it,' he insisted. 'It's Mum's Gap Year now, remember. Which reminds me.'

He took out his phone. 'I hope you don't mind but I took a photo of you earlier. I know I should have asked you first, but I posted it on Instagram.'

He held it out for me to see the screen.

The photograph was of me at Echo Point looking out across the Blue Mountains. It had been taken from behind, so my face wasn't visible, but there was something hopeful and brave about the way I was looking outwards, my chin tilted towards the sky, hands on hips.

'That's beautiful,' I breathed. 'Thank you.'

'I wrote a post to go with it telling my followers who you were. So far there have been one hundred and fifty comments. You're a big hit, Maggie! Want to read it?'

I held out my hand in response and he gave me his phone.

There's a special visitor to my place in the Blue Mountains today. Meet Maggie, Brontë's mum. I only knew Brontë for three years and the strength of my grief is overwhelming. Maggie brought Brontë into this world. Imagine the pain of seeing her leave it far too soon. Brontë's relationship with her mum was special. Maggie is an incredible woman, mother and role model. She was the first person Brontë wanted to talk to when something good or bad happened. Maggie is yet another gift I have to thank Brontë for and I am honoured to have her visit me while I'm in Australia. And guess what? The gap-year travels that my girl planned in such detail have not been abandoned – because Maggie is doing them for her. She's chosen action as her way to work through her grief and I'm here for it. #MumsGapYear

Brontë, Brontë, Brontë . . . clearly he was able to write the word, but not speak her name yet, I noticed. Harry's post was followed by a stream of comments. I scrolled through them, my heart lurching as I read about the pain of other people's losses.

I handed his phone back to him and hugged him tight. 'Thank you for those beautiful words. I'm honoured to know you too.'

'Thank you.' He hung his head and exhaled a weary breath, after a moment adding, 'Want to know what my favourite thing to do at night is?'

I nodded and he pointed upwards.

'Stargazing?' I asked.

'Yep. No light pollution out here. Wait there a sec.'

He fetched a large blanket and a pair of giant binoculars from inside. 'Uncle Pete's found his phone but the battery's flat, and then once he gets talking he doesn't stop. So he'll be ages.'

We snuffed out the candles, turned off the outside lights and spread the blanket on the ground. For the next few minutes while I got myself comfy and removed all the stones sticking in my back, I let my eyes grow accustomed to the dark.

'I miss her like crazy. We were kids when we first met, but I think my relationship with her is probably going to be one of the most important of my whole life.'

'Being young doesn't make love any less important.' I stole a sideways glance at him; there was a single tear trickling down his face. 'I fell in love when I was the same age you and Brontë were. And I've never loved anyone as much as that since. That's not to say you won't,' I added swiftly. 'I chose not to, that's all.'

'Can I tell you something weird?'

'Of course.' I put the binoculars to my eyes. Stars in their millions appeared instantly, and the sight of them all took my breath away.

'When I see all the stars shining in the sky, I imagine that they are all the people who died and whose love still shines down on the ones they left behind.'

'Oh Harry.' A lump formed in my throat. 'That's not weird at all. It's lovely.'

'Thank you,' he mumbled. 'And I think that she's up there, sparkling – probably the sparkliest. And when I'm on my own I talk to her. I tell her the truth that I don't like telling anyone else: that life is shit without her.'

'I talk to her too,' I told him. 'I've been writing on the blank pages in her notebook. It helps me to write things down instead of bottling them up. Life was shit for me too, but . . .' I paused and felt a smile growing on my face. 'I think it's less shit than it was.'

'Semi-shit.'

We both laughed.

'And I think Brontë is up there, cheering us both on, hoping we'll remember to celebrate life, fill it with happy moments. And in your case, fall in love with someone new.'

'Hmm.'

'I mean it, Harry, don't be afraid to love again. Here, your turn.' I handed him the binoculars.

'What about you?' he asked. 'I've always wondered why you've stayed single.'

'I nearly married once,' I told him. 'I met a guy when Brontë was three. He was great, loved Brontë, loved me. But I couldn't take the risk. His income wasn't stable, his work schedule was erratic; he was a freelance photographer and never knew where he was going to be from one week to the next. He would have been happy living out of a suitcase for the rest of his life. So even though I loved him, and he made me happy, when he proposed I turned him down. I needed a steady, reliable presence in our lives; he couldn't provide it. Since then I've kept the few relationships I've had casual.'

'She used to wish you'd got someone to love. She used to worry about you.'

I looked at him sharply. 'Really?'

He lowered the binoculars and looked at me. 'Yeah. She thinks you never got over her dad.'

'Yes, I . . .' My voice trailed off. 'I guess she's right, in a way. Was right. I never felt that way about anyone else.'

'He sounds cool. She would have liked to have met him.'

'I know.' I felt a knot of guilt in my stomach. I'd let my daughter down. I should have done more to find him, but I'd been overwhelmed with life at the time, I reminded myself. 'The older she got, the worse I felt about it. But then it got to the point where it was too late to track someone down and gatecrash their life with that sort of news. You know, remember me? Oh, and here's your daughter. There was too much risk involved, and I didn't want Brontë to end up getting rejected, or disappointed if we couldn't find him.'

'Maybe.' He stared up at the sky again. 'I guess she'll never know now. I sort of feel the same about her as you did about Brontë's dad. That no one will replace her. That she was my person. Yeah, that about sums it up: Brontë was my person.'

My heart lurched at the sound of her name on his lips. He'd finally been able to say it. I reached towards him and squeezed his hand, and we stayed like that until I heard his breathing steady.

'Harry?'

'Yeah?'

'I understand exactly how you feel, but all I ask is that you don't rule out love forever.'

He laughed softly. 'Tell you what, I won't if you won't.'

He made it sound so easy, as if meeting someone you sparked with, and opening your heart to them, twining your life with theirs, was simply a matter of choice. Either way, I couldn't very well give him advice that I wasn't prepared to take myself.

'I guess I can't argue with that, so it's a deal.'

The kitchen door crashed open and the outdoor lights came on again.

'Good news, my starry-eyed little poms,' cried Pete, marching towards us, arms outflung. 'Jono is all for some help and says how soon can you come.'

'Fantastic!' I jumped to my feet and kissed his bristly cheek. 'How about tomorrow?'

I hadn't been this spontaneous for a long time and it felt bloody amazing.

# Chapter 22

## Maggie, Bali, 2000

Thailand and Jackson and me. Every time I thought about it, my insides fluttered with a thousand butterflies. It felt right, and I had no reservations as I gripped onto the side of the rickshaw which would take me into the nearest town to find a phone to call home. I was on my own today. Jackson was scuba diving, doing his final test for his PADI licence. My other friend, Hannah, had flown home yesterday. I had been here a month! When I'd booked this trip, I'd worried that a month so far away from England would be too much. How wrong could I have been? If anything, it wasn't long enough.

Now there were only two days left in Bali, but instead of going home, I'd be heading to actual Thailand with my amazing Jackson. So much for telling him that I did not 'do boyfriends'. I very much did boyfriends now. I'd been walking on air since deciding to go with him. Being with Jackson was exciting; he was changing my outlook on life for the better. He was impulsive where I was cautious; he expected everything to turn out well while I'd learned to look over my shoulder, always waiting for something to come along and ruin my fun. I liked the new me: this girl who for once in her life was following her heart and taking a risk and letting spontaneity be her guide.

We'd be travelling by train all the way north and starting our trip in Ko Tao, which he promised I would love; I already knew I would.

The only flaw in my plan to extend my trip was that it was going to be so much harder to leave him behind. I kept having to remind myself that I was only twenty-two, still a student, that I'd fallen fast and deeply in love with him precisely because we were in paradise. There was literally nothing not to love about being here with him. But then every so often, my inner romantic whispered in my ear that I'd fall in love with Jackson even if we met at a bus stop in the rain and I had a hole in my shoe. My inner romantic was big on detail, and it was hard to ignore her.

I'd left it until the last minute to tell my mum and my sister that I wasn't coming straight home after my month in Bali. I knew Kat would be disappointed and if I hadn't got my new ticket sorted before speaking to her, I'd probably cave in and go home after all. It hadn't been easy rearranging my flights, but there had been a very patient travel agent in Denpasar who'd managed to do it for me at very little cost.

I hadn't brought my mobile phone to Bali with me. It probably wouldn't work; it had been third-hand when I bought it and had very limited battery life. Anyway, God knows how much it would have cost to call the UK. Which was why I was on my way into town, where there was a funny little phone shop where you could sit in a booth and pay to make a call.

The rickshaw driver dropped me right in the centre of town. I had a wander around first, stocking up on jewellery and buying one last T-shirt with a Balinese design on it. I'd probably never come back, and if I did, it would be decades from now. Not that I wouldn't want to come back here, but this trip had given me a taste for exploring the world. There was so much of it to see, so much to do that when I did get the chance to travel, I knew I'd want to go to new places and not revisit the old. I stopped at a fresh coconut stall where the stallholder lopped off the top with a huge knife and dropped a straw into it for me. I headed to the phone shop sipping on the sweet coconut water and was shown into a booth.

*Okay, Mags, brace yourself,* I thought as I dialled the land-line number at home. No one was going to be thrilled that I wasn't coming straight home: Kat because she'd be fed up dealing with Mum on her own, and Mum because I'd told her I didn't have any spare money to give her, and now she'd be annoyed that I clearly did.

The phone didn't even ring. Instead an automated voice said, 'Sorry, we can't connect your call.'

Frowning, I tried again, this time concentrating on the number, making sure I got the international code right. Still no joy, just a repeat of the message.

I paused for a few seconds, considering my options and not wanting to rack up more cost by trying a third time. Maybe the phone line was down or, perhaps even more likely, we'd been cut off again. Either way, I didn't have an option to abandon the task. Time was running out. Tomorrow was our last full day in Bali and Utt had organised for his cousin to take us out on his boat. He'd become quite fond of Jackson and me and had suggested the trip to thank us for our hard work. I didn't want to miss that.

I was going to have to call my father instead and ask him to get in touch on my behalf. If it came to it, and our phone line didn't get fixed, he'd have to do the ninety-minute journey and deliver my message himself. I didn't have a choice; his was the only other number I knew off by heart. I recited his number aloud to make sure and then dialled.

'Hello, Magnolia.' I could hear the surprise in his voice, and not in a good way. 'Aren't you off on holiday somewhere?'

'Bali, yes,' I spoke quickly, conscious of the cost of the call.

'All right for some,' he grumbled. 'And I thought students complained about being poor.'

I bit my tongue, not having the time to get into my finances right now.

'Dad, I need your help. I can't get hold of Mum or Kat. Their phone isn't working. Can you get a message to them?'

'It wouldn't be working.' He sniffed. 'Because they've been evicted. Phone line's probably been cut off too. I saw it coming. Your mother seems to lurch from one—'

'Evicted!' I gasped with a surge of panic. 'When? What happened? Where are they now?'

'Unpaid council tax, unpaid rent, taking housing benefit and not passing it on to the landlord. Bailiffs turned up last week, so that's that. Perhaps the shock will do your mother good, teach her a lesson in acting responsibly.'

*Last week.* I put a hand to my throat, gulping for oxygen, feeling as if I couldn't breathe. Mum would breeze through this, but Kat . . . She'd be devastated. 'How did you find out?'

'Kat rang me to tell me, although I'm not sure what she thought I could do about it. They're staying with a neighbour for the time being.'

I clenched my jaw angrily. Wasn't it obvious what he could do about it? 'They'll be at Phyllis's.'

'That's the one.'

She was a kind lady who'd often stepped in over the years with small gifts of a cake, or a casserole she claimed had been going spare. Her husband had died years ago, and she said doing things for others made her feel needed. Taking in Mum and Kat was exactly the sort of thing she'd do.

'Poor Kat, have you seen her?'

'No, I haven't seen her. I'm busy with my allotment this month. And the grass – I turn my back and it's grown two feet.'

The grass was his priority? Unbelievable. 'But you're going to help out?'

'Not this time, Magnolia.' His tone was curt. 'I've helped your mother enough over the years.'

'Jesus Christ, Dad!' I blew up at him. 'You just said you saw it coming, so why didn't you step in? We are your *children*. I can look after myself, but Kat is still at school.'

She'd finished her A-levels but officially she was at school until 31 August.

'Is she? Blimey,' he muttered. 'I've got Phyllis's number if you want it. I'm sure Kat would like to hear from you.'

'How helpful of you,' I seethed.

The thought of Kat trying to pack her things, leaving her home, nowhere to go, with only Mum to look after her . . . I started to sob, huge wrenching sobs. My poor sister. Meanwhile, here I was in paradise, blissfully in love, oblivious to her ordeal. The guilt came crashing down, burying the freedom, the happiness, the laughter of the last few weeks. And alongside it, anger. I was angry with Mum for not staying on top of the bills, for not putting her youngest daughter's security at the top of her list; and with Dad for not caring enough to be there – if not for his ex-wife, then for his kids.

I ended the call with Dad and phoned Phyllis immediately. Mum wasn't there but Kat came on the line.

'Oh Mags,' she wailed. 'I was so scared. The bailiffs only gave us a few hours to leave. Mum tried to talk them out of it for ages, but they weren't interested. I had to pack all your stuff too.'

'I'm so sorry I wasn't there, sis. Sounds like you need a hug.'

'It's okay. At least it has happened at the end of your trip. When are you coming home?'

My throat burned with disappointment as I mentally waved goodbye to my dreams of Thailand with Jackson and gave her the answer she needed to hear. 'Tomorrow, Kat, I'll get a flight home tomorrow.'

## Mum's Gap Year

My sweet girl, this trip has taught me so much; thank you for showing me the way. It's proved to me that I can cope without checking my emails every five minutes, that I can make snap decisions and be excited about what might come next. I can keep busy, see new places, have new experiences. Life shouldn't be about marking time, waiting for it to pass so that I can get into bed and close my eyes and my mind to the world. And I see now that that's what I've been doing since you died.

But even a full diary can't make up for the fact that there's so much emptiness in my heart. I shared my life with you, sweetheart. I rejoiced at every achievement, pushed you to do the hard stuff as you moved through the phases of your life, so mine changed along with you.

What next for me? One day I'm going to read the last page of your gap-year book and from then on, I'll be travelling alone without you. That heart of mine needs filling – I need someone to love, and I want someone to love me back.

I know this will make you happy, and I think it might make me happy too.

Love always
Mum xxx

P.S. Harry is such an amazing young man.
P.P.S. I've got myself a hashtag – #MumsGapYear!

# Chapter 23

## Australia

The taxi dropped me and my suitcase off at the entrance to the Ruby Creek winery. I brushed the creases out of my linen dungarees and pushed my sunglasses up onto my head. The Hunter Valley was several degrees warmer than the mountains I'd left behind this morning, and there was little breeze.

In front of me was a low building made of attractive yellow stone, an open door at each end, both with signs above them: *Ruby's Bar* on one and *Cellar Door* on the other. In front of the building, there were picnic tables and parasols set up on the grass and a long table and chairs to seat upwards of twenty people under the shade of a wooden porch. Oak barrels served as taller tables with high stools set around them. The impression was of a rustic restaurant, homely and welcoming. I couldn't see anyone but there was laughter coming from inside.

I gave myself a moment to breathe. Two weeks on an Australian vineyard: how spontaneous and exciting. I took a quick selfie with the Ruby Creek sign in the background and sent it to Kat and Harry to let them know I'd arrived. I wandered over to one of the benches and sat down, putting my sunglasses back on to shield me from the glare.

A flare of happiness lit me from the inside, taking me by surprise. I was happy to be here, happy to be doing something new. Happy to be alive.

Meeting up with Harry had changed so much for me. My heart was lighter. I'd set myself free of the guilt I'd been carrying from the moment Brontë had left my house for the last time. She didn't hate me for challenging her gap year at all. She'd welcomed it. I'd always feel the pain of losing her, but at least I could finally set down the burden of guilt. And as for Harry, I felt sure that he had waved to me this morning with a brighter, more positive outlook for the future. We'd helped each other, and I could only imagine how pleased Brontë would have been to see us together.

Pete had wanted to drive me to the Hunter Valley, but I'd declined his offer of a lift further than the train station. I was enjoying plotting my own path. There was satisfaction to be had in successfully navigating train timetables and platform changes, even if my suitcase seemed to get heavier as I dragged it on and off the train. And the lengthy journey had given me time to read and write, and take in the ever-changing landscape, from the blue-hued mountains, through the suburbs and city and finally, following the coastline north, into the lush lime greens of the wine region.

I was fortunate to be here. Life wasn't perfect and I knew I would still hit plenty of bumps in the road ahead. But for now, I was going to give myself up to enjoying this moment. I closed my eyes and focused on the sounds and smells of my new environment.

'You found us okay, then?' A low gravelly voice accompanied by steady footsteps approached and I blinked my eyes open. 'Maggie?'

'Hi, yes, I'm—' I faltered, taking in the tall, tanned man in front of me. I felt myself blush and hoped he'd assume it was because of the strong sunlight catching my cheekbones. 'Jono. I mean, you're Jono. I'm Maggie.'

Worn jeans, cotton shirt, chunky boots and a leather bush hat. He looked like a cowboy. A good-looking cowboy. I'd been expecting Pete's friend to look like Pete, a grizzled Santa Claus with a roving eye. I'd got that wrong.

'Correct.' He looked amused, but there was an unmissable weariness in his face, a hint of sadness which his eyes couldn't hide. 'Sorry I didn't collect you from the station. Busy day.'

He offered me his hand and I shook it, feeling the rough skin of his palm, his grasp so much larger and stronger than mine. He pulled his hand away, making me notice that I'd held onto it a beat longer than he'd expected.

'No worries!' I replied. Had I said that with an Australian accent? My blush deepened. 'I got to see my first kangaroos in the taxi. I wouldn't have wanted to miss that.'

'Kangaroos in the taxi, eh?' A teasing smile played on his lips and he folded his arms. 'Man. I'd have liked to see that myself.'

'Under a tree,' I clarified. 'A big gang of them.'

'Gotcha, that makes sense.' He nodded. 'There are loads of them around here. Shame they can't pick grapes, it'd save me a lot of effort. Righto, Maggie, come with me, let's get you settled in.' He scooped up my suitcase as if it weighed no more than a matchbox and strode off towards the back of the building. The path took us past the winery, and I caught sight of a trailer piled high with red grapes and behind it a row of large stainless-steel vessels.

'Thanks for letting me come at such short notice.' I was half jogging to keep up with him. 'It's really good of you.'

He opened a gate and gestured for me to go through it. 'No bother. Pete told me you'd been through a shit time. Excuse my language. Happy to help. If I lost my daughter, well, I dunno, but I probably wouldn't look as good as you.'

He pulled his bottom lip between his teeth as if annoyed with himself. Too late. I'd registered the compliment long enough to feel even warmer. 'Cheerful, I mean. I don't know you, but taking off from the UK, travelling the world solo – that's impressive.'

'Not really,' I argued, pleased nonetheless. 'I got banned from work, so it seemed like a good thing to do.'

He gave a laugh of disbelief. 'I'm going to need to hear the rest of that story.'

'Well, maybe over a glass of wine one night.'

The look of surprise on his face matched my own reaction; I'd been here five minutes and I'd already asked him out for a drink. I hardly recognised myself.

'Pete told me you'd had a shit time too,' I continued. 'I chose to run away from my home life. Sometimes I think staying to work through your problems is the harder thing to do.'

'Yeah, well, I didn't have any choice,' he said with a low growl to his voice. 'I have a business to run and a daughter to look after.' His eye met mine and he swore under his breath. 'I didn't think. I'm sorry.'

'For having a daughter? Don't be.' I touched his arm. 'There's no need to censor yourself around me. My loss isn't any greater because you still have your daughter. I'm looking forward to meeting her.'

'Daisy is great.' He grinned, and this time there was no mistaking the light in his eyes. 'And pretty much the boss around here. Okay, this is you.'

Jono set down my suitcase with a thud outside a small chalet the colour of a Tuscan sunset. Climbing plants with pink and orange flowers scrambled over trellises either side of the front door, hiding a sign announcing that this was Creek Cottage.

'Wow. Are you sure? It's beautiful.'

'Yeah.' He brushed a spider's web away from the porch and unlocked the door.

I stepped inside to find a charming studio space: a small galley kitchen at one end, a sleeping area at the other with white furniture and pretty pink and green bed linen; a two-seater sofa facing a TV in the middle. The space was charming and feminine and made Jono look very masculine in comparison.

'It's lovely.' I peered out of the kitchen window. In the distance a group of kangaroos were lying under the shade of some tall trees. 'Look, kangaroos!' I whirled around to him, thrilled with my discovery, but of course, he simply looked mildly bemused. 'Sorry, they're still a novelty. Thanks for letting me stay here, I wasn't expecting anything as grand.'

He waved a hand. 'This place was going to be an Airbnb. My ex-wife's idea. Weddings, parties, even offering working holidays in the winery. Clever idea, extra income and free labour. But like a lot of things around here, it got abandoned. Maybe one day—' The sound of a diesel engine out in the yard outside disturbed him. 'Excuse me. That's the pickers' transport. Come and say hi.'

I followed him out to the yard where a minibus had pulled up. A crowd of young people appeared from inside the winery and began piling their rucksacks into the back of it.

'You did great today, fellas.' Jono folded his arms, rocking back on his heels. 'We're picking Shiraz tomorrow, and Maggie's staying here for a while and will be helping us too.'

'Hey.' I gave them a little wave. 'Looking forward to it.'

'Hey, Maggie!' A girl in her early twenties in T-shirt, shorts and trainers waved back. 'Remind him that he promised us an amazing breakfast tomorrow, will you?'

'Um.' I looked at Jono for confirmation.

He pressed a hand to his forehead and groaned. 'Sure. I hadn't forgotten.'

'An army doesn't pick grapes on an empty stomach, Jono,' said one of the boys.

'I hear you.' He high-fived them as they piled into the minibus, and we waved them off. 'I'm going to make some tea. Want one, or do you want to unpack?'

I had a message to respond to from Kat, who wanted a full update on the Blue Mountains and what I was up to next; and Anna had emailed with a couple of questions. But I decided that spending more time with my new host ought to be top of my list. 'Tea sounds great.'

He showed me round the back of the winery to a modest colonial style house, with a wraparound porch, and steps covered with herbs and plants in terracotta pots. There was a dog lying in front of the door, his tail thumping faster and faster the nearer we got.

'Hey, buddy,' Jono called out to him 'This is Max. Max, say hi to Maggie.'

Max got up, stretched luxuriously and wagged his way towards me. I bent to make a fuss of him and while Max and I became acquainted, Jono led me inside, apologising for the state of the place.

'The harvest is our busiest time. We barely get a chance to eat and sleep, so cleaning up takes a back seat.'

The kitchen was large and rustic and one of the most chaotic spaces I'd ever been in. It looked like someone had emptied out the cupboards and left everything on the surfaces. The sink was piled high with pans to be washed. However, the view through the window above it of the rows of green vines, stretching away as far as the eye could see, more than made up for the mess.

Half of the room was taken up with a long table and chairs, each with different coloured cushions on them. A huge floor-to-ceiling wine rack dominated one wall. Next to it was a double American-style refrigerator.

Max the dog settled himself on the tiled floor and I took a seat at the table. 'No need to apologise. It's lived-in, that's all, and I imagine it's a lovely room to spend time in.'

He laughed and took off his hat. 'Thanks, it has its moments. As you can see, I've been having a sort-out. I thought we had a bread maker somewhere, but I can't find it.' He held up the kettle. 'Mint, camomile or black?'

I opted for black and quizzed him about the conversation I'd overheard regarding breakfast for the pickers.

Jono gave a wry smile. 'We've always offered lunch, but now our website states that we offer breakfast on picking days too. Another bright idea from Andrea. The kids who pick stay at nearby hostels. There are kitchens, but most of the kids would rather stay in bed a bit longer than eat. Feeding them breakfast here means at least we know they're not out in the sun working on an empty stomach.'

'Andrea is your ex-wife?'

'Yeah.' He nodded grimly. 'This morning, the fan belt on the tractor needed fixing, I lost track of time, so unfortunately breakfast was bananas and a big bag of chocolate freckles. They'll never let me forget it.'

'What time is breakfast?' I smiled my thanks as he set a mug on the table for me.

'Why, do you like the sound of the menu?' he asked, sitting opposite me. 'Seven-thirty usually. We start picking at eight.'

'Never heard of chocolate freckles, but as I haven't met a chocolate I didn't like, they sound delicious. But I was thinking that maybe you put me in charge of breakfast, that way you can concentrate on the vineyard?'

'Maggie.' He chinked his mug against mine. 'You got yourself a job.'

We both looked up at the sound of a vehicle pulling up and a door slamming. Max trotted off to greet whoever had arrived, his tail already thumping.

A teenage boy popped his head into the kitchen. 'Hey Jono, is Daisy ready?'

'Hi, Tom!' Jono seemed surprised to see him. 'Er, sure, I'll give her a shout.'

He'd only taken a few paces towards the hall when footsteps came running down the stairs.

'Hi, Dad, bye Dad.' Jono's daughter flew into the kitchen, kissed his cheek and paused when she saw me. 'Oh, hey. Maggie, right?'

I nodded. 'Lovely to meet you, Daisy. I'm cooking breakfast tomorrow. Will you be around to show me where everything is, if Jono's busy?'

'Sure, there's no school tomorrow, so I'll be slaving away for Dad anyway,' she told me.

'That would be really helpful,' I said, but her attention had already moved to the boy jingling his car keys in the hallway.

'Ready?' she said, sidling up to him.

'Are you two going somewhere . . . together?' Jono asked, waving a finger between the two of them.

'No, Dad, we're going to sit in Tom's car in the yard. Duh.' She was attempting to be cool, but the tell-tale pink circles on her cheeks gave her away.

'My Auntie Sue's dog has had a litter of pups. Daisy wants to see them,' Tom explained.

*Do you like puppies?* In a flash, Jackson's face appeared to me in my mind's eye. Our first date. In a dark forest by torchlight, the ebb and flow of the distant ocean waves creating our own personal soundtrack.

Jono relaxed. 'Gotcha. Well, have fun. Drive safely with my daughter on board, Tom.'

Daisy grabbed Tom's hand. 'Then we're going out for food. Bye, see you at breakfast, Maggie.'

After they'd gone, Jono puffed his cheeks out and ran a hand through his hair. 'Jesus.'

'Pretty girl,' I said, sipping my tea. 'How old is she?'

'Fourteen.' He smiled wistfully. 'And growing up fast.'

Young to be dating a boy who already held a driver's licence, I thought, but it was none of my business, so I kept my opinion to myself.

'My girl is the best thing to come out of my marriage,' said Jono, settling back in his chair. 'What did Pete tell you about me and Andrea?'

Max returned from seeing off Daisy and Tom and chose to sit next to me, his chin on my knee. I stroked his head and bopped his black nose with my fingertip. He must have liked that because he stood on his hind legs and tried to lick my face.

'The bare minimum. That you'd split up, that Daisy was living with you and that you could use a spare pair of hands during the harvest.'

'Not only the harvest, to be honest. And we didn't split up; she left me.' He narrowed his eyes. 'I should never have employed a Frenchman.'

'What do you mean?' I gave him a quizzical look, hoping he wasn't about to blame an entire nation for his wife's defection.

'She couldn't resist his accent,' he explained. 'Even when he said, "Your dog has eaten his own shit," he sounded romantic.'

I moved Max's face away from mine, in case that had been a real quote from the Frenchman.

'I can forgive her for leaving me. But leaving Daisy? Never.' A muscle in his neck twitched. 'I lost all respect for her the day she walked out. There's no coming back from that. Daisy cried for weeks. I can handle the dent to my ego, but Daisy doesn't understand why her mum has chosen not to be in her life anymore. Poor kid.'

Max removed his paws from my knee, padded over to Jono and gave a single low woof.

'I know, boy, it's time.' He set his mug down and got to his feet. 'Time for his walk. I'm going to head out to the vines, check we're on track for tomorrow's picking. I'll leave you to enjoy the view.'

It was on the tip of my tongue to ask if I could go with him, but something told me he didn't want company.

'I'm not here to just enjoy the views, Jono,' I said, as he put his hat back on. 'Put me to work.'

'Okay.' He looked at me evenly. 'Can you drive a forklift truck?

'Um . . .' I winced. 'I'll give it a go?'

He laughed. 'Kidding. Don't worry, there's plenty to do, but for today, relax, okay? Make yourself at home. Come on, Max.'

I watched them head out, silhouetted by the setting sun, Max's nose to the ground exploring the scent of his surroundings, Jono's attention fixed on the field of vines beyond the fence. Cold and frosty England seemed a long way away right now, and I had no rush to get back.

# Chapter 24

**Maggie, Bali, 2000**

My last night in Bali was my worst. I was devastated. After one perfect month, the freshest memories I'd be taking home with me were the hours of tears I'd cried after agreeing to return to the UK.

I spent most of the afternoon and evening frantically rearranging my travel plans and paying a lot of money for the privilege. I'd seen Jackson arrive back from his dive with the others and heard on the grapevine that he'd gained his PADI licence. I'd hidden in my room, feigning a headache, to avoid having to tell him my news and ruin his moment.

He'd been drunk when I'd caught up with him later that night in our favourite bar, and a party was in full swing. He was wearing his snorkel and mask and one of the other guys was pouring alcohol down the breathing tube for him to drink. Everyone was cheering and whooping, clapping him on the back and telling him how amazing he was. I'd seen this before – it was a traditional drinking challenge bestowed on everyone who passed their PADI exam. As soon as I'd got him on his own, I'd told him what had happened, shouting above the dance music, holding his face, trying to make him understand that I'd rebooked my flight home again. His eyes were unfocused, and he couldn't stop laughing. I wasn't sure he even believed me. I left the party early, and predictably cried myself into a fitful sleep.

By the time he surfaced the next day, I'd packed my ruck-sack, let Utt know that I couldn't make the boat trip after all, and said goodbye to my friends. I'd barely slept. I felt sick with worry about Kat back home, and every cell in my body was leaden with sadness at the prospect of letting Jackson go.

He took one look at me and held his arms out. I collapsed into his embrace, tucking my head under his chin and letting the tears flow.

'So you meant it?' he murmured softly. 'I was hoping it was a bad dream.'

'I'm so, so sorry to let you down,' I said. 'I promise you, if there was any other way, I'd take it.'

'This isn't your mess, Mags.' He hugged me tighter. 'If you go back now, you'll always be the one to solve your family's problems.'

'That's why I have to go, because there is only me.' I pulled back to look at him, willing him to understand.

But why would he? He was the only son of two loving parents, who'd brought him up to give him wings. He had the freedom to fly, but my wings had been clipped.

'This has been amazing. The best month of my life.' I kissed him and held him tight. I could feel his speeding heart and I wondered whether I'd ever know this feeling again. I loved him, no getting away from it. But it was an impossible love, and an impossible situation. As well as my responsibility to my family, I still had to finish my university course. 'I'm so grateful I met you, and that we were both in Bali at the same time.'

'Stay, Maggie,' he implored. 'Stay and live the dream.'

I blinked the tears away and shook my head. 'I can't, but you must. Keep being your gorgeous, kind, amazing self. Live the dream for both of us.'

'I'll never forget you, Mags.'

'Me neither. Thank you for everything.'

'We could try and keep in touch?' He stroked my face, as if imprinting my skin on his fingers.

For a moment I let the possibility burn like a flame of hope in my heart, but I shook my head. I was tempted, but I couldn't live my life waiting for the next phone call, or the next letter. Our paths had crossed briefly, serendipitously, pleasurably, but to try to make that happen again would mean sacrifices for one or both of us. I wanted us to remember each other with joy, not frustration.

'I don't think we should make promises that neither of us is in a position to keep. We're so young, and so different.'

'Oh, okay.' His eyebrows lifted at that, and I could see I'd hurt him. But better to make a clean break than face heartache further down the line.

I sobbed when the minibus arrived to take me and another couple of volunteers back to the airport.

Jackson was my first love. At this point in my life, I couldn't imagine ever loving anyone as deeply as I loved him.

*Brontë's Gap Year*

---

If my expectations are even halfway met, I'm betting that I'm in love with the Aussie lifestyle by now. A swim in the ocean before breakfast, your entire life lived outdoors, and so much less busy than the UK. Sounds sooo amazing. Not quite sure how I'll cope with living in London when this gap year is over. Honeybourne is a lovely place to grow up – pretty Cotswold cottages, lovely old pubs, friendly people . . . I'm not sure I'm going to be cut out for big cities.

Maybe this trip will give me time to work out what I want my life to look like. Could I emigrate to Australia? I reckon Harry would come in a heartbeat. It's got the beaches, the sunshine, and I wouldn't even have to learn a new language. We could have such a cool life together.

Sometimes I feel like there are two opposite sides to me: the ambitious one who wants the steady career, moving up the ladder with the salary to match; and the other one who only works to live, who wakes up to a view of the ocean. I wonder if Saatchi would let me work in their Sydney office . . . ?

Who even am I, with all this talk of living abroad?? As if I could EVER leave Mum. I'm even determined to get her to join me on this trip. I'd give anything to see her let her hair down and relax for five minutes instead of worrying about work, or me, or the interest rates or energy bills or whatever. At home, she's only happy if she has something to feel responsible for. I'm going to make it my mission to change that!

# Chapter 25

## Maggie, England, 2000

I was going to have a baby. Jackson's baby. In six months' time, I'd be somebody's mother. Since taking a pregnancy test and having it confirmed by a doctor, I'd alternated between fits of panic that I couldn't cope and heady waves of love for my unborn child.

This new development changed everything. I was going to have to rethink my last year at uni, where I lived, how I was going to earn enough money to support a child . . . There was no question that I wasn't going to keep it. Being heavily pregnant wasn't quite how I planned to spend my twenty-third birthday next spring, but some kernel of self-confidence told me I could do it.

The biggest thing gnawing at my conscience was Jackson. He was going to be a father and I couldn't tell him.

If I hadn't had to cut my summer short, maybe I'd still be in touch. But no, instead of going to Thailand with him, I'd scurried back home to sort my mother's mess. Why hadn't we swapped numbers or home addresses? I didn't even know his last name, or his parents' names or where exactly he lived in the US. For the first and probably only time in my life I'd existed entirely in the moment, in our bubble of paradise, and now I was paying the price.

Would he be pleased about the baby? Deep down I knew the answer. Jackson wanted adventure, and freedom; to live on a beach, spending his days surfing and scuba diving. I could almost hear him telling me that one day he'd love children, but he was too young to be a father when he still felt like a kid himself.

So maybe it was for the best. I'd bring up our baby as well as I could, and tell him or her what a lovely man their dad was.

Predictably, Mum had been crap.

'Well, well, well.' She had shaken her head, bemused. 'You really did have fun on that trip, didn't you?'

'Mum,' I'd warned, willing my cheeks not to heat up. I wasn't going to let her embarrass me. I was twenty-two, my body was my own, and it wasn't as if Jackson and I had been a one-night thing. I'd been in love with him. Still was.

'At least it'll be easier for you than it was for me. There was no chance of a termination when I got pregnant the first time.' She pulled a face as if she had a nasty taste in her mouth. 'Your father wouldn't even discuss the idea of getting rid of you. Biggest mistake of my life.'

'Mum!' I stared at her, speechless. The last vestige of respect for her leached away.

'Oh, my mistake wasn't just getting pregnant,' she said, squeezing my arm, as if that made it better. 'Getting married, settling down –the whole thing. A couple of years later, I gave up pretending to get along with your dad, but in some bizarre twist of fate, ended up pregnant again with your sister.'

'So you never wanted either of us.' I could feel a pulse throbbing in my neck. I couldn't believe my own mother could be so matter-of-factly cruel to me. 'And you choose to tell me this now, when I'm having a baby of my own?'

'Well, no, I didn't really want children at all,' she said apologetically. 'But we all got along all right, didn't we? Anyway, the point is, you don't have to go through with an unwanted pregnancy.'

'I'm not having a termination.' I gave her a challenging look. 'I'm keeping the baby.'

'As you wish, but don't expect me to look after it,' she warned. 'I've only just got rid of Kat. I'm not ready to be a grandmother yet.'

'It didn't cross my mind that you would look after my baby,' I said, fuming. 'You haven't even looked after your own children. I had to cut my trip short to sort a place for you to live.'

'Oh, not this again.' She sighed. 'You do exaggerate.'

I bit my lip, determined not to rise to the bait. I'd been home for almost three months now and the memories of those first few weeks were still raw.

As soon as I'd arrived back, after seeing how she and Kat were cramped up in a small double bed at Phyllis's house, I'd berated Mum for not getting help sooner.

'The Aikwoods don't take charity,' she'd replied, referring to her own family name.

Posh but poor had been her throwaway line ever since I could remember. Her own mother passed away when she was only six. She died giving birth and the little boy died too, which must have been harrowing for her. Her dad had remarried twice since then, each time heaping more misery on my mother, and giving away half of his estate with each divorce. He'd died when I was four. I had only sketchy memories of visiting him in his big old draughty house with bare floorboards, damp patches on the ceilings and an overbearing smell of mould.

'Granddad Aikwood left thousands of pounds of debt,' I'd reminded her at the time, 'so maybe he should have. And, I should point out, you're now accepting charity from Phyllis.'

But she wouldn't be drawn, preferring to bury her head in the sand as ever, and I gave up trying. I'd tried to reason with our old landlord too, but he'd point-blank refused to take us back. Too many chances already given, too many promises broken, Mum was too much trouble.

Now at least, after a lot of door-knocking on my part, she was in social housing and Kat had been accepted onto an Art Foundation course. So they were both okay. I'd taken on more shifts to give Kat money to help her through the expense of her first few months of uni, all the while nursing my own post-holiday blues.

And yet despite doing all that, Mum's response to my pregnancy was an immediate refusal of help.

What I needed was a hug from my mum. For her to tell me that everything was going to be all right, and that she'd look after me. And she couldn't even offer me that. Anger flared in my chest, and it took all my self-control not to cry.

'Oh darling, don't get all touchy,' Mum said now airily. 'I'm being honest with you, that's all. I want you to understand what you're getting yourself into with motherhood. What about finishing your course, and money? And where are you going to live?'

She gave me a telling look as if to say, *You hadn't thought about that, had you?*

'I'll work it out,' I replied.

What I did know was that I'd been given the blueprint from my own mother on how not to do it. My child would be able to come to me with their problems and know that I would help. They would always know that Mummy would keep them safe and provided for and teach them how to live an independent life. I would love my child fiercely, encourage them to be curious and hopeful, and always, always protect them until they were big enough to protect themselves.

I also knew one more thing; I wasn't going to let Mum treat me like this anymore. And I didn't want her to have the chance to treat her grandchild like this either. We were done.

## Mum's Gap Year

My darling girl,

I've never been able to look at you without thinking of your father. You had his beautiful smile, and his soft dark curls. What you wrote about living next to the ocean made me think of him straight away. The two opposite sides of you are essentially Jackson and me. I've always been about having a plan and sticking to it – I had life all mapped out. He, on the other hand, wanted to let life unfurl, go with the flow. He imagined spending his days diving and surfing, because that was what made him happy. You get your adventurous side from him! My plans changed with the arrival of you – absolutely no regrets, I hasten to add. But I do sometimes wonder whether his dreams worked out.

I'm sorry that you haven't had a father figure. Jackson was a free spirit and would not have chosen fatherhood at that age, but he was a good man. He would have moved on quickly romantically no doubt – he was too good-looking not to have caught the eye of another girl. But I'm sure he would have loved to have known you.

I have a confession. Do you remember when you were about fifteen and got angry with me for not trying to find him when you were born? You told me that you could find anyone on the internet if you really tried.

But I didn't tell you the whole truth. I did try to find him. I rang the volunteering agency that I'd used to book my turtle conservation project in Bali. But they told me that the project had closed down and that they were having to send volunteers to other places instead. So the trail quickly went cold. Maybe I could have tried harder, but I was a single mum, no one to help me. I was working and trying to be good at everything. Jackson didn't even have a mobile phone. I didn't know his last name, or whereabouts in America he was from. At the time, I knew I'd never forget him, but little did I know that I'd be blessed with a baby girl who'd remind me of him every second of every day.

Leaving you with a childminder so I could start working again was one of the scariest things I'd ever done. I'd really loved being at home with you in our tiny flat in those early months after you were born. It had been the first time in my life I hadn't had exams or homework or deadlines. You were tiny and vulnerable and completely dependent on me. I was more determined than ever to do well at work. I wanted to be your role model, to show you that hard work paid off. So I started work in a sales office, feeling guilty for leaving you to be cared for by others. Then I began enjoying my job and felt guilty for that too.

At the back of my mind was the knowledge that I was providing for us, so that you'd always know you were safe and that you'd have a home. It wasn't perfect, but I was proud that I was doing it on my own. We didn't always have time to do the fun stuff in those early years. I saved my money for the important things like a deposit on a house for us both.

You're right when you say I'm not happy if I don't have something to worry about. Take, for example, when you told me about your gap-year plans and I reacted badly. I told myself – and you – it was because I didn't want you to give up your dream job at Saatchi. I thought you'd regret it after working so hard to get through all the interviews. But now with the hindsight of the awful months that have passed since then, I can admit that my reaction was about me and not you.

I panicked at the thought of you being out of reach, thousands of miles away on the other side of the world where I couldn't protect you. I know, I know – you were an adult and perfectly capable of looking after yourself. But I'd still been coming to terms with letting you go, with watching you taking your own path instead of following mine.

My trip to Bali changed the course of my life, and ultimately caused the breakdown in my relationship with your grandmother. I guess deep down a small, irrational part of me was worried that it might happen to us. I didn't want to lose you. But fate had other ideas and I lost you anyway.

Saying goodbye to Jackson in Bali knowing I'd never see him again was the second-saddest thing I've ever done. The saddest was organising my girl's funeral. The two people who've meant the most to me gone, but always in my heart.

Love, always and forever

Mum xx

# Chapter 26

## Australia

'I thought we could make banana bread.'

It was seven in the morning, and I was in the main house with Daisy. I'd been awake since six and already had two strong cups of coffee. I'd had a quick look around the kitchen yesterday evening and there was a bunch of overripe bananas in a bowl looking desperate for attention.

She was dressed in shorts, a T-shirt and yawning sleepily. 'Good choice. We've got yogurt and fruit to serve with it.'

'Plus tea, coffee and juice, yeah?'

'Better than Starbucks,' said Daisy, twisting her hair up into a bun.

'Thanks for helping out,' I said, tying on an apron over my sundress. 'Especially as we're catering for twelve, including both of us and Jono. I've found this recipe.' I showed her one I'd found online.

'Hmm.' She glanced at it. 'I think Mum's is better. More banana-y.'

'Your mum's it is. Do you have it written down somewhere?'

'It's up here,' she replied, tapping the side of her head. 'She taught me how to do it.'

In an instant I was back in my mum's kitchen as a little girl, gathering the ingredients for something like her favourite raspberry buns while Mum recited the recipe. There were still some things I could make on autopilot, all because I'd learned them at my own mother's knee. I'd forgotten about that. I'd forgotten the happy times when we'd cooked together. Somehow my brain had filtered them out and only recalled the occasions when she hadn't been bothered to cook, and Kat and I had had to fend for ourselves.

We decided to make two loaves, and Daisy put the oven on and found tins while I peeled and chopped eight bananas.

'Did you teach your daughter to cook?' she asked.

'I did. She loved baking. Although she was more into the eating than the cooking. Decorating everything with icing and sprinkles was her favourite part – she would spend ages making patterns on the top of cakes. Then always had a good excuse when it came to doing the dishes and clearing up.'

'Sounds like she was a lot of fun.' She bit her bottom lip. 'I'm sorry she died. You must really miss her.'

'I do. But I'm very lucky to have had her in my life. I have lots of happy memories of her, so in a way she is still with me.'

My words took me by surprise. For once, the first emotion I'd had was not of anger that she'd gone, but gratitude that she'd lived. The thought filled me with joy.

'And you have her gap-year itinerary too,' she added.

'You know about that?' I said, surprised.

'I follow Harry on Instagram. All my friends do; he's adorable. He really loved Brontë. We all hope he can find someone else one day . . . Oh, sorry!' She cringed. 'That sounds bad. I hope I haven't upset you.'

I smiled, feeling the familiar ache in my throat when I thought about what he and I had both lost. 'Don't apologise.

I hope he does too. He's only twenty-three, too young to give up on love.' *So why did you?* nagged a voice inside my head.

The banana bread mixture was too big for one bowl, so we made it in two batches. Once the batter was ready, we scraped it into loaf tins and put them in the oven and I set a timer for fifty minutes.

'The pickers eat outside Ruby's Bar under the porch,' Daisy told me as we stacked the dishwasher. 'The plates and stuff are already over there.'

'Thanks for helping. I can manage from here if you've got stuff to do.'

'Can I ask you something? I'll understand if you say no.' She stumbled over her words. 'But would it be okay to see the book Brontë made, the gap-year one?'

For a moment I hesitated. Brontë's messages to herself, her drawings and anecdotes, were so precious to me that I was loath to share them with someone I didn't really know. Plus, of course, I'd begun my own journalling in it too. I wouldn't want anyone else reading that. But then I thought that if Brontë were standing here now instead of me, she'd be flattered and fetch the book straight away.

'Sure. Come over to the cottage. We'll do it now.'

We left the kitchen and headed to Creek Cottage.

'So tell me about last night,' I prompted. 'How were the puppies?'

'Adorable. I took some photos.'

She wiped her hands on her shorts and got her phone out to show me, swiping through the images. Brontë used to wipe her hands on her clothes too. You could always tell when she'd been painting by the state of the pockets on the back of her jeans. She had loads of paintings in her room and I made a mental note to look for some when I got home. I would get them framed and hang them, so I could see them every day. They deserved to be admired, not shut away.

'The puppies were so tiny and their eyes were still closed.' Daisy grinned. 'Like Max was the first time we saw him. More like a guinea pig than a dog. Mum wanted one of the others, but Max had the prettiest little face.'

'What about your dad?' I asked. 'Which one did he want?'

'He wasn't there. Me and Mum were choosing a puppy for Dad's birthday as a surprise. He and Max are best friends now. Inseparable.'

'Tom seemed nice,' I said. 'Is that your boyfriend?'

Daisy blushed. 'He is nice but we're friends. Not even that, really. It's his sister who's my friend. She was in the car when Tom came to pick me up.'

'So why didn't she come in instead of him?'

She shoved her phone away, looking sheepish. 'Because Tom's obviously too old for me and I wanted Dad to say something.'

'And he didn't,' I said.

'Nah.' She shook her head. 'He says he trusts me. But sometimes I want a dad who cares about what I'm doing.'

'I'm sure he does,' I said. 'I only met him yesterday, but I already know how much he loves you.'

She looked sceptical. 'He's too busy. Especially now that the winery manager and my mum have left.'

'You must be the only teenager on the planet who wishes their dad was stricter,' I said, to get a smile out of her.

It worked and she giggled. 'True. Maybe I should make the most of it. Go a bit wild.'

I held my hands up, laughing in horror. 'That was not what I meant!'

We entered my cottage, and she sat down while I fetched Brontë's notebook.

'There's a bookmark in it,' I said, handing it to her. 'I haven't looked beyond this page and I don't want to either. The rest of my trip is a mystery.'

'This is so cool.' She gave me an appraising look. 'You're cool too. I miss my mum.'

I sat beside her so that our knees were touching. I wanted to give her a hug, but I wasn't quite sure we were on hugging terms yet. 'I'm sure she misses you too.'

She shook her head. 'Then why did she leave me? She's been gone three months. I haven't seen her since. She left me a letter telling me she would always love me, but it doesn't feel like it.'

My heart broke for her, poor kid. 'I don't know enough about your parents to comment, but maybe she felt she didn't have a choice.'

'She did.' Daisy's eyes flashed. 'She had a choice between me and Pierre – and she chose him.'

'I felt the same when my dad left home,' I told her. 'My little sister and I stayed with my mum. I thought that he didn't care about us, but the truth was that it was my mum he'd fallen out of love with, not us. He still loved us.'

This was in fact debatable, but there was no point in digging into that particular wormhole. He had loved us – I felt sure of that – but as time had gone on he'd gradually distanced himself from us, only getting involved when either Kat or I forced him to. It wasn't the greatest demonstration of fatherly love, and his actions following Mum's eviction had shown me that he wasn't a man who could be relied on. But this wasn't about me, it was about Daisy and her parents.

'I wouldn't have wanted to leave Ruby Creek and go with Mum and Pierre,' she said. 'All my friends are here, and my school, and I love Dad. But sometimes you want a hug from your mum, you know?'

'I do know,' I confirmed.

While I watched Daisy examine Brontë's book, marvelling at her clever illustrations and reading her anecdotes and observations, I let my mind examine my emotions surrounding my mother.

I did know about wanting a hug from your mum. Despite everything. There'd been so many times over the years when I'd needed just that. Not because a hug could solve anything, but because occasionally you needed to be reminded that someone loved you unconditionally, that when you were hurting or overwhelmed or lost, someone understood and would happily share your burden.

My memory of the day I told Mum I was pregnant was as sharp as it had always been. How her response had been to inform me that she'd regretted becoming a mother. I'd shut her out from that day onward. I'd never told Kat what she'd said. I didn't want her relationship with our mother ruined by me. To give her her due, Mum had apologised. In cards, in phone messages, by leaving gifts outside my door. I hadn't let her back in my life, but oh how I'd been tempted to.

Those difficult early weeks and months with a newborn, feeling clueless, exhausted and lonely. The years of being a proud mum as Brontë had grown into an energetic, happy child, through the wilful teenage years and finally revealing the impressive young woman who floored me with her enthusiasm and excitement for her life to come. I'd wanted to share my pride; I'd wanted a mum who would revel in Brontë's achievements and tell me what a good job I'd done with her. But I couldn't trust my mum to be that person, so I'd kept her at arm's length.

Mum had been at Brontë's funeral. I'd spoken to her, although I have no recollection of what I said. She'd looked old and grey, a tissue twisted up in her hand. I'd allowed her to hug me, as I let everyone hug me, but I wanted to scream at her. How dare you mourn her now, when you didn't even want her to exist in the first place?

'Daisy, I'm not your mum, and I'm only here for two weeks, but I do give great hugs,' I said, holding her gaze.

'Thanks.' She dipped her chin. 'I bet you were a great mum.'

Her use of the past tense brought tears to my eyes, and I hurriedly blinked them away. She was young and had yet to know the mother-child bond from the other side.

'I like to think I still am,' I said. 'Brontë will always be my daughter, I will always be her mum.'

She thought about that for a moment and nodded. 'I guess you never stop being someone's mum, do you? Like you never stop having a mum, even if they're not there anymore.'

I nodded. 'I'm sure your mum thinks about you all the time. Have you told your dad that you miss her?'

She scrunched up her pretty face. 'Whenever I try to talk about her, he changes the subject. When she left, he said she wasn't welcome here ever again. He's really mad about her and Pierre. I think he's humiliated too. Do you think my dad is good-looking?'

I was taken aback by the sudden question and found myself floundering for words. 'Jono? Yes. Your dad is a very handsome man.'

She shrugged, throwing her hands out to the sides. 'Exactly! Pierre is old, like ten years older than dad, and really grumpy. Why would Mum . . . ?' She broke off, shuddering. 'I don't even want to think about it.'

I smiled to myself, remembering Jono's words about Pierre's French accent. I wondered about Andrea, and what had been going through her mind when she ran off with Pierre and left Ruby Creek and this lovely girl behind. Was she regretting her decision, missing Daisy?

'Jono loves you, and he seems like a really nice guy. He's hurting too. My advice is to keep talking to him, let him know how you feel. Maybe he and your mum could work out a way for you to see her.'

Daisy looked speculatively at me. 'Do you think?'

Before I could answer, Max bounded through my open door, leaping up onto the sofa and knocking Brontë's book out of Daisy's hand. Jono appeared next, his broad shoulders filling the door frame.

'The oven timer's going off in the kitchen, ladies, and something smells really good.'

'The banana bread! I'll go!' Daisy squealed and raced out of the cottage, followed by Max.

I stood up too and picked up my hat and sunglasses.

'Looks like you two are getting on well,' said Jono.

'Daisy's a lovely girl. You're obviously doing a great job with her.' I closed the door behind me and together we strode back towards the main house.

Jono's pace slowed as we approached the door. 'I worry that I'm not enough on my own, that she needs a mother figure in her life.'

'She's got a mum, Jono.'

He shook his head, his jaw as hard as stone. 'She needs someone who's present for her. Not the other side of the country. If it's not too much to ask, I'd like it if you could take her under your wing, you know, talk to her.'

'While I'm here, I will, gladly,' I told him.

'I appreciate that.' He smiled with relief. 'I'm not very good at the talking stuff.'

'Sometimes all you need to do is be willing to listen.'

'Okay, yeah, I hear you,' he said earnestly, making me laugh.

In the distance, a minibus turned into the track leading to the winery. The pickers had arrived.

'Ready for your first day as a winemaker?' said Jono.

'Can't wait,' I replied, and then took a sharp breath as his hand lightly touched the small of my back to guide me inside. I hadn't been affected like this by a man for a long time and it felt new and exciting. I had a sudden urge to capture the moment.

'Stay right there. Selfie time.' I pulled my phone from my shorts pocket.

'Seriously?' he moaned, but then stepped close enough to feel the heat emanating from his T-shirt.

I took a picture of us both with the porch of his house behind and a perfect blue sky above us.

'For the 'Gram,' I said, laughing at his bemused expression. 'Hashtag Mum's Gap Year.'

## Mum's Gap Year

Dear B,

I can't believe I've been at Ruby Creek for nearly a week already. I LOVE it. Physically the toughest job I've ever done, working out in the vineyards, but I feel fitter than I have for years, I've actually got muscles, and the fresh air means I'm sleeping through the night for the first time since I lost you. I've even got a tan, although Daisy is very strict about hats and sunscreen and makes sure we all slap on the factor 50 several times a day. She's a great kid, missing her mum of course. We make a good pair, because I'll be missing you for the rest of my life. Hopefully her situation won't take as long as that to get sorted!

I've stopped shouting 'Kangaroo!' every five minutes, which Jono is pleased about. I still love seeing them but the novelty has worn off. There isn't much more picking to be done now – the harvest is mostly in. Jono says we should be finished by the time I leave. But there's always so much to do here, I'm tempted to stay a bit longer. We'll see . . .

Ruby Creek sells its wine from the cellar door, so we get people turning up all the time. Some are touring the area and will pick up one or two bottles, but one lovely old couple came yesterday from two hundred miles away. I sold them three cases of wine and they told me they'd been coming to the Hunter Valley every year since they'd been married to stock up on their favourites. It did my heart good to see a relationship still flourishing after such a long time. It made me want the same. There's also a bar here, but Nora, the woman who runs it, is off visiting her first grandchild, and Jono decided it was easier to close it while she's away. The days fly by, especially the picking days. After breakfast cooked by me, assisted by Daisy, we set the pickers to work with scissors and big plastic buckets, one on each row. When the buckets are full, I swap them for empty ones and tip the grapes into the trailer on the tractor. When the trailer is full, I drive the tractor back to the winery. Yes. ME!! It's a bumpy ride, and I learned the hard way that a good sports bra is essential, but I'm quite good on the tractor now. I know I say this all the time, but I wish you were here.

Love
Mum xx

# Chapter 27

## Australia

It was only eight a.m. and Ruby Creek was already shimmering under a glorious blue sky. Inside, the pickers were washing their hands and topping up their water bottles after a breakfast of fluffy pancakes with maple syrup and crispy bacon.

I'd been here nearly a week and had slipped into an easy morning routine. I'd get the breakfast and then enjoy a cup of coffee under the shade of the porch. This morning Jono had joined me and was endeavouring to revive a weary bumble bee with a teaspoon of sugar water.

For a large man, he was surprisingly gentle. I'd been instantly attracted to him that first day, and getting to know him had only strengthened my feelings towards him. I hadn't met Pierre, but I was instinctively on Jono's side and wondered what on earth Andrea could have been thinking.

'Dad!' Daisy called, holding out his mobile to him. She was in her school uniform ready to leave for the day. 'Tim McGuinness is on the phone for you.'

'Thanks, love.' He kissed her cheek, picked a flower from a bush and tucked it behind her ear before taking the phone from her. 'Have a good day, gorgeous.'

'You too,' she said, and gave me a brief hug on her way towards the gate. 'Bye.'

A school bus picked her up from the end of the road every morning and dropped her off later. She was inevitably late, and seeing her sprinting to meet it – rucksack bouncing on her back, her hair flying – made me smile every morning.

'G'day Tim, mate, what can I do for you?' Jono listened and frowned. 'You're kidding? I'm sorry to hear that, buddy.'

Daisy stopped in her tracks and turned back. 'What's wrong?'

He covered the microphone with his hand. 'Sickness bug. The whole team has come down with it.'

She looked at me and we both grimaced.

'A wine tour?' Jono continued into his phone. 'No can do, I'm afraid. Don't have the manpower, Nora's away. Sorry about that. No worries, get well soon.'

'What did he want?' Daisy wanted to know.

'He's got a wine tour booked in for today and he's going to have to cancel. He wondered whether we could take the booking instead.' Jono turned to me to explain. 'McGuinness winery is a couple of miles from here. The guy who runs the tour is a mate and Tim doesn't want to let him down.'

I'd seen the minibuses full of day-trippers from Sydney on my forays to the nearest supermarket in the neighbouring town of Cessnock. They followed a route around the Hunter, stopping off at several wineries sampling the wines on the way. Jono had told me that they can be big business for the smaller wineries if you made the tasting experience fun.

'I'll do it if you pay me.' Daisy's eyes lit up with hope.

'You've got school.' He laughed. 'And your mother would kill me if I started letting you bunk off to work for me.'

'Since when did you care what Mum thinks?' she challenged him, tilting her chin up defiantly.

233

Jono exhaled. 'Where you're concerned, your mum and me will always be on the same side.'

'Are under-eighteens even allowed to serve wine?' I pointed out.

'No, they're not,' Jono replied.

'Maggie!' Daisy pretended to pout.

'So, get going then!' Her dad gestured towards the driveway. 'Vamos. Scoot.'

'Ugh, so unfair.' She rolled her eyes but did as she was told.

I was conscious that the pickers were loitering, ready to start work. There were six of them today: four boys and two girls. The girls were Swedish, attractive and aloof. The boys were younger, full of fun and clearly infatuated with the girls. We needed to round them up and get them out to the Merlot vines, but I couldn't stop thinking about that wine-tasting tour. I liked a challenge, and it seemed a shame to turn away business.

'I'll handle the wine tasting for you, if you like?' I suggested.

I'd tasted all the wines produced at Ruby Creek. Each evening we'd sit outside with a couple of opened bottles, and Jono would tell me a little bit about the history of the winery and about the wines we were tasting. As darkness fell, we'd listen to the birds tweeting their evening tunes, and watch the bats swooping through the warm night air. I'd fallen under the spell of this place; it was vast and beautiful, and I loved the contrast of the neat vineyards set amidst the wilderness of the bush.

Jono looked sceptical. 'That's kind of you, but some of these folks can be real wine snobs. They get a hint that they know more than you about wine and they can be patronising suckers.'

'I'm a professional sales executive,' I told him with a glint in my eye. 'Awkward customers are my favourite.'

'You're a better man than me.' He gave me a lazy smile. 'Thanks for the offer, but I've already turned him down.'

'Call your friend back!' I nodded to his phone. 'Come on. How long will it take, an hour? I'll set up, you can waft in, talk about the wines and go back to the vines, and I'll work my charm on the punters, and everyone leaves a happy bunny.'

He grinned. 'I can *waft*?'

I held his gaze. 'Okay, swagger then. Is that better?'

'Much. Okay, you win.' He shook his head, smiling and tapped a number on his phone screen. 'Tim? Me again. Change of plan. We'll do the tour.'

Two hours later, the tour group had arrived and were seated under the porch. They were a mixed bunch: four Germans; a mother and daughter from Sydney who'd immediately wandered off to try and photograph a family of dozing kangaroos under the trees; a couple on their honeymoon, whose bodies were so entwined that it was hard to see which was him and which was her; and an American family from California with three grown-up children.

'Keep an eye on the youngest American boy; this is our third vineyard and he's starting to slur his words.' The tour guide tipped me a wink and retreated to his minibus to wait.

'We've all been there.' Jono smirked.

'Welcome to Ruby Creek.' I handed out a sheet of tasting notes to everyone. I'd already set the table with a flight of glasses, jugs of water and a batch of cheese straws which I'd knocked up out of ready-made pastry from the freezer. 'Today, we're going to be tasting the sparkling Chardonnay, our 2022 Sauvignon Blanc, a new Chenin Blanc, our best-selling rosé and two of our reds, one of which is my favourite Ruby Creek wine. And then for those who still have room, we've got a Bacchus which is almost sold out – so if you like it, make sure you don't leave without a bottle.'

'So you were listening, I'm impressed,' Jono murmured, tearing the foil off the first bottle. 'Full marks for attention to detail.'

'But of course,' I replied. 'I hang on your every word.'

He laughed under his breath, shaking his head.

Jono had divided the pickers into two teams, each headed by one of the girls. They'd decided to have a competition to see who could fill their trailer first. It was probably going to be the fastest-ever pick and result in a lot of bruised grapes, but from the hoots of laughter drifting to us on a warm breeze, it sounded like they were having fun.

'My parents started this vineyard when I was a baby,' Jono began, popping the cork. He handed the bottle to me. Our fingertips brushed and a frisson of pleasure fluttered down my spine. 'Their passion for fine wine must be in my blood because I've been lucky enough to live and work here my whole life. Our heritage is in our Semillons, which have won international awards, but over time we've added premium reds to our portfolio and now our name is as synonymous with robust Cabernet Sauvignons as it is with our sought-after whites.'

I went around the table with the sparkling wine, pouring everyone a sample, ignoring the American boy when he swigged his straight down and held his glass out for more.

'We're particularly proud of our sparkling wines,' Jono continued. 'This one has vibrant floral aromas, intense citrus flavours, balanced by a mineral acid backbone.'

'What do you think?' I asked, once everyone had had a taste. 'Did you like that?'

The group nodded their assent, already eyeing up the next bottle. I pulled the cork out of a bottle of Semillon.

'At Ruby Creek we like to think of ourselves as more than quality wine producers. We make good times in a glass, an opportunity to make memories with family and friends. We believe that you can taste our love for what we do.' He turned to me and caught me gazing at him. 'Isn't that right, Maggie?'

I was mesmerised by his passion for his family's business, by his obvious love of his home. And if I was honest with myself, I was mesmerised by the sheer presence of him. I'd teased him about his manly swagger, but I'd meant it. I hadn't felt this affected by a man since I'd bumped into Gordon Ramsay coming out of a boutique on Bond Street and asked him if we'd met before. Gallantly, he'd said no, but he was sure he'd remember if he had. It was only after he'd walked away that I'd realised who he was.

'Yes,' I stuttered, my mouth dry. What would his lips feel like? Would he be as tender with me as he'd been with that thirsty bumble bee? Would I find out? I wanted to find out, very much. What had been his question? 'Yes. Absolutely.'

'Maggie?' said one of the Germans. 'You are pouring that wine on my shoe.'

'That was a success,' I declared once the group had finally left.

We'd sold out of the Bacchus and organised to have two cases of Merlot delivered to Germany; and the mum from Sydney had placed an order for Ruby Creek wines for her daughter's wedding later this year. The Americans had been about to make a purchase when their son turned green and vomited. The boy blamed the wines; his parents clearly blamed themselves. They had bought a case of rosé and proceeded to slink back to the minibus, avoiding eye contact with the rest of the group.

'It was.' Jono nodded. 'We make a good team, you and me.'

We collected up the glasses and loaded them into the dishwasher in Ruby's Bar.

He reached a hand to my face. I held my breath, heart pounding, hoping he was going to kiss me.

'Eyelash,' he said, touching a fingertip to my cheek. 'There, gone.'

'Oh. Thanks.' Hope vanished as quickly as it had come.

'Maggie? Can I ask you a question?'

'Sure.' I felt my heart race again.

'Would you . . . ?' He frowned and shook his head. 'No, no, nothing.'

'Would I what?' I prompted. 'Just ask.'

He looked away and then back again. 'Okay, okay. Daisy clearly loves you, Max prefers you to me these days, and I was wondering if you'd stay a bit longer. Here, working for me. I'd pay you, of course.'

'A job?' I blinked at him, not sure how to deal with my disappointment. And then a split second later deciding that maybe, for once in my life, I should go after what I wanted for a change. 'For a moment there, I thought you were going to ask me for a kiss.'

He slapped a hand to his forehead and took a step back. 'Sorry. My fault entirely. Look at me, invading your personal space.'

'No worries.' I was doing that weird Australian accent again. My face was probably purple with embarrassment. 'We'd better get back to the vines, see what the pickers are up to.'

'Yeah, good plan.'

The two of us walked back to the vineyard, an awkward silence humming between us.

Jono stopped just before the gate and caught hold of my hand. 'I think I'm being a bit slow here. So just to be clear, did you want me to kiss you? Because if you did then—'

My answer came in the form of a kiss, my hands sliding upwards across the muscles in his back. He responded immediately, the heat of his mouth making me heady with longing.

'Clear enough?' I pulled back to relish the look of surprise on his face.

'Almost,' he replied with a glint in his eye.

I laughed and kissed him again to make sure. I was slowly coming back to life and my goodness, did it feel good.

# Chapter 28

## Australia

'Seven a.m. and we're already winning,' I said to Max, sending a sheet of address labels to print from the laptop in front of me.

The dog and I were on the veranda. I'd processed the online orders that had come through overnight while he dozed under the table, one eye permanently open on the lookout for approaching vehicles and people to make friends with.

Today was officially the last day of the harvest. There was only one small parcel of vines still to pick. They were in the shadiest spot in the vineyard, Jono had explained, and always the last to ripen. This season's harvest had been the best since before the bush fires, and Jono said that there was a feeling across the Hunter Valley that the yield was going to produce some amazing wines. He deserved his success after the months he'd had. I knew only too well how hard it was to get up each morning and get going when life did its best to throw you off course.

As well as harvesting coming to an end, today was officially my last day at Ruby Creek. My two weeks were up, and in theory I'd be heading back to Sydney tomorrow.

My last few days had flown by in a blur of fresh air, warm sunshine, starry nights spent on the veranda with Jono, Daisy and Max, and the blissful sleep of someone who was living her best life. Each day we picked grapes until mid-afternoon, at which point the pickers were sent home and work began in the winery. Jono's two presses were at full capacity. The grapes were pressed and juice pumped into the waiting stainless-steel tanks. He was working well into the evenings, anxiously checking the grape juice, taking samples and cataloguing every detail. Other people had begun to turn up at Ruby Creek to help him: members of the Ruby Creek club who owned a stake in the vineyard, friends of Jono's he'd known since school, and even his cousin and her husband – all coming to lend a hand at the busiest point in a winemaker's calendar.

The longer I was here, the more I was able to help. From selling direct at the cellar door, and updating the winery's website, to preparing bedrooms in the main house for visitors. I felt part of the Ruby Creek team and I was going to miss them all so much.

Should I stay longer? The question played on a loop in my head. The chemistry between Jono and me was rising with each passing encounter, like the pressure and heat building before a thunderstorm that you know with absolute certainty is heading your way. We flirted and made eye contact at every opportunity, we deliberately brushed against one another, fingers intertwining briefly and breaking away before we were spotted.

The kiss had changed the dynamic between us. Now if I stayed I wasn't sure whether he wanted me as a worker or something more. And what about my travels? There were still plenty of pages left unturned in Brontë's book, which meant she had more places she'd wanted to discover. If I stayed, would there be time to do it all before I was due back at work? Surely Bronte's trip should be my priority? After all, she was the reason I was here to begin with.

'Maggie.' Daisy's voice cut into my thoughts. Her cheeks were flushed, and she checked around before continuing. 'I need to tell you a secret.'

'Morning, love.' I patted the space beside me. 'Sit down, tell me all about it.'

She reminded me so much of Brontë at that age; full of energy and ideas, veering erratically from worldly-wise one minute to self-conscious and unsure of herself the next. I often thought about her mother and how sad it was that she and Jono had not been able to work out a way for Daisy to keep in touch. I'd miss her when I left, and felt a rush of warmth that she knew she was safe to confide her secrets in me.

'Okay, so here's the thing.' She slid onto the bench. Max perked up, nudging her with his nose until she gave him some fuss.

She looked different today. Her hair fell in glossy waves instead of its casual ponytail and there was a pair of sunglasses perched on her head.

She looked cool and stylish, and I could see flashes of the woman she was becoming.

'You're not wearing school uniform,' I said, taking in her jeans and T-shirt.

She dismissed that with a flap of her hand. 'There's some travelling theatre coming into school today, doing workshops about diversity. We're allowed to wear what we want to express our individuality. Best of all, there's no proper lessons.'

'Lucky you!' I smiled at the glee in her eye, remembering how much Brontë had loved school days like that. Her favourite had been World Book Day. She'd have to pick a character from a book to dress as and I'd endeavour to create an outfit that vaguely resembled it. I'd grumbled then at the effort I'd have to go to for one day. Now, of course, I'd give anything to sit up half the night transforming an old sleeping bag into the Very Hungry Caterpillar.

'Which is why,' Daisy continued, lowering her voice, 'today is the perfect day to do what I'm going to do.'

'Go on,' I prompted. Alarm bells began to ring.

'I'm not going to school.' She chewed her lip. 'I've got it all planned out. I'm getting the train to Sydney to meet Mum.'

'And this is the secret you want me to keep?' I said warily.

She nodded. 'I've been thinking about what you said on that first day we made breakfast together. Mum left my dad, not me. So, I thought that maybe she might want to hear from me after all. I sent her a text yesterday telling her that I needed her. She sent me one straight back saying how much she missed me and that she's so sorry about leaving me behind. Isn't that amazing?'

'I'm glad you two are in contact again. And the bit about your mum missing you is lovely to hear,' I agreed, squeezing her hand. 'But bunking off school and going behind your dad's back isn't.'

'I can't tell him,' she said, firmly. 'He'd try and stop me; I know he would. I love him, but I love Mum too. She still loves me, but she said she didn't have any choice about leaving me. What if she's regretting it? That's why I want to see her. Maybe I can be the one to get them talking again. Maybe deep down they still love each other. Imagine if I could get them back together! Everyone was so much happier before Pierre came to work here. We could be happy again.'

My chest swelled with affection for her youthful optimism. If only life's issues were so easy to solve. Even if Jono did still have feelings for Andrea, I was sure he'd be wary of letting her back into his life.

'That's a lovely thought,' I said carefully. 'But your dad was very upset when your mum left with Pierre. His pride was hurt, and he was angry with her for upsetting you. Your mum arranging to see you behind Jono's back is not the way to go about this.'

'It's the only way,' Daisy protested. 'It's not as if I'm missing anything useful at school, and Mum was coming to Sydney anyway. It's too good an opportunity to pass up.'

I could see how much this meant to her. But what was Andrea thinking to encourage her fourteen-year-old child to lie to her father and travel to Sydney on her own? It was ridiculously irresponsible of her and, if it went wrong, Jono would be even more angry with his ex-wife.

'You won't keep my secret, will you,' said Daisy hotly, getting to her feet. 'I thought I could trust you, and that you'd be on my side, but you're like every other adult. You don't take my feelings seriously.'

Her words hit me like a blow to the stomach. This took me right back to my last conversation with Brontë. I hadn't listened to her when she'd tried to tell me about her gap year. I didn't want to make the same mistake twice; I wanted to do better.

'Oh, Daisy. That's not true,' I told her. 'I'm putting myself in Jono's shoes. You're the most precious thing in his world. He'd be devastated if anything happened to you. And he'd be furious with me for not telling him where you'd gone – rightly so.'

She picked up her bag and slung it over her shoulder. 'It's an easy train ride. Nothing's going to happen.'

'That's probably what Brontë thought the last time she left her house with Harry,' I said, meeting her eye. 'The thing is, we never know what's around the corner. I wouldn't be being a good friend to you if I didn't point out the possible dangers of this trip.'

Daisy appeared to consider this for a moment. 'Fine. Let's swap numbers. I'll let you know when I arrive.'

'Your dad needs to know too. If you won't tell him now,' I said. 'Then at least text him from the train so he knows where you've gone. It'll be too late for him to do anything about it, and he might be angry with you, but at least he'll have had a chance to calm down by the time you come home.'

She sighed with relief. 'Cool. Thanks. And it's the end-of-harvest dinner tonight, so Dad will probably have a few beers. He'll be so happy and caught up with celebrating that I'll be back before he even notices that I've gone.'

'What's the end-of-harvest dinner?' I asked.

Before she had the chance to reply, the sound of the metal sliding doors on the winery made us both look up and Jono came loping towards us.

'Please don't say anything,' Daisy hissed, clutching my shoulder. 'I'll text him, I promise.'

'Make sure you do.' I really didn't want to get involved in this, but it looked like I already was. I hoped I didn't live to regret it.

'What are you two looking so serious about?' He looked from his daughter to me, an eyebrow raised.

'You haven't told Maggie about the end-of-harvest dinner,' Daisy gave him a peck on his cheek and sent me one last pleading look. 'I've got to go.'

'How exciting,' I said, smiling up at him. 'What's the dress code, ballgowns and tiaras?'

'Not exactly. More like clean feet and a good sense of humour. You'll love it,' he said with a grin. 'It's Daisy's favourite thing, isn't it?'

She mumbled something about possibly being late back, avoiding his eye.

'Can't wait,' I said, my stomach twisting uneasily.

The two of us watched as Daisy did her usual sprint down the driveway to catch the school bus. I had an awful feeling that he'd be the one in need of a good sense of humour by the end of today. I already regretted my promise to her and cursed Andrea for putting me in this position.

# *Chapter 29*

**Australia**

By mid-afternoon, the harvest was finally in. The last batch of grapes had gone into the press, with a few crates stacked in the yard beside a wooden trough.

I hadn't been able to relax all day and had been checking my phone regularly. I'd sent Daisy a text reminding her of her promise to message her father but hadn't received a reply. Even more concerning was that Jono hadn't said a word about Daisy's antics. He didn't seem distracted, or angry, or worried. I couldn't help but wonder if perhaps she'd reneged on her promise and he was still in the dark.

If that was the case, he'd be asking questions soon enough. The school bus should have been dropping her back here within the next hour or so, and when she failed to return he'd remember that she'd hinted that she might be late and would want to check up on her.

For the time being, a party atmosphere had taken over at Ruby Creek and Jono seemed to be enjoying himself. Nora was back from visiting the new baby and had come in to work especially to tend the bar, and the wine was flowing. I'd contacted as many of the pickers as I could reach to invite them back to celebrate with us, and with them and Jono's assorted friends and family, the picnic tables outside Ruby's Bar were the busiest I'd seen them. Country and western music played from speakers and people were wolfing down platters of cheese, olives and fresh bread as quickly as Jono's cousin, Tara, and I could ferry them out from the kitchen.

I paused from my catering duties for a breather under the shade of the porch and Jono joined me, a mischievous sparkle in his eye.

'I have a special job for you.' He held out a hand to me. 'Would you like to kick off the foot-stomping?'

'The what?' I asked, taking his hand automatically.

'Foot-stomping time!' cried one of the pickers, drumming his hands on the table.

A cheer went up and everyone trooped across the yard to the wooden trough, which had been filled to the top with grapes.

'It's a Ruby Creek tradition.' Jono indicated for me to take my shoes off. 'We stomp the last of the grapes and give everyone some of the juice in a bottle to take home as a memento.'

'You are honoured,' said Nora slyly. 'Andrea got first stomp last time.'

'Don't ruin my mood, Nora,' Jono said lightly. 'I'd rather not think about last year's harvest, if it's all the same to you. Let's enjoy the moment, shall we?'

He looked over his shoulder briefly towards the drive. 'Shame Daisy's not back yet, she loves this. Never mind, she can join in when she arrives.'

'When are you expecting her?' I asked, hoping he'd know what train she was coming back on.

'Late, which was as much as I got out of her this morning,' he said with a grin. 'Now, are you ready?'

He helped me into the trough, and everyone cheered again. The grapes were slippy underfoot. I'd expected them to pop in their skins, but instead my feet slid over them, and I lurched sideways. Jono caught hold of me to steady me and I held on tightly to his hands, facing him.

'What do I have to do?' I said, giggling.

'Clue's in the name, Maggie,' he teased. 'What d'you think you do?'

'Stomp,' cried Nora, 'just bloody stomp!'

I did as she said, stamping as hard as I could, marching up and down on the spot, squishing the grapes with my feet. The juice was sticky and it was trickier than it looked to stay upright, but it was a lot of fun, and the way Jono's strong hands tightened around mine to stop me from slipping only added to the experience.

'Feels good, doesn't it?' Jono said with a grin.

'*Very* good,' I responded. 'But please don't let go.'

He met my eye. 'I'm not going anywhere. You're safe.'

My heart had speeded up; whether from the exertion of the task or from his proximity to me, I couldn't be sure, but I was very much enjoying the sensation. How long had it been since I'd felt safe, I wondered, and how long could I make this feeling last?

'Everything okay?' I asked.

I'd washed my feet, put my shoes back on and taken a couple of fresh beers to where Jono was leaning on the fence, looking out across the valley. The shrieks of the two Swedish girls who'd jumped into the trough after me made us both smile. 'Everything's great.' He tapped his beer bottle against mine. 'It's been a good day.'

In the distance, a few grey clouds hovered over the horizon. It was the first time I'd seen anything but unbroken blue sky since I'd arrived in Ruby Creek.

'Does that mean rain, do you think?' I pointed my beer towards the clouds.

Jono studied the sky and wrinkled his nose. 'Maybe. Won't bother us. The grapes are in safe and sound, rain can only be a good thing from now on, for us at least.'

I nodded, selfishly hoping that the wet weather stayed away for another day until I was safely back in Sydney.

'Last year was a different story,' Jono said, grimly. 'Pierre and I had had a disagreement about harvesting. He wanted to pick, I wanted to leave it another couple of days. And because I was the boss, I got my way. The weather forecast had failed to pick up an electric storm which came in overnight and destroyed a good proportion of our Semillon. Those we did salvage were wet and we had to work fast before rot set in. Pierre didn't let me forget it. That was probably where the rot set in between him and me too.'

Jono hadn't told me much about his relationship with Pierre before now and I was curious to know more. 'Is that when their affair started?'

He shrugged. 'I don't know, and I have no intention of finding out. She disliked him at the beginning, complaining that I shouldn't have employed him, that he was a know-all and was rude to everyone. We even argued about it, can you believe. Somewhere along the line that changed without me noticing. I remember hearing her laughter coming from the winery and, when I went inside, he had his arms around her, supposedly helping her pull a cork from a bottle. When I challenged them, she admitted it straight away and said she couldn't help herself. I sacked him on the spot and told him to get off my property. Twenty-four hours later she'd gone too. Without a word, no explanation, or apology, nothing. I stumbled through those first few weeks not knowing which way was up. I was so shocked that I didn't know how to feel, then came the feelings of hurt and anger about what she'd done to me. But above all else I was furious about the way she'd disappeared into the sunset without a backward glance at Daisy.'

'I'm sorry you had to go through that,' I said, taking a step closer so that my arm touched his.

'It makes you think, you never know what's around the corner, do you? Your life can change in a fraction of a second. One minute you think you have it all figured out. The next you're right back at the bottom of the ladder.'

I'd said more or less the same thing to Daisy this morning and I felt a twinge of guilt for keeping a secret from him.

'You don't have to tell me that,' I replied. 'Mine changed when a police officer rang my doorbell and informed me my beautiful girl had gone forever.'

He put his arm around my shoulders and gave my arm a rub. 'Of course, sorry.'

I allowed myself to relax against him. I could get used to this, I thought, having another adult to lean on, particularly one as kind and attractive as Jono.

'I blame myself,' he said, clearly still thinking about Andrea. 'Looking back, I could have paid her more attention. I was always so busy with the business that I neglected us. I talked about "when" a lot, promising that things would be different "when", like when Daisy was older, or when bottling was finished, or when we'd got more staff to help. Eventually she got tired of waiting.'

It was hard to listen to him beating himself up without leaping to his defence. I wanted to point out that it takes two to make a marriage work, and that if Andrea hadn't wanted to put in any effort to keep their love alive, then she deserved as much blame as him.

'Do you still love her?' I asked.

He pondered the question for a few seconds and shook his head. 'I'll never take her back.'

Which didn't answer the question. I suspected that he was still conflicted in his feelings towards her. Which meant that he wasn't ready to start a new relationship. Not that he'd ever suggested he was, I mused, hoping that my thoughts weren't written on my face.

He looked at his watch. 'I'm surprised Daisy hasn't been in touch yet.'

'You haven't heard from her today?'

'Nope.' He took out his phone and double-checked. 'Nothing.'

*Oh Daisy*, I thought, groaning inwardly. Why had she not texted him as she'd promised?

'I'm sure she's fine,' I said. 'She's a sensible girl.'

'I guess,' he muttered. 'But do parents ever stop worrying about their kids?'

'Of course not.' Even now, I'd probably never stop worrying about Brontë. I could conjure up an event from long ago and worry about that, even though there was nothing I could do to change it. 'Shall I text her and see where she is?'

I was beginning to get worried about Daisy, and annoyed with myself for agreeing to her plan. What if something had happened to her? What if Andrea hadn't been able to meet her after all, or she'd had trouble with the trains? The thought of her being out of her depth in Sydney and too worried to let her dad know where she was made me feel sick.

'You have her number?'

I nodded and his face softened.

'It's okay, Maggie. I'll ring her. But thanks. It's been good for her having you here. She's missed a woman around the place. I do my best to be both parents, and I'll try to discuss any topic with her, but there are some things – periods, for example – that she point-blank won't talk about. And I know my eyes glaze over when she talks about clothes. I'm a jeans and T-shirt man; I can't get into fashion.'

He didn't need to get into fashion when he looked so hot in jeans, I mused. I gave myself a shake, recalling how he wouldn't be drawn on whether he still loved Andrea or not.

'I know it's a touchy subject,' I said, 'but maybe the best person for Daisy to speak to about that sort of stuff might be her mum. Is there a way the two of them can rekindle their relationship? Even regular phone calls might help.'

'I'm with you there.' Jono's face set in a grim line. 'But Daisy wants nothing to do with her. Maybe time will soften the blow, but she shuts down whenever I mention her mother's name.'

It seemed there was simply a misunderstanding between father and daughter: Daisy wanting to see her mum but worried about appearing disloyal to Jono; Jono not wanting to force his daughter to see Andrea before she was ready. An impasse fuelled by love for each other.

'Time will help,' I agreed. 'Even the bitterest of feelings lose their sharpness eventually.'

'I hope you're right. Okay, let's see where she is.' He dialled his daughter's number and held the phone to his ear while it rang. He gave a sigh. 'Voicemail . . . It's Dad. Drop me a quick text, sweetheart, let me know where you are. You're missing the foot-stomping, you know.' He ended the call and put the phone back in his pocket.

My stomach twisted; I didn't like being part of this deception one bit. I was going to drop her one last message too, hoping that both of us getting in touch would entice her to reply. If she didn't reply, I was going to tell him myself, because it wasn't fair.

I set down my beer bottle, took out my own phone and found her number, turning the screen away from him.

Daisy, your dad is getting worried. You promised you'd tell him where you were going. I'm sorry but I'm going to have to tell him the truth. xx

'Has she texted you?' Jono asked, watching me.
'Er, no,' I replied.

I attempted to press *send* quickly but the phone slipped out of my grasp and onto the ground.

I bent to pick it up, but Jono got there first.

'Whoops, here you go.' His eyes glanced at the screen, he saw the unsent message and froze. 'What the . . . ? I'm going to have to . . . ?' he read. 'Maggie, what's going on here?'

'Okay, I can explain,' I said hurriedly.

The intensity of his stare stopped my heart for a second. In my panic, I grabbed the phone from him and sent the message.

'Is it that boy, Tom?' he growled. 'I knew I should have said something.'

'It's not Tom,' I reassured him. 'But I'm afraid that Daisy didn't go to school today.'

'Okay.' He frowned, not taking his eyes off me for a second. 'And? Where is she?'

'She's gone to meet Andrea.'

'She what?' His eyes widened with disbelief. 'I didn't even know they were in contact.'

'I don't think they were until yesterday. Daisy sent her mum a message and they arranged to meet up today,' I told him as calmly as I could.

'Let me get this straight,' he said, running a hand through his hair, his tone curt. 'You knew about this all day today and didn't think to tell me? For God's sake, Maggie. How would you feel if it was your daughter?'

My face burned with shame. 'I'm so sorry. She made me promise to keep her secret and in return I made her promise to tell you. But she evidently decided against that part.'

'Do you know what? Whatever.' He held his hands up, his eyes hard and cold. 'Where the hell are they meeting?'

'Sydney. Daisy got a train there.'

'Jesus Christ.' He started pacing, both hands in his hair now. 'On her own? She's fourteen!'

He strode off across the yard, swearing so loudly that everyone stopped in their tracks, alarmed. Max started barking and jumping up at him, sensing his master's distress.

'What's up, boss?' Nora asked, catching hold of his arm. But he shook her off and opened the door to his truck.

'Wait,' I cried, reaching the truck as he slammed his door. 'Where are you going?'

'To fetch her,' he growled through the open window. He looked at me as if I was a stranger. 'I'll drive to Sydney if I have to. I'm not letting Andrea get away with this.'

He put the keys in the ignition and started the engine.

'Jono, please.' I gripped the side of the truck. 'Go easy on Daisy. The only reason she didn't tell you about this trip is because she didn't want to upset you. She's protective of your feelings, and trying to keep everyone happy.'

Before he could reply, his phone rang and connected to the car's Bluetooth.

'It's Daisy,' he said curtly, stabbing at a button on his steering wheel.

'Hey, Dad,' came a small voice.

'Sweetheart, where are you?'

'At the train station, I get into Cessnock in forty minutes. Are you mad at me?'

I stepped away from the truck as Jono turned off the engine.

'I'm annoyed that no one told me where you were going.'

His eyes slid to mine, his anger clearly aimed at me. I shrank away, wracked with guilt.

'But I'm glad you're safe. Do you want me to collect you?'

'Jono,' said an older female voice. 'It's me.'

'Andrea.' He gave a harsh laugh. 'I would say, how could you act so irresponsibly? But then I remembered who I was talking to. The woman who was shagging my manager behind my back and then buggered off without a single thought for her own child. Nothing you do can surprise me now. My expectations are already rock bottom where you're concerned.'

'Come on, let's talk about this like adults,' she replied.

'Adults? Are you kidding me?' Jono thrust himself back against his seat, his arms outstretched in disbelief. 'I'm the only adult left in this broken marriage. You behaved like a teenage girl with a crush last year and you have the nerve to suggest I'm not being adult about this. I can't do this.'

'Tough shit,' came the response. 'We have to because our daughter needs us to.'

I suddenly realised I was eavesdropping on their private conversation – frozen to the spot, my pulse thrumming to a guilty rhythm. I should have told him sooner, let him know that Daisy had been missing her mum and had considered this to be her only option. She'd grasped at the chance to see Andrea again, regardless of the consequences.

I forced myself to move away from what was turning into a bitter row between Jono and his ex-wife, and I stumbled back to Creek Cottage feeling terrible about being a part of it.

Thank goodness tonight was my last night. There would be no more talk about me staying longer, I was sure about that. Tomorrow couldn't come soon enough.

# Chapter 30

**Australia**

It was dark when I heard a light knock on the door of Creek Cottage later that evening.

I'd seen Daisy getting out of Jono's truck earlier. He must have been to collect her from the station. I'd stayed out of their way. If either of them wanted to talk to me, they'd know where to find me. Until then, I guessed they needed space to talk.

I opened the door and there he was, a respectful distance from the doorway.

'Jono?' My breath caught as my mouth formed his name.

'I hope I'm not disturbing you?' His voice was gravelly and gentle and I felt a flush of hope that he was no longer angry with me.

'You're not. I'm packing.' I nodded towards the bed, where my suitcase was open, neat piles of clothes waiting to go in.

'Ah.'

We smiled at each other. His handsome face was lit by the porchlight, hands slung low on his hips, toe scuffing the dust of the path. I had an urge to put my arms around his neck, press my body to his and kiss him like I'd done before. Did he feel it too? Had the moment passed us by?

'You got caught in the crossfire today and I'm sorry.' He shifted his stance, dipping his head, but still holding my eye. 'I had no right to talk to you the way I did. And I'm sorry Daisy put you in a difficult position. None of it was your fault.'

'It's fine, I promise.' I dismissed his apology. 'I should have done better. You asked me how I'd feel if it had been my daughter. The answer is, I'd have been hurt too.'

I leaned on the frame of the door, wondering if I should invite him in. Was he waiting for me to? The studio was small and the only place to sit was the little sofa or my bed. Either option felt too intimate. I probably shouldn't. We might have apologised to each other, but I doubted we would be able to recapture the flirtiness of our previous conversations. Besides, I was leaving for Sydney in the morning and had booked a cab to take me to the train station after breakfast.

'I feel such a fool.' Jono shook his head. 'I thought she told me everything. But of course she doesn't. What teenager does? And on top of that, it's such a blow to the ego to find they don't need to run everything by you any more to make a decision.'

'It is a blow,' I agreed. 'But it's also an indication that you've done your job as a parent.'

He grinned. 'You know how to cheer a man up.'

'I don't have a relationship with my own mother. And growing up, neither did Brontë. But one year, Mum gave her a pair of vintage boots for her birthday and Brontë loved them. I made sure she messaged her grandmother to say thank you.'

'My dad drummed it into us to write thank-you letters,' said Jono, leaning on the other side of the door frame. 'He drummed rules in and drummed information out, never trusting me, always suspicious that I was up to no good. There was no way I could keep anything private. I wanted to be a different sort of father.'

'Sounds familiar,' I said. 'Anyway, unbeknownst to me, Brontë and my mother started speaking to each other regularly after that. I was hurt when I found out. It felt as if Brontë was siding with her. But the truth was that she was as entitled to have a relationship with her grandmother as I was entitled not to. It didn't change things between Mum and me, although I think Brontë hoped it would bring us closer.'

He nodded thoughtfully. 'That's the point Daisy and I are at now. She was hiding how much she misses her mum to avoid hurting my feelings.'

'Things are much more straightforward when people are honest with each other about how they feel,' I said, looking directly at him.

Jono met my gaze and the words hung between us for a second. He was the one to look away.

'Andrea and I are going to have to work out something more formal for Daisy. As you can imagine, I'm not thrilled at that prospect.' He gave me a wry smile. 'But neither do I want Daisy disappearing off God knows where without telling me.'

'What happened between you and Andrea is really sad, and you're fully entitled to be angry at how she behaved.'

'How she's still behaving,' he retorted. 'Today's escapade shows she'll always do what suits her and to hell with everything and everyone else.'

I couldn't argue with that. Encouraging her daughter to lie to her father, bunk off school and travel alone to a city she didn't know well was fraught with risk, not least to Daisy.

'Luckily you can move on from the marriage, start over,' I said. 'But Andrea will always be Daisy's mum, just as you will always be her dad, so she will be in your life whether you like it or not. Today was a bump in the road you weren't expecting, but your relationship with Daisy has survived. If you can protect your own feelings and try not to let Andrea rile you, I'm sure it will get easier.'

He nodded slowly and laughed softly under his breath. 'Are you always this wise?'

I laughed too. 'Yes, actually.'

My hand found the edge of the door ready to close it. The conversation felt like it had come to an end, although I didn't want to say goodnight.

'Thanks for coming over,' I said, breaking the silence. 'You should never go to bed on an argument – isn't that the saying?'

He rubbed a weary hand over his face. 'Crikey, I almost forgot why I came over. I haven't even got to the point yet. I've got something special to show you, if you're not too busy.' He nodded to my bare feet. 'You'll need your trainers on.'

Two minutes later we were walking away from the winery and towards the forest that lined Ruby Creek's driveway. It was pitch black and I turned on my phone torch to light my path.

'You won't need a torch,' said Jono, slipping his hand into mine. 'I know every inch of this place.'

My heart skipped a beat as I looked up at him. This was unexpected. Nicely unexpected.

'Even the location of the snakes?' I teased, nonetheless turning it off and pocketing my phone.

I'd seen several snakes since I'd been here and had learned not to scream and run away. But encountering one in the dark was way beyond my comfort zone.

He stamped his feet and led me off the path and into the trees. 'There. Gone. Trust me.'

'Obviously, I do,' I replied. 'Or I wouldn't be out at night in the Australian bush without even asking what we're doing.'

He gave a low rumbly laugh and squeezed my hand gently. 'That's one of the things I like about you, Maggie. Nothing fazes you.'

'I'm not sure that *nothing* fazes me,' I countered, loving the gentle ways that he made me feel good about myself. 'But I'll take it.'

'We never really finished our conversation about you staying longer, did we?' he said.

I sucked in a breath. 'No. I seem to remember interrupting you by asking for a kiss. Sorry about that,' I added in a way which implied that I wasn't sorry at all.

'Don't be. A beautiful woman, smart and sexy, wanting to kiss me did wonders for my ego.'

His compliments were making me heat up. Not so much with embarrassment but with desire. When was the last time I'd been told I was sexy? My breath was shaky when I answered him. 'And not turning me down was a boost to mine.'

'Then we're even. But you've packed your case, so I guess that's my answer.'

Was I wrong to be leaving? No, I decided, it was the right thing to do. As much as I enjoyed flirting with him, he was still in pain about Andrea and not ready to have a relationship with anyone new. If I stayed there was a real danger of falling in love with this man – and that wouldn't be the right thing for either of us.

I was ready to love again, I recognised that now. But there were still places to go, pages of Brontë's thoughts to read and ultimately new things to add into my life to make sure I would always know moments of joy like this. Because, I thought – as he led me through the trees, the dry twigs on the forest floor snapping beneath our feet – that was what this was: an intoxicating moment of joy.

'Yes, I am going to leave,' I confirmed. 'I've booked two more nights in Sydney from tomorrow and then after that, I shall turn the page in Brontë's book and find out where she's sending me next.'

He reached for my hand and brought it to his mouth, grazing his lips against my skin. 'I hope wherever it is, it's somewhere that makes you very happy.'

I gave him a sideways glance. 'It's worked out that way so far . . . Oh wow, look at that!'

The velvet darkness of the forest had changed. Suddenly it was filled with golden specks of light, like the sparks from a bonfire glittering in the night.

'What is it?' I breathed.

'Fireflies.' Jono was so close to me now that I could feel the hairs on his arms brush against my skin.

'I've never seen anything so beautiful,' I murmured, almost too scared to speak in case I chased them away. 'Thank you for bringing me here. I wouldn't have missed this for the world.'

'I'm glad. Be careful.' He let go of my hand and put his arm around my waist, steering me around a tree stump and pulling me close.

The fireflies danced and swirled around us as we walked deeper into the forest; it was like walking through gold dust. I waved my fingers through the air, watching as the tiny dots of light darted away like shoals of shimmering fish.

'Those on the ground are the females.' Jono pointed them out as we came to a stop. 'The boys are the ones showing off their moves to attract the best girls.'

'No change there,' I mused. 'So all this is a mating dance? Incredible.'

'Yep, a light show to find a mate for the night.' He paused and caught my eye. 'Unfortunately, they only get one night and then they die.'

'What?' I was horrified. 'That's the most dramatic one-night stand ever.'

He laughed. 'I can think of worse ways to go.'

'I guess,' I agreed. 'Although one-night stands have never really appealed to me. I prefer making a deeper connection with someone.'

'Same here. But I think if I knew I'd only got one chance at it, and I'd never see her again after tomorrow, then maybe I would.'

'Yeah,' I whispered. 'Maybe I would too.'

For a moment neither of us spoke; I slid my arm around his waist and moved in close enough to feel the rise and fall of his breathing, and we stood in silence watching the show. I'd never forget tonight, I realised. Never. How lucky I was to be here with this gorgeous man, experiencing such a beautiful sight.

We turned to each other, he put his hands on my hips and drew me towards him. The fireflies created a halo around us both, and it felt otherworldly and magical and incredibly hot.

I touched the tip of my tongue to my lips, scarcely believing what I was about to propose.

'Jono,' I began, 'shall we—'

'Yes, Maggie.' He lowered his face, and his lips brushed mine. 'The answer is yes.'

---

## Brontë's Gap Year

If I'm not tanned by now, I'll be seriously pissed off. I want to be golden and gorgeous when I'm lying on those beaches with Harry. How long will I have been away by now? Six weeks? Two months? Factor fifty on my face and the backs of my hands though. I do not want wrinkles.

So, my itinerary ... I make zero apologies for keeping it loose for Australia. I think it's the right vibe for down under. I haven't even decided how long I'll stay. If I fall in love, maybe I'll stay longer. If I think it's time to move on, I will. Having a plan and being like Mum is great but occasionally I'm going to go with my gut and see where it takes me. Perhaps I'll get sick of cold beers and beaches and bikinis. Or maybe I'll love it so much I'll want to stay forever. Who knows. If I stayed longer, would Harry stay with me, I wonder?

Imagine if Mum and my dad had stayed together and spent their lives by the beach like he said he was going to do. Where would I be now? I'll never know. But I do know that Mum has a certain smile when she talks about that summer when she met my dad. Like she's lit up from inside. I wish she smiled like that all the time. Maybe that should be my mission, to find a place on the planet which lights me up like a firefly too.

## Mum's Gap Year

My darling daughter,

I realised something this morning. A good/bad thing, depending on what sort of mood I'm in.

For the first time in my life there's no one I need to check on, no one reliant on me for money, or support or well-being. There's no reason to keep my phone on during the night, in case you were to end up stranded somewhere and don't know how to get home (remember that train strike in France?), or woke up with food poisoning (the last time you ever ate tinned ravioli). Even for those closest to me, like Auntie Kat, I would only be – at most – the second person they'd call in an emergency.

After you died, I'd only been able to see the negatives in this life of no responsibility. But there are positives, I can see that now. Do I still wish you were here to ring me in the night in a panic? Yes, one hundred per cent. But you never will again, and every so often, I can appreciate the peace which comes from having no one to please except myself. I can be entirely selfish if I want to be without taking anyone else into consideration. Last night I lay in the bath in my hotel for an hour and listened to music, completely relaxed because I knew no one was going to knock on the door and tell me to hurry up because they needed the loo. This morning I watched the sun come up behind the

Opera House, taking photo after photo to make sure I captured the most glorious colours. Later, I sat and listened to a young girl with a guitar and a hauntingly beautiful voice busking near Circular Quay, and her singing brought me to tears. Then I took my Kindle and a blanket from my room and lay in the Botanic Gardens for a couple of hours being blissfully lazy.

The big things are still scary and sad. I'll never get to experience the exquisite sweetness of holding your newborn child – my grandchild – for the first time, or cry tears of joy at your wedding. I've sneaked down on Christmas morning for the last time to take a bite out of the mince pie and carrot you would still religiously set out for Santa and Rudolph. However, doing your gap-year trip has shown me that there's still so much joy to be found in everyday moments.

I've laughed with the Nepalese children as elephants squirted them with water while bathing in the river; I've seen the snow-spangled tops of the Himalayas; and I've made love in a forest lit solely by fire-flies. (I'd never have told you that in person, by the way, but I did and it was amazing and I have zero regrets.)

My heart still aches for you, but I've noticed that my grief isn't linear – I don't wake up expecting that today will be less painful than yesterday. But at least now I don't wake up with dread at having to face another day without you.

Love from
Your healing, tentatively happy, with a boosted ego Mum xxx
P.S. Thank you for putting this trip together, you're incredible xxx

# Chapter 31

**Australia**

'Mums taking a gap year could be the next big thing, Maggie. You're a trendsetter.'

Harry held his phone across the table to show me, scrolling through the comments on the picture he put up of me in the Blue Mountains.

I was touched reading some of the lovely words of encouragement from Harry's followers. 'Gosh, I see what you mean. Look at that one: "Maggie has inspired me to do a solo trip for the first time. Why should my kids have the monopoly on seeing the world?" My little gap year does seem to have captured people's imagination, doesn't it?'

'An inspiration,' Harry said. 'It's true, you are, Maggie. Brontë would be so proud of her mum.'

'She'd be proud of you too, of how well you're dealing with life without her.' We smiled at each other, reflecting on how far we'd both already come. 'Mind you, it took a major life trauma for me to take time out from work. Hopefully all these people commenting won't wait as long. At least I've got the bug now. Once this trip is over, I'll be planning more.'

I told him that Tiff had been in touch, asking if I could go back to Nepal in November to help Meena set up some new adult reading classes. I'd said I would be delighted.

'You should ask some of these mums if they'd like to volunteer,' Harry said. 'There are more than five thousand posts using the Mum's Gap Year hashtag already. Most of them are connected with you.'

'I've been swamped with direct messages on Instagram,' I admitted, stunned by the numbers. 'But I've been too busy with the grape harvest to reply.'

He laughed. 'You're going to need a social media manager now that you're an influencer.'

'Stop it.' I grinned. 'Can you imagine?'

Harry and I had met at Watson's Bay, a short ferry ride from Circular Quay. It had been his suggestion because he was staying with a friend that night who'd got a job at the hotel beside the quay. After a breezy walk around the lighthouse, a fit of immature giggling at a canoodling couple on the nudist beach and a frantic wriggle under a gigantic spider's web crossing our path, we'd arrived back at the quay. Now it was late afternoon and with plates of fish and chips on order, we were sitting at a waterside table at Doyles restaurant, with Sydney's iconic skyline gracing the horizon.

'You look great, by the way,' said Harry, pouring a Coke Zero into a glass. 'Relaxed and happy. You look like Brontë, actually.'

'That's kind of you to say.' I was touched, although I'd always thought that she resembled her father more than me. But perhaps the eye sees what it wants to see.

'The Hunter Valley was good then?'

'Loved it,' I confirmed, taking a sip of my sparkling water. 'I could have stayed longer. Jono asked me to, but I want to see where Brontë was planning to go next.'

'You got on well with him?'

'Jono?' I said with a grin. 'He's a love.'

'Uncle Pete said he's been very bad-tempered since his wife ran off with the Frenchman.'

I'd rung Kat before dawn yesterday morning after Jono had crept out of Creek Cottage and gone back to his house. Before I could say a word, she'd launched straight into a story about Mum and the trouble she was in with a credit card company. To get her attention I'd had to resort to yelling that I'd just had amazing sex with a hot Australian. The whole of Honeybourne probably heard her shrieks of excitement. It had only been a brief chat; Sam had come into the room in search of a snack and interrupted us.

'He isn't grumpy anymore,' I said coyly. 'Jono and I got on very well. Very well indeed.'

'Good.' Harry nodded enthusiastically. After a beat the penny dropped and he blinked hard. 'Oh, right. I see. *Good!*'

'So, thanks for suggesting spending time at Ruby Creek. It worked out very well – for everyone.'

'Well, gosh,' he stammered, clearly stuck for a suitable response. 'I'm pleased for you.'

'And what about you?' I gave him a questioning look. 'You and I had an agreement that we are going to be receptive to love, not rule it out forever. Not that what Jono and I shared was motivated by love; it was pure lust. But we enjoyed each other, if you know what I mean, and it's given me the confidence to think that one day . . .'

Harry choked on his fizzy drink and his glass clunked down on the table.

'Sorry, too much info,' I said, laughing. 'What I'm saying is that I've kept my end of the deal. How about you?'

'Well, you win, progress-wise. I've downloaded a couple of dating apps and I've been talking to a few girls. You met one of them, actually.'

I raised an eyebrow. 'Oh?'

'The waitress in the café in Leura.' He cleared his throat, and I noticed a slight blush to his face. 'Lola.'

'I remember her!' I'd thought I'd sensed a spark between them. 'She's lovely.'

He shrugged. 'I'm not sure. We'll see.'

'Baby steps,' I patted his arm. 'But steps all the same.'

Our food arrived and for the next few minutes we busied ourselves with condiments and more drinks and Harry taking photos of our plates with the picturesque bay as a backdrop.

'I've been thinking about work,' said Harry, once our plates had been cleared away. 'And what I might want to do for a career.'

'Go on.' I nodded encouragingly.

He told me that he'd been looking into courses back in the UK, and that he was thinking of training to be a counsellor. That the popularity of his Instagram posts had made him realise how many people out there were hurting and how much he felt drawn to help them through their trauma. He'd also been contacted to appear as a guest speaker on a couple of high-profile podcasts.

I was impressed with the way he was getting his life together, and told him so.

'Do you mind?' he asked warily.

'Why would I?' I gave him a blank look.

He shifted in his seat. 'Because none of this would have occurred to me if Brontë hadn't died. Sometimes I worry that I'm somehow profiting from losing my girlfriend.'

'Oh, love.' I covered my hand with his. 'No one could ever accuse you of that. The truth is that life does go on. We have both been changed by losing her. The things we took for granted have gone, the goalposts have shifted. In fact, I don't even know where my goalposts are any more. But I do know that my future will always be shaped by the absence of my daughter. If a path is emerging for you from what you have experienced, embrace it.'

He smiled with evident relief. 'Thanks. It feels good to be doing something positive. Like it's given me a purpose.'

'That's what I need,' I said wistfully. 'A new sense of purpose. Following Brontë's itinerary has given me one for the time being. But soon I'll get to the last page and then what?'

'Create your own?' suggested Harry. 'Now you've got the travel bug, what's to stop you planning the sort of itinerary she did? You've just said Nepal is on the cards for winter.'

He got up from the table to find the bathroom, leaving me to think that through. 'There's more to life than work, Mum,' Brontë had said during our last conversation. She would hardly recognise this version of her mother. I'd barely thought about work at all since the day I talked George out of resigning. I'd had one text from him saying that Anna and her family had gone on a skiing holiday and bumped into Lee and his family and they had come back best buddies – but nothing else. That had shaken me a bit, if I was honest. Anna had always been my friend. Not that she wasn't allowed to have more than one friend, obviously. But I supposed I'd been relying on our bond to help strengthen my route to the boardroom. Now that Lee had established himself as her friend too, that link no longer seemed so secure.

My Honeybourne life seemed so far away now, inhabited by a sepia version of me, a woman living half an existence. The idea of spending every day at a desk only to go home, eat, sleep and repeat, felt so alien that I wondered how I'd cope when the day came to don smart clothes and proper shoes and head to the office. I smiled to myself, recalling that this was exactly what I'd predicted for Brontë. That she'd get a taste for travelling and not want to come home. Would it have been so bad if that had happened to her? Or *did* happen to me?

I shrugged off the notion. Of course I'd be going back to work, I had bills to pay, a pension to build. But the woman who'd be stepping back into her career was going to be setting boundaries. Emails received at the end of the work day would go unanswered, annual leave would be taken; no letting it roll over to the next year. There was a world out there, and I was going to explore it while I had the chance.

Once Harry returned, we settled the bill and gathered our things. The next ferry to Circular Quay wasn't for another half an hour, so we took a stroll along the beach and ogled the beautiful properties lining the shore.

'Listen, there's something I'd like to do while I'm here with you, if you don't mind.' I reached into my bag and took out the small pot of Brontë's ashes I'd brought from home. I told him the story of sprinkling some of them at the temple in Nepal and that I wanted to do the same here.

'I'd like that,' he said. 'Let's do it.'

Together we walked to the edge and each took a pinch of the ashes.

'I miss you, darling,' I whispered under my breath as I flung the ashes out into the water. 'Thank you for bringing me here; thank you for bringing Harry into my life. I love you.'

I glanced sideways at Harry as he did the same. He wasn't speaking but there were tears in his eyes. After a few minutes, I tucked my arm through his and we continued walking for a while before sitting down on the shingle beach. His legs were dotted with old scars. Brontë always used to say that he could trip over his own shadow. Now both of us had scars, although the new ones weren't on our skin, but on our hearts.

'You're going to be okay, you know,' I told him, bumping my arm against his.

'So are you.' He grinned shyly. 'Maybe I can come and see you when we're both back at home.'

'You must. Any time. I'll hold you to that,' I replied.

He and I shared a deep connection now. I got him and he got me.

'Any tips you can give me for my next Instagram post?' he asked, getting his phone out. 'I thought I'd use these pictures.'

He showed me a selection of the photographs from our day together. The lighthouse; the rocks; a hazy one of me smiling, with the sun a golden halo behind my head, that I liked so much I got him to send it to me.

'What sort of tips?'

He shrugged. 'Whatever comes to mind. Life after loss, maybe? Taking a gap-year trip when you're—'

'Old?' I shot him a teasing look.

'Sorry. More mature?'

'Better. Okay, what about this,' I suggested. 'Things I've learned about grief.'

'Good shout.' Harry opened the voice recorder on his phone and I started to talk.

'Grief is a lonely place. However much your friends and family want to share that burden, no one can carry it for you. Grief is utterly unique. You and I have lost the same person, but we'll grieve at different times and in different ways. I've realised that love is forever; Brontë may not be here where I can see her, but she remains as loved as she always was. I will be her mother for eternity. Lastly, don't make the mistake I made for so long and lock your grief for your loved one away. Tell their stories, say their name, celebrate the good times, remember what they gave you. Grief will be a part of your life forever, but so will love.'

'That was amazing. You're amazing.' He scrubbed the tears from his face roughly and gave a self-deprecating laugh. 'And I'm such an idiot.'

The ferry was pulling up to the quay. We hugged and said our goodbyes, renewing our promises to keep in touch, and I watched him lope away.

Within an hour I was back at my hotel. I made a cup of tea and prepared myself to read the next entry in Brontë's itinerary. It was time to find out where I was going next. I pulled my backpack onto my lap and looked inside. The book wasn't there.

I checked again, searching in every pocket, every compartment.

*Shit, shit.* Where was it? It had to be here somewhere. It couldn't simply vanish.

I was ninety-nine per cent sure that I'd taken it out with me this morning. It went everywhere with me because it was too big for the tiny hotel safe. I'd blithely thought that it would be secure with me. How wrong I was.

The third search of my backpack was fruitless, so I searched my room, checking all the places it might be: the nightstand, the bathroom, my suitcase. I stripped the sheets off the bed, got down on my hands and knees and looked under the bed. My throat felt tight and I was having to hold back my tears of frustration. I checked the backpack again, this time tipping the contents on the floor, becoming increasingly frantic.

My mind skipped back across the hours of the day. I'd seen it in my room this morning because I'd finally peeked at the inside back cover and looked at the weather wheel Harry had told me about. I'd smiled with delight at the spinning cardboard wheel she'd made of the continents and their wet and dry seasons.

The coffee shop, I recalled with a surge of fear. I'd stopped to get a coffee before boarding the ferry and it had definitely been in my backpack then. I was certain of that because I'd spilled my flat white and had seen the book when I'd reached into my bag for a tissue.

So where was it now? *Think, Maggie, think!* It could be anywhere between here and Watson's Bay. Did someone steal it? Surely not. Could I have dropped it in the water getting on or off the ferry?

Possibly. It had been quite a step; there'd been a man there at the quay giving smaller people a hand. The idea that her beautiful book had dropped into the ocean didn't bear thinking about.

For the next few minutes, I was gripped by panic, unable to think straight or do anything sensible.

Finally, my brain kicked in and I called Harry.

'Harry, something terrible has happened,' I blurted out.

'Maggie? What is it? Are you okay?'

'No. I've lost Brontë's book,' I sobbed. 'I had it when I left the hotel this morning and it's gone. I don't know what to do.'

'Oh no. Where did you last see it?' There were voices in the background and music playing and Harry had to shout to make himself heard.

'This morning in Sydney before catching the ferry to meet you. After that, I'm not sure if it was still in my bag or not.'

'Right. There's a good chance you dropped it somewhere at Watson's Bay. I'm still here at the bar,' he said. 'I'll retrace our steps; it's got to be somewhere.'

'But what if we don't find it?' I wailed. 'What am I going to do then?'

'Try not to panic. And keep on looking at your end.'

'I'm already panicking, I've searched everywhere in my room. More than once.'

'I'll get my mate to help me. We'll set off now and we won't stop until we're sure we've checked everywhere.'

'Thank you, Harry,' I said tearily.

He ended the call and I sank down onto the floor and cried tears of guilt and frustration. My most precious possession. Brontë's book, her words, her thoughts, her plans. Brontë's trip and now mine too. All gone.

# Chapter 32

## Australia

It was three hours before I heard from Harry again.

'Please say you've found it,' I said shakily.

I was all cried out by then, exhausted and angry with myself. I'd been down to reception and checked with housekeeping to see if it had been collected with the used linen, and I'd even been to the lost property at Circular Quay in case I'd left it on board one of the ferries, but no luck.

'I wish I could,' said a weary-sounding Harry. 'But we've searched as much of Watson's Bay as we could before it got dark, and there was no sign of it.'

'Oh God, no.' I couldn't believe this was happening. How stupid of me.

'Hey, don't worry. I'll have another look in the morning,' Harry said optimistically. 'Don't give up yet.'

'Thank you for trying.' I reached for a tissue and blew my nose. 'I do appreciate it.'

'No problem,' he said. 'We've left messages at the hotels and restaurants, and if I hear anything I'll let you know straight away.'

'How could I have been so careless?'

'You weren't careless,' he insisted. 'Sometimes accidents happen. Don't beat yourself up about it.'

'I don't know what I'll do if we can't find it,' I said.

'Maybe this is your sign to go home,' Harry suggested. 'You've been away a long time.'

That made me sit up straighter. I gripped the phone.

'No. I'm not ready,' I told him firmly. 'I don't want to leave yet, Brontë's journey can't be over. Not while I know she still had pages left for me to read.'

Harry remained silent on the other end of the line. I wondered what was going through his mind. It was different for him, I thought. He could travel for as long as he liked, should he so wish. I had responsibilities to get back to. This was my one chance, possibly the longest break from the rat race I'd ever get until I retired. I had to make the most of my sabbatical; and more than that, I had to keep following in Brontë's footsteps and take the journey that she'd been so determined to take for herself.

'But let's say you don't find her book,' Harry said finally. 'You won't have much choice.'

He had a point. Except . . . I had a sudden flash of inspiration. Hadn't Harry said he'd helped Brontë with her research?

'You know!' I said. 'You know where she was going next.'

'Um. I . . . Well, I guess . . .' Harry's voice faltered down the line. 'I'm not sure I've got the details.'

'Can't you look on your laptop?' I pleaded. 'You must have some idea.'

He let out a long sigh. 'Honestly, Maggie, I'd rather not.'

'But why?' I cried, frustrated. 'Come on, Harry, you know how important this is to me, why don't you want me to know?'

'Okay, okay,' he retorted. 'Hold on. Let me think.'

I chewed my lip, not really understanding why he was so reluctant.

'I do know the next destination,' he said gently. 'It's actually her last one, but—'

'Yes! Fantastic! I could kiss you,' I gasped. 'Where is it?'

'It's somewhere she was always fascinated with,' he began.

I racked my brains. 'She was obsessed with the giant turtles in the Galapagos Islands for a while. Is that it? Or Los Angeles? She wanted to see for herself if every waiter really was an actor waiting to be discovered.'

'Neither of those,' said Harry.

I detected a smile in his voice; he must have heard her talk about both those places too.

'So?' I prompted. 'Where is it?'

'Bali,' he replied simply. 'She planned to go to Bali.'

I stared at the phone, speechless. Of course she'd want to go to Bali. I pressed a hand to my chest as emotion hit me in waves. 'I want my Bali moment,' she'd told me. And quite literally, she had planned to have it. My life had changed beyond recognition since I'd last been there – I was a different person now and I couldn't imagine how I'd feel to be there again. But it looked as if I'd be finding out very soon because, courtesy of my daughter, I was going back to Bali where it had all begun.

# Chapter 33

## Bali

The hotel porter glided along the corridor ahead of me, showed me into my room and bowed.

'We hope you enjoy your stay, Miss Maggie,' he said, handing me the key.

'Thank you. I'm sure I will.' I shut the door behind me and sank onto my bed, relieved that my long journey was over. I closed my eyes for a moment, allowing the softness of the bed to work its magic on my weary body.

I had travelled to Bali without Brontë's book, and this part of my trip already felt lonelier because I didn't have her to guide me.

I'd landed in Bali a couple of hours ago and had taken a taxi from the airport to the town of Ubud. We'd driven around the outskirts of Denpasar, Bali's biggest city, through villages populated by houses so ornate that they could have been mistaken for temples, past roadside stalls piled high with watermelons and papaya, and kiosks selling roasted cobs of corn. As we travelled further inland, the landscape gave way to tropical forest, green fields and neatly sculpted rice terraces. There were signs for waterfalls and temples and monkey sanctuaries, with the summit of Mount Batur ever present on the skyline. The country had changed in the two decades since my last visit. There was more traffic, more people, more development. But its beauty was as dazzling as ever.

Subconsciously, I knew I was fortunate to be here. Some people would never get the chance to experience such an incredible place. But I was so angry with myself. I couldn't stop thinking about how I careless I'd been with Brontë's precious book. I'd been torturing myself with trying to remember where I'd last seen it and at what point in the day I could have mislaid it.

It had been so much more than an itinerary. It had become a talisman, a piece of her, every page imprinted with her DNA. It was my last link to her, a way of staying connected. Her presence in book form had cast a golden light over my time in Nepal and Australia, and without her some of the joy of my trip had slipped away.

Now I was here in the last destination. Bali. The place where Jackson and I had met and fallen in love. Where Brontë was conceived. I wanted her with me more than I'd ever done before, and it felt like I had lost her for a second time.

I knew of Brontë's vague plans for the first few days: Harry had been able to tell me that. But no details. He said he knew other things too and would share those when I was ready. I wasn't. In my heart I knew Brontë's book was gone for good, but miracles did happen and in case one happened for me, and her precious book was found, I wanted to be able to turn the last pages, read the words written by my daughter and take the final steps of the journey with her. Because I had a feeling that I knew exactly where she would be drawn to.

I'd always been open with her about how she'd come into the world. I'd told her so much about my month doing turtle conservation that she'd known almost as many facts about releasing turtles into the wild as I did. But what had captured her imagination most was her parents' love story. How we'd fallen under each other's spell – both too young to make a solid commitment at the time, but with a love so strong it had stayed with me for a lifetime.

From time to time, she'd asked me to take her and show her the Bali I'd spoken so fondly of. And, stupidly, I'd put her off, making excuses about money and not being able to take too long off work. But the truth was that I'd been scared to revisit the place I'd been truly happy, in case it didn't live up to my memories. How short-sighted I had been. Even if my memories were viewed through rose-tinted glasses, I'd still have enjoyed showing Bali to Brontë. I'd missed my chance. If one thing else came out of this trip, it was that if another opportunity for happiness should ever cross my path I'd embrace it with open arms.

For the next few days, I had very little planned. It had been non-stop in Australia, and I needed some time to catch my breath and process what had happened. I was staying in the Adiwana Hotel, a restful oasis in the centre of bustling Ubud. Brontë's own choice had been an Airbnb. I'd looked it up online and it was lovely, tranquil and private with a view of the river and the rice fields. But now was not the time for solitude. I couldn't remember a time when I'd felt as lonely. I needed to have people around me. I was craving company, even that of strangers.

I got off the bed and explored my room, trailing my fingers over the crisp white bedsheets, the fluffy pile of towels. The bed itself was vast. Two cotton robes hung side by side on the back of the door. There was a vase of fresh flowers, a wooden bowl filled with fruit and a selection of snacks beside a fancy coffee machine. It was gorgeous. I only wished I had someone to share it with.

I walked to the end of the room and slid open a wide glass door. My patio was shaded by tall palm trees and led directly into fragrant gardens lush with hostas and ferns and other plants I didn't recognise. Through the greenery, I glimpsed a sparkling blue swimming pool, surrounded by sunloungers and deserted except for a woman floating in an inflatable ring, and a sunburned man asleep on a bed with a paperback over his face, the front of his shins and arms the colour of strawberry ice cream.

The water looked so inviting that within a couple of minutes I had slathered myself in sunscreen, changed into my bikini, and taken one of the towels plus my phone down to the pool.

The water felt delicious against my skin, cool enough to revive me, but warm enough not to shock my lungs. I dipped down under the surface and swam, enjoying the stretch in my legs and the pull across my shoulders after the seven-hour flight.

When I reached the wall I came up for air. It was an infinity pool and once I'd brushed the water from my face, I leaned over the edge and looked down into the tropical green valley below.

'Isn't it awesome?' said an American voice.

I flipped onto my back. The woman in the ring was swimming my way.

'Perfect.' I smiled, glad for the opportunity to talk, hoping it would distract me from my thoughts. So far today, the sum total of my conversation had been brief exchanges with cabin crew, taxi drivers and hotel staff. Not even Kat had responded to the voicemail of woe I'd sent her last night.

'I'm Barb. That's my husband Stanley over there, passed out. Poor chick got up early with me this morning to do yoga and now he can't stay awake.' She laughed, cherry-red lips parting to reveal large white teeth. She wore a long-sleeved rash vest and shorts and most of her face was hidden by oversized sunglasses. I guessed she was in her sixties.

'He looks very relaxed,' I said, wondering whether to mention his sunburn. 'I'm Maggie.'

Barb glanced over to the sunlounger where I'd left my folded towel. 'Travelling by yourself?'

'I wish I wasn't but yes, I am.' I suppressed a sigh.

'Oh honey, that's sad.'

'I should have come with my daughter while I had the chance. She wanted to, but it would have been an expensive trip.'

Even as the words were leaving my mouth, I was aware how ridiculous my priorities had been for so much of my life. What good was money or a successful career now?

Barb nodded. 'And now she's all grown and too busy to come along with her mom, huh? On holiday, or are you one of the health nuts, here to "detox"?'

'She was almost grown-up. I mean, twenty-three is still a baby adult, right?' I kept eye contact with her. I needed to talk about Brontë. If I didn't have her book to keep her memories alive then speaking about her would have to do instead. 'She passed away last year. I'm taking some time out to get over her death. Or rather, get through it; I don't think I'll ever get over it. I'm calling it Mum's Gap Year.' My words had come out in a rush and I could see that I'd startled Barb.

After a moment, she flipped herself off the inflatable ring, paddled her way to me and enveloped me in a hug. I thought back to what Daisy had said, that sometimes you needed a hug from your mum. My mum hadn't been the huggy type, but I loved hugs, both giving and receiving. Even when they were off bosomy wet strangers.

'You're awesome,' she said, placing her hands on my shoulders.

'I don't feel awesome,' I told her.

'Get outta here!' she protested, shoving my arm. 'Oh look, here comes Indra for our cocktail order. Will Long Island Tea do you?'

'Oh, sure.' I didn't think I'd have much choice in the matter either way.

A young woman with shiny hair and a yellow flower tucked behind her ear approached the edge of the pool. 'Miss Barb, you would like a drink?'

Barb ordered our drinks and a pot of tea for the sleeping Stanley to be put on her tab. Indra returned almost immediately with a tray and Barb and I moved to the shallow steps to sip our cocktails.

'I'm not a mom,' said Barb. 'Stanley and I weren't blessed, but I sure am in need of a gap year. I was caring for my mom for years, until she died last fall, and now Stanley's dad has dementia and he's had to move in with us. I think I've shrunk two inches from tensing up so much. My sister is looking after him while we're on vacation. We go home tomorrow. Goodness knows when we'll get away again.'

'That sounds tough, I'm sorry,' I said, stirring my drink with the fruit from the side of the glass. 'And you certainly don't need to be a mom to deserve a break. Perhaps I mean taking time out, putting yourself first, no responsibilities, no expectations. Lots of adult women care for others, but who cares for them?'

'I hear ya,' said Barb, chinking her glass against mine. 'We could all do with a little mothering now and again.'

'Will someone answer that goddamn phone!' yelled a voice.

Barb's sun-wizened husband pushed himself up onto his elbows and was scowling in our direction.

'It must be mine.' I levered myself out of the water and hurried to my sunlounger.

I'd had several missed calls from a number I hadn't seen for a long time. My shoulders tensed automatically.

'Hello Mum?' I wrapped the towel around my waist as I answered.

'Maggie, at last! I've been trying you for ages.'

'I was in the pool,' I said, calmly. 'I didn't hear the phone.'

She harrumphed. 'All right for some.'

'Did you call for a specific reason, Mum, or just to wind me up?' I perched on the end of my sunlounger and sipped my ice tea, doggedly keeping my temper.

'I know you're having a lovely long holiday but I'm afraid I need you to come back and help me. I'm in a bit of a mess and there's no one else I can ask.'

'What do you mean, a mess?' She was my mother and, regardless of our past history, of course I'd help her if she really needed me to.

'I kept putting it off and putting it off and by the time I made an appointment the situation was too far gone.'

'Oh Mum.' I set my drink down on the table beside me and pressed a hand to my chest. 'I'm so sorry.'

So she was ill. I felt awful for being so brusque, for not taking her calls or making an effort. And now it looked as if I might have left it too late.

'Thank you. I've been trying to tell you about it, but you wouldn't engage with me.'

'I know, I know, I should have listened.' I closed my eyes and shook my head sadly. When would I learn to tune into those around me and be there for them when they needed it? Maybe it wasn't too late with Mum. Maybe I could make amends.

'How are you feeling?' I asked gently.

'Wretched. Annoyed with myself. Hopeless.' She sounded very down, and my heart went out to her.

'Have you told Kat?'

'God, no!' Mum replied. 'She'll only worry, and she's been busy with Sam anyway, he hasn't been well. High temperature and whatnot, you know how kids are. I'm keeping well away if he's got the lurgy.'

Poor Sam. I pricked my ears up; this was the first I'd heard of it. I'd send Kat a message immediately to check up on him.

Probably wise of Mum to keep away though, if her immune system was already vulnerable.

'Do you want to talk about it, Mum?' I probed. 'Your situation, I mean. I won't push you on the details, if you'd rather not.'

'There's no need to rake it all up. The question is, could you come home and help me make arrangements?'

Did she mean as in final arrangements, a funeral, last wishes, and so on? The thought of another funeral sent waves of dread through me. This was a lot more serious than I realised. 'Of course I will, Mum. Of course.'

'Thank you, Magnolia, I knew I could rely on you. Eventually. And I'm sure you must have a fair sum saved by now.'

I was confused. What had money got to do with it? Not to pay for a funeral service, surely. It had to be because there was some sort of private treatment available, I realised. I didn't have unlimited funds, but I'd do what I could, obviously. 'Anything your doctor thinks might help is definitely worth considering.'

'Doctor?' She gave an exasperated huff. 'What are you talking about?'

'Well, if you're ill then—'

'I'm not ill, for heaven's sake,' she snapped. 'I'm in a financial muddle, that's all. My lovely new car has been repossessed and I've got into arrears with the rent. I can't bear the thought of eviction at my age, so if you could—'

My jaw dropped in disbelief. Unbelievable. She wasn't at death's door, she wasn't even ill. No, she was simply repeating her bad habits from decades ago. Ignoring demands for payment of bills until finally the control was taken out of her hands. I was incensed, and annoyed with myself for almost being taken in again and coming to her rescue.

'No.'

I could almost hear my mother's shock. 'Pardon?'

'No, I'm not coming back. The last time I was in Bali I had to leave early to look after Kat because you'd messed up. This time, you can sort yourself out. You can face your own problems. Because God knows it's about time you did. And as for little Sam – he's your grandson, go over there and help Kat out. You never get enough sleep when your kids are ill.'

'Ha!' my mother retorted. 'Always back to this. Change the record, Magnolia. You love pointing out my faults, don't you? You weren't always perfect either. I knew all about Brontë's gap-year plans long before you. She confided things in me that she probably never told you.'

How could she? I was seething with rage. 'And what did you confide in her, that you told me to get rid of her when I was pregnant? That you wanted her dead? Well, you got your wish: she *is* dead. She's dead and it isn't fair. She was the centre of my world. I barely scratched the surface of yours. I wish it had been you, Mum. I wish it had been you who died instead of her.'

My heart thundered against my ribs as the awful words poured out of me. Years of resentment, disappointment, and a longing to be mothered – they were no longer prepared to remain hidden.

The heavy silence on the other end was replaced by the dialling tone. She'd hung up on me. I turned to see Barb and Stanley staring at me in horror. And no wonder. I picked up my things and strode back to my room, sending Kat a message about Sam as I walked. I didn't want to be here; in fact I wasn't sure I wanted to be anywhere. I drew the curtains and lay on my bed in the dark, willing the earth to swallow me up. I had to have hit rock bottom. There couldn't possibly be anywhere lower to fall.

## Mum's Gap Year

My darling Brontë,

It's day two in Bali and other than some walking around Ubud to explore, I've been very lazy. And gosh, it has felt good to relax and slow down for a while. I have got a trip planned tomorrow, though, so don't think that I'm not making the most of being in such a beautiful place.

I don't mind admitting that I've been feeling low since losing your itinerary, so I thought I'd cheer myself up this afternoon by writing to you.

I know that you'll never read this letter, but it does my heart good to share my thoughts and feelings with you. I can't explain how; all I know is that this keeps us connected, and the bond we have is as close as it ever was. I've been thinking a lot about the diary I kept when I was in Bali last time. I didn't know it then, but I was recording the events which brought you into my world. Now here I am again. The wheel of life has turned, and you are gone. Being here has brought the memories flooding back. My head is full, and my heart is sore, and I can't not write things down. I'm so, so sad that I don't have your book to write in. For now, a few sheets of hotel note-paper will have to do.

First things first. Sam's fine. Auntie Kat says it was the scariest thing she's ever been through when Sam's temperature spiked, and they had to rush him into hospital. But it was only a virus and once they'd dosed him up, he started to improve. I've spoken to him on FaceTime and he was his perky little self already. Thank goodness.

Unfortunately, I probably can't say the same of my relationship with your gran. It wasn't strong to begin with and now it might be over for good.

My pen usually scribbles like crazy, but I'm struggling to put these words on paper. That's because if you were in front of me, I'd be too ashamed to tell you about the row we had on the phone.

I said some terrible things. Only a monster would wish another person dead, and it's even worse if that person is your mother.

Something's holding me back from making the apology. This time she pushed me too far. I know what I said was bad, but I'm not ready to say sorry and I guess Gran isn't either because she hasn't called since. I've spoken to Auntie Kat again and she didn't mention our row, which means she doesn't know about it. But she did say that Gran had offered to do some shopping for her while Sam was ill if it would help. Which is progress.

I would have gone home for Gran if she'd really needed my help, but I'm glad I don't have to yet. Now I'm in Bali, there are places I want to go. I wish I had your book to see where you had planned to visit, but I think I can guess which places would have been of interest to you.

Following your path across the world has given me a purpose at a time when I was feeling lost. I'm scared of taking the final few steps you've set out for me, because I don't know what will happen once your journey ends and mine has to continue alone. It's almost time to face the future without you, so please forgive me if I slow down while I take these final steps. Wish me luck, my darling

All my love
Mum xx

# Chapter 34

## Bali

I leaned on a wall beneath a crumbling archway, angling my body to get as much of myself into the shade as possible. Far below was the sea, a constant muffled roar, crashing onto the rocky cliffs. In front was a set of ancient stone steps leading down into a fountain surrounded by gardens. Directly opposite on the balustrade was a lone monkey, tucking into a mango while staring at me, occasionally pulling his lips back to reveal long yellowed teeth. There were signs everywhere warning visitors to the Uluwatu temple to keep shiny objects hidden from the monkeys; they were such dreadful pickpockets that staff kept catapults and long sticks handy to protect unsuspecting tourists. I had a scarf covering my shoulders and backpack, and although I had my phone out, I was keeping a tight hold of it.

It wasn't the ideal spot to take a Zoom call from my employer, but the message I'd received earlier had stressed the importance of the meeting and this was the only place at the temple that I'd been able to get a phone signal.

I had a couple of minutes spare, so I scrolled to my saved messages and replayed the voicemail I'd woken up to from Jono.

'I've heard you're in Bali. It's all right for some! Daisy saw your update on Instagram, and that you've lost your daughter's book. I know how important it is to you and I hope you're okay. You never know, it might turn up; it's got to be somewhere. But if it doesn't, don't let it ruin your trip by beating yourself up. You can still have a good time. Bali is a great place; I went with a bunch of mates years ago. Head down to Uluwatu and visit the temple. There's a spirituality to the place that I think will appeal to you.

'If you're into surfing, go to Canggu – the waves are enormous. In fact, go anyway, even if you're not. It's fun to watch the surfers, and every other café is owned by an Aussie, so the coffee is great. Daisy says hi and Max misses you. He goes to Creek Cottage every morning to look for you. I've told him you're not coming back yet, but we can always hope.'

There was a pause down the line.

'To be honest, I miss you too. There's a Maggie-shaped hole at Ruby Creek, so if you get fed up with beach life in Bali, I'd love to have you back. Anyway, something to think about. Enjoy the rest of your trip and don't forget us.'

Listening to his voice made me smile again. His suggestion to come to Uluwatu was a good one. I had booked a driver for the day who'd brought me here and was waiting outside the temple to take me back afterwards. I'd arrived early and had had the place almost to myself, wandering along quiet paths dressed in the sarong I'd been given, planning my next move. Jono was a good man and I'd enjoyed our fling, but Australia was a long way from home. Besides, there was still unfinished business with his ex-wife. So, I wouldn't be going back, but it felt good to be wanted.

Right on cue, my phone screen kicked into action and my boss started the meeting.

'Hi, Anna. How's things?' I took my sunglasses off so I could see the screen better.

She was sitting in the boardroom, a coffee mug in her hand. She looked pale and there was something about her posture which hinted at weariness and set my alarm bells ringing. Something wasn't right.

'Look at you, all tanned and relaxed. Australia suits you,' she said. 'I'm very envious. We were skiing a couple of weeks ago and I don't think the temperature rose above zero the entire time.'

No mention of bumping into Lee Masters and his family, I noticed. I didn't let on that I knew about it, in case it caused problems for George, but it did strike me as odd that she hadn't told me. Perhaps I was reading too much into it, but it was unsettling. For the first time since being away from the office, I felt nervous about my standing within the company. This call, whatever it was about, was a chance for me to demonstrate to Anna that she'd be right to recommend me for a place on the board when I returned.

'Thanks. I'm in Bali now. Australia was so last week.' I gave an exaggerated flutter of my eyelashes, making her smile. 'Although I'm not relaxed. I've been worried ever since I got your message. Is everything okay?'

Before Anna had time to answer, her dad took a seat beside her.

'Maggie, hi,' Ron Swift said with a faint smile. 'Nice to see you taking some time for yourself after the year you've had. I'm sure it's given you a new perspective on life. Good decision.'

'It was Anna who suggested I take a sabbatical,' I said, realising too late that I'd probably just reminded them about the keys in the canal incident. 'But travel certainly broadens the mind.'

Ron nodded. 'Wendy and I are planning on doing the same; we're going on a cruise. Got to make the most of what time she's got left.'

His voice cracked and he looked at his daughter for support. I frowned. The last time I'd seen Wendy Swift was when she'd popped into the office with mince pies in December. She'd been fine then as far as I'd known, and we'd had a quiet chat about Brontë.

'Mum's had some bad news.' Anna pressed a tissue to her eyes. 'Health-wise.'

'Oh no, I'm so sorry.' My heart sank. This was so unfair. 'Please give her my love.'

Anna's mum was the antithesis of mine: a stay-at-home wife who had been the heart of the home, always on hand with a cuddle or a kiss for a grazed knee. Endless ideas for rainy-day activities. And since Anna's son was born, a willing babysitter.

'No need to go into details,' said Ron, rubbing his daughter's shoulder. 'Suffice to say that my priorities have changed, and I've brought forward my retirement date to be with Wendy. Wanted to tell you myself.'

'Of course,' I nodded. 'Family comes first, always.'

'It does. Right, best get on. I'll leave the rest with Anna.'

We said our goodbyes and Ron got up and disappeared from view.

'Oh Anna,' I said heavily once we were alone.

'I know. It's awful.' She stared down at the tissue in her hands. 'Look, can we stick to work stuff or I'll be more of a mess than I already am?'

'Sure.' I understood the need to remain professional even when your heart was breaking.

'I'm stepping up to the role of chairperson with immediate effect,' she told me.

Poor Anna. She'd worked so hard to prove herself at ShopSwift so that no one would resent her eventual elevation to the top job. It had been a role she'd long been looking forward to: the chance to take her father's company to even greater heights. Now her promotion would be tinged with regret that it had come at a price. Poor Ron too. He had been talking for years about his impending retirement and how Wendy was looking forward to having him at home. This would be a big blow to all the family.

'You can count on me to support you as much as I can,' I said. 'Under the circumstances, you'll want me to cancel my sabbatical and return to the office as soon as possible.'

'There's no need for that.' Anna held her hands up. 'You've given a lot to this company over the years. I have been going back over the personnel files. Your record is incredible, Maggie. No sickness, never more than five consecutive days' annual leave and only a short stint of compassionate leave when Brontë passed away. No, you deserve this break, I won't hear of you cutting it short.'

Her comment worried me. Why would she have been checking my file? 'But a decision will have to be made about your replacement?'

'Dad and I have been thinking about restructuring,' said Anna with a tight smile, skirting past my question.

'Oh?' That was a word which struck fear into a senior manager's heart. It was normally accompanied by the word *redundancy*.

She nodded. 'I'm going to be introducing a new training and mentoring strand to the business. You excel at bringing on new talent, and you're brilliant with people, so I thought you'd be a great choice to lead it. Senior manager initially, with potential to join the board in the future. Dad has already approved it.'

One phrase stood out: in the future. How many times had I been promised a seat on the board? And now the goalposts were shifting again.

'I've trained staff for my sales team, yes,' I said calmly. 'Sales is where I excel, not training.'

My boss leaned forward on her elbows, her gaze firm. 'I want a strong and united team in place to take the company forward with me, Maggie. I hope I can count on you.'

'What about my shot at the job of sales director?' My voice trembled with frustration. Was I being sidelined? 'Anna, what's going on?'

'Lee is going to be heading up sales. He's done a terrific job and the profits in his division confirm that. We think it makes sense to streamline and so rather than having two divisions, yours and his, he'll be absorbing your team and your clients.'

I stiffened. 'My division has always been profitable, offering him the job on that basis doesn't stack up. You said you'd support my application for a promotion to the board.' I could hear the hurt in my voice as it climbed an octave. I'd trusted her; she was supposed to be my friend. 'It was a condition of me taking the time off in the first place. You aren't even giving me a chance.'

'Mum's illness has come out of the blue and it's changed everything.' Anna winced guiltily. 'We have had to make some difficult decisions. Lee is a steady pair of hands, a family man—'

'A family man?' I gave a shocked laugh. 'I'm being penalised for my lack of relatives now?'

'No, no, no!' Anna's eyes widened and then she covered her face with her hands. 'That wasn't what I meant. I'm sorry, Maggie. I take that back. Everyone has equal opportunities at ShopSwift, I hope you know that.'

'It doesn't look like that to me,' I replied.

Anna sighed heavily. 'I'm saying all the wrong things. My brain is in overdrive, I'm not sleeping because I'm so worried about Mum.'

'Don't worry, I'm not going to sue you over it,' I said flatly. 'I value our friendship too much for that.'

'Thank you.' She looked sheepish. Promotion should be awarded on merit, not friendship, but even so, she clearly knew she'd let me down. 'As Dad said, there's no need to rush back. He's doing a quick handover while Lee deputises for me. You can set up the new strand as and when you return.'

The phrase *as and when* didn't fill me with confidence. This new department felt as if it had been manufactured simply to find a role for me.

'Thank you very much,' I replied, unable to keep the petulance from my voice.

Her eyes lit up with gratitude. 'So you'll accept the restructure?'

'Of course,' I said, faking a smile. What else could I do? I needed a job to go back to and it looked like I didn't have much choice.

'Thank you, Maggie.' Anna's shoulders slumped with relief. 'I hope you know that you are very valued here and I'm looking forward to working with you when you return.'

'Likewise,' I replied, tightly. 'And do give my very best wishes to your mum.'

After we ended the call, I sat there, stunned, phone in my hand. I could barely believe what had happened, and what I'd agreed to, but I certainly didn't feel 'valued'.

An ear-piercing screech, followed by a tug on my hair, made me leap out of my skin. With a flash of teeth and the stench of foul breath, the monkey grabbed hold of my scarf and tugged it off my back.

'Get off me!' I yelled, pushing myself away from the wall. I tripped, one foot twisted out of my flip-flop, and my phone flew out of my hand. Another monkey appeared so fast that I didn't even have the chance to react. It pounced on my flip-flop and hissed at me.

'Yah,' I shouted, swinging my backpack at it. 'Give me that back.'

It bared its teeth, and the thought of those yellow fangs sinking into my skin made me back away. Instead I put my foot on my phone and tried to slide it towards me.

'Okay, fine, take the shoe, but you're not having this.'

A flash of pink caught my eye, and I looked up. My scarf was disappearing through the trees, a trail of fabric weaving through the branches.

'No,' I wailed. 'I loved that scarf.'

The monkey seized its moment and pulled the phone from under my foot.

'Not my phone! No, not my phone!'

The monkey swung itself out of reach, taking my mobile phone with it. I sank down on the wall, wondering how, in the space of two minutes, I'd managed to lose so much: my phone, a shoe, a scarf and even the job I loved. Then, picking up my backpack I hobbled back to the car park, my bare foot burning on the hot tarmac.

'Monkeys take your shoe ?' asked Ayu, my concerned driver, as I dived into the taxi.

'Yes,' I gulped. 'And my phone.'

I knew it was a coincidence, but since I'd lost Brontë's book, everything seemed to be going wrong. I'd had enough. No more loss. I couldn't take it.

'Oh Miss Maggie,' said the driver, passing me a box of tissues for my tears. 'Don't worry. I have shoes for you. But they are not smart like yours.'

He retrieved a worn and dusty pair of leather sliders from under the front seat and handed them to me. A long-forgotten memory surfaced: Utt had had a pair just like these. In a flash I was back at that turtle sanctuary, watching Utt mend the nesting bed after one of the volunteers had crashed into it. Dear, grumpy Utt, who'd known exactly who he was and what he'd wanted to do with his life. The thought made me smile as I wiped away my tears.

'Thank you, Ayu, you are very kind.'

He shook his head. 'You come to my country, and we are very grateful. It has been hard for drivers like me to earn money without visitors. We are glad you are here. Keep my shoes and remember Ayu.'

'I will, thank you.' I dabbed away fresh tears.

'Miss Maggie, I can't give you my phone, but my cousin has a shop in Ubud where you can buy one. Special price for my VIP guests. I take you?'

'Yes please, that would be wonderful.' I hid my smile. On the drive here, I'd heard about a cousin who could give me a Balinese cookery class, a cousin who gives such good massages that she has a waiting list and a cousin who would take me up Mount Batur to see the sunrise.

My heart had been beaten and battered today, as if I was losing at life. I was a middle-aged woman with the weight of the world on her shoulders. A far cry from the brave and adventurous and free-spirited Maggie I'd been last time I was in the village on the beach. Brontë would have made a beeline for that part of Bali; I knew she would. I wondered whether she would have had her own 'Bali moment' where I had done. Suddenly I knew that I had to go there too. I needed to recapture the magic of my first time on this beautiful island.

I leaned forward and touched Ayu's shoulder.

'I've changed my mind, Ayu. There's somewhere else I'd like to go, if that's okay with you.'

'No problem, Miss Maggie. Ayu will take you anywhere.'

I felt a rush of nerves as I gave him the name of the village; it was time to go back.

# Chapter 35

**Bali**

We had been driving for forty minutes when Ayu took a left turn at a mini roundabout and pulled into a parking space in front of a bakery store.

'Here, Miss?'

'This is it?' I looked uncertainly at the shops and restaurants that lined the street.

His face fell. 'Don't you like it? I can take you some-where else. Ubud Swing, or the waterfall, for nice photos? No problem.'

'No, this is the right place,' I reassured him. 'It has been a long time since I was here, that's all. I was only young.'

'Everything changes, miss, nothing stays the same. Except the ocean, that is always the same.'

My heart squeezed. 'Yes, I'm sure I'll recognise the beach. That's where I'll start.'

He pointed across the street to a narrow road. 'Follow the path and you will come to a beautiful beach.'

I got out of the car, and realised that without my phone I was entirely reliant on my driver to wait for me and take me back to Ubud. 'I'll see you back here in one hour?'

He flipped his car seat back until he was almost horizontal and pulled his hat over his eyes. 'Take your time, miss. Ayu rests his eyes.'

I set off down the narrow road that Ayu had promised led to the water. I passed a hostel, a scooter rental place and a pharmacy. Cars and bikes were parked bumper to bumper on either side. But as I walked on, the buildings became houses, the road became an unmade track and the traffic noise from the main street faded to nothing. All the houses had offerings on their doorsteps: bamboo mats decorated with flower petals, marigold heads, coloured rice and a burning incense stick. Offerings made as a sign of gratitude, I remembered.

I leaned closer, breathed in the delicious scent of sandalwood and vanilla and was hit with a sense of nostalgia. The aroma reminded me of home. Not my cottage in Honeybourne, but here. There was something about this place that resonated with me on a deep level.

Though I still didn't recognise my surroundings, I felt drawn onward, every cell in my body urging me forward as if it knew the way. My head buzzed as snatches of long-forgotten images emerged from my past. Another Maggie, a younger, lighter version of me, appeared in my mind's eye like an apparition. She was laughing, a flower tucked behind her ear, hair loose and tangled from swimming in salt water. Cut-offs, bikini top and flip-flops. She was carefree and ridiculously happy. Oh to be that happy again, I thought fondly.

The track narrowed again until it was no more than a footpath with trees on either side.

I heard the ocean before I saw it. The path changed to soft sand beneath my feet, and then I was out in the open on the palm-fringed perfect beach, the water lapping softly at the shoreline. I slipped off Ayu's sandals to feel the soft white sand between my toes. It was just as I remembered. There were a few people dotted here and there, lying on towels; a group of young people laughing and playing cards, a mother watching her toddler in the shallows and several people swimming.

I set my bag down beside a driftwood log and shimmied out of my dress, unable to wait a single moment more; the ocean was calling me. I walked down the beach and straight into the crystal turquoise water, revelling at the feel of the water on my skin. I thought of the baby turtles Jackson and I had released onto this beach all those years ago, and how they'd made their way so instinctively to the water's edge. Imprinting their birthplace into their DNA. I felt the same. This place was in my bones, part of my soul even. I walked further out until my feet couldn't touch the bottom and I swam and I swam.

Paradise.

I turned over onto my back and floated like a starfish, closing my eyes against the sun.

For a few minutes I let my mind wander. To the moment I met Jackson on my first morning. To the idyllic month we'd had, getting to know each other, falling in love; the delicious nights spent together on this beach. That summer had felt endless, magical, perfect.

Where was he now? Did he get to live his dream beach life, surfing and diving as he'd planned? Or was he a family man with a brood of children who'd inherited his beautiful skin and liquid brown eyes? Like Brontë's.

Flipping over, I started swimming again. A shoal of miniature fish flashed by me, the water so clear I could see their vivid stripes. I swam parallel to the shore, searching the beach for memories. The old turtle hatchery had gone, of course; I'd known about the project closing down years ago. There was a beach bar and a couple of restaurants, with chairs and beanbags set up on the sand facing the ocean. Much further along the beach, too far to make out much detail, was a rack of surfboards and some wetsuits hanging from a rail. That might have been the dive school Jackson had been to, I couldn't be sure.

Finally, I waded out of the water, dried myself on my little travel towel and sat down in the sun, allowing the memories to roll over me like gentle waves.

It was bittersweet to be here without Brontë. I cursed myself for staying away, for not bringing her here when I had the chance.

Why had I always been so sensible? It was a long way to go for a week when that was all I could spare away from work; the flights would cost a fortune . . . Excuses. Excuses.

How foolish I'd been, letting worry get in the way of doing something wonderful. I dug my toes into the sand to the cool layer beneath and vowed that I wouldn't hold myself back again. What was that saying? Feel the fear and do it anyway? Maybe I should get some business cards made with that on it. I smiled at the thought before remembering my phone call with Anna. I *would* be needing new business cards. Head of training and mentoring, I mused. There was something appealing about the role. It would be more people-focused than sales, and what I liked most about sales was getting to know our customers, what made them tick, what was important to them . . . I stopped myself in my tracks. What was I thinking? I shouldn't be taking this lying down. Anna had made a commitment to support my application for the job of sales director if I agreed to the sabbatical. I understood that Ron's earlier retirement had changed things now that Wendy was ill. But I was still me, Lee was still Lee. We should have been given an equal chance. I shouldn't have said yes so quickly; I should have asked for some time to think about it.

I flicked sand from my legs, brushing away the negative thoughts along with it. I was here now, thousands of miles from home, and work could wait. A new phone couldn't wait, though. For starters I hadn't brought a separate camera with me, and without a phone I couldn't take any photos of this beautiful place. Then there was my sister and her family to keep in touch with, and I'd got really into Instagram and following the Mum's Gap Year hashtag. The direct messages from women my age telling me that I'd inspired them to go travelling were lovely to read too. And I also needed to reply to Jono; he'd no doubt find my monkey business amusing.

I was still smiling about our night together when I was joined on the sand by a man carrying a wooden tray of bracelets.

'Australia?' he asked, straightening his jewellery deliberately.

A good salesman, I thought; engaging me in conversation while simultaneously drawing attention to his bracelets.

'UK,' I replied.

One of the bracelets had a tiny shell in the centre, a row of blue and green beads either side. It matched my bikini perfectly. I was tempted, but I'd already bought so many bracelets this trip.

He noticed which one I'd spotted. 'You want to look? I made them all myself.'

'They're very beautiful. But no thank you.'

The man untied the bracelet anyway and held it in his palm, gesturing for me to take it. 'First time in Bali?'

'Second.' I told him. 'I came here, this exact place when I was young, as a volunteer. There was a turtle conservation project on this beach, but it isn't here anymore.'

He smiled broadly. 'It is still here. It is new. A big building but still the same management.'

I sat bolt upright. 'Is it? Where?'

He tied the bracelet onto my wrist. 'You buy bracelet and I tell you.'

I laughed too and dug my purse out of my bag. 'You are a good salesman; I'd give you a job.'

He shook his head. 'No, no, no, you English persons all work, work, work. You want to be rich. But look.' He waved a hand around him. 'These are my riches.'

It had been a throwaway comment, intended as a compliment, but I saw his point. My driving goal had been financial security for Brontë and me. I'd defined myself by my job, as well as by my role as mother. I'd lost Brontë and now it seemed the job I'd left behind had been lost too. So where did that leave me? By comparison, the bracelet maker's life seemed to be working out great for him.

'You win,' I said, paying him for the bracelet, which was now firmly fixed around my wrist. He adjusted the length and snipped off the loose ends of string. 'So where is the turtle sanctuary now?'

He started to laugh, and pointed to a hand-painted sign fixed to the next palm tree along. I'd been sitting right next to it.

I read it and shook my head, grinning. *'Turtle rescue and conservation centre this way.* You have to be kidding me.'

I thanked my new friend, picked up my things and followed the path along the edge of the beach. I passed a dive and surf school where a charming young man tried to sell me a course of lessons. So charming, in fact, that I almost signed up. I laughed at my own behaviour as I continued on my way. I blamed Jono for my sexual renaissance; I never used to be all fluttery in the presence of an attractive man.

Far, far too young for me, I scolded myself, but I definitely had a type: the similarity to Jackson was irrefutable.

A couple of minutes later I walked through a set of gates and was greeted by a giant sculpture of a sea turtle. Tourists milled around while children climbed on the turtle's back to have their pictures taken.

'Wow!' I took my sunglasses off for a better look around.

Behind the entrance was a low, whitewashed building with open sides, a proper concrete floor and tiled pools for the turtles.

It was very smart; a million miles away from the ramshackle place I'd volunteered at.

A young woman in staff uniform greeted me. 'Welcome to the turtle conservation and education centre!' She ushered me to a kiosk. 'Please buy your ticket and enjoy your visit.'

I paid my entry fee and wandered around, looking at the pools of sea turtles and reading the information boards. The only activity on offer when I was last here was to collect the eggs from the beach and release them back into the ocean safely. Now they did dive trips, they'd constructed underwater feeding areas out in the wild, and they ran an emergency rescue service for injured turtles.

The new hatchery was a sophisticated construction: a solid concrete base enclosed with mesh fencing to protect the unhatched eggs from inquisitive fingers. The piles of sand covering the eggs were the same as last time, and there were still flags poking out of the sand with details of the eggs buried below. I smiled to myself, recalling the lanky volunteer who'd arrived late to our induction and proceeded to smash the perimeter of the wooden sandpit – and Utt, ordering us all out, angry with us for laughing.

I was still smiling when one of the guides approached me.

'We will be releasing new hatchlings this evening, if you want to help?' he said. 'All we ask is a donation to our centre.'

'I would love to,' I replied. 'But I'll be back in my hotel in Ubud by tonight.'

'Ah, that is sad. It is a wonderful experience to see the little turtles go into the waves for the first time.'

'It is,' I agreed. 'I did it when I came here twenty-four years ago.'

'Oh wow.' The guide's eyes widened. 'I was not even born then.'

'I was very young,' I said, touchily. 'The turtle conservation project was tiny then. And it was further along the beach.'

'You were volunteer?' he said, looking interested. 'At the first turtle project?'

'I was.' I sighed happily. 'Best summer of my life.'

'My grandfather was here all those years ago too. He was the boss of the volunteers.'

My breath caught. 'Your grandfather isn't called Utt is he, by any chance?'

'Yes!' he nodded excitedly. 'That is him. I am also Utt, named after him. You knew my grandfather!'

My jaw dropped. 'I did! That's incredible! Is he still alive?'

The young man threw his head back and laughed. One of his colleagues shouted across to find out what was going on and young Utt answered back in Indonesian. Other staff came to join us and they laughed too.

'What is it? What's so funny?'

'Oh yes,' he said finally. 'He is very alive. He still works at the centre.'

At once, the hairs on my arms and the back of my neck stood up. I gave an incredulous laugh. 'Utt – he's still here?'

'Of course,' said his grandson. 'This is his home. Why would he leave?'

'Please can you take me to him? I'd love to say hello, if he remembers me after all these years.'

He looked sceptical. 'There were lots of volunteers and he didn't like them very much.'

'It's definitely the right Utt. But I'd like to say hi anyway, my name is—'

'Miss Margaret,' said a gruff voice from behind. 'Welcome back to Bali.'

I spun around with a gasp. And there was Utt, standing right behind me, a big smile on his face, with a small sleeping baby in the crook of his arm. He'd hardly changed at all; a few more silver hairs maybe and less teeth. But still recognisable as the man I'd known all those years ago.

'Utt!' I exclaimed, taking his hand. 'It's Maggie, short for Magnolia rather than Margaret, but I'm delighted that you remember me. I can't believe it! It's so good to see you.'

'Magnolia? Ah, I see.' Utt shook his head. 'Of course I remember you. How could I forget two love birds like you and Mr Jackson.'

He called over to one of the other members of staff, who came and took the baby from him.

'We were love birds, weren't we?' My heart lurched at the mention of Jackson. Utt was the only other person I knew in the world who'd met him too. I wanted to stay in this moment and talk about him, reminisce about my month-long love affair with him.

'Always volunteering for the night shift so you could be alone in the dark together. Utt knew what you were doing.' He wagged a finger.

I felt myself blushing. 'Oh stop . . . Don't embarrass me in front of your grandson.'

'No, no. Love is good, it's good.' Utt put a hand on his grandson's shoulder. 'I always knew this lady would come back to see us. She was so pale and serious when she arrived in Bali, but when she was here, she blossomed like a lotus flower, full of life and love.'

I felt my eyes sting with tears, amazed that he had noticed that about me. 'I'm only sorry that it took me so long to come back.'

'Don't be sorry,' he said softly. 'The universe only shows you the right path when you are ready to follow it.'

His wise words touch my heart. 'Thank you.'

He bowed his head. 'You are welcome. I told Jackson the same thing when he returned.'

'You've seen him again since that summer?' I froze, every nerve in my body suddenly alert. 'He's been back too?'

I was taken aback. Jackson was an American. Bali had been simply one stop of his summer of travelling.

'Oh yes, Miss Maggie.' His eyes looked deep into mine. 'For him Bali is home.'

Home.

Less than an hour ago when I'd inhaled the smell of the incense, I'd felt the same. There was something about this place that got under your skin. Of course Jackson would have come back. He had always said he belonged by the water. He'd loved it here even more than me.

Waves of regret washed over me. If only, if only . . . Maybe if I'd brought Brontë here, as she'd asked me to, our visit might have coincided with his and he'd have met his wonderful daughter. Deep down, I knew how unlikely that would be, but things like this did happen. You read about it all the time.

'Was he . . . was he well and happy when you saw him?' I swallowed, my mouth suddenly bone dry. Did Utt know where Jackson lived now? Did I want to find him? It would mean telling him that he'd had the most beautiful daughter, who'd made me proud every single day – but that now she was gone. What if he was married, settled, happy? What would this new knowledge do to him? Maybe it would make his life worse.

Seeing him again might make my life worse too, and that scared me. Right now I held the memories of our time together in a perfect golden light. Maybe my imagination had run wilder and wilder over the years and there hadn't really been anything special after all in what we'd had. Maybe.

I'd never been able to forget the time we'd spent together because Brontë had been the result of it. But he might have completely forgotten the girl he had a holiday romance with many moons ago. The prospect of dimming the happy memory I had of him felt too risky, and I'd given up being risky a long time ago.

'He has lived a full life,' Utt replied, 'and a full life brings with it many chapters, some happy, some not so happy.'

I nodded. 'I can sympathise with that.'

'Are you with family, friends, husband?' he asked.

'I never married,' I told him. 'I'm here alone, I've been travelling since the beginning of the year.'

'No husband?' Utt looked surprised.

'Never been tempted,' I said with a shrug. 'But my life has been good on the whole.'

He had his hand on my shoulder and gently led me towards the exit. 'I am glad. How long are you in Bali?'

'I'm not sure. But I'm not ready to leave yet.'

'Then come back again, Magnolia.' He gave a bow to say goodbye.

I hesitated, wanting to press him for more information about Jackson, but Utt seemed keen for me to leave.

'I will,' I said, touching his arm gently. 'Goodbye.'

There was a taxi parked outside. Ayu was leaning up against it and we waved at each other. I didn't know how he'd found me but my legs were shaky and I was glad he had.

'What's up, Utt!' Ayu shouted.

The two men exchanged greetings in Indonesian while I got into the car.

'Don't tell me,' I laughed, doing up my seat belt. 'Utt is your cousin, right?'

'No, no, no,' Ayu cried. 'Utt is too old. He is my mother's cousin.'

*Silly me*, I thought, hiding my smile.

'But I have good news, about *my* cousin, Miss Maggie. The one with the phone shop. He has a beautiful phone for you, and he will be waiting for you at your hotel.'

'That is good news, Ayu. Thank you. Can you drive me back there now, please?'

I leaned my head back against the head rest and closed my eyes. I was exhausted. My past and my present had collided in the most extraordinary way today. I mulled over what Utt had said about the universe only showing you the right path when you were ready to follow it. I'd waited a long time to revisit this beautiful country and I had a feeling that I was ready for the universe to show me what it had in store for me next.

# Chapter 36

**Bali**

I ran my fingers through my hair, still damp from my shower. As promised, Ayu's cousin had been here when we arrived. I was now in possession of a second-hand iPhone and Ayu had left with a hefty tip for being such a wonderful driver. As soon as both men had gone, I'd headed to my room.

Today had been a lot to deal with. It felt as if a cyclone had whirled through my life and turned everything upside down. The conversation with my boss about the 'restructuring' would have been enough on its own to unsettle me, but the trip down memory lane and meeting Utt had ignited a restlessness in me that I didn't know what to do with.

Being on *our* beach, swimming in the ocean where I'd first met Jackson and then learning from Utt that he'd been back to Bali not once, but multiple times – all this had propelled Jackson from being buried deep in my past to here in the present. My head was full of if-onlys and what-nexts.

Could Utt contact Jackson for me, and if so, did I want him to? I needed to organise my thoughts properly. If only I hadn't lost Brontë's book, I'd probably be journaling in it now. So my next job was to go into town and buy a new notebook.

Ten minutes later, I left my room and headed out.

My new phone was in my bag, but I hadn't yet set it up properly. I could make calls, I could surf the internet, but after logging into Facebook I'd stopped.

There was something liberating about being disconnected for a while. I needed to stop scrolling and checking emails; and I did not want to be available should Anna decide to call me again. I wanted to find some stillness, look inwards, and figure out what the hell I was going to do with the next year or two of my life.

The street my hotel was on was crammed with interesting places, from crystal and reiki healing to massage parlours and sound bath classes. Any of these would give me respite from my inner turmoil, but the time had come to face up to some things and stop escaping from them.

Because that was what I'd been doing ever since Brontë died. I'd thought that I was protecting myself by carrying on as if my world hadn't shattered. In fact, I had done the opposite. I'd put myself, my heart, my life on ice, refusing to acknowledge that I faced a future without her in it.

I picked up a little notebook from a gift shop, found a table inside a highly Instagrammable café and ordered a fruit smoothie. The café was full of lush greenery and had a spiral wooden staircase suspended by what looked like jungle vines. The words *Open up to the magic of life* were written on the floor in marigold flowers. The vibe was relaxed and peaceful and I couldn't have picked a more zen location to pin down my whirling thoughts.

'Terima kasih,' I said to the waitress delivering my drink, hoping I'd got the translation for *thank you* right.

'You're welcome.'

As she walked away, I picked up my pen and turned to the first page in my new notebook.

I put the date in the right-hand margin, as I had at school, and after a hesitation wrote a heading: *What do I want?*

Where to start? I sipped my smoothie.

*Don't overthink, Maggie, write . . .*

to love my life
to love other people
to be loved

I stared at what I had written. Goose pimples tickled my arms and tears pricked at my eyes as the message I'd written to myself stared back at me. I'd been starved of love, I knew I had; but in return I hadn't given love to others either and I needed to change that.

I thought of Tiff. Now there was a woman who loved her life. She'd walked away from the things that didn't make her happy and replaced them with things that did. That was oversimplifying, of course, and her new life had come with a price.

*But you've already paid your price*, said a small voice.

I put down my pen, blinked away my tears before they had a chance to fall, and let out a long breath.

'Oh honey, that's a big sigh,' said a chirpy voice.

I swivelled round to see a woman with bright inquisitive eyes looking at me.

'Sorry,' I replied, feeling embarrassed at being caught at such a melancholy moment. 'I didn't mean to be so loud. I've got a lot on my mind.'

'Not at all.' She held her hands up, sending many bangles jingling down her arms. She nodded to my open notebook. 'You're journaling, which is very sensible if you're feeling a bit muddled. I'll leave you in peace.'

'Thank you.' I returned her smile. 'I think better when I have a pen in my hand.'

'Although, I have to say, I am a very good listener. So . . .'

She left her sentence hanging and I bit back a smile. She had no intention of leaving me in peace at all.

'I'm not really someone to unburden themselves to a stranger,' I replied. 'But thanks for the offer.'

She got up from her own table and joined me at mine, her bird-printed kaftan wafting as she moved.

'I'm Lisa,' she said, offering me her hand. 'And you are?'

'Maggie.' I put my hand in hers and instead of shaking it, she squeezed it softly before turning it over and studying my palm.

'Hmm,' she said thoughtfully.

'What is it?' I retracted my hand.

'Not entirely sure.' She cleared her throat. 'I'm still learning. Anyway, now we're not strangers anymore, so I'm all ears.'

I puffed out my cheeks. 'Where to begin?'

She glanced at the words on my page. 'Maggie, honey, if you don't mind me stating the obvious, whatever the question, it looks as if love is the answer.'

I closed the book, feeling self-conscious.

'Whoops, sorry. I didn't mean to look.' She pressed her lips together, suppressing a smile. 'Actually that's not true. I'm incredibly nosy.'

'It's fine,' I said. 'I left the UK to go travelling, thinking it would solve all my problems. But all that's happened is that the problems tagged along for the ride and now I've lost my map and I'm at a crossroads and don't know which way to turn for the best. I could do the easy thing and go home, but if I did, I'd probably regret it later. On top of that I think my job is being phased out and I'm being shunted sideways instead of upwards.'

Lisa blinked. 'You are in a pickle.'

'That's not all.' I hesitated. 'I've said a terrible thing to my mum.' Despite our turbulent history, tears sprang to my eyes.

'Oh, my love. Okay.' Lisa sat up taller. 'I know what you need.'

'Is it alcohol? Because if so I agree.' I glanced at my phone to see the time; a drink would go down nicely.

She gave a tinkly laugh. 'No! My body is a temple. At least until I finish work.'

'You work in Bali?'

She gave me a smug smile. 'I do! Aren't I lucky? I'm a freelance journalist officially, with one or two sidelines. It's my dream job.'

'Good for you,' I said, meaning it. 'I thought my dream promotion would be waiting for me when I got back to the UK, but it seems like fate has other plans, or at least my boss does.'

'What's for you won't pass you by; I'm a firm believer in that.' She wagged a finger.

'So if it's not alcohol, what is it I need?'

Lisa's eyes sparkled. 'I'll do you a tarot card reading.'

'Um.' I gave her a look of surprise. 'Thank you for the offer. I need practical thought processes, not psychic powers. No offence.'

'Oh, none taken. It's not for everyone. And I fully agree. The cards can't predict the future, but they can help you to pay attention to what you already know.'

'Sorry.' I shook my head. 'But it's not my thing.'

Lisa pouted. 'Drat. But could I do you a reading anyway? I'm still learning, and I need the practice.' She saw me hesitate. 'Go on. If you don't believe in what the cards tell you then you can ignore them. I'd be very grateful, and I won't charge.'

'In that case, how could I refuse?' I couldn't help but laugh.

'Yes! My first customer.' She got to her feet and signalled to the waitress that we were ready to leave. 'Come on, let's go back to my apartment and see if we can't get you over this crossroads.'

We paid our bills and I followed her out of the café. I seriously doubted my future would be solved on the turn of a card, but at this point what did I have to lose?

# Chapter 37

**Bali**

'So.' Lisa had a pack of cards in her hand. 'I'm going to pull out some cards for your reading and then we'll talk about what they mean.'

We were sitting cross-legged on the floor of her apartment with a low footstool in between us. On it was a manual on how to read tarot cards. She'd poured us both a glass of water and placed a box of tissues on the floor beside us.

'Okay.' I didn't for one second imagine that the tarot cards would reveal anything useful, but it would be fun, and for an hour or so it was a good distraction.

Lisa turned over the first three cards and flicked through her manual.

'Ah, right,' she said briskly. 'So the three of swords, the five of cups and the death card represent the recent past. These are telling me a story of grief and death. Someone has gone over, perhaps?'

'Correct.' A fair guess; not many people are fortunate enough to get to my age without suffering the loss of a loved one.

'Okay, my lovely,' she continued. 'This person means a great deal to you and grief has become a part of who you are.'

'My daughter,' I croaked. 'I've lost my daughter, Brontë.'

She placed a hand over mine. 'The path out of pain might not be clear now, but take a look at the death card.'

The card showed a battle scene and a knight in armour on a white horse, and at the very back, a golden sun.

'In the distance, the sun is rising,' she pointed out. 'A new day *does* dawn. You see? The sun *will* rise again.'

'Thank you,' I swallowed, my eyes blurred with tears. 'I do believe that; but at the moment it seems so far off. Everything keeps going wrong.'

She pulled a tissue out of the box and blew her nose. 'Sorry, I don't usually get upset, but, oh Maggie, I'm so sorry. No wonder the words in your notebook were all about love. Let's see which card represents your present. Ah, the Hanged Man.'

I recoiled at the card, which revealed a man hanging upside down from a tree; not exactly what I wanted my present to be.

'This card means that you're stuck, uncertain about what to do next.'

'Maybe this is the crossroads I told you about,' I said. 'That's how I feel about everything. I've been working towards promotion for years and now I don't know if I even want to stay at that company. My role as a mother feels complicated too. I'm still Brontë's mum and I don't know how to fill that space that she left behind. I don't know how to be myself.'

Lisa turned over another card. 'This one shows us who influences you. You've got the Empress, but the card is upside down, which means it's reversed.'

She checked in her manual again.

'So the Empress represents a woman who loves you, but can't express her love, she can be austere and critical.'

I gave a bark of laughter. 'My mum. I based my mothering skills on doing the reverse of her.'

'She's important to you,' Lisa insisted, waving her hand across the cards. 'Does your relationship with this woman need attention, perhaps?'

'It does.' I felt a niggle of shame for having left things the way I had between us. 'Let's move on.'

She held my gaze. 'Sure. These next ones represent what your heart and soul needs.'

I inched forward, curious to see the next cards.

'The Queen of Wands, the World and the Moon. Nice.'

She explained that the queen was a figure who would encourage me to find my purpose; the world card told her that I was searching for something that mattered deeply to me; and the moon meant I'd need to go deep inside myself to find out what it was I wanted.

'Okay, next up is your near future. The lovers' card, the Six and Three of Cups. A soulmate is coming back into your life. This person will remind you of who you once were and who you can be again.'

I thought of the photo of myself in my old diary. That brave and adventurous girl, confident and sure of who she was and what she wanted. Who'd travelled to Bali alone, spending her savings to fulfil a dream. Immersing herself in that moment on the beach and giving herself up to joy.

She was the one I needed to reconnect with most. Not anyone else.

She turned over three more cards and her eyes sparkled with unshed tears. 'Ooh.'

'What?' I felt my own eyes tingle.

'The last three cards represent your future: The Sun. The Wheel of Fortune and the Ace of Cups.'

'Are they good or bad?' I asked, feeling nervous.

'The sun will rise again, you will be happy again, the wheel of life goes around and around, bringing change and, with it, freedom and happiness. The Ace of Cups is reminding us that we can't fill from an empty cup; we must fill our own cup with love first. And the more love you give away, the more you will receive.'

'That's what I want,' I said shakily. 'More than anything. I want somewhere to channel all the love I have.'

'You'll find the right place, I know you will.' Lisa's eyes were full of compassion. 'Focus on finding your way back to *you* and the rest will take care of itself.'

I took a deep breath, and nodded. 'Thank you.' I reached into my bag to pay her but she held up her hand.

'Follow me on Instagram and tell all your friends about me.' She winked and folded a business card into my hand. 'I can do readings on Zoom, so I'm fully global.'

'I will, I promise,' I said.

We hugged for a long time, and she showed me to the door.

I left her apartment, descended the stairs and found myself back outside the massage parlour, blinking as my eyes readjusted to the afternoon light. I stood for a moment, steadying myself against the dark wood of a doorway, and let Lisa's words wash over me.

*Focus on finding your way back to you and the rest will take care of itself.*

I sent myself back in time to the day I left Jackson to begin my journey back to the UK. A girl who desperately wanted to stay beside her boy, whose every breath fought to ignore the pull from home and family. My duty to my younger sister had won out then and I'd held on tight to the reins of responsibility ever since, never quite having the courage to pursue any goals solely for myself. But I had no such demands on my time anymore. I could be selfish and go after what I wanted.

And what I wanted – or rather *who* I wanted – felt more within reach now than for years. No sooner was the thought in my head than I found myself running back to my hotel. I was going to do everything in my power to find him.

I had to find Jackson.

# Chapter 38

## Bali

The heat from the late afternoon sun was strong and the back of my neck was burning, but I didn't slow my pace. The turtle sanctuary was an hour away and I had to order a taxi to get me there. I wanted to get there before it closed so I could ask Utt if he knew where I could find Jackson.

The sign for the hotel was in sight. The entrance was tucked away down a slope. I ran down the hill, almost colliding with a minibus pulling out of the car park. The reception desk was swamped with new arrivals; a sea of suitcases blocked my path.

I swore under my breath at being forced to wait. These people would be filling in their registration forms for ages yet. I glanced around for any spare staff, but couldn't see anyone. My breath was ragged from running and my hair was damp with perspiration. A headache was building in my temples and wished I had some water.

'Excuse me,' I shouted over the crowd to the receptionist. 'Could you order me a taxi?'

'Can't she see there's a queue?' someone grumbled.

A shrill siren blared out from my bag, startling me. It was such an awful noise that people turned to see where it was coming from. It was the default ring tone on my new phone. I pulled the phone from my bag, anxious to silence it as quickly as possible, and saw that it was Harry calling via Facebook Messenger.

'Maggie! Finally! I've been trying to get hold of you for hours.' His words tumbled over each other and he sounded relieved. 'Haven't you been checking Instagram?'

'No. A monkey stole my phone. I've got a new one, but it's not completely up and running yet. And then I've been in a tarot card reading this afternoon. Is everything okay?'

Beside me, two children started to yell and cry at each other. I jammed a finger into my ear to concentrate on what he was saying.

'What?' He gave a laugh of disbelief. 'No way! That was not what I expected to hear. Yeah, I'm great. Listen, I've got some amazing news. Guess what it is?'

'Oh my word.' I pressed a hand to my heart, hardly daring to voice my biggest wish. 'Is it what I think it is?'

'It is. Someone has found Brontë's book!' he exclaimed. 'You're going to get it back.'

My chest felt tight with gratitude. 'I don't believe it. Thank you, thank you!'

'It's in Watson's Bay near the nudist beach. You must have dropped it when we were trying not to stare at the naked sunbathers.'

'Oh my God.' I felt myself sway, my head dizzy from the heat and the running I'd been doing. 'I feel a bit faint.'

The lobby was making me feel claustrophobic amongst the tangle of tourists with their suitcases and pushing and shoving, and I couldn't get any air.

'Isn't that great?' Harry continued.

'It is.' Tears streamed down my face. 'I really thought . . . I really thought . . .'

Dots swam in front of my eyes and I shook my head to clear them. I needed to sit down.

'I'm heading into Sydney now to collect it.'

'Thank you,' I croaked. I pressed a hand to my mouth. My face felt clammy and cool despite the heat. 'But there's no need to rush; it must be getting late in Australia?'

'The cool thing is that a girl I've been talking to is coming to Bali tomorrow, so there isn't much time to get it organised. I'm going to send her your contact details. You've met her actually. Lola? Do you remember?'

'Excuse me,' I mumbled, edging past an elderly couple bickering over who'd got the passports. They were blocking the path to a spare seat on a sofa and I needed it. I needed to sit down – now.

'Maggie? You sound weird, are you okay?'

'Hot. That's all.' I took a couple of breaths as I sat down on the sofa. 'Harry, I need to know something. Did Brontë plan to come to Bali to trace her dad?'

There was a silence down the line.

'Please. Tell me the truth.'

'She planned to do a bit of digging, yes,' Harry admitted. 'She didn't have anything major to go on, but she had found an old man who you knew when you were in Bali. She was going to start there.'

'Was his name Utt?' I suggested.

'Yes, I think so.'

She had planned to do exactly what I was doing now. My gorgeous girl, two steps ahead of me, as she had been on this entire trip. And now I was to be the one to complete the task on her behalf, in her final destination. I felt her gentle presence beside me then, like a silk scarf around my shoulders. I needed to book a taxi, I had to get moving, I was doing this for both of us.

Intent on flagging down a taxi myself on the street, I got to my feet quickly – and felt my knees begin to buckle. Dancing spots appeared before my eyes and I tried to blink them away.

'Maggie?' I heard Harry shouting. 'What's going on? Are you still there?'

'Air,' I gasped, pressing a hand to my chest. 'I can't breathe.'

I staggered forward to escape the hotel lobby and get myself into the open air. A couple more paces, that's all it would take . . . My bag slipped off my shoulder and hit the marble floor, followed a second later by my phone.

And then the world went silent.

'Can someone get this lady some water, please?' I heard someone shout.

Bodies pressed around me. Someone fanned my face.

"She's out cold.'

'Do you have a nurse in the hotel?'

'Call an ambulance.'

*I don't need an ambulance.* I wanted to speak, but my mouth wasn't working properly and all that escaped was a tiny moan.

'I'm a first-aider,' said a man with a voice that sounded familiar. One I hadn't heard for twenty-four years. But it couldn't be him, could it? It was my imagination conjuring him up. 'Please let me through.'

It had to be him. He sounded more gravelly, richer, but I'd recognise that voice anywhere. My eyes flew open and there he was, kneeling beside me.

'Oh my God, Maggie, it is you!'

The sound of my name on his lips stirred a thousand butterflies in my stomach.

'Jackson!' I struggled to sit up, and despite my dizziness my face broke into a smile. His face was as handsome as I'd remembered, his gaze just as striking. 'I can't believe it.'

'Whoa, take it easy, Mags.' He caught hold of my arms to steady me.

'How are you here? I mean, why are you in Bali at my hotel?'

He smiled lazily. 'You mean right now? Looks like I've come to your rescue again, like the first time we met, when you decided to go off swimming in strong currents by yourself.'

'I didn't need rescuing then,' I replied, 'and I don't now either.'

He threw his head back and laughed properly. 'Here she is. My feisty girl. You haven't changed a bit.'

'Neither have you.'

'Here, drink.' He handed me a glass of water and I gulped it down. 'Okay, thanks, everyone,' he said. 'I'll take it from here.'

The other hotel guests melted away until it was just him and me. We held eye contact, his hand was still on my arm, mine was gripping my glass. Two middle-aged people meeting again after over twenty years.

'Thanks.' I trembled as he took the glass back from me and for a second or two, we allowed our fingers to touch. I wanted to hold his hand, feel his arms around me and melt into him, as I'd always done.

I pressed my palm to my thudding chest in an attempt to calm myself. In theory, he was a stranger to me now. And yet at the same time, how could he be, when the connection between us was so strong that I could almost feel it? 'Is it really you?'

'It's definitely me.' His eyes were full of concern, but a smile was tugging at his lips.

'And I'm here because Utt called me as soon as you left the turtle sanctuary.'

I shook my head, bemused. 'That explains why he ushered me out of the building so quickly.'

Jackson laughed. 'He couldn't wait to tell me. I came as quickly as I could.'

More than two decades had passed since we'd said goodbye, yet he'd dropped everything to see me again. This was surreal, and wonderful, and possibly the biggest compliment he could pay me.

'You came from where?' I asked.

'From home,' he said, his lips twisting into a half-smile. 'Or to be more accurate, from work.'

My eyes widened. 'You live in Bali?'

'Sure do,' he grinned. 'For the last twenty years.'

'Wow.' If only I'd come back sooner and brought Brontë with me, maybe . . . I had to tell him about her, I realised. And soon.

I let out a long breath and Jackson touched my arm. 'Are you okay?'

I nodded, unable to drag my eyes from his face.

'*Magnolia*,' he murmured. 'No wonder I couldn't find you. I should have known you wouldn't have been an ordinary Margaret, there was never anything ordinary about you.'

I swallowed. 'You looked for me?'

'For two years. But then, life moved on.' He broke off, rubbing his jaw. 'I had a hunch you'd come back one day, but you sure took your time. So what brings you back to Bali now?'

I needed to stand up, look him in the eye. I didn't want to say this sitting on the floor in the hotel lobby. Jackson steadied my arm as I rose to my feet, and handed me my bag and my phone.

'I . . . I . . .' I stared at him, my heart thudding erratically.

He tilted his head, his gaze never wavering from mine. 'Hey, take your time.'

'Okay.' I blew out a breath and pressed my hands together to stop them from shaking. 'Your daughter, Jackson, that's what brought me here.'

His brow furrowed. 'But I don't have a daughter.'

I caught my lip between my teeth and stared at him, waiting for him to understand.

'Wait. No.' He waved a finger between him and me, and gave a half-laugh, visibly shocked. '*You* have a daughter. Did we . . . you and me . . . ?'

'We did.' I bowed my head as a torrent of sorrow threatened to drown me. 'We did. I had your baby. And, oh Jackson, I'm so, so sorry, but I've got some terrible news.'

# Chapter 39

## Maggie, Bali, 2000

'Oh shit. Disaster.' Jackson shifted his weight to the edge of the narrow bed.

'Exactly what every girl wants to hear after sex. Thanks,' I teased. 'And there was I thinking I was incredible. Like you.'

We were in his dorm, squashed into his single bed. He'd got the room to himself until tomorrow, when a batch of new volunteers were due to arrive, and we were making the most of being able to spend a whole night together.

It hadn't happened often, but the times when I got to wake up beside him and watch him sleep were the best. This boy had awakened something new in me, a softer side. He made me feel safe and so I had let down my guard. Moments like this when we were completely alone, in our little bubble, gave me the perfect opportunity to reveal my vulnerable heart.

Tomorrow we'd be back to sneaking down to the rocks at the far end of the beach to get some privacy. We'd been for a romantic midnight swim earlier and then he'd smuggled me in here. That was an hour ago.

He laughed, a low, sexy laugh. Everything about this boy was sexy. There was a full moon tonight and the muscles in his back gleamed where slivers of light filtered through the shutters.

He turned back to me, sliding his hand into my hair. 'I don't mean *you*. You were . . .' He leaned down to kiss me. 'Amazing.'

I felt blissed out, alive, deliriously happy.

'What is the disaster then?' I hitched myself up onto my elbows, trying to see what he was doing.

He pulled a face. 'The condom has split. I'm sorry. I feel terrible.'

I giggled. 'Is that all? Don't worry about it, I'm on the pill.'

He stared at me, amused. 'Now you tell me. So I needn't have bothered with a condom at all.'

For a fraction of a second, I felt a squeeze of panic; I had taken it today, hadn't I? I should probably go and check, but then the other girls in my dorm would tease me mercilessly about it. Also, it would break the mood; I didn't want to do that. I gave myself a shake. Of course I'd taken my pill; I was being paranoid.

He got up, put the condom in the trash and lay back down beside me.

'Better safe than sorry,' I said.

'What's that supposed to mean?' He pretended to be insulted.

'I mean double protection.' I put my hand on his hip, feeling the jut of his hipbone hard against my palm. I tugged him towards me. 'We don't want any accidents, do we? A little Maggie or Jackson making an appearance and turning our lives upside down. Anyway, thank goodness I am on the pill, given what's just happened.'

'I dunno.' He grinned. 'A little girl with your brains and beauty would be cool. Or a boy. We would make awesome babies.'

'Jackson!' I punched him in the chest playfully. 'No thank you. Besides, I thought you wanted to roam free, explore the world one beach at a time. No responsibilities.'

He laughed. His breath soft against my mouth. 'You're right, as always.'

He kissed me then, pulling my leg over his hip and easing his body against mine.

'Maybe we should meet up in ten years, when we're proper grown-up adults, make some beautiful babies then.'

I traced my fingertip lightly along the lean muscles of his arm. I delighted in feeling his breathing hitch, knowing the effect I had on him.

'So,' I drawled. 'We have to wait ten years until you're ready to do it again? Is that what you're saying?'

'Hell no,' he growled, his eyes dark with desire.

He rolled onto me, pinning my arms above my head and pressing a line of hot kisses down my stomach. I closed my eyes, arching my back.

A future together. For a moment I let myself dream. There was nothing I wanted more than to keep Jackson in my life forever. For us to stay like this, blissfully in love and wrapped up in each other. But I forced myself to think logically, even though it pained me to do so. It was a delicious fantasy but in ten years' time this precious boy would belong to someone else, I just knew it. No, this was my time, right now, and I was going to enjoy every second of it while it lasted.

# Chapter 40

## Bali

Jackson and I had moved to my patio for some privacy. There, sitting on sofas opposite each other, a pot of mint tea on the table between us, I told Jackson everything about the wonderful young woman we'd made together. From the joyous moment of her birth to the devastating news of her death.

He listened without interruption, emotions lightening and darkening his features. Features still familiar to me despite the passage of so many years. He wiped away tears, smiled at the funny stories of her childhood, quizzed me about Harry, and marvelled at Brontë's academic achievements and dream job offer.

For a long time after I'd finished talking, Jackson said nothing. He had a lot to process; he'd gained and lost a daughter today, not to mention having me walk back into his life. As we sat in reflective silence, I studied his face, watching him blot tears with the back of his hand. He leaned forward, hands clasped, elbows to knees, and dropped his head. His dark hair had a few silver threads running through it, the veins on the back of his hands were more prominent, his forehead not as smooth, but his presence was every bit as magnetic as I remembered.

Brontë would have adored him.

Finally, he looked across at me, his face etched with sadness. 'Can I join you on that sofa? I feel a long way away over here.'

'Sure.' I scooched over to make room.

He sat facing me, took my hand and held it between both of his. My insides sparked with nerves as I tried to work out what was running through his head.

'I can't imagine how tough this was – *is* – for you,' he said gruffly. 'I've only just learned about her, and I already feel her loss. From now on, a part of me will always be missing. I wish I'd known her. My daughter.' He whistled between his teeth. 'I had a daughter.'

'I'm so sorry.' By now I'd lost count of the number of times I'd said it. And it would never be enough. Never make up for the child he hadn't had the opportunity to love. 'She was incredible. She looked a little like you. Wait, I've got a picture beside my bed.'

I went inside to fetch it and noticed that a weight had shifted from me. I felt as if I'd found the missing piece to complete the jigsaw of Brontë's life. Perhaps this might be the start of a new friendship for the two of us; but even if that wasn't to be, I felt better, knowing that both of her parents had had this chance to grieve for her together.

With a sudden burst of clarity, it occurred to me that this was the conversation my heart had been burning to have since her death – with him, her other parent, the most important person she'd never know. Finding him, telling him her truth was going to give me the sense of peace that I hadn't known I needed.

I returned with the framed photo and let Jackson see his daughter for the first time.

'Taken in our garden last summer.'

'Hello, beautiful.' Jackson examined it for what felt like an age. 'Brown eyes?'

'Like yours, yes.'

'She looks happy in this picture. Was she happy?'

My chest tightened. 'Oh yes. Apart from when it was her turn to wash the dishes.'

He gave me the ghost of a smile. 'She probably got that from me.'

'She had a wild, adventurous streak,' I told him. 'She got that from you too.'

'The Maggie I met in the year 2000 was pretty adventurous,' he pointed out. 'And you're here travelling solo like you did back then.'

'Well, yes, but only because that was what she planned to do. I'm here because of her, doing the trip that she never got the chance to take for herself.'

'So when you said your daughter brought you here, that was what you meant?' His eyes were liquid pools and I could see he was on the edge of tears. 'She would have been here, in Bali?'

'She would, and according to her boyfriend she was hoping to find you through Utt.'

'What?' he said, half laughing with shock. 'That would have been . . .' He pinched the bridge of his nose. 'That would have made me so happy.'

'She had her whole itinerary planned out in a book. I'll be able to show you tomorrow.'

I explained about the loss of Brontë's book and how it was being flown from Australia to Bali.

'How about I take you to the airport, we can fetch it together?' he suggested.

His obvious interest to learn more about his daughter made me want to cry; I couldn't have asked for a nicer response. 'I'd love that.'

He stretched his legs out in front of him. 'Listen, I'm starving. Have you got plans for dinner, or shall we go and pick up some nasi goreng and bring it back here? There's a great place not far from here.'

'No plans,' I confirmed. 'But I can't believe you still love nasi goreng.'

'What's not to love?' He spread his hands out. 'Is that a yes?'

'Yes, but are you sure you don't you have to be back for someone?' I held my breath.

'Shit.' He slapped a hand to his forehead. 'Yes, I do.'

The disappointment hit me like a brick. I tried not to show it. Of course he was going to have responsibilities. He wasn't a kid anymore, surfing his way around the world, footloose and fancy-free.

'I can sort that out with a quick phone call,' he continued. 'I don't want to leave you yet, I've still got loads more questions. But if you feel uncomfortable answering them, let me know.'

I was too wound up to eat, but I didn't want him to leave yet either.

'For months after the accident, I could hardly bring myself to say her name. Even now, whenever I talk about her in the past tense I feel an anxiety in me like a low buzz. But this is different; you have a right to know everything about her. It feels good to share her stories with you. And . . .' I paused. 'Thank you for not being angry.'

'I'm angry with the guy who's responsible for causing her accident. I'm not sure I'd be able to keep my temper if I was to find myself down a dark alley with him.' He tensed his jaw. 'But not with you. How could I be? It sounds like you and she had an incredible bond.'

I smiled wistfully. 'We did. I was her North Star, her constant. Even when she was a teenager and she would throw me a look of pure contempt for setting a perfectly normal boundary, she still knew I'd be there, loving her unconditionally. I was her place of safety and I loved it.'

'I bet you were a great mom.'

'Am,' I corrected him. 'I still am her mother.'

'Oh Maggie.' He looked stricken at his error and pulled me into his arms. 'Of course you are.'

I leaned into him, savouring the feel of his hands rubbing my back. I rested my cheek on his chest. I reached my arms around him, the cotton of his T-shirt soft, the muscles in his back taut and firm. The scent of his aftershave teased my nostrils. He didn't smell as I remembered, but my body still curved into his as it once had.

With a flash of alarm, I realised what I was doing. He'd literally just told me that someone was waiting for him at home. I jerked away, embarrassed by my own response to him.

'I'll leave you to make your call in private,' I said, hurriedly. I collected the tea things and took them inside.

He joined me a minute later.

'Okay, that's all sorted. Ready when you are.' He tucked his phone in his pocket.

He wasn't free, that was clear, but he was all mine for the next couple of hours, and that was much more than I could have dreamed of when I'd woken up this morning.

'Come on then,' I grinned, beckoning him in so I could lock up. 'Let's revisit our nasi goreng era.'

It was dusk and the streets were busy with tourists and ticket touts drumming up business for the nightly traditional dance show at Ubud Palace. We walked side by side, his hand sometimes reaching to my back as we negotiated people and scooters and stray dogs.

'This is weird, isn't it?' he said, directing me into a side street. 'You and me, out on the town again after all these years.'

'Weird in a good way I hope,' I teased, raising an eyebrow.

'In a very good way,' he replied. 'So, do you mind if I ask you more about Brontë?'

I smiled up at him under the streetlight, watching shadows play across his face. 'Of course not.'

'Okay, what were some of her favourite things?'

'That's easy,' I said. 'Art, especially drawing, which you'll see tomorrow. Sushi; she loved sushi.'

'What about music?'

'All sorts. Everything from Abba to country and western.'

He grinned. 'Now we're getting somewhere. A country girl, huh?'

'Yes, like you!' I'd forgotten that about Jackson, how much he'd loved his country music. So many moments, so many memories were coming back to me by being close to him again. This felt like a dream. I reached out and touched his arm to reassure myself that this was real, that I was here with him. Wordlessly he took my hand and our fingers found their groove just as they had all those years ago, and we continued along the narrow path in silence. There was so much still to learn about each other, so many gaps to fill in about our lives since the summer we met.

But tonight was about us, our past and the beautiful girl we had created together. Tomorrow was another day. The future could wait for a few delicious hours.

# Chapter 41

**Bali**

The next morning, I was up and raring to start the day after the best night's sleep I could remember for months. Today was going to be huge and I was excited, nervous and terrified. Jackson would be arriving in a couple of hours and I couldn't wait.

*Jackson.* I kept having to pinch myself to check that this wasn't a dream, that I really had reconnected with him after all this time.

We'd be heading straight to the airport to collect Brontë's book from Lola. I was desperate to have it back in my possession, read the Bali pages and see what she had planned to do when she got here. I wanted Jackson to see the book too, for him to get to know his daughter through it. Each page was infused with her personality: her words, her thoughts, her dreams. I was already brimming with pride, knowing how much he'd enjoy looking at it.

Jackson and I had brought our food back to the hotel last night and eaten outside at a table by the pool. There'd been no on else around and only the light of the moon and its pale silver reflection on the water to see by. We'd talked some more, mostly about Brontë, and I'd managed to log into my iCloud on my phone and show him all the photos I had stored of her. The temptation to quiz him about his life grew stronger by the minute, but I'd forced myself to hold back, not wanting reality to intrude into such an incredible night.

Jackson had finally left me at one a.m., saying he needed to get back. Get back to whom, I'd wondered; a girlfriend, a wife? We'd bid each other goodnight with a kiss on the cheek before he left, and I'd floated off to bed on a cloud, emotional, exhausted and, above all, filled with gratitude that Brontë had led me back to this man.

Now, I made a cup of coffee and opened the patio doors. Instantly the room was filled with birdsong and the scent of tropical flowers, I savoured the warm air on my face, a sharp contrast to the air-conditioned cool behind me. It was a beautiful day, this place was a paradise, and I was so, so lucky to be here. I thought of yesterday and how everything had felt bleak. Now, less than twenty-four hours later, there were chinks of light appearing in the darkness.

'A new day is dawning,' Lisa had said yesterday. 'The sun *will* rise again.'

It felt very much as if her prediction was already coming true.

I fetched my phone, and settled down in the shade on my terrace to send Kat a message.

Call me when you wake up x

My phone rang immediately.

'What's wrong?' Kat demanded. She was puffing and panting as if she was out running.

'Nothing,' I assured her. 'Only good stuff.'

'I'm so pleased,' she wheezed. 'You've sounded so down since losing Brontë's book.'

'Good news on that front. It's been found and I'm being reunited with it later.' I gave her an update and she shrieked down the phone with joy.

'Where are you? You sound out of breath.'

'I'm walking next door's German shepherd with our dogs today. I say walk, but it's more of a sprint.'

'Isn't it only five a.m. in the UK?'

'Yes, and dark and bloody freezing. But I volunteered to help out on Sam's school trip to the museum with the big dinosaurs. We're leaving at seven and I haven't done the packed lunches yet. Or had a shower.'

'Sounds exhausting.' I sipped my coffee and noticed a bee zigzagging lazily between hibiscus flowers. 'You need a mum's gap-year trip, if only for one week. Seven days of me-time without running around after everyone else.'

'I like doing it all.' She sounded tetchy. 'I'm the hub of the family and I love being the one they rely on.'

She and I had very different lives, but our crushing need to nurture was the same.

'I know you do, but everyone needs to stop and fill their own cup every so often. You can't fill from an empty cup,' I said, quoting Lisa.

'That's true, I suppose. Is that why you called? To make me jealous of your sunlounger-and-cocktail day ahead?'

'Not quite. I'm . . .' I paused to savour this moment, knowing how my sister was going to react. 'Kat, you'll never guess who I was with last night.'

'You're right, I won't. Tell me. It's too early and I don't have the headspace to guess.'

'Jackson.'

Silence down the line and then, 'Shit the bed.'

'I fainted in the hotel lobby and when I came to, I heard his voice. And there he was, larger than life and sexier than ever.'

'Oh my God, Mags. I bet you nearly fainted again.'

'Correct. And then I cried because the first thing I had to tell him after all these years was . . .' A lump formed in my throat as I recalled how his look of happiness faded to dismay.

337

'About Brontë,' Kat finished for me. 'His daughter.'

'Yes,' I whispered.

'And how did that go?'

My heart ached at the memory. 'I felt like I was losing her all over again by seeing it through his eyes. He was amazing; he took it so well. He wanted to know everything about her. He stayed with me for hours and I showed him all my photos. And now her father knows about her. I feel . . . I feel . . . I don't even know how to explain it.'

'Oh Mags,' she soothed. 'You probably feel a lot of things right now, and that's okay, you don't have to say. But I'm glad he knows; it has always niggled me that the man who stole my sister's heart didn't know about our lovely girl.'

'Me too,' I replied. 'But it would have been so much better if they'd met.'

We were quiet for a few moments, but it was a companionable silence and I felt comforted by her being on the end of the line.

'So: Jackson?' she quizzed, breaking the mood. 'Still good-looking by the sound of it. Married? Single? Handsome? Tell me everything.'

'My hormones are in major overdrive,' I admitted, 'he is every bit as gorgeous as I remembered. As for the rest, I don't know.'

'What?' she screeched. 'How did you not ask if he's single or not?'

'Because last night needed to be about Brontë. He's grieving for a child he didn't even meet, and I needed to give him space to process everything.' I sighed. 'We'll have more time to talk today after we've collected the book. He had to make a call yesterday to make arrangements to be home late, so I'm guessing there's someone in his life. He's too much of a catch to be single.'

'So are you, but you're single,' she pointed out.

'By choice.'

'Imagine, though.' She sighed dreamily. 'Imagine he's been waiting for you to come back all these years.'

'I have been imagining that, believe me.'

'Look, I'd better go, but let's talk again later, once you've been reunited with Brontë's book.'

'Before you go, how's Mum?' I asked, unsure if I really wanted to know.

'Funny you should ask about her. She offered to have Sam to sleep overnight for the first time ever, which he's looking forward to. She has sold her car though, which is a shame.'

Mum hadn't told Kat about her latest money issues for some reason. So neither would I.

'I was very unkind about her mothering skills when she rang me.'

Kat laughed. 'I'm not sure she even had any when we were kids. But she's making an effort now at least. Whatever you said to her worked.'

'I'm glad.' Even if the end didn't justify the means.

'Maybe the two of you should try again,' my sister suggested. 'She's not getting any younger, and if she's changing her ways then perhaps you could let her in?'

'Hmm, maybe,' I said vaguely.

'Think about it. Now I've really got to go and thaw out before getting Sam up.'

'Bye, sis. Kiss Andy and Sam for me. I love you all.'

'Go get your man. If he's single. Oh God, I really want him to be single.'

'Kat!' I laughed. 'Actually, yes, so do I. Bye!'

I was still laughing when the phone rang again, and Tiff's name flashed up on the screen.

'Jeez, you're a toughie to get hold of.'

'Sorry, a monkey stole my phone, and I've been too busy ever since to catch up on my messages.'

'Ah, that sucks. Still, we've all been there.'

I grinned. 'Coming from most people that would be a joke, but with you, it's probably true.'

'Listen, I've been watching the drama unfold on Insta with Brontë's book and your travels and I might be reading this completely wrong, but I get the feeling that you're never going to be satisfied with returning to the UK at the end of your trip and knocking out your nine-to-five again. Am I right?'

'Er, yes,' I replied, taken aback. 'I've been thinking a lot about what I want my future to look like now that Brontë's gone. I need to make some changes. I want things to look forward to and not wake up every morning with a feeling of dread that today will be as bad as the last.'

'I knew it!' She sounded triumphant. 'You need a challenge and I have one for you. Now, I'm a lone wolf and I like to do things my way, but I like you, Maggie. I don't think you'd annoy me.'

'Thanks.' I smirked. 'What praise.'

'You're welcome,' she replied without a trace of irony. 'You're as sweet as candy on the outside, but rustle that candy wrapper and boy, do you get a shock. So will you join me as a trustee of the One World Project? I want to expand our reach, in terms of services we offer in the Chitwan valley; but also in the future, I want us to open more centres in other places, maybe even other countries. And I need someone I can trust to help with that.'

'If you're offering me a position, your timing is impeccable.'

I told her about the call I'd had with Anna yesterday and how even though I still had a job, it wasn't the one I wanted.

'What? Get your lawyer onto them,' she spluttered, indignantly. 'That's constructive dismissal. They owe you big time.'

'I might like the new role,' I countered. 'I should at least give it a go.'

'No you should not! They don't deserve you. Ditch 'em. Do something that sets your heart racing. Tell you what, I'll draft you a letter to send them, see if we can't squeeze some severance pay out of those cowboys.'

She was absolutely right. ShopSwift didn't deserve me. Why hadn't I thought of that? 'Thank you, I appreciate that. And to clarify, are you offering me a job?'

'Yes. I mean the pay is terrible – by that I mean that it's non-existent – but the perks are phenomenal.'

'What perks?' I asked, already knowing that I was going to accept her offer regardless. At some point I was going to need a job that paid the bills, but I had savings to tide me over while I worked out what that could be, and working with Tiff would be fun.

'Well, let's think,' she paused for a second. 'You get me emailing you all hours of the day and night. You'll get your travel expenses paid to visit the project and you get to help me expand the project. And, of course, you get the heart-warming knowledge that you're doing good in the world.'

'Would I be able to have an input on locations?' Such as Bali, I thought.

'Sure. Absolutely.'

'Could I help with fundraising?' I'd never done that, but it required similar skills to selling and I could do that in my sleep.

'Oh my God, *yes!*' came the reply. 'And you're a big hit on Insta, so your first job will be taking over the social media.'

I frowned. 'I wouldn't say that's true, but I could give it a go.'

'By the way, do you ever check your Instagram? There are so many questions on your last post all waiting for answers.'

'I will later, I've been offline for a while.'

'Oh yeah, the monkey. Okay, I'll get that letter to your employer done and the details of the trustee agreement drawn up and emailed over.'

'Assuming I accept this well-paid opportunity.'

There was a silence which went on so long that I had no choice but to fill it.

'I'd be delighted to become a trustee.'

'Great.' Tiff drew a breath. 'Brontë was a lucky young woman to have you in her corner. And now I'm very glad to have you in mine. Take care in Bali – and no more monkey business.'

An hour later, Jackson and I, with his dog, Scout, were on the way to the airport in Denpasar. Scout, it transpired, was the reason he'd had to call home last night, because she couldn't be left on her own for too long. Not a girlfriend, or a wife, but a dog. That knowledge alone had put an extra shine on my morning.

He had an open-top khaki-coloured jeep which bounced over every pothole but on the plus side, afforded me an amazing view of the scenery as we headed out of the town past ornate temples, terraced rice fields and shady forests.

'I've got the whole day free,' he told me. 'Once we've been to the airport, we can do whatever you want. I can be a tourist for the day and show you around.'

'That's really good of you, but I have been here before, you know.'

'I know,' he said with a grin. 'Because I have very fond memories, but Bali has changed a lot since then.'

'The turtle sanctuary for starters,' I agreed. 'Oof, careful Scout!'

Scout had her bottom on my leg, her two front paws on the door and her head sticking out of the vehicle, ears flapping in the breeze. Every so often her back legs would slip and dig into my thigh, making me wince.

'Sorry about her.' Jackson patted the dog's back. 'She insists on sitting there whether I have a passenger or not. She likes you, by the way.'

'I like her,' I said, stroking her head. Our hands touched for a split second, and I felt a frisson of heat as if someone had flicked a switch inside me.

He'd always had an air of confidence about him; it had been one of the things that had attracted me to him. But he'd matured into a man who I instinctively felt was one of life's good guys: strong-minded, determined, with a gentleness in his manner that spoke directly to my heart. Also, his good looks were playing havoc with my pulse rate. Today he wore shorts and a cotton shirt, several buttons of which were undone, and every so often I caught a glimpse of his toned brown chest. I was in my favourite sundress and beaded flip-flops; and I'd piled my hair into a bun, allowing just enough tendrils to escape to soften the look. I'd even put on mascara and lip gloss.

I glanced sideways at him, still not quite believing that I was here with him, in Bali, where we first met. He stole a look at me, and we both grinned at being caught staring.

'Thanks for doing this,' I said. 'You probably have a lot better things to do than drive me to the airport.'

'Are you kidding me?' he said playfully. 'The first girl I fell in love with turns up after twenty years? You bet I'm going to spend as much time with you as I can. You'll be begging me to leave you alone by tonight.'

The *first* girl.

'I doubt that,' I said boldly, my eyes challenging his.

Of course there'd been others, it would have been odder if there hadn't been. And besides, I wanted him to have found love in his life. I hadn't, at least not a deep enough love to want to commit to. Although I was beginning to think that maybe I hadn't been receptive to love. I'd been so devoted to providing Brontë with the stability and security my own childhood had lacked that I'd left no heart space for romantic love.

343

'I did, you know,' he said after a pause. 'Fall in love with you, I mean. I didn't say it at the time because I was too scared to tell you in case it wasn't reciprocated.'

There was a crushing tightness across my chest. He'd felt the same about me as I had about him. It was wonderful to hear, but at the same time, absolute torture.

'It was reciprocated,' I said quietly. 'I could hardly admit it to myself, let alone you, because it had seemed impossible that a holiday romance stood a chance in the real world. I'd never felt like that with anyone before.'

*Or since.*

'No way. D'you hear that, Scout?' He reached across me to scratch behind the dog's ears and grinned, his teeth pearly white against his tanned skin. 'I remember you telling me that you didn't do boyfriends, and I thought there was no way you were going to fall for my limited charms.'

'Oh come on,' I scoffed. 'You were blessed with plenty of charm, you had me at "Do you like puppies?"' We both laughed at the memory. 'I wonder what would have happened if we'd told each other the truth.'

'I wouldn't have let you get on that plane back to the UK by yourself, that's for sure. I'd have come with you.'

'Seriously?' I stared at him in disbelief. 'But you were so set on going to Thailand. You'd wanted to travel and see the world.'

He shrugged. 'I would have happily traded Thailand for the UK; it still would have classed as travelling. I haven't been there even now. It's on my list though.'

'So, let me get this straight. If you'd known at the time how much I loved you, you'd have come home with me?'

'Yeah.' He gave me a sheepish smile. 'I guess it serves me right for not saying anything.'

'Oh my God,' I murmured.

We fell silent for a while then, both lost in our thoughts. All I could think was that if he'd been in the UK when I found out I was pregnant, my whole life, and Brontë's, would have been entirely different. I blinked tears away and when I looked across at him he was doing the same.

Neither of us spoke until we approached the signpost for the airport and Jackson turned off the main road.

'I suppose there's no point regretting things we can't change,' I said. 'We have to believe that things happened for a reason. And that we were destined to go our separate ways.'

I wasn't sure I believed this myself, but the conversation felt like it needed a positive spin.

'I guess you're right,' he said wistfully, 'but I'd sure like to have known my daughter.'

'And she would have loved to have known you too.'

We pulled into the airport car park, and he slowed down while we looked for a parking spot.

'Well,' he said, reversing smoothly into an empty space. 'I'm not too scared to talk about my feelings anymore. So let me say how happy I am that you're here.'

My heart could have burst with joy. 'I'm happy to be here too.'

My phone buzzed with a message. It was from Harry's friend, Lola, to say she had landed. Brontë's book was finally in Bali.

# Chapter 42

## Bali

We'd arranged to meet Lola outside the terminal where the taxi drivers wait for their passengers. We found a space at the barriers and scanned every face. Scout sat down good-naturedly between us, Jackson keeping a tight hold of her lead. The flow of passengers pouring out of the doors was fast and furious. I'd met Lola once in the coffee shop in Leura but even so I wasn't sure I'd be able to pick her out in a crowd.

'Maggie?' called a voice eventually.

Scout jumped to her feet and began wagging her tail.

A petite girl in linen dungarees stood at the opposite side of the barrier, waving. Her hair was arranged in two long braids; a layer of frizz had escaped, revealing little curls all along her hairline.

'Yes! Lola, lovely to see you.'

She shrugged off her rucksack and pulled out Brontë's book.

My eyes welled up with tears at the sight of it. 'I thought I'd lost this for good.'

She handed it to me immediately. 'You have no idea how scared I was in case I got my bag stolen. I mean, can you imagine the pressure to return this amazing book to you in one piece? Well, of course you can – you were the one who lost it in the first place.'

'Thanks for reminding me.' I clasped it to my chest. I was never letting it out of my sight again.

Jackson hooted with laughter. 'Brutal.'

Lola blushed. 'Sorry. I'm nervous.'

'It's fine, I'm nervous too. Thank you, thank you.' I closed my eyes for a brief second, overwhelmed with relief. I'd got my girl back. I couldn't wait to immerse myself back in her world again.

Lola looked at Jackson and back to me.

'This is Jackson,' I said. 'And his dog Scout.'

'I'm Brontë's father,' he added. 'Pleased to meet you.'

There was the slightest crack in his voice as he said it. It would have been the first time he'd introduced himself as that and it looked like the experience had really moved him. Seeing his reaction moved me too.

Her eyes widened. 'That is so cool. So you managed to find him without Brontë's guidance? That is so . . . so romantic.'

'You've read her book ?' It was so personal to her and me. And then of course, there were my own journal entries, words written from the heart, a love letter to my daughter, meant only for her.

'Yes,' she squeaked, slapping a hand over her mouth. 'I'm sorry, but it was a long flight and I read the whole thing. Brontë is amazing; you must be so proud of her.'

'We are,' said Jackson gruffly, squeezing my hand.

I loved that he'd said *we*. All through my pregnancy and throughout Brontë's life, there had been no *we*, only *I*. Whatever happened now, even if I left Bali and never saw him again, I'd know that we were both her parents; we shared a special connection.

'I'll come round,' said Lola, and darted off to join us on our side of the barrier.

'You're so kind to do this for me,' I said, giving her a hug.

'Harry asked me and . . .' She looked down at her feet. She was wearing a pair of the Birkenstocks that Brontë got for her last birthday, the ones with the closed-in toes. 'And I kinda like being part of the story. You're Insta-famous now.'

I raised a sceptical eyebrow. 'I don't think so, but thank you, and thank you for agreeing to bring the book back to me.'

She bent down to give Scout some fuss, who promptly rolled onto her back to get her tummy tickled. 'Seriously. Like, you have almost as many followers as Harry now.'

I stared at her in disbelief. 'I have?'

She nodded. 'The whole Mum's Gap Year thing has caught on. Even my mum knows who you are, and she only follows Michael Bublé and the Royal Family. Can we get a selfie?'

'Sure.' I tucked my arm around her waist to get in close.

'You too, Jackson, and Scout,' Lola said, waving him to stand next to her.

Jackson picked up his dog and we all huddled together for the picture.

'I'm gonna get us something to drink. Scout's thirsty. Anyone else?' he asked.

We both asked for water and he and the dog wandered over to the vending machine.

'I'm sending this to Harry,' said Lola, tapping at the screen. 'He's waiting to hear from me.'

'He's very lucky to have you as his friend.'

'Yeah,' she said quietly.

'But you'd like to be more than friends?' I guessed, observing the wistfulness in her voice.

Lola blinked at me. 'This is so awkward. I mean, you're Brontë's mum.'

I nodded. 'Which is why I know what a decent guy he is and why he deserves a lovely girl in his life.'

'I think he still loves her.' She wrinkled her nose. 'Which is cool, but there's no way I want to come between him and her. Oh God, that sounds crazy.'

I thought about Harry and I stargazing in the Blue Mountains and how we'd agreed that we'd both try to find love again.

'He might be feeling nervous about starting another relationship, maybe not knowing what a long enough gap is after losing Brontë. So my advice is to tell him how you feel when you get back. What's the worst that can happen?'

'He freaks out and runs a mile?'

'That won't happen; he's a nice boy. I'm sure that even if he says no, he'd let you down gently.' I gave her my most reassuring smile. 'And the best?'

She visibly melted. 'He says yes, and we fall in love and . . . well, you know what I mean.'

I nodded to where Jackson was pumping money into a vending machine. 'I wished I'd told him how I felt when I had the chance twenty-four years ago.'

She pulled a face. 'That's so sad, but it's not too late, is it? You two seem comfortable with each other, like you've been together for, like, forever.'

'Honestly? I don't know whether it's too late or not,' I said.

Jackson returned with three bottles of water and we both took one. 'Lola, can we give you a lift somewhere? It's the least we can do.'

*We.* He'd said it again. My breath hitched at the implied *coupleness* of his words. I wondered whether my feelings were as obvious to him as they were to me. Were my pupils dilating, was my chest visibly rising? I needed to make more of an effort to play it cool, at least until I found out more about his personal life.

'Thanks, but I'm waiting for the rest of my family to arrive,' Lola told him. 'Their flight lands any minute. We're here for my granddad's third wedding.' She rolled her eyes. 'Are you okay for me to post this picture?' She showed us her phone. She'd captured the second that Jackson and I had looked across at each other smiling. Scout was trying to lick Lola's face. 'I mean, it kinda looks like we're a family, which is cool and weird at the same time.'

'Fine with me,' I told her.

Jackson approved too and asked her to send it to him.

'Maggie, you won't tell Harry about our chat, will you?' Lola bit her lip.

'Absolutely not, I promise, as long as you promise to tell me how it goes.'

'Deal. You're awesome,' she said, flinging her arms around my neck again. 'Bye, both of you. So great to meet you.'

'What was that about?' Jackson asked as we watched her walk back into the terminal, her head bowed over her phone.

'She fancies Harry and worries that he might not feel the same way as her,' I explained.

'And what did you tell her that was so awesome?' He squatted down to Scout's level and tipped his water up so she could drink from the bottle.

'That she should tell Harry how she feels and that I wished I'd done that twenty-four years ago,' I said casually. 'With you.'

Jackson shot me a surprised look. 'That's very good advice.'

I smiled. 'Hindsight is a marvellous thing. You might want to stop pouring water now, by the way.'

'What?' He looked down at the puddle of water at his feet and grinned. Scout was licking it straight from the floor. 'Oh hell. I was distracted for a second there.'

*By me*, I thought. Two decades on and there was still something there between us.

'Listen, do you mind if we find somewhere to sit for a few minutes?' I asked. 'I'm dying to read what Brontë's written about Bali in her book.'

'Sure.' He got to his feet and looked awkward. 'Do you want to be alone?'

We both looked at the book in my hands, her illustrations so familiar to me and as yet unknown to him. I could sink into her world by myself, or I could share the next chapter – and possibly the most important – with the man she'd wanted to meet. It was an easy decision.

'Absolutely not!' I tucked my arm through his. 'I think Brontë would love us to be reading it together.'

The three of us found a shady bench and Scout promptly flopped down underneath it.

I gave the book to Jackson to flick through and let his daughter introduce herself through her words and art while I drank my water. Once he'd found the page headed *Bali*, he held it between us so that we could both see the words.

'Okay?' I asked.

'More than okay,' he said, wiping a tear from his eye. 'What a girl.'

'Indeed. Let's see what she has to say about Bali.'

*Brontë's Gap Year*

Everyone my age wants to go to Bali. It's Instagrammer heaven. If it's not digital nomads, it's backpackers or volunteers working at kids' nurseries or turtle conservation or people having the holiday of a life-time. But I've got a special reason for going. I'm going to try and trace what happened to my dad.

Mum has never had one bad word to say either about Bali or about Jackson, my father. Their story is probably the most romantic I've ever heard, and it's always made me sad that they never got to meet up after I was born. I love to hear Mum telling me how she and he got together. There's this golden glow to her face when she talks about him and about Bali. The older I've got, the more curious I am to know more. Maybe I won't find my dad on this trip, and if I don't, I'll keep looking. The path to success is paved with failures, as Mum is always saying.

But one thing's for sure, I bet I fall in love with Bali as much as Mum did in 2000.

I feel so sorry for the older generation trying to do stuff without social media. It was so easy to lose touch with people in the old days. Now it's the other way around. Like the boy from my junior school called Richard who moved to Vancouver when he was eight who still messages me. I didn't even like him back then. Now it's rare that I meet someone who I don't have at least one mutual connection with. Anyway, all Mum knew was his name and age and that he was American, that he loved surfing and scuba diving, wanted to travel the world and spend his life living by the sea. I love to imagine that that was what he ended up doing and it wasn't the random dreams of a twenty-three-year old. Having a surfer dude for a dad would be so cool. Mum only has about six photos of him because phones didn't take pictures then. But I've seen enough to think that he looks a bit like me. I think if I meet him, I'll know straight away whether I've got the right man or not.

So I don't have much to go on. Or so I thought . . . Because although the turtle conservation project that Mum stayed at is gone, there's another new one close by. Even better, there's a man Mum used to talk about called Utt and there's a really old man called Utt who works at the new one. Coincidence? Maybe. But there's only one way to find out. So Utt might have some info on Jackson, and even if he doesn't, it'll be cool to meet someone else who knew my dad. I've searched Bali and Thailand (just in case) for anyone with Jackson as his first name but came up with a big fat zero. I did find one possible, a man whose *surname* is Jackson, the owner of a hotel for surfers. So not ruling him in or out at the moment. But I'm romantic enough to hope that it's all going to work out happily ever after.

# Chapter 43

**Bali**

My face was aching from smiling by the time I got to the bottom of the page. It felt so good to be back in her world, seeing her familiar handwriting and her scratchy little doodles in the margin. I felt a tug at my heartstrings at the thought of her researching her own father by herself. This must have been why she wanted to finish her itinerary completely before coming to me with it. I conjured up her expression that day when she'd come over with it; excited, eager to share but nervous too. At the time, I'd put her jitters down to the prospect of telling me she wanted to defer her job, but now I saw I was wrong.

Jackson was still reading, his eyes roving over every detail on every page, drinking her in.

Finally, he closed the book and exhaled. 'Smart girl. First to find Utt and then to find me and the hotel. So if she'd made it to Bali, I'd have met her. How cool would that have been?'

'But your name?' I said, confused.

'I was baptised Eugene Jackson, Gene for short. My dad was a big fan of the Apollo missions. Remember Gene Kranz, from the Apollo movie, who wore the waistcoats?'

'Vaguely.'

'Everyone has called me by my last name since kindergarten. There was a girl in my class called Jean; you can imagine the teasing I got for having a girl's name. So I became Jackson and it stuck.'

I stared at him, trying to reconfigure my brain with this new information. 'You never told me.'

He shrugged. 'It honestly never occurred to me. Like I guess it never occurred to you to tell me you're a Magnolia.'

'Touché,' I said with a laugh. 'I like my name now, but growing up it felt so pretentious. My sister Kat's name is short for Katalina. Our mother thought we'd sound grander if she gave us unusual names.'

'Magnolia is a beautiful name, it suits you.'

'And Eugene is very . . .' I searched for a suitable word and Jackson's eyes danced with amusement. 'Unique?'

'Exactly,' he said. 'Unique is every high school kid's nightmare.'

'And the surf hotel?'

'That's me,' he confirmed.

'Are we going to read on ?' I said, nodding to Brontë's book.

He pondered that for a moment and shook his head. 'Do you remember Tegenungan Waterfall?'

A shiver ran down my spine. 'Our first proper date. How could I forget?'

We'd hired a scooter and gone off exploring by ourselves. We'd come across the waterfall by chance and had ended up climbing down steep steps and diving into clear cold water below the falls. We'd swum and laughed and kissed and had to lie on the rocks to dry off because we hadn't taken towels. It had been the most romantic day of my life.

'Fancy a trip down memory lane?' He cocked an eyebrow.

'Now?' I asked.

He shrugged. 'Why not? I've loved getting to know Brontë through your stories and now in her own words, but I think it's time we talked about ourselves, don't you? There are things I need to say, things I want to tell you, and ask you too, if I may?'

There was a sombre note to his voice which sent a wave of panic through me. But he was right. We couldn't put it off any longer. I had to find out what he'd been doing for the last two and a half decades – and more importantly, with whom.

I attempted a smile. 'Okay. Let's go.'

We set off again. This time, thankfully, Jackson persuaded Scout to settle on the back seat where it was shadier. I think I'd have melted if I'd had to ride with a hot, panting dog on my lap again. We'd only been driving for a few minutes when I got a call from Harry.

'You got the book back!' He sounded thrilled. 'I saw Lola's story on Instagram.'

'I have, thank you. Lola is *lovely*,' I added.

'Yeah,' Harry agreed. 'I really like her.'

'As a friend, or do you think she could be more?' I probed.

'More, maybe?' He groaned. 'I don't know, Maggie. Is it too soon? The moment I start seeing someone else, I'm worried I'll feel as if I've broken my tie with Brontë. I'm scared of letting go.'

What a sweetheart he was. He was so worthy of somebody's love. But I understood how he felt and my heart ached for him. 'Think of it like this. Life is made up of chapters. Some people will appear all the way through while others will only be in a few of them. The chapter with Brontë has ended, but it's not the end of your story, not by a long way. She'll always be there; you can look back at the time you had and know that she loved you and that you made each other happy. But don't be afraid to start a new chapter. Don't miss out on what life has waiting for you on the next page.'

355

'That's cool, thank you.' He cleared his throat. 'And you wouldn't mind?'

'Oh, Harry,' I said, my voice thickening. 'Why would I mind? You deserve to be happy. Everyone does.'

There was silence for a moment and then, 'You're right. Okay, I'm doing it, I'm asking her out on a date. As soon as she gets back from Bali.'

'Or,' I suggested, knowing how pleased Lola was going to be. 'You could message her now and ask her; make the date for a couple of weeks' time. Give you both something to look forward to.'

'I'll think about it,' he said. 'Have you seen your Instagram recently, you've got loads—'

'I know, I know.' I laughed. 'Everyone keeps telling me.'

'There's a travel company trying to get hold of you. They've commented on your last post multiple times. They are super interested. Check your DMs.'

'Yes, boss! I'll look now.'

'Lovely boy,' I said, ending the call.

'Our daughter made good choices with men, then?' Jackson asked.

I smiled at him, enjoying the chance to talk about her. 'She did. She learned from her mother.'

He started to laugh and focused his gaze on the road. 'I didn't doubt it for a second.'

I opened up Instagram on my phone. 'Right, I'd better see what all the fuss is about . . . Oh my goodness!'

Since the last time I'd checked, my followers had leapt to thirty thousand. I scrolled in amazement through the hundreds of comments on my last couple of posts.

'What is it?' Jackson asked, trying to squint at my screen.

I told him about Harry's Instagram account and how he'd started helping people who were struggling with grief and that he'd tagged me in one of his pictures along with the Mum's Gap Year hashtag.

'I posted that I'd lost Brontë's book and asked people to look out for it, not thinking for a moment that it would help me to find it.'

'But it did, huh?' Jackson grinned, 'and now you're Instagram famous, as Lola put it.'

'Apparently so. I think older women taking a gap-year-style trip has fired a lot of people's imaginations. The travel market is geared towards young people taking these life-changing trips to far-flung places, but there's a lot to be said for letting go of your responsibilities for a while and enjoying some freedom from everyday life.'

'Is that what *you're* doing?'

'Now that Brontë's gone, I don't have any responsibilities to let go of,' I admitted. 'Not even a dog. This trip started as a way to honour Brontë. There were things she wanted to do, places she wanted to go and people she wanted to meet. Since she could no longer go, I decided to go in her place with this itinerary as my guide.'

He gave me an appraising look. 'That's really cool, you know. And you're glad you did?'

'Oh yeah. I was stuck in a rut, telling myself I was dealing with my grief by accepting it and getting on with life. But I wasn't dealing with it at all. If anything, I was in denial. I wouldn't even let people at work mention her name.'

'That doesn't sound healthy.'

'I've learned a lot about myself in the last few months. I'm going to be making some changes when I get back. Starting with finding things that set my soul on fire.'

The thought of going back to the UK made my stomach flip and I fell silent, mulling over what lay ahead for me when I got home. At the moment, the answer was: not much. But I was going to be a trustee for Tiff, which I was excited about, and I was planning to do more travelling. I was determined to take this new energy back home with me and stay open to where life took me.

'I liked what you said to Harry about chapters and turning over a new page. I can tell you studied psychology. You always said you wanted to be an expert in human behaviour.'

'But I didn't finish my degree. Once I knew I was pregnant, I had to start earning money. And I wouldn't have been able to sit my exams anyway: Brontë was born in May.'

Jackson swore under his breath. 'I'm sorry, that sucks. I wish . . . It's no good me wishing things could have been different because they weren't, but it's a shame you had to quit. Couldn't your parents have helped?'

'No.' I stiffened. 'I don't really have much to do with either of them. Not anymore. What about you? How are your mum and dad?'

'Mom sadly passed away. Dad was heartbroken and lost without her. I persuaded him to join us out here for a month.' He smirked. 'Five years later, and he's still here.'

'I'm so sorry about your mum,' I said softly, remembering how fondly he used to talk about her.

He nodded grimly. 'The worst thing was that I'd been talking about going back to the States to see her for months, but I was so busy that I didn't make the trip. Then she died and I flew straight back for the funeral.' He looked at me. 'Isn't that crazy? I couldn't make time for her when she was alive, but as soon as she was gone, back I went. I was so angry with myself about that. I'd give anything for one more chat with her, one more hug, one more slice of her famous sticky ginger cake. But I left it too late.'

His words hit home. That could so easily happen to me. If Mum died, of course I would go to her funeral. Which begged the question that if I would pay my respects on her death, couldn't I find it in me to repair our relationship while she was alive?

'We never know, do we,' I mused, 'how long we have. We always assume that there'll be enough time for everything. When so often life shows us that there isn't.'

I thought of Brontë and how I'd taken for granted that she'd be back at my dinner table a week from that last sushi takeout. How I presumed I would have time to listen to her tell me about her gap year. Now I was doing the same with my own mother. Brontë's death should have been a wake-up call for me to not put off saying and doing the important things. I'd go and see Mum, I decided, as soon as I got back home, and I'd work to repair some of the fences which we'd both damaged over the years. Maybe we'd never have the close bond that Brontë and I had, but it had to be worth a shot. It was the right thing to do, and I felt a load slip from my shoulders by coming to this decision.

While we'd been talking, I'd been scrolling through my Instagram messages looking for the one from the travel company Harry had told me about. I found one from Independent Travel Club and opened it.

I laughed in disbelief as I skimmed through it. 'That's interesting.'

'Good news?' Jackson glanced at me.

'Possibly, it's from a travel company who'd like to collaborate with me to curate some holidays under the Mum's Gap Year brand. A *brand*!' I laughed. 'How did that happen?'

'That's genius.'

'They say they've been following my journey and think I may have discovered an untapped market. I think I have too.'

My head buzzed with the idea. This could work. The feed-back on my Instagram posts proved how much interest there was in a trip like mine. We could do short trips for those who worked and longer ones for those looking for a sabbatical. I might even be able to weave in Tiff's One World Project and tie in some volunteering and fundraising.

Beside me Jackson laughed, bringing me back to the moment. 'Look at your face! Sounds like you've found something to set your soul on fire.'

I beamed at him. 'This is insane, but yes, I just might have.'

By the time I'd finished typing a message back to them to express my delight and to arrange to speak to them on Zoom, we'd arrived at our destination.

'I don't remember any of this,' I said, after we'd parked the car and headed downhill past a café and a collection of gift and snack shops.

'Bali has grown up,' said Jackson.

'Haven't we all,' I replied.

'But you've improved with age,' he replied. 'The same can't be said for these tourist spots.'

'Very smooth, *Mr* Jackson.'

Already I could hear the tantalising roar of the waterfall in the distance. I peeled my dress away from my hot skin, desperate to get into the water. There were several steep flights of stone steps to the water and we joined a steady stream of people downwards. Scout, tugging on her lead, seemed as keen to get in as I was.

At the bottom, we took off our shoes and put our feet in the cool clear water.

'Bliss,' I groaned, taking Jackson's hand for support.

Scout plunged straight in, her muzzle in a wide smile as she doggy-paddled to and fro. Once she'd had enough, Jackson secured her lead to a shady post and she lay down with her head on her paws, panting. We stripped off and waded out into the deep water and closer to the waterfall. I dived under the surface. The noise of the waterfall thundered in my ears and the water was effervescent with bubbles.

'It's just as beautiful as I remember it,' I said, coming back to the surface and pushing my hair off my face.

Last time we were here, he had dived beneath me, grabbed hold of my ankles and tugged me under, and we had burst through the surface gasping for air, laughing and splashing at each other. It had been fun, romantic and sexy too. I wondered if he remembered it the same way I did.

It was too deep for me to touch the floor but not for Jackson and as I swam back to him, he caught me around my waist.

'I'm not going to dunk you this time,' he said with a smile.

'You remember!' My eyes sparkled at him.

'Of course I do,' he murmured. 'I thought you were the most beautiful girl I'd ever met. And you're even more beautiful now.'

I braced myself against the taut muscles in his arms to prevent his chest from touching mine. If there was someone else in his life, I'd back away now. I'd be devastated, but I didn't want to put temptation in his way. That wasn't my style.

But being so close to him was torture. I didn't know how much longer I was going to be able to keep my distance. I wanted to wrap my arms around his neck, press my body against his, kiss him . . . I had to know. I had to know now.

'Are you—'

'Do you—'

We both spoke at once and laughed.

'You go first,' he said.

'Okay.' I let go of his arms and floated away to put some space between us.

'Actually, no,' he said, swimming after me and catching my hand again. 'I've gotta go first, this is killing me.'

He pulled me to him, his eyes flashing with longing, and I grabbed hold of his shoulders to steady myself.

'Maggie, do you have a partner waiting back home for you? Because now that you've walked into my life again, I don't want to let you go. And if there's any chance, any tiny chance at all of kissing those delicious lips of yours, I want to take it.'

Was this really happening? It felt like a dream. 'I'm single. Are you?' I rasped. 'Is that what you're saying?'

He gave a slow nod and that was all it took. Our bodies collided, hands cupping faces, fingers tangled in hair, lips on lips, my legs wrapped around his hips as he crushed my chest against his.

The taste of his mouth made me weak with longing and only the sound of nearby giggling forced us to pull apart.

'You've done it to me again, Maggie,' he whispered soft against my lips. 'Twenty-four hours in your company and I'm a lost cause.'

'Count yourself lucky,' I retorted, barely able to contain my joy. 'I've been a lost cause for twenty-four years.'

'I've dreamed about you so many times over the years,' he murmured. 'Wondering where you were, what sort of life you've had. Who you loved after me. Those weeks we had together were so perfect that whenever I met someone new, I couldn't help but compare them to you.'

'Jackson.' I touched his face, his shoulders, his chest. Now that I knew he felt the same, I couldn't get enough of him. 'That was how it was for me. I couldn't bear to bring anyone else into our little family of two because I knew he would never be you.'

'Why didn't we try harder to stay in touch, Maggie?' he groaned.

'Because we were young?' I said. 'Because we didn't realise then how special what we had was? Who knows.'

He gave me a wicked smile. 'You became a sort of fantasy woman to me.'

'Me?' I forced myself not to ruin the moment by saying something self-deprecating. The girl he met all those years ago would never have done that. She'd have met his eye, letting him know how good it felt to be desired. 'Tell me more,' I said.

'As crazy as it sounds, whenever I thought about my dream woman, an image of you, in your bikini on the beach, would appear. You were hard to get over, Mags. I guess I never did.'

'It doesn't sound crazy at all. Because I've never got over you either.'

'When Utt called to tell me you were in Bali, I was in such a rush to get to you that I struggled to get the key in the ignition of the jeep. On the drive from Canggu, I told myself I had to play it cool, you'd probably be here with your partner. And even if you weren't, would you even want to see me?'

'I did want to see you, Jackson, I've never stopped wanting that.'

'Oh Maggie.'

I watched his face as he spoke, his lips forming my name, his eyes burning into mine as if I was the only person in the world. 'I've fantasised about you too. But fantasy can only take you so far. The reality is so, so much better.'

A plaintive woof from the bank made us turn back to Scout and we both laughed.

'And right on cue, real life beckons,' said Jackson. 'We'd better give her some attention.'

'As long as that's your only other woman,' I teased, 'I can handle sharing you.'

'I've got some special people in my life who I can't wait for you to meet.' We waded out of the water hand in hand, and he brought my fingers to his lips to kiss them 'But honestly? There's never been anyone who came close to you.'

This man: he melted my heart. I sent up a silent prayer of gratitude to Brontë for bringing us back together via her planning. None of this would have happened without her.

'Like who?' I asked. 'Do you have kids?'

He hooked an arm around my shoulders as we crossed the pebbles towards the dog. 'Two sons. The eldest is in Jakarta at uni and the other now manages the diving school I set up after I decided to settle in Bali. It's really near the turtle sanctuary. Their mother and I never married, but we're still friends and she's married to one of Utt's nephews now. I focus on the hotel these days as Brontë found out.'

Scout rolled over onto her back as we reached her and Jackson tickled her belly.

My heart swelled with love for him. 'I'm so proud of you. Seems like you got exactly the life you dreamed of.'

He stepped towards me, a smouldering look in his eyes as he lowered his mouth to mine. 'I have now. I love you, Mags.'

A gasp formed in my throat and he pulled back.

'Too soon?' he whispered, his breath soft against my lips.

'Not soon enough.'

I closed my eyes and surrendered to Jackson's kiss, and it was every bit as intoxicating as it had always been.

As our kiss deepened, all thoughts of work and the UK and Tiff and the Mum's Gap Year idea floated away. For now, all that mattered was this wonderful man and the certainty that this time, I was never letting him out of my life again.

*Thank you, Brontë*, I thought. *Thank you for bringing me home.*


*Brontë's Gap Year*

---

I have never felt like such a stalker before, but once you start digging into someone's background, you can't help yourself.

So let's say my dad is Mr Jackson the hotel owner, then there's a chance that the two young Jacksons in Bali on Insta could be family too: Kai studying oceanography at uni and Regan who won an award for young business owner of the year for his dive school. Both super cute. Although (a) potentially my half-brothers and (b) I'm team Harry for ever. Couldn't find anything about their mum, but their dad Eugene (no wonder he goes by Jackson) popped up in a post about the Beach Break Hotel in Canggu. They run surf camps where you stay for a week and learn to surf. So guess who'll be booking in for lessons?? ME!

I'll do a recce and if he seems nice, I'll separate him from the crowd and ask if he remembers Maggie Jones. I'll probably take her year 2000 diary along too to jog his memory. I mean, it might not work, it might not even be him, but stranger things have happened, right? Then all I need to do is to somehow persuade Mum to come out and join us. I know it's her happy place, and if I end up finding my dad, it'll be mine too.

## Mum's Gap Year

My darling girl,

For once I'm struggling to find words to adequately express how much I love and appreciate you. I set off on this trip three months ago with no plan other than to follow your itinerary. My world had grown so small and I didn't want to imagine a future without you in it. I'd been merely existing, doing enough to get myself through each day, avoiding my feelings, even avoiding your bedroom. I'd lost my purpose, the one that had sustained me for the last twenty-four years – to be the best possible mother I could to my beautiful girl, to be your role model.

I thought you were crazy to defer your job to go travelling, but now I see that you had your priorities right. It was me who had mine wrong. All along it was you who had the answers I needed. You showed me the way. With your encouragement, page by page, you led me across the world to wonderful places, opening my heart and my mind to new experiences, new ideas.

And now you have led me back to Jackson, your wonderful dad. Quite simply, you have turned my world upside down.

I've been in Bali for three weeks, most of the time staying with your dad in his villa near the Beach Break Hotel. It's all Balinese carved wood and outdoor showers with a pool that I've taken to floating in, while Scout paces the edge of the pool in lifeguard mode. I've met his sons – your half-brothers – who are full of fun and call their dad Eugene to wind him up and constantly compete against each other in everything. You'd love them. And you'd love your granddad Errol, who is the sweetest man. He's seventy-five but you should see him on his surfboard – he puts us all to shame.

Tomorrow, we head back to the UK. Jackson wants to see our house and meet the family – and yes, that does include your gran. She and I have a lot to talk about. Losing you has made me realise that you have to make the most of the people you love while they're alive. And I do love her, even if she drives me mad. Also, I've got some ends to tie up with ShopSwift. Tiff secured me a decent severance payout, which will tide me over while I put together the plans for a new business. I'm so excited about that – I keep having to pinch myself.

And it's all because of you. You've taught me so much, my sweet girl. You will be with me always, your light and energy showing me the way.

Love, always

Mum xxx

# Epilogue

## Six months later

The sun was setting in Bali, and the sky glowed pink and orange. The ocean was still and the row of traditional fishing boats close to the shore barely stirred against their moorings. Further up the beach towards the bar, a DJ played a mix of laid-back tunes while people relaxed on beanbags under rows of brightly coloured silk parasols.

I spotted my group standing on the soft white sand close to the water's edge and my stomach fluttered with nerves. Their chatter and laughter drifted over to me on the warm breeze and it sounded like everyone was happy. The relief that all was going well so far was immense. I picked up a champagne glass from the member of staff and made my way over to them.

As I approached, the group opened up to include me and gradually the chatter died down.

'Good evening, ladies. My name's Maggie and I am thrilled to welcome you all to the first-ever Mum's Gap Year Trip.'

There was cheering and whooping, and my heart soared, knowing what a wonderful experience lay in front of them. Their faces already radiated happiness and they'd only been here a couple of hours.

'I hope you've all settled into your rooms and found the copies of your itinerary?'

'Yes!' they chorused.

'I've already decided I'm never going home,' one woman declared, making the others laugh.

I raised my glass to her. 'I've got a convert already. Okay, as you know, Mum's Gap Year Trip is a travel company with a difference,' I said. 'I am passionate about making every day count and filling our lives with things, people, and experiences which make our hearts sing. You all know my story, and I'm looking forward to hearing yours over the next three weeks. I know you're not all mums, but you are women who've decided to invest in a little bit of time for yourselves, to escape your busy lives and put real life on hold. We will be exploring Bali, scuba diving, doing some yoga, as well as volunteering at the turtle sanctuary. I hope you'll get what you need from this trip, whether it's to open yourselves up to new experiences and challenges, to see the world from a different perspective, or get away from looking after everyone else for a change.'

I pressed a hand to my heart. 'I am so blessed to have you here. And I hope you'll have the time of your lives. To Mum's Gap Year!'

I raised my glass, and everyone followed suit. I made my way around the group learning names, listening to their funny stories and reassuring those that needed it that nothing was compulsory and that their sole duty was to enjoy themselves. When I was confident that everyone was happy, I made my way up towards the bar where my family were waiting for me. Sam and Scout were playing with a piece of old driftwood in the sand while Kat was looking very cosy and loved-up on Andy's lap. Kai and Regan, Jackson's sons, were entertaining Harry and Lola with one of their stories. My mum was fanning herself while Errol showed off the scar from his monkey bite and Tiff, who was only here on a flying visit, was in deep conversation with Utt. Jackson walked across to me and met me with a kiss, sliding his arm around my waist.

'Ready?'

I blew out a breath and nodded. 'Let's do it.'

'Okay everyone,' Jackson announced. 'The boat is waiting.'

The mood was reflective as all of us boarded the boat that Utt had borrowed from his cousins. We were united by love and loss, and I made a point of hugging everyone and thanking them for being part of this special night.

'Are you all right, darling?' said Mum, hooking her arm through mine.

I exhaled and smiled at her. 'I'll never get over the loss of my child, but I was so glad to have had her, so fortunate to have those memories to look back on.'

'I'm sorry for what I said when you told me you were pregnant,' she said meekly. 'It was unforgivable, I know, but it was motivated by fear and ultimately love, you know.'

I gave her a quizzical look.

'The only memory I have of my mother is that she died giving birth to the brother I never knew. It broke my father's heart, and he never recovered; and, of course, it completely turned my world on its head. I was terrified that I would die during labour too when I had you and Kat. I was never cut out to be a mother, I barely had any experience of being a mother, or any maternal love. I knew that, but your father persuaded me it would be different.'

'It's okay, Mum, I understand. And we didn't turn out too badly in the end.'

Her eyes filled with tears. 'I'm very proud of my girls and I'm sorry it's taken me this long to tell you.'

'Thank you, I'm sorry for what I said too, about wishing you were dead.'

'Well.' She sniffed. 'That was a bit close to the bone admittedly. You've always been hot-headed. Mind you, you probably get that from me.'

'Mum,' I warned her, inwardly rolling my eyes. She would probably always be quick to criticise. But I was beginning to understand that it came from a place of insecurity and not malice. We'd spent more time in each other's company in the last six months than we had in the previous twenty years, and we were both working on our relationship. I'd persuaded her to talk to her bank too, to set up some better financial habits. No more spending money she didn't have, and proper budgeting for the things she really needed. I was determined to make her more independent and accountable. We were getting there. Slowly.

The engine of the boat cut out and I looked for Jackson. He was with Utt and the captain at the helm and I went to join them.

'Is this okay, here?' Jackson asked.

I took his hand and squeezed it and gazed around me. The sun had disappeared for the day and in its place a crescent moon hung in a wash of soft lavender sky. We had sailed about a hundred metres from the shore and the festoon of lights along the beach twinkled like stars in the distance.

I was surrounded by my favourite people and they were looking at me with love in their eyes, waiting for the signal.

'It's perfect,' I replied, my voice shaking as Jackson picked up the urn containing Brontë's ashes that we'd brought back to Bali with us.

'Okay, I think we're ready,' he announced.

Everyone gathered around us and I felt their eyes on me. I stepped close enough to Jackson to feel his heartbeat through his shirt.

'You can do this, Mags,' he murmured. 'I got you.'

I took a deep breath and removed the lid from the urn.

'Darling Brontë,' I said, 'you will always be the best part of me. You made me who I am, and I will be forever grateful to have had you here in my world for the last two and half decades. Because of you, I know how strong I am, how resilient I am, and that whatever life throws at me, I'll always survive. Because I've survived the loss of you, my beautiful child.

'And yet you will never be truly gone, because I see you in the stars at night, I feel you in the warmth of the sun, and I'll keep you forever in my heart.

'Bali is mine and Jackson's happy place, and I'm sure it would have been yours too. It is the place you chose as your final destination for your gap-year trip, and it's where your life began. It seems right that it is your final resting place too. Even though you were never here, this beautiful island is imprinted in you, like it was for the baby turtles your dad and I once released into the world. And now we release you, with all our love.'

In turn, we each took a handful of Brontë's ashes and sprinkled them into the ocean until the urn was almost empty and her ashes had been carried away by the breeze and into the water.

'That was beautiful, honey.' Jackson hugged me to him, tears running unashamedly down his face. 'I love you so, so much.'

'I love you too.' I leaned into him, drawing strength from his presence as I sprinkled one last pinch of our daughter's ashes overboard.

'Fly high, my darling girl, fly high.'

# The Thank Yous

There's a saying that it takes a village to raise a child, and sometimes it feels as if that's also true of writing a book. I think the whole world helped me with this one.

Firstly, I'd like to thank my readers, many of whom have been loyal fans right from my very first book. Your little messages of support and kind words about my books really do make all the difference.

To my daughters, Phoebe and Isabel, thank you for being the real inspiration for this story. Your dad would be so proud of you. You are both adventurous and independent, you embrace challenge and overcome adversity and throw yourselves into new experiences with boundless zest for life. I hoped that you would get out and see the world, and that is exactly what you are doing (although don't forget to come home sometimes, girls). My trips to Bali and Australia were made all the more wonderful by doing them with you. Phoebe, thanks for the weather wheel, and all the anecdotes from Sri Lanka and Bali. Being chased by a pack of wild dogs wasn't all bad – that story made it into the book.

To Linda Lawler, my roommate in Nepal, thank you for encouraging me to volunteer with you, it still remains one of the best trips of my life. Let's not talk about the cockroach nest under my mattress. Still itching.

Thank you to someone who doesn't even know me: Brontë King, you inspire me on social media with your adventures. It is your 'Gals Who Travel' community that gave me the idea for the Mums Gap Year trips. If we ever get to meet IRL, I owe you a coconut.

Thank you to Peter de Jong, from One Guide Tours for an incredible trip to the Blue Mountains, I'll treasure the memory of that day always.

Isabelle Broom, you will probably always get a mention in the 'thank yous' in my books, because I'm not sure I can write a book without you. You are such a brilliant brainstormer and cheerleader especially when the words aren't flowing. In those first few months of 2023, you were the one who kept me going, who came to stay so I wouldn't be alone, worked by my side, fed me and made me laugh. I owe you a lot. You're in Thailand as I write this and I'm very jealous, although I'm not jealous of the trench foot, the cold showers or John, the dirty old monkey.

To my dear friends, Lisa and Alison. I love you both very much and am proud to be part of the Nottingham Three, thank you.

Thanks to my brother, Andy for all that you did for me during a very difficult year. Also thanks to Max for his habit of eating his own . . . I'll leave that to readers' imagination.

Thanks to Harriet Bourton for the spa days and the mini breaks when I needed a pick-me-up. Love you. Let's keep doing those forever.

Thanks to my family down under: John, Skye and Kara Hatton, thank you for helping me fall in love with Australia.

Thanks to Milly Johnson for staying in touch and checking up on me, those little messages meant a lot. You are ace.

Thank you to Kat Robson for donating to Young Lives versus Cancer Good Books Campaign in exchange for having your name, Kat Winkleberry in the story.

Thank you, as ever, to my wonderful agent, Sheila Crowley for being as passionate as I am about this book and for your mentoring, support and kindness always. Thank you Sam Eades, you are a very special person, and I'm lucky to have you on my team. Thank you to Victoria Laws, you are never allowed to leave. Ever.

Finally, thank you to Jon, for bringing the sunshine back to my life. I can't wait to have more adventures with you. I love you.

# *Credits*

Cathy Bramley and Orion Fiction would like to thank everyone at Orion who worked on the publication of *Somewhere Only We Know* in the UK.

**Editorial**
Sam Eades
Snigdha Koirala

**Copyeditors**
Francine Brown
John Garth

**Proofreader**
Jenny Page

**Audio**
Paul Stark
Louise Richardson

**Contracts**
Dan Herron
Ellie Bowker
Oliver Chacón

**Design**
Charlotte Abrams-Simpson

**Editorial Management**
Anshuman Yadav
Charlie Panayiotou
Jane Hughes
Bartley Shaw

**Finance**
Jasdip Nandra
Nick Gibson
Sue Baker

**Marketing**
Cait Davies
Hennah Sandhu

**Publicity**
Francesca Pearce
Sarah Lundy

**Production**
Ruth Sharvell

**Sales**
Dave Murphy
Esther Waters

Victoria Laws
Rachael Hum
Ellie Kyrke-Smith
Frances Doyle
Georgina Cutler

**Operations**
Jo Jacobs